EVERYBODY
DIES

ALSO BY LAWRENCE BLOCK

THE MATTHEW SCUDDER NOVELS
The Sins of the Fathers · Time to Murder and Create · In the Midst of Death · A Stab in the Dark · Eight Million Ways to Die · When the Sacred Ginmill Closes · Out on the Cutting Edge · A Ticket to the Boneyard · A Dance at the Slaughterhouse · A Walk Among the Tombstones · The Devil Knows You're Dead · A Long Line of Dead Men · Even the Wicked

THE BERNIE RHODENBARR MYSTERIES
Burglars Can't Be Choosers · The Burglar in the Closet · The Burglar Who Liked to Quote Kipling · The Burglar Who Studied Spinoza · The Burglar Who Painted like Mondrian · The Burglar Who Traded Ted Williams · The Burglar Who Thought He Was Bogart · The Burglar in the Library

THE ADVENTURES OF EVAN TANNER
The Thief Who Couldn't Sleep · The Canceled Czech · Tanner's Twelve Swingers · Two for Tanner · Tanner's Tiger · Here Comes a Hero · Me Tanner, You Jane · Tanner on Ice

THE AFFAIRS OF CHIP HARRISON
No Score · Chip Harrison Scores Again · Make Out with Murder · The Topless Tulip Caper

OTHER NOVELS
After the First Death · Ariel · Coward's Kiss · Deadly Honeymoon · The Girl with the Long Green Heart · Hit Man · Mona · Not Comin' Home to You · Random Walk · Ronald Rabbit Is a Dirty Old Man · The Specialists · Such Men Are Dangerous · The Triumph of Evil · You Could Call It Murder

COLLECTED SHORT STORIES
Sometimes They Bite · Like a Lamb to Slaughter · Some Days You Get the Bear · Ehrengraf for the Defense

BOOKS FOR WRITERS
Writing the Novel from Plot to Print · Telling Lies for Fun & Profit · Write for Your Life · Spider, Spin Me a Web

Lawrence Block

EVERYBODY

DIES

Lawrence
Block

WILLIAM MORROW AND COMPANY, INC. | NEW YORK

Library of Congress Cataloging-in-Publication Data

Block, Lawrence.
    Everybody dies / by Lawrence Block.—
  1st ed.
      p. cm.
    ISBN 0-688-14182-X (alk. paper)
    I. Title.
  PS3552.L63E97   1998
  813'.54—dc21   98-10529
                    CIP

Printed in the United States of America

First Edition

1 2 3 4 5 6 7 8 9 10

BOOK DESIGN BY DEBBIE GLASSERMAN

www.williammorrow.com

This is for
KNOX BURGER *and*
KITTY SPRAGUE
and in memory of
ROSS THOMAS

ACKNOWLEDGMENTS

The author is pleased to acknowledge the considerable contribution of the Ragdale Foundation, in Lake Forest, Illinois, where this book was written. He is grateful, too, to the following venues, all in Greenwich Village, where some of the early work was done: the Writers Room, Caffè Lucca, Caffè Vivaldi, Peacock Caffè, Homer's Restaurant, the Jefferson Market branch of the New York Public Library, and the coffee shop of Barnes & Noble on Astor Place.

From too much joy of living,
  From hope and fear set free,
We thank with brief thanksgiving
  Whatever gods may be
That no life lives forever;
That dead men rise up never;
That even the weariest river
  Winds somewhere safe to sea.
                    —A. C. SWINBURNE, "The Garden of Proserpine"

Everybody dies.
                    —JOHN GARFIELD in *Body and Soul*

Everybody dies.
                    —RANDY NEWMAN, "Old Man"

At the door of life, by the gate of breath,
There are worse things waiting for men than death.
                    —SWINBURNE, "The Triumph of Time"

EVERYBODY DIES

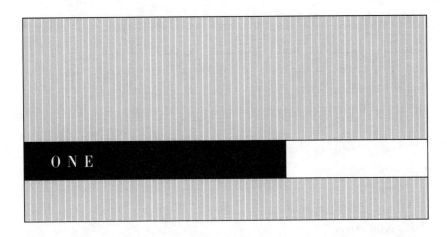

ONE

ANDY BUCKLEY SAID, "Jesus Christ," and braked the Cadillac to a stop. I looked up and there was the deer, perhaps a dozen yards away from us in the middle of our lane of traffic. He was unquestionably a deer caught in the headlights, but he didn't have that stunned look the expression is intended to convey. He was lordly, and very much in command.

"C'mon," Andy said. "Move your ass, Mister Deer."

"Move up on him," Mick said. "But slowly."

"You don't want a freezer full of venison, huh?" Andy eased up on the brake and allowed the car to creep forward. The deer let us get surprisingly close before, with one great bound, he was off the road and out of sight in the darkened fields at the roadside.

WE'D COME NORTH on the Palisades Parkway, northwest on Route 17, northeast on 209. We were on an unnumbered road when we stopped for the deer, and a few miles farther we turned left onto the winding gravel road that led to Mick Ballou's farm. It was past midnight when we left, and close to two by the time we got there. There was no traffic, so we could have gone faster, but Andy kept us a few miles an hour under the speed limit, braked for yellow lights, and yielded at intersections. Mick and I sat in back, Andy drove, and the miles passed in silence.

"You've been here before," Mick said, as the old two-story farmhouse came into view.

"Twice."

"Once after that business in Maspeth," he remembered. "You drove that night, Andy."

"I remember, Mick."

"And we'd Tom Heaney with us as well. I feared we might lose Tom. He was hurt bad, but scarcely made a sound. Well, he's from the North. They're a closemouthed lot."

He meant the North of Ireland.

"But you were here a second time? When was that?"

"A couple of years ago. We made a night of it, and you drove me up to see the animals, and have a look at the place in daylight. And you sent me home with a dozen eggs."

"Now I remember. And I'll bet you never had a better egg."

"They were good eggs."

"Big yolks the color of a Spanish orange. It's a great economy, keeping chickens and getting your own eggs. My best calculation is that those eggs cost me twenty dollars."

"Twenty dollars a dozen?"

"More like twenty dollars an egg. Though when herself cooks me a dish of them, I'd swear it was worth that and more."

Herself was Mrs. O'Gara, and she and her husband were the farm's official owners. In the same fashion, there was somebody else's name on the Cadillac's title and registration, and on the deed and license for Grogan's Open House, the saloon he owned on the corner of Fiftieth and Tenth. He had some real estate holdings around town, and some business interests, but you wouldn't find his name on any official documents. He owned, he'd told me, the clothes on his back, and if put to it he couldn't even prove those were legally his. What you don't own, he'd said, they can't easily take away from you.

Andy parked alongside the farmhouse. He got out of the car and lit a cigarette, lagging behind to smoke it while Mick and I climbed a few steps to the back porch. There was a light on in the kitchen, and Mr. O'Gara was waiting for us at the round oak table. Mick had phoned earlier to warn O'Gara that we were coming. "You said not to wait up," he said now, "but I wanted to make sure you had everything you'd need. I made a fresh pot of coffee."

"Good man."

"All's well here. Last week's rain did us no harm. The apples should be good this year, and the pears even better."

"The summer's heat was no harm, then."

"None as wasn't mended," O'Gara said. "Thanks be to God. She's sleeping, and I'll turn in now myself, if that's all right. But you've only to shout for me if you need anything."

"We're fine," Mick assured him. "We'll be out back, and we'll try not to disturb you."

"Sure, we're sound sleepers," O'Gara said. "Ye'd wake the dead before ye'd wake us."

O'Gara took his cup of coffee upstairs with him. Mick filled a thermos with coffee, capped it, then found a bottle of Jameson in the cupboard and topped up the silver flask he'd been nipping from all night. He returned it to his hip pocket, got two six-packs of O'Keefe's Extra Old Stock ale from the refrigerator, gave them to Andy, and grabbed up the thermos jar and a coffee mug. We got back into the Cadillac and headed farther up the drive, past the fenced chicken yard, past the hogpen, past the barns, and into the old orchard. Andy parked the car, and Mick told us to wait while he walked back to what looked like an old-fashioned outhouse straight out of Li'l Abner, but was evidently a tool-shed. He came back carrying a shovel.

He picked a spot and took the first turn, sinking the shovel into the earth, adding his weight to bury the blade to the hilt. Last week's rain had done no harm. He bent, lifted, tossed a shovelful of earth aside.

I uncapped the thermos and poured myself some coffee. Andy lit a cigarette and cracked a can of ale. Mick went on digging. We took turns, Mick and Andy and I, opening a deep oblong hole in the earth alongside the pear and apple orchard. There were a few cherry trees as well, Mick said, but they were sour cherries, good only for pies, and it was easier to let the birds have them than to go to the trouble of picking them, taking into account that the birds would get most of them whatever you did.

I'd been wearing a light windbreaker, and Andy a leather jacket, but we'd shucked them as we took our turns with the shovel. Mick hadn't been wearing anything over his sport shirt. Cold didn't seem to bother him much, or heat either.

During Andy's second turn, Mick followed a sip of whiskey with a long drink of ale and sighed deeply. "I should get out here more," he said. "You'd need more than moonlight to see the full beauty of it, but you can feel the peace of it, can't you?"

"Yes."

He sniffed the wind. "You can smell it, too. Hogs and chickens. A rank stench when you're close to it, but at this distance it's not so bad, is it?"

"It's not bad at all."

"It makes a change from automobile exhaust and cigarette smoke and all the stinks you meet with in a city. Still, I might mind this more if I smelled it every day. But if I smelled it every day I suppose I'd cease to notice it."

"They say that's how it works. Otherwise people couldn't live in towns with paper mills."

"Jesus, that's the worst smell in the world, a paper mill."

"It's pretty bad. They say a tannery's even worse."

"It must be all in the process," he said, "because the end product's spared. Leather has a pleasant smell to it, and paper's got no smell at all. And there's no smell kinder to the senses than bacon frying in a pan, and doesn't it come out of the same hogpen that's even now assaulting our nostrils? That reminds me."

"Of what?"

"My gift to you the Christmas before last. A ham from one of my very own hogs."

"It was very generous."

"And what could be a more suitable gift for a Jewish vegetarian?"

He shook his head at the memory. "And what a gracious woman she is. She thanked me so warmly that it was hours before it struck me what an inappropriate gift I'd brought her. Did she cook it for you?"

She would have, if I'd wanted, but why should Elaine cook something she's not going to eat? I eat enough meat when I'm away from the house. Home or away, though, I might have had trouble with that ham. The first time Mick and I met, I was looking for a girl who'd disappeared. It turned out she'd been killed by her lover, a young man who worked for Mick. He'd disposed of her corpse by feeding it to the hogs. Mick, outraged when he found out, had dispensed poetic justice, and the hogs had dined a second time. The ham he'd brought us was from a different generation of swine, and had no doubt been fattened on grain and table scraps, but I was just as happy to give it to Jim Faber, whose enjoyment of it was uncomplicated by a knowledge of its history.

"A friend of mine had it for Christmas," I said. "Said it was the best ham he ever tasted."

"Sweet and tender."

"So he said."

Andy Buckley threw down the shovel, climbed up out of the hole, and drank most of a can of ale in a single long swallow. "Christ," he said, "that's thirsty work."

"Twenty-dollar eggs and thousand-dollar hams," Mick said. "It's a grand career for a man, agriculture. However could a man fail at it?"

I grabbed the shovel and went to work.

I TOOK MY turn and Mick took his. Halfway through it he leaned on his shovel and sighed. "I'll feel this tomorrow," he said. "All this work. But it's a good feeling for all that."

"Honest exercise."

"It's little enough of it I get in the ordinary course of things. How about yourself?"

"I do a lot of walking."

"That's the best exercise of all, or so they say."

"That and pushing yourself away from the table."

"Ah, that's the hardest, and gets no easier with age."

"Elaine goes to the gym," I said. "Three times a week. I tried, but it bores me to death."

"But you walk."

"I walk."

He dug out his flask, and moonlight glinted off the silver. He took a drink and put it away, took up the shovel again. He said, "I should come here more. I take long walks when I'm here, you know. And do chores, though I suspect O'Gara has to do them over again once I've left. I've no talent for farming."

"But you enjoy being here."

"I do, and yet I'm never here. And if I enjoy it so, why am I always itching to get back to the city?"

"You miss the action," Andy suggested.

"Do I? I didn't miss it so much when I was with the brothers."

"The monks," I said.

He nodded. "The Thessalonian Brothers. In Staten Island, just a ferryboat ride from Manhattan, but you'd think you were a world away."

"When were you there last? It was just this spring, wasn't it?"

"The last two weeks of May. June, July, August, September. Four months ago, close enough. Next time you'll have to come with me."

"Yeah, right."

"And why not?"

"Mick, I'm not even Catholic."

"Who's to say what you are or aren't? You've come to Mass with me."

"That's for twenty minutes, not two weeks. I'd feel out of place."

"You wouldn't. It's a retreat. Have you never done a retreat?"

I shook my head. "A friend of mine goes sometimes," I said.

"To the Thessalonians?"

"To the Zen Buddhists. They're not that far from here, now that I think of it. Is there a town near here called Livingston Manor?"

"Indeed there is, and 'tis not far at all."

"Well, the monastery's near there. He's been three or four times."

"Is he a Buddhist, then?"

"He was brought up Catholic, but he's been away from the church for ages."

"And so he goes to the Buddhists for retreat. Have I met him, this friend of yours?"

"I don't think so. But he and his wife ate that ham you gave me."

"And pronounced it good, I believe you said."

"The best he ever tasted."

"High praise from a Zen Buddhist. Ah, Jesus, it's a strange old world, isn't it?" He clambered out of the hole. "Have one more go at it," he said, handing the shovel to Andy. "I think it's good enough as it is, but no harm if you even it up a bit."

Andy took his turn. I was feeling a chill now. I picked up my windbreaker from where I'd tossed it, put it on. The wind blew a cloud in front of the moon, and we lost a little of our light. The cloud passed and the moonlight came back. It was a waxing moon, and in a couple of days it would be full.

Gibbous—that's the word for the moon when there's more than half of it showing. It's Elaine's word. Well, Webster's, I suppose, but I learned it from her. And she was the one who told me that, if you fill a barrel in Iowa with seawater, the moon will cause tides in that water. And that blood's chemical makeup is very close to that of seawater, and the moon's tidal pull works in our veins.

Just some thoughts I had, under a gibbous moon . . .

"That'll do," Mick said, and Andy tossed the shovel and Mick gave him a hand out of the hole, and Andy got a flashlight from the glove compartment and aimed its beam down into the hole, and we all looked at it and pronounced it acceptable. And then we went to the car and Mick sighed heavily and unlocked the trunk.

For an instant I had the thought that it would be empty. There'd be the spare, of course, and a jack and a lug wrench, and maybe an old blanket and a couple of rags. But other than that it would be empty.

Just a passing thought, blowing across my mind like the cloud across the moon. I didn't really expect the trunk to be empty.

And of course it wasn't.

T W O

I DON'T KNOW that it's my story to tell.

It's Mick's, really, far more than it's mine. He should be the one to tell it. But he won't.

There are others whose story it is as well. Every story belongs to everyone who has any part in it, and there were quite a few people who had a part in this one. It's none of their story as much as it's Mick's, but they could tell it, singly or in chorus, one way or another.

But they won't.

Nor will he, whose story it is more than anyone's. I've never known a better storyteller, and he could make a meal of this one, but it's not going to happen. He'll never tell it.

And I was there, after all. For some of the beginning and much of the middle and most of the end. And it's my story, too. Of course it is. How could it fail to be?

And I'm here to tell it. And, for some reason, I can't *not* tell it.

So I guess it's up to me.

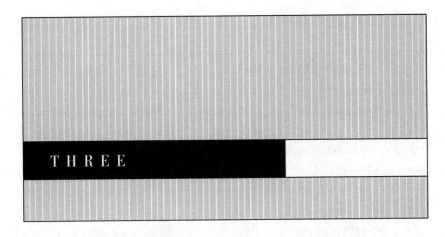

THREE

EARLIER THAT SAME night, a Wednesday, I'd gone to an AA meeting. Afterward I'd had a cup of coffee with Jim Faber and a couple of others, and when I got home Elaine said that Mick had called. "He said perhaps you could stop in," she said. "He didn't come right out and say it was urgent, but that was the impression I got."

So I got my windbreaker from the closet and put it on, and halfway to Grogan's I zipped it up. It was September, and a very transitional sort of September, with days like August and nights like October. Days to remind you of where you'd been, nights to make sure you knew where you were going.

I lived for something like twenty years in a room at the Hotel Northwestern, on the north side of Fifty-seventh Street a few doors east of Ninth Avenue. When I moved, finally, it was right across the street, to the Parc Vendôme, a large prewar building where Elaine and I have a spacious fourteenth-floor apartment with views south and west.

And I walked south and west, south to Fiftieth Street, west to Tenth

Avenue. Grogan's is on the southeast corner, an old Irish taproom of the sort that is getting harder and harder to find in Hell's Kitchen, and indeed throughout New York. A floor of inch-square black and white tiles, a stamped tin ceiling, a long mahogany bar, a matching mirrored backbar. An office in the back, where Mick kept guns and cash and records, and sometimes napped on a long green leather couch. An alcove to the left of the office, with a dartboard at the end of it, under a stuffed sailfish. Doors on the right-hand wall of the alcove, leading to the restrooms.

I walked through the front door and took it all in, the mix of slackers and strivers and old lags at the bar, the handful of occupied tables. Burke behind the bar, giving me an expressionless nod of recognition, and Andy Buckley all by himself in the rear alcove, leaning forward, dart in hand. A man emerged from the restroom and Andy straightened up, either to pass the time of day with the fellow or to avoid hitting him with a dart. It seemed to me that the fellow looked familiar, and I tried to place the face, and then I caught sight of another face that drove the first one entirely out of my mind.

There's no table service at Grogan's, you have to fetch your own drinks from the bar, but there are tables, and about half of them were occupied, one by a trio of men in suits, the rest by couples. Mick Ballou is a notorious criminal and Grogan's is his headquarters and a hangout for much of what's left of the neighborhood tough guys, but the gentrification of Hell's Kitchen into Clinton has made it an atmospheric watering hole for the neighborhood's newer residents, a place to cool off with a beer after work, or to stop for a last drink after a night at the theater. It's also an okay place to have a serious drink-eased conversation with your spouse. Or, in her case, with someone else's.

She was dark and slender, with short hair framing a face that was not pretty, but occasionally beautiful. Her name was Lisa Holtzmann. When I met her she was married, and her husband was a guy I hadn't liked and couldn't say why. Then somebody shot him while he was making a telephone call, and she found a strongbox full of money in the closet and called me. I made sure she could keep the money, and I solved his murder, and somewhere along the way I went to bed with her.

I was still at the Northwestern when it started. Then Elaine and I took the Parc Vendôme apartment together, and after we'd been there for a year or so we got married. Throughout this period I went on spending time with Lisa. It was always I who called, asking her if she wanted company, and she was always agreeable, always happy to see me. Sometimes I'd go weeks and weeks without seeing her, and I'd begin to believe the affair had run its course. Then the day would come when I wanted the escape that her bed afforded, and I would call, and she would make me welcome.

As far as I've ever been able to tell, the whole business didn't affect my relationship with Elaine at all. That's what everybody always wants to think, but in this case I honestly think it's true. It seemed to exist outside of space and time. It was sexual, of course, but it wasn't *about* sex, any more than drinking was ever about the way the stuff tasted. In fact it was like drinking, or its role for me was like the role drinking had played. It was a place to go when I didn't want to be where I was.

Shortly after we were married—on our honeymoon, as a matter of fact—Elaine gave me to understand that she knew I was seeing somebody and that she didn't care. She didn't say this in so many words. What she said was that marriage didn't have to change anything, that we could go on being the people we were. But the implication was unmistakable. Perhaps all the years she'd spent as a call girl had given her a unique perspective on the ways of men, married or not.

I went on seeing Lisa after we were married, though less frequently. And then it ended, with neither a bang nor a whimper. I was there one afternoon, in her eagle's nest twenty-some stories up in a new building on Fifty-seventh and Tenth. We were drinking coffee, and she told me, hesitantly, that she had started seeing someone, that it wasn't serious yet but might be.

And then we went to bed, and it was as it always was, nothing special, really, but good enough. All the while, though, I kept finding myself wondering what the hell I was doing there. I didn't think it was sinful, I didn't think it was wrong, I didn't think I was hurting anybody, not Elaine, not Lisa, not myself. But it seemed to me that it was somehow inappropriate.

I said, without making too much of it, that I probably wouldn't call for a while, that I'd give her some space. And she said, just as off-handedly, that she thought that was probably a good idea for now.

And I never called her again.

I'd seen her a couple of times. Once on the street, on her way home with a cartful of groceries from D'Agostino's. *Hi. How are you? Not so bad. And you? Oh, about the same. Keeping busy. Me too. You're looking well. Thanks. So are you. Well. Well, it's good to see you. Same here. Take care. You too.* And once with Elaine, across a crowded room at Armstrong's. *Isn't that Lisa Holtzmann? Yes. I think it is. She's with somebody. Did she remarry? I don't know. She had a bad run of luck, didn't she? The miscarriage, and then losing her husband. Do you want to say hello? Oh, I don't know. She looks all wrapped up in the guy she's with, and we knew her when she was married. Another time . . .*

But there hadn't been another time. And here she was, in Grogan's.

I was on my way to the bar, but just then she looked up, and our eyes met. Hers brightened. "Matt," she said, and motioned me over. "This is Florian."

He looked too ordinary for the name. He was around forty, with light brown hair going thin on top, horn-rimmed glasses, a blue blazer over a denim shirt and striped tie. He had a wedding ring, I noted, and she did not.

He said hello and I said hello and she said it was good to see me, and I went over to the bar and let Burke fill a glass with Coke for me. "He should be back in a minute," he said. "He said you'd be coming by."

"He was right," I said, or something like that, not really paying attention to what I was saying, taking a sip of the Coke and not paying attention to that either, and looking over the brim of my glass at the table I'd just left. Neither of them was looking my way. They were holding hands now, I noticed, or rather he was holding her hand. Florian and Lisa, Lisa and Florian.

Ages since I'd been with her. Years, really.

"Andy's in back," Burke said.

I nodded and pushed away from the bar. I saw something out of the corner of my eye, and turned, and my eyes locked with those of the man I'd seen coming out of the bathroom. He had a wide wedge-shaped face, prominent eyebrows, a broad forehead, a long narrow nose, a full-lipped mouth. I knew him, and at the same time I didn't have a clue who the hell he was.

He gave me the least little nod, but I couldn't say whether it was a nod of recognition or a simple acknowledgment of our eyes having met. Then he turned back to the bar and I walked on past him to where Andy Buckley was toeing the line and leaning way over it, aiming a dart at the board.

"The big fellow stepped out," he said. "Care to throw a dart or two while you wait?"

"I don't think so," I said. "It just makes me feel inadequate."

"I didn't do things made me feel inadequate, I'd never get out of bed."

"What about darts? What about driving a car?"

"Jesus, that's the worst of it. Voice in my head goes, 'Look at you, you bum. Thirty-eight years old and all you can do is drive and throw darts. You call that a life, you bum, you?'"

He tossed the dart, and it landed in the bull's-eye. "Well," he said, "if all you can do is throw darts, you might as well be good at it."

He got the darts from the board, and when he came back I said, "There's a guy at the bar, or was, a minute ago. Where the hell did he go?"

"Who are we talking about?"

I moved to where I could see the faces in the backbar mirror. I couldn't find the one I was looking for. "Guy about your age," I said. "Maybe a little younger. Wide forehead tapering to a pointed chin." And I went on describing the face I'd seen while Andy frowned and shook his head.

"Doesn't ring a bell," he said. "He's not there now?"

"I don't see him."

"You don't mean Mr. Dougherty, do you? Because he's right there and—"

"I know Mr. Dougherty, and he's got to be what, ninety years old? This guy is—"

"My age or younger, right, you told me that and I forgot. I got to tell you, every time I turn around there's more of 'em that are younger."

"Tell me about it."

"Anyway, I don't see the guy, and the description doesn't ring a bell. What about him?"

"He must have slipped out," I said. "The little man who wasn't there. Except he *was* there, and I think you talked to him."

"At the bar? I been back here the past half hour."

"He came out of the john," I said, "just about the time I walked in the door. And he looked familiar to me then, and I thought he said something to you, or maybe you were just waiting for him to get out of the way so you didn't stick a dart in his ear."

"I'm beginning to wish I did. Then at least we'd know who he was. 'Oh, yeah, I know who you mean. He's the asshole wearing a dart for an earring.' "

"You don't remember talking to anybody?"

He shook his head. "Not to say I didn't, Matt. All night long guys are in and out of the men's room, and I'm here tossing darts, and sometimes they'll take a minute to pass the time of day. I'll talk to 'em without paying any attention to 'em, unless I get the sense that they might like to play a game for a dollar or two. And tonight I wouldn't even do that, on account of we're out of here the minute he shows, and what do you know? Here he is now."

HE IS A big man, is Mick Ballou, and he looks to have been rough-hewn from granite, like Stone Age sculpture. His eyes are a surprisingly vivid green, and there is more than a hint of danger in them. This night he was wearing gray slacks and a blue sport shirt, but he might as well have been wearing his late father's butcher apron, its white surface marked with bloodstains old and new.

"You came," he said. "Good man. Andy'll bring the car round. You wouldn't mind a ride on a fine September night, would you now?"

Mick had a quick drink at the bar, and then we went out and got into the dark blue Cadillac and drove away from what a reporter had called "the headquarters of his criminal empire." The phrase, Elaine once pointed out, was infelicitous, because Mick's whole style wasn't remotely imperial. It was feudal. He was the king of the castle, holding sway by the sheer force of his physical presence, rewarding the faithful and drowning rivals in the moat.

And he was, I've always realized, an unlikely friend for a former policeman turned private investigator. The years have left his hands as bloodstained as his apron. But I seem to be able to recognize this without judging him, or distancing myself from him. I'm not sure whether this represents emotional maturity on my part, or mere willful obtuseness. I'm not sure it matters, either.

I have quite a few friends, but not many close ones. The cops I worked with years ago are retired by now, and I've long since lost touch with them. My saloon friendships wound down when I quit drinking and stopped hanging around bars, and my AA friendships, for all their depth and solidity, center on a shared commitment to sobriety. We support one another, we trust one another, we know astonishingly intimate things about one another—but we're not necessarily close.

Elaine is my closest friend and by far the most important person in my life. But I do have a handful of men with whom I have bonded, each in a different and profound way. Jim Faber, my AA sponsor. TJ, who lives in my old hotel room and serves as my assistant when he's not clerking in Elaine's shop. Ray Gruliow, the radical lawyer. Joe Durkin, a detective at Midtown North, and my last real hook in the Department. Chance Coulter, who once trafficked in women and now deals instead in African art. Danny Boy Bell, whose own stock-in-trade is information.

And Mick Ballou.

They don't run to type, these friends of mine, not as far as I can see. By and large, they wouldn't have much fondness for one another. But they are my friends. I don't judge them, or the friendships I have with them. I can't afford to.

I thought about this while Andy drove and Mick and I sat side by side in the big back seat. We talked a little about the new Japanese pitcher for the Yankees, and how he'd been disappointing after a promising start. But neither of us had a great deal to say on the subject, and mostly we sat in silence as we rode along.

.   .   .

WE TOOK THE Lincoln Tunnel to New Jersey, then Route 3 west. After that I didn't pay much attention to the route. We found our way through a sort of suburban industrial sprawl, winding up in front of a massive one-story concrete-block structure perched behind a twelve-foot woven wire fence topped with concertina wire. ROOMS 4 RENT, a sign announced, which was hard to credit, as I'd never seen a more unlikely rooming house. A second sign explained the first: E-Z STORAGE / YOUR EXTRA ROOM AT LOW MONTHLY RATES.

Andy drove slowly past the yard, turned at the first driveway, coasted past the place a second time. "All peace and quiet," he said, pulling up in front of the locked gate. Mick got out and opened the big padlock with a key, then swung the gate inward. Andy drove the Cadillac in and Mick secured the gate behind us, then got into the car.

"They lock up at ten," he explained, "but they give you a key to the lock. You've got twenty-four-hour access, with no attendant on hand from ten at night to six in the morning."

"That could be convenient."

"Why I picked it," he said.

We circled the building. There was a roll-up steel door every fifteen feet or so, each of them closed and padlocked. Andy pulled up in front of one and cut the engine. We got out, and Mick fitted another key into this lock and turned it, then gripped the handle and raised the door.

It was dark within, but information was coming my way before the door was all the way up. I sniffed the air like a dog with his head out the car window, sorting the rich mixture of scents that came my way.

There was the smell of death, of course, of lifeless flesh spoiling in a warm unventilated space. With it was the smell of blood, a smell I've often heard described as coppery, but it has always reminded me more of the taste of iron in the mouth. An ironic smell, if you like. There was the burnt smell of cordite, and another burnt smell as well. Singed hair, for a guess. And, as unlikely background music for all these sour notes, I breathed in the rich nostalgic bouquet of whiskey. It smelled like bourbon, and good bourbon at that.

Then the light came on, a single overhead bulb, and showed me what my nose had led me to expect. Two men, both wearing jeans and sneakers, one in a forest green work shirt with the sleeves rolled up, the other in a royal blue polo shirt, lay sprawled just a few feet left of the center of a room some eighteen feet square and ten feet high.

I walked over and had a look at them, two men in their late twenties or early thirties. I recognized the one in the polo shirt, although I couldn't remember his name, if in fact I'd ever heard it. I'd seen him at Grogan's. He was a fairly recent arrival from Belfast, and he had the accent, with his sentences turning up the slightest bit at their ends, almost like questions.

He'd been shot through the hand, and in the torso, just below the breastbone. He'd been shot again, and conclusively, just behind the left ear. That shot had been fired at close range, the blast singeing the hair around the wound. So it had indeed been singed hair that I smelled.

The other man, the one in the dark green work shirt, had bled abundantly from a bullet wound in the throat. He lay on his back, with the blood pooled around him. Again, there'd been a coup de grace, a close-range shot into the middle of the forehead. It was hard to see the need for it. The throat wound would have been enough to kill him, and, judging from the blood loss, he may well have been dead before the second shot was fired.

I said, "Who killed them?"

"Ah," Mick said. "Aren't you the detective?"

ANDY WAITED OUTSIDE with the car, guarding our privacy, and Mick lowered the steel door to screen us from any chance passerby. "I wanted you to see them exactly as I found them," he said. "I didn't care to walk away and leave them like this. But how could I tell what clues I might be disturbing? What do I know of clues?"

"You didn't move them at all?"

He shook his head. "I didn't have to touch them to know they were beyond help. I've seen enough dead men to know one on sight."

"Or even in the dark."

"The smell was less a few hours ago."

"Is that when you found them?"

"I didn't note the time. It was early evening, with the sky still bright. I'd say it was between seven and eight."

"And this is exactly what you found? You didn't add anything or take anything away?"

"I did not."

"The door was lowered when you got here?"

"Lowered and locked."

"The cardboard carton in the corner—"

"Just some tools in it that it's useful to keep here. A pry bar for opening crates, a hammer and nails. There was an electric drill, but I guess they took that. They took everything else."

"What was there for them to take?"

"Whiskey. Enough to fill a small truck."

I knelt down for a closer look at the man I recognized. I moved his arm, lined up the wound in the hand with the wound in the torso. "One bullet," I said, "or at least it looks that way. I've seen that before. It seems to be instinctive, holding up a hand to ward off a bullet."

"And have you ever known it to work?"

"Only when Superman does it. He was beaten up, did you notice that? Around the face. Pistol-whipped, probably."

"Ah, Jesus," he said. "He was just a lad, you know. You must have met him at the bar."

"I never got his name."

"Barry McCartney. He would be telling you he was no relation to Paul. He'd not have bothered saying that at home in Belfast. There's no lack of McCartneys in County Antrim."

I looked at the hands of the other dead man. They were unmarked. Either he hadn't tried catching bullets with them or he'd tried and missed.

He looked to have been beaten around the face and head as well, but it was hard to be sure. The bullet to the forehead had distorted his features, and that was enough to explain the discoloration.

To me, at any rate, if not to someone who knew what he was looking at. I'd been to my share of crime scenes, but I wasn't a medical examiner, I wasn't a forensic pathologist. I didn't really know what to look for or what to make of what I saw. I could pore over the bodies all night and not pick up a fraction of what an expert eye could tell at a glance.

"John Kenny," Mick said, without my having to ask. "Did you ever meet him?"

"I don't think so."

"From Strabane, in the County Tyrone. He lived in Woodside, in a rooming house full of North-of-Ireland boys. His mother died a year ago. Saves having to tell her." He cleared his throat. "He flew home, buried her, and came back here. And died in a room full of whiskey."

"I don't smell it on them."

"The room was full of whiskey, not the lad himself."

"But I smelled whiskey when I walked in the door," I said, "and I smell it now, but not on them."

"Ah," he said, and I looked where he was pointing. Broken glass covered a few square feet of the concrete floor at the base of the wall. Five or six feet above the heap of shards the wall was stained, with the stain trailing down the wall to the floor.

I went over and had a look at it. "They were stealing your whiskey," I said, "and they broke a bottle."

"They did."

"But it didn't just slip out of their hands and break on impact," I said. "Somebody deliberately smashed the bottle against the wall. A full bottle, too." I poked around in the debris, found the piece of glass with the label on it. "George Dickel," I said. "I thought I smelled bourbon."

"You still have the nose for it."

"McCartney and . . . Kenny, is it?"

"John Kenny."

"I gather they both worked for you."

"They did."

"And it was your business that brought them here?"

"It was. Last night I told them to drive out here sometime today and pick up half a dozen cases, scotch and bourbon and I don't remember what else. I told them and they wrote it down. John had a station wagon, a big old Ford consumed with rust. Plenty of room in it for a few cases of whiskey. Barry would give him a hand. They'd be coming during the day, so they wouldn't need a key to the padlock. I had extra keys to this unit, and I gave them one."

"They knew how to get here?"

"They'd been here before, when we unloaded the truck the whiskey came in. They weren't part of the taking of the truck, but they helped in the unloading. And they were here another time or two over the months."

"So they came to pick up some whiskey. And they were to deliver it where?"

"To the bar. When they didn't show up I called around looking for them. I couldn't find hide nor hair, so I got in my own car and came out here myself."

"You were worried about them?"

"I'd no cause for worry. The errand I sent them on was of no great urgency. They might have put it off for a time."

"But you were worried all the same, weren't you?"

"I was," he admitted. "I had a feeling."

"I see."

"My mother always said I had the second sight. I don't know if it's so, but sometimes I'll have a feeling. And we needed whiskey at the bar, and I'd nothing else to do, so why not run out and have a look?"

"And this is how you found them?"

"It is. I added nothing and took nothing away."

"What happened to the station wagon?"

"I've no idea, beyond that it was nowhere to be seen. I'd say whoever killed them drove off in it."

"But there was more whiskey than would fit in a station wagon," I said. "That would do for the half dozen cases, but to clear out the whole room—"

"You'd need a panel truck."

"Or a couple of station wagons, each making several trips. But they'd want to get it all in one trip. They wouldn't want to come back to a room with dead men in it. They had a truck, and one of them drove away in it and the other drove off in Kenny's station wagon."

"You couldn't sell the thing," he said. "Not even for parts. Take away the rust and there'd be nothing holding it together."

"Maybe they needed the space. Maybe the truck or van they brought wouldn't take the whole load, and they had to stuff the extra cases into the station wagon."

"And had one bottle left over," he said, "and smashed it against the wall."

"It's hard to make sense out of that, isn't it? It's not as though the bottle just dropped. Somebody heaved it against the wall."

"If there was a scuffle—"

"But there's no sign of one. The killers got the drop on your boys and pistol-whipped them and shot them. That part seems clear, and it's hard to fit a broken bottle into that scenario." I bent down, stood up. "The bottle was opened," I said. "Here's the neck, and the cap's off and the seal's broken." I closed my eyes, trying to reconstruct the scene. "Kenny and McCartney are in here. They've loaded the cases and they're having a drink before they head out. The bad guys come in with guns in their hand. 'Calm down, have a drink,' Kenny says, or McCartney. He hands over the bottle, and the gunman takes it away from him and heaves it against the wall."

"Why?"

"I don't know, unless you got knocked off by Carry Nation and the Anti-Saloon League."

"All this talk of whiskey," he said, and dug out his flask and took a short drink. "They wouldn't have found an opened bottle, man. All the cases were sealed. They'd have had to open a case if they wanted a drink, and they wouldn't have done it."

I returned to the bodies. There was a little flake of glass floating on top of the blood that had gushed from John Kenny's throat. "The bottle was broken after the men were killed," I said. "They killed them, then broke open a case and had a couple of drinks while they loaded the whiskey. And smashed the bottle. Why?"

"Mayhaps they didn't care for the taste of it."

"In some localities it's a violation to drive around with an opened bottle of liquor. But somehow I don't think that would have worried them. It's a gesture of contempt, isn't it? Smashing a bottle against the wall. Or maybe it's like tossing your glass in the fireplace after you drink a toast. Whatever the reason, it was a stupid thing to do."

"Why is that?"

"Because glass takes fingerprints beautifully, and there's a good chance one of those chunks of glass has a usable print on it. And God only knows what else a lab technician might find here." I turned to him. "You were careful not to disturb the integrity of the crime scene, but it's largely wasted if I'm the only one to see it. I haven't got the training or the resources to do a good job. But I don't suppose you want to call this in to the cops."

"I do not."

"No, I didn't think so. What happens next? Are you planning to move the bodies?"

"Well, now," he said. "I can't leave them here, can I?"

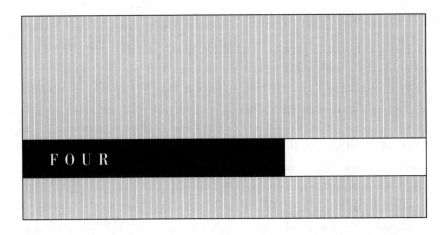

FOUR

WE LAID THE two bodies in the single grave we'd dug. We'd shrouded each in a pair of black plastic Hefty bags before loading them in the trunk, and we left the bags on when we transferred them to the grave.

"There ought to be a prayer over them," Mick said, standing awkwardly at the side of the grave. "Would you ever have a prayer you could say?"

I couldn't think of anything appropriate. I remained silent, as did Andy. Mick said, "John Kenny and Barry McCartney. Ah, you were good boys, and may God grant you glory. The Lord giveth and the Lord taketh away. In the name of the Father and of the Son and of the Holy Ghost, amen." He made the sign of the cross over the grave, then dropped his hands and shook his head. "You'd think I could think of a fucking prayer. They ought to have a priest, but that's the least of it. They ought to have a proper funeral. Ah, Jesus, they ought to have thirty more years of life, as far as that goes, and it's too fucking bad what they ought to have because this is all they're after getting, a hole in the ground and three men shaking their heads over it. The poor bastards, let's bury 'em and be done with it."

It took a lot less time to fill in the hole than it had taken to dig it. Still, it took awhile. We had only the one shovel and took turns with it, as we'd taken turns before. When we'd finished there was earth left over. Mick shoveled it into a wheelbarrow from the toolshed and dumped it fifty yards away, deep in the orchard. He brought the barrow back, returned it to the toolshed along with the shovel, and came back for another look at the grave.

He said, "Spot it a mile away, wouldn't you? Well, there'll be no one back here but O'Gara, and it won't be the first one he's seen. He's a good man, O'Gara. Knows when to turn a blind eye."

The light was still on in the farmhouse kitchen. I rinsed out the thermos and left it in the strainer, and Mick put back the unopened cans of ale and topped up his flask from the Jameson bottle. Then we all got back in the Cadillac and headed for home.

It was still dark when we left the farm, and there was less traffic than there'd been before, and no bodies in the trunk to hold us to the posted speed limit. Still, Andy didn't exceed it by more than five miles an hour. After a while I closed my eyes. I didn't drift off, but thought my own thoughts in the stillness. When I opened my eyes we were on the George Washington Bridge and the eastern sky was beginning to brighten.

So I'd had a white night, my first in a while. Sometimes Mick and I would sit up all night at Grogan's, with the door locked and all the lights off but the shaded bulb over our table, sharing stories and silence until the sun came up. Now and then we rounded off the night with the eight o'clock Mass at St. Bernard's, the Butchers' Mass, where Mick was just one of a whole crew of men in bloodstained white aprons.

As we came off the bridge and onto the West Side Drive, he said, "We're in good time for it, you know. Mass at St. Bernard's."

"You read my mind," I said. "But I'm tired. I think I'll pass."

"I'm tired myself, but I feel the need for it this morning. They should have had a priest."

"Kenny and McCartney."

"The same. The one's family is all in Belfast. All they need to know is there was trouble and he died, the poor lad. John Kenny's mother died, but he had a sister as well, didn't he, Andy?"

"Two sisters," Andy said. "One's married and the other's a nun."

"Married to Our Lord," Mick said. It wasn't always clear to me where reverence left off and irony began. I'm not sure it was clear to him, either.

ANDY LET US out at Grogan's. Mick told him to drop the Cadillac at the garage. "I'll take a taxi to St. Bernard's," he said. "Or I might walk. I've time enough."

Burke had closed the place hours ago. Mick opened the steel accordion gates and unlocked the door. Inside, the lights were off, the chairs perched on top of the tables, so they'd be out of the way when the floor was mopped.

We went into the back room he uses for an office. He spun the dial of the huge old Mosler safe and drew out a sheaf of bills. "I want to hire you," he announced.

"You want to hire me?"

"As a detective. It's what you do, isn't it? Someone hires you and you undertake an investigation."

"It's what I do," I agreed.

"I want to know who did this."

I'd been thinking about it. "It could have been spur of the moment," I said. "Somebody with an adjoining cubicle sees two guys standing around and all that booze there for the taking. What did you say it ran to?"

"Fifty or sixty cases."

"Well, what's that worth? Twelve bottles to a case, and how much a bottle? Say ten dollars? Is that about right?"

Amusement showed in his eyes. "They've raised the price of the creature since the day you stopped drinking it."

"I'm surprised they're still in business."

"It's hard for them without your custom, but they manage. Say two hundred dollars a case."

I did the math. "Ten thousand dollars," I said, "in round numbers. That's enough to make it worth stealing."

"Indeed it is. Why do you think we stole it in the first place? Though we didn't feel the need to kill anyone."

"If it wasn't somebody who just happened to be there," I went on, "then either somebody followed McCartney and Kenny or else they had the place staked out and waited for somebody to come and open up. But what sense does that make?"

There was an opened bottle of whiskey on his desk. He uncapped it, looked around for a glass, then took a short drink straight from the bottle.

"I need to know," he said.

"And you want me to find out for you."

"I do. It's your line of work, and I'd be entirely useless at it myself."

"So it would be up to me to learn what happened, and who was responsible."

"It would."

"And then I would turn the information over to you."

"What are you getting at, man?"

"Well, I'd be delivering a death sentence, wouldn't I?"

"Ah," he said.

"Unless you're planning on bringing the police into it."

"No," he said. "No, I wouldn't regard it as a police matter."

"I didn't think so."

He put a hand on the bottle but left it where it stood. He said, "You saw what they did to those two lads. Not just the bullets but a beating as well. It's no more than justice for them to pay for it."

"Rough justice, when you mete it out yourself."

"And isn't most justice rough justice?"

I wondered if I believed that. I said, "My problem's not in the action you take. My problem's being a part of it."

"Ah," he said. "I can understand that."

"What you do is up to you," I said, "and I'd be hard put to recommend an alternative. You can't go to the cops, and it's late in life for you to start turning the other cheek."

"It would go against the grain," he allowed.

"And sometimes a person can't turn the other cheek," I said, "or walk away and leave it to the cops. I've been there myself."

"I know you have."

"And I'm not sure I chose the right course, but I seem to have been able to live with it. So I can't tell you not to pick up a gun, not when I might do the same thing myself in your position. But it's your position, not mine, and I don't want to be the one who points the gun for you."

He thought that over, nodded slowly. "I can see the sense in that," he said.

"Your friendship is important to me," I said, "and I'd bend what principles I have for the sake of it. But I don't think this situation calls for it."

His hand found the bottle again, and this time he drank from it. He said, "Something you said, that it might have been men acting on impulse. Lads with a storage bin of their own, seeing a chance for a fast dollar."

"It's certainly a possibility."

"Suppose you were to look into that side of it," he said evenly. "Suppose you did what you do, asked your questions and made your notes, and learned enough to rule that possibility in or out."

"I don't understand."

He went over to the wall and leaned against it, looking at one of the hand-colored steel engravings mounted there. He has two groups of them, three scenes of County Mayo in Ireland, where his mother was born, and three others showing his father's birthplace in the south of France. I don't know which ancestral home he was looking at now, and I doubt he was seeing it.

Without turning around he said, "I believe I have an enemy."

"An enemy?"

"The same. And I don't know who he is or what he wants."

"And you think this was his doing."

"I do. I believe he followed those boys to the storage shed, or got there first and lay in wait for them. I believe the whiskey he stole was the least of it. I believe he was more intent on shedding blood than in stealing ten thousand dollars' worth of stolen whiskey."

"There have been other incidents," I guessed.

"There have," he said, "unless it's my imagination. It could be I've turned into an old maid, checking the cupboards, looking under the bed. Perhaps that's all it is. That, or else I've an enemy and a spy."

I have a license now, issued by the State of New York. I got it awhile ago when one of my lawyer clients told me, not for the first time, that he'd be able to give me more work if I were licensed. I've worked a lot for lawyers lately, and more than ever since I picked up the license.

But I haven't always had a license, and I haven't worked exclusively for members of the legal profession. I had a pimp for a client once. Another time, I worked for a drug trafficker.

If I could work for them, why couldn't I work for Ballou? If he was good enough to be my friend, if he was good enough to sit up all night with, why couldn't he be my client?

I said, "You'd have to tell me how to find the place."

"And what place would that be?"

"E-Z Storage."

"We were just there."

"I wasn't paying attention once we got out of the tunnel. I'll need directions. And you'd better let me have a key for the padlock."

"When do you want to go? Andy can drive you."

"I'll go by myself," I said. "Just tell me how to get there."

I jotted down the directions in my notebook. He proffered the roll of bills, his eyebrows raised, and I told him to put his money away.

He said this was business, that he was a client like any other, that he expected to pay. I said I'd be spending a couple of hours asking questions that most likely wouldn't lead anywhere. When the job was done, when I'd done as much as I felt comfortable doing, I'd tell him what I'd learned and how much he owed me.

"And don't your clients usually pay you something in advance? Of course they do. Here's a thousand dollars. Take it, man, for Jesus' sake! It won't obligate you to do anything you don't want to do."

I knew that. How could money obligate me more than friendship had? I said, "You don't have to pay in advance. I probably won't earn all this."

"Little enough you'd have to do. My lawyer gets as much every time he picks up the telephone. Take it, put it in your pocket. What you don't earn you can always give back."

I put the bills in my wallet, wondering why I'd even bothered to argue. Years ago an old cop named Vince Mahaffey told me what to do when somebody gave me money. "Take it," he'd said, "and put it away, and say thank you. You could even touch your cap if you're wearing one."

"Thanks," I said.

"It's I should be thanking you. Are you certain you don't want some-one to drive you?"

"I'm positive."

"Or I can let you have the use of a car, and you can drive yourself."

"I'll get there."

"Now I've hired you, I'd best leave you alone, eh? Just let me know if you need anything."

"I will."

"Or if you learn anything. Or if you determine there's nothing to be learned."

"Either way," I said, "it shouldn't take more than a day or two."

"Whatever it takes. I'm glad you took the money."

"Well, you pretty much insisted on it."

"Ah, we're a fine pair of old fools," he said. "You should have taken the money without an argument. And for my part, I should have let you refuse it. But how could I do that?" His eyes caught mine, held them. "Suppose some wee fucker kills me before you finish the job. How would I feel then? I'd hate to die owing you money."

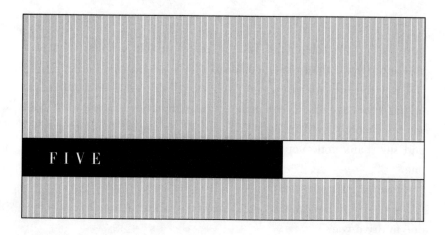

F I V E

I WAS UP a little before noon, and by one o'clock I had picked up an Avis car and found my way to E-Z Storage. I spent the afternoon there. I talked to the man in charge, one Leon Kramer, who started out wary and turned into Chatty Cathy before he was done.

Elaine rents a storage cubicle in a warehouse a few blocks west of our apartment—she stores artwork and antiques there, the overflow from her shop—but the system at the E-Z facility in New Jersey was different, and a good deal more casual. We have to sign in and out whenever we visit our bin, but E-Z, unattended at night and offering twenty-four-hour access, can't attempt anything like that level of security. A sign over Kramer's desk insisted in large print that all storage was entirely at the customer's risk, and he made the point himself three times in the first five minutes I spent with him.

So there were no records kept of comings and goings, and nothing stronger than the tenant's own padlock to keep others out of his storage bin.

"They want to be able to come here any hour of the day or night," Kramer said. "Their brother-in-law needs to store some stuff, they can hand him the key without worrying did they put his name on a list of persons authorized to have access. They don't want to sign in each time, clip on a security badge, fill out a lot of forms. What we got here is more convenience than security. Nobody's renting one of our bins to stash the crown jewels. Anything really important or valuable's gonna go in your safe deposit box at the bank. What we get is your mother's dining room set and the files from Dad's old office, before you went and put him in the home. All the stuff you'd keep in the attic, except you sold the house and moved to a garden apartment."

"Or things you'd just as soon not keep around the house," I suggested.

"Now that I wouldn't know about," he said, "and I wouldn't want to know. All I need to know's your check cleared the first of the month."

"A man's storage space is his castle."

He nodded. "With the exception that you can live in a castle, and you can't live here. There's a lot of other things you can do. We call it storage, but it's not all storage. You see that sign, 'Rooms 4 Rent'? That's what we're offering, the extra room your house or apartment hasn't got. I got tenants'll store a boat here, boat motor and trailer, 'cause they got no room to garage it where they live. Others, the room's their workshop. They set up their tools and do woodworking, work on their car, whatever. Only thing you can't do is move in and live here, and that's not my rule, it's the county's, or the township's, whatever. No living. Not that people don't try."

I'd shown him my business card and explained that I was working for a tenant of his who'd had some goods disappear. He didn't want to make it a police matter until he'd ruled out the possibility of employee pilferage. That was probably what it was, Kramer said. Somebody who already had a key, went and made himself the boss's silent partner.

By the time I left him I had a list of the tenants on the side of the building where John Kenny and Barry McCartney had been shot to death. I'd fumbled my way to a pretext—maybe another customer had seen or heard something—and Kramer went along, either to get rid of me or because we were old friends by then. Ballou's cubicle, I noted, was officially leased to someone named J. D. Reilly, with an address in Middle Village, in Queens.

I had a sandwich and fries at a diner across the road, asked a few questions there, then returned to E-Z Storage and used Mick's key to have another look at the murder scene. I could still detect all the odors I'd smelled the night before, but they were fainter now.

I'd brought a broom and dustpan, and I swept up the broken glass and dumped the shards into a brown paper bag. There was a reasonably good chance that one of those chunks of glass held an identifiable fingerprint, but so what? Even if it did, and even if I found it, what good would it be to me? A single print will nail a suspect, but it won't produce a suspect out of thin air. For that you need a full set of fingerprints, and you also need official access to federal records. What I had was useless from an investigative standpoint, and would be useful only when a suspect was in custody and a case was being made against him.

But it wasn't even good for that. The crime scene had been compromised beyond recognition, with the murders unreported, the bodies spirited away and tucked in an unmarked grave. What I held in my hand was evidence that a bottle had been broken. I knew people who'd call that a crime, but nobody who'd want to run prints to hunt down the man who'd broken it.

I stood inside the doorway, listening to traffic sounds, then lowered the steel door all the way down. I couldn't hear anything now, but it was hard to say what that proved; the traffic hadn't been all that loud.

What I was wondering about was the noise of the gunshots. I was assuming the killers had lowered the door before opening fire, but that wouldn't necessarily render the cubicle soundproof.

Of course they could have used suppressors. If so, that made it a little less likely the incident had been a spur-of-the-moment response to an unexpected opportunity for gain. A couple of resourceful sociopaths could have been on the scene, could have seen all those cases of booze. And they could have been carrying weapons at the time— some people, more than you'd think, never leave home unarmed.

But who routinely carries a silencer? No one I'd ever known.

I raised the door, stepped outside and looked around. Half a dozen units away, a man was shifting cartons from the back of a Plymouth Voyager, stowing them in his cubicle. A woman in khaki shorts and a green halter top was leaning against the side of the van and watching him work. Their car radio was playing, but so faintly that all I could tell was that it was music. I couldn't make it out.

Aside from my Ford, theirs was the only vehicle on that side of the building.

I decided the killers probably hadn't needed to muffle their gunfire. The odds were there hadn't been anyone around to hear it. And how remarkable would a few loud noises be? With the steel door shut, anyone within earshot would write off four or five shots as hammer blows, somebody assembling or disassembling a packing case, say. This was suburbia, after all, not a housing project in Red Hook. You didn't expect gunfire, didn't throw yourself on the pavement every time a truck backfired.

Still, why shoot them?

"NAMES AND ADDRESSES," TJ said, and frowned. "These be the dudes renting alongside where the two dudes got shot."

"According to the storage company's records."

"Somebody's bad enough to shoot two dudes and steal a truckload of liquor, you figure he'd put his real name down when he rents storage space?"

"Probably not," I said, "although stranger things have happened. There was a fellow a couple of months ago who robbed a bank, and his note to the teller was written on one of his own printed deposit slips."

"Stupid goes clear down to the bone, don't it?"

"It seems to," I agreed. "But if the shooters used a false name, that's a help. Because if one of the names on our list turns out to be phony—"

"Yeah, I get it. So we lookin' for one of two things. Somebody's got a record, or somebody that don't exist at all."

"Neither one necessarily proves anything," I said. "But it would give us a place to start."

He nodded and settled in at the keyboard, tapping keys, using the mouse. I'd bought him the computer for Christmas, at the same time installing it—and him—in my old room at the Northwestern. When Elaine and I moved in together I'd kept my hotel room across the street as a combination den and office, a place to go when I wanted to be alone, sitting at the window and thinking long thoughts.

I'd met TJ on Forty-second Street long before they prettied up the Deuce, and early on he appointed himself my assistant. He turned out to be not merely street-smart but resourceful. When Elaine opened her shop on Ninth Avenue, he took to hanging out there, filling in for her on occasion and revealing a talent for retail sales. I don't know where he lived before he took over my old room—the only address we ever had for him was his beeper number—but I guess he always found a place to sleep. You learn a lot of survival skills in the street. You'd better.

He'd since then learned computer skills as well. While I leafed through *Macworld* magazine, trying to find something written in a language I could understand, he tapped keys and frowned and whistled and jotted down notes on the sheet of paper I'd given him. Within an hour he'd established that all the names Leon Kramer had supplied belonged to living human beings, and he was able to furnish telephone numbers for all but two of them.

"This don't necessarily mean that all the information's straight dope," he pointed out. "Could be somebody rented a bin and put down a real name and address, only it's a name and address belongs to somebody else."

"Unlikely," I said.

"Whole deal's unlikely. I'm at my storage locker, and I happen to see you got all this liquor in *your* storage locker, and there I am with a gun in my pocket and a truck parked alongside?"

"The first part's plausible enough," I said. "You're there and you spot the whiskey. But why shoot me?"

"On account of you might not care to stand idly by while I load your booze onto my truck and drive off with it."

"Why not wait?"

"Come back later, you mean."

"Why not? I've got a station wagon, I'm not going to haul off more than a few cases. The rest'll be there when you come back with a truck and somebody to help with the heavy lifting. You can even do it at night, when it's less likely anybody'll see what you're doing."

"You go away and come back, you got the padlock to contend with."

"So? You drill it out or hacksaw it. Or spray it with Freon and take a hammer to it. What do you figure is trickier, getting past a padlock or taking out two men?"

He tapped the sheet of paper. "Sounds like we wastin' our time on these here."

"Unless somebody on the list happened to see or hear something."

"Long odds against that."

"Long odds against most things in life."

He looked at the list of names and numbers, shook his head. "Guess I got some calls to make."

"I'll make them."

"No, I'll make them. They mostly in Jersey. You make them, they go on your phone bill. I make them, they be free."

A couple of years ago I'd used the talents of a pair of high school computer hackers, and in gratitude they'd given me an unrequested perk. By doing some backing and filling within the phone company's labyrinthine computer system, they had so arranged things that all my long-distance calls were free. By leaving their handiwork in place, I was technically guilty of theft of services, but somehow I couldn't get too worked up about it. I wasn't even sure which long-distance carrier I was defrauding, and hadn't a clue how to go about straightening it out.

The free calls went with the hotel room, so TJ inherited them when he moved in. He'd installed a second line for the computer modem, so he could talk and tap keys at the same time.

That's the future, and I guess it works. I'm old-fashioned, and take perverse comfort in telling myself I'm too old to change. All I know how to do is knock on doors and ask a lot of questions.

"Use your Brooks Brothers accent," I said.

"Oh, you think, Dink? What I was figuring was I'd try to sound like a dude with a 'tude." He rolled his eyes. In the voice of an NPR announcer he said, "Let me assure you, sir, that neither asphalt nor Africa will register in my speech."

"I love it when you talk like that," I told him. "It's like watching a dog walk on his hind legs."

"That a compliment or an insult?"

"Probably a little of both," I said. "One thing, though. Remember you're talking to people from Jersey. If you speak too clearly, they won't be able to understand you."

ELAINE AND I went out for dinner and a movie, and I wound up telling her what I'd been doing. "I don't think TJ's going to learn anything," I said. "It's not too likely any of the other tenants were around yesterday when the shit hit the fan. If they were, I'd be surprised if they saw or heard anything."

"Where do you go from here?"

"I probably give him his money back, or as much of it as I can get him to take. The money's the least of it. I think he's afraid."

"Mick? It's hard to imagine him afraid of anything."

"Most tough guys are afraid a lot of the time," I said. "That's why they take the trouble to be tough. At the very least, I'd say he's anxious, and he's got reason to be. Somebody executed two of his men for no good reason. They didn't have to shoot anybody."

"They were sending him a message?"

"It looks that way."

"But not a very clear one, if he doesn't know what to make of it. What happens next?"

"I don't know," I said. "He didn't tell me much and I didn't ask. Maybe he's in a pissing contest with somebody. Maybe there'll be a certain amount of pushing and shoving before things sort themselves out."

"Gangsters fighting over territory? That kind of thing?"

"Something like that."

"It's not really your fight."

"No, it's not."

"You're not going to get involved, are you?"

I shook my head. "He's my friend," I said. "You like to talk about past lives and karmic ties, and I don't know how much of that I believe in, but I don't rule it out. Mick and I are connected on some sort of deep level, that much is clear."

"But your lives are different."

"Utterly. He's a criminal. I mean, that's what he does. I'm hardly a candidate for canonization, but essentially he and I are on opposite sides of the law." I thought about that. "That's if the law is something with only two sides to it, and I'm not sure it is. The job I did for Ray Gruliow last month was designed to help him get a client acquitted, and I know for a fact the son of a bitch was guilty as charged. So my job in that particular case was to see that justice wasn't done. And when I was a cop I gave perjured testimony more times than I can remember. The men I testified against had done what they were accused of doing, or else they'd done something else that we couldn't pin on them. I never framed an innocent man, or one who didn't damn well belong in prison, but what side of the law was I on when I lied to put him there?"

"Deep thoughts," she said.

"Yes, and I'm the Old Philosopher. But no, I'm not going to get involved in Mick's problem. He'll have to get through it on his own. And he probably will, whatever it is."

"I hope so," she said. "But I'm glad you're out of it."

THAT WAS ON Thursday. There was a message from TJ when we got home, but it was late and I didn't call him until the following morning, when I learned that he'd reached everybody on the list, including the two whose phone numbers he'd been previously unable to obtain.

"Computer gives you the world's longest arms," he said. "You like Plastic Man, you can reach out and touch someone and pick their pockets while you at it. But what good's it do you if their pockets is empty?"

And in fact his report was that he had nothing to report. Only one of the people on our list had paid a visit to E-Z Storage on the day in question, and she hadn't seen or heard anything memorable, let alone suspicious. If there'd been a truck there with men loading boxes onto it, she hadn't noticed. If there'd been gunshots, or loud noises of any kind, she hadn't heard them.

I called Mick at Grogan's and left word for him to call me. I tried the other numbers I had for him and nobody answered. He has a few apartments around the city, places he can go when he wants to sleep, or drink in private. I'd been to one of them once, an anonymous one-bedroom apartment in a postwar building up in Inwood, the furnishings minimal, a change of clothes in the closet, a small TV set with a rabbit ears antenna, a few bottles of Jameson on a shelf in the kitchen. And, almost certainly, someone else's name on the lease.

I'm not sure why I bothered trying those phone numbers, and I hung up not much concerned that I'd been unable to reach him. All I had to report, really, was that I didn't have anything to report. Nothing terribly urgent about that. It would keep.

WHEN I STOPPED drinking and started going to AA meetings, I heard a lot of people say a lot of different things about how to stay sober. Ultimately I learned that there are no rules—it's a lot like life itself in that respect—and you follow the suggestions to whatever extent you choose.

Early on I stayed out of bars, but when Mick and I became friends I found myself spending occasional long nights with him in his saloon, drinking Coke or coffee and watching him put away the twelve-year-old Irish. That's not generally recommended—*I* certainly wouldn't recommend it—but so far it hasn't felt dangerous to me, or inappropriate.

I've followed the conventional wisdom in some respects and ignored it in others. I've paid some attention to the program's Twelve Steps, but I can't say they've been in the forefront of my consciousness in recent years, and I've never been much good at prayer or meditation.

There are two areas, however, in which I've never strayed. A day at a time, I don't pick up the first drink. And, after all these years, I still go to meetings.

I don't go as often as I once did. In the beginning I damn near lived in meetings, and there was a time when I wondered if I might be abusing the privilege, attending too frequently, taking up a seat somebody else might need. I asked Jim Faber—this was before I asked him to be my sponsor—and he told me not to worry about it.

These days it's a rare week when I don't get to at least one meeting, and I generally manage to fit in two or three. The one I'm most regular at attending—I'm almost always there unless we go out of town for the weekend—is the Friday night step meeting at my home group. We meet at St. Paul the Apostle, three blocks from home at Ninth and Sixtieth. In the old drinking days I lit candles in that church, and stuffed spiritual hush money into the poor box. Now I sit in the basement on a folding chair, drinking sacramental coffee out of a Styrofoam chalice and dropping a dollar in the basket.

In the early days I could scarcely believe the things I heard at meetings. The stories themselves were extraordinary enough, but more remarkable to me was the willingness people demonstrated day after day to tell their most intimate secrets to a roomful of strangers. I was even more surprised a few months later to find myself equally candid. I've since learned to take that stunning candor for granted, but it still impresses me when I stop to think about it, and I've always enjoyed listening to the stories.

After the meeting I joined Jim Faber for coffee at the Flame. He's been my sponsor for all these years, and we still have a standing dinner date on Sunday nights. One or the other of us has to cancel occasionally, but we get together more often than not, meeting at one of the neighborhood's Chinese restaurants and talking from the hot and sour soup straight through to the fortune cookies. Nowadays we're as apt to discuss his problems as mine—his marriage has had its ups and downs, and his printing business almost went belly-up a few years ago. And we always have the problems of the world to solve if we're ever fresh out of problems of our own.

We drank our coffee and paid our separate checks. "C'mon," he said. "I'll walk you home."

"I'm not going home," I said, "although I'll pass the place. I've got a call to make and you won't want to go there."

"Some gin joint, would be my guess."

"Grogan's. I did a day's work for Ballou, and I've got to drop by and tell him what I found out."

"That what you were talking about earlier?"

During the meeting I'd shared about my occasional difficulties in setting boundaries. I'd been referring to the business at hand, although I'd avoided saying anything at all specific.

"It's hard to do the right thing," I told Jim, "when you're not sure what it is."

"That's the great advantage the religious fanatics have," he said. "They always know."

"Puts them way ahead of me."

"Me too," he said, "and the gap is ever widening. Every year there's a few more things I'm not sure of. I've decided that a wide-ranging uncertainty is the mark of the true maturity of man."

"Then I must be growing up," I said, "and it's about time. Are we on for Sunday night?"

He said we were. At the corner of Fifty-seventh we shook hands and said goodnight, and he turned right while I crossed the street. I started to turn automatically toward the Parc Vendôme's entrance, caught myself, then came close to going on in anyway. I was tired, and could call Ballou and tell him what I had to tell him over the phone.

But instead I stayed with the original plan and skirted the building, heading downtown on Ninth Avenue. I walked three blocks, passing Elaine's shop, then crossed to the west side of Ninth when the light turned and walked another block. I was just stepping off the curb at Fifty-third Street when a stocky guy with dark hair plastered down across his scalp popped up smack in front of me and stuck a gun in my face.

My first reaction was chagrin. Where had he come from, and how had I managed to be wholly unaware of his approach? The crime rate's down these days and the streets feel a lot safer, but you still have to pay attention. I'd been paying attention all my life, and what was the matter with me now?

"Scudder," he said.

I heard my name and felt better. At least I wasn't a random patsy, sufficiently oblivious to blunder into the role of mugging victim. That was reassuring, but it didn't do anything to improve the short-term outlook.

"This way," he said, and pointed with the gun. We moved onto the sidewalk and into the shadows on the side street. He stayed in front of me and kept the gun in my face, while a second man, behind me throughout, was behind me still. I hadn't had a look at him yet, but I could sense his presence and smell his beer-and-tobacco breath.

"You ought to quit sticking your nose into storage sheds in Jersey," the one with the gun said.

"All right."

"Huh?"

"I said all right. You want me out of it and I want out myself. No problem."

"You trying to be smart?"

"I'm trying to stay alive," I said, "and to save us all a headache. Especially me. I took a job that's not going anywhere and I was just on my way to tell the man to find himself another boy. I'm a married man and I'm not a kid anymore and I don't need the aggravation."

His nostrils flared and his eyebrows went up a notch. "They said you were a tough customer," he said.

"Years ago. See how tough you are when you get to be my age."

"And you're ready to forget the whole thing? Jersey, the cases of hooch, the two Irish guys?"

"What Irish guys?"

He looked at me.

I said, "See? It's forgotten."

He gave me a long look, and I read disappointment in his features. "Well," he said. "Turns out you're easier than you figured to be, but I still got to do what I got to do." I had an idea what that meant, and I knew I was right when the man behind me took hold of my upper arms and held on tight. The one in front tucked his gun under his belt and made his right hand into a fist.

"You don't have to do this," I told him.

"Call it a convincer."

He hit me right at the belt line, putting some muscle behind the blow. I had time to tense my stomach muscles, and that helped some, but he threw a good punch, getting his shoulder into it.

"Sorry," he said. "Just a couple more, huh?"

The hell with that. I didn't want to take a couple more. I set myself, visualizing my move before I made it, and he drew back his fist, and I shifted a foot and bore down full force on the instep of the son of a bitch who had my arms pinned. I felt bones snap. He cried and let go, and I stepped forward and threw a quick right, hitting the other son of a bitch a glancing blow on the side of the face.

I guess he didn't care for boxing when his opponent could hit back. He stepped back himself and tugged at the gun wedged under his belt, and I moved in on him, feinted with my right, and put everything I had into a left hook aimed at his right side just under his rib cage.

I hit what I aimed at, and it worked the way it was supposed to. I've seen boxers go down and stay down from a single blow to the liver. I don't hit as hard as they do, but I wasn't wearing gloves to cushion the blow, either. He dropped as if he'd been cut off at the knees and rolled on the sidewalk, clutching his middle and moaning.

The gun hit the sidewalk. I snatched it up and whirled around in time to catch the second man, the one whose foot I'd stomped, bearing down on me. He pulled up short when he saw the gun.

"Beat it," I said. "Come on, move! Get the hell out!"

His face was in the shadows and I couldn't read it. He looked at me, weighing the odds, and my finger tightened on the trigger. Maybe he noticed, maybe that made his decision for him. He drew back, deeper into the shadows, and scuttled around the corner and out of sight. He was limping a little, favoring the foot I'd damaged but moving quickly all the same. He had sneakers on, I noticed, while I was wearing a pair of regular leather shoes. If it had been the other way around, I might not have been able to break his hold on my arms.

The other guy, the one with the plastered-down hair, was still on the ground, still moaning. I pointed the gun at him. It had looked much larger when it had been aimed at me than it felt now in my hand. I stuffed his into my own waistband, wincing at the soreness where his opening shot had landed. My middle was tender already, and it would be ten times worse in the morning.

He didn't have to hit me, the son of a bitch.

My anger flared, and I looked down at him and caught him looking back up at me. I drew back a foot to kick him in the head. Kick his fucking head in, the son of a bitch.

But I overruled myself and held back. I didn't kick him.

My mistake.

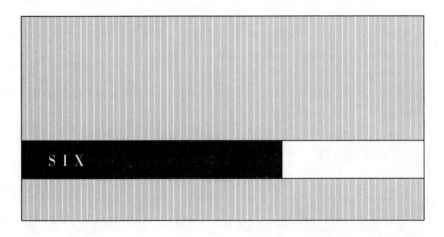

S I X

"**W**HEN I TOLD him I was out of it," I said, "I was telling the simple truth. I'd have said the same thing anyway, because I've never seen the point of talking back to a gun, but this time I wasn't just shining him on. I'd already decided I was done with the case, and I was on my way here to tell you as much when they braced me."

He'd been spelling Burke behind the stick when I came in, and I guess something must have shown in my face, because he was out from behind the bar before I could say a word, shepherding me to his office in the rear. He pointed to the green leather sofa but I stayed on my feet, and so did he, and I talked and he listened.

I said, "I'd already decided I was wasting my time and your money. I couldn't absolutely rule out the possibility that whoever killed your men and stole your whiskey was there by chance and acted on impulse. But I couldn't turn up anything at all to support that premise. And I wasn't comfortable trying to investigate from the other end. That would mean poking around in your business affairs, and I didn't want to do that."

"You did what you said you'd do."

"I guess so, even if all I learned was that there was nothing to learn. Then two clowns turned up with a gun, and in an eye blink they confirmed the conclusion I'd already drawn. If they were part of the package, then you couldn't possibly write off what happened across the river to coincidence and bad luck. You've got an enemy, and that's why Kenny and McCartney wound up dead."

"Ah, I think I knew as much all along," he said. "But I wanted to be certain."

"Well, it got certain for me the minute they showed up to warn me off. I was already off. That's what I said to them, and the hell of it is I think they believed me."

"But the fucker hit you all the same."

"He was apologetic about it," I said, "but that didn't make him pull the punch. So it didn't feel much like an apology."

"And you stood and took it."

"I didn't have a lot of choice. But one punch was as much as I wanted to take."

"And so you showed them what you could do. Jesus, I wish I'd been there to see it."

"I wish you'd been there to give me a hand," I said. "I'm too old for this shit."

"How's your stomach, man?"

"Not as bad as it'd be if I'd let him hit me again. You know, I was damn lucky. If I don't come down just right on his foot, he doesn't let go. And then all I've done is irritate them, and then where am I?" I shrugged. "On balance it was probably a mistake to fight back. He had a gun, for Christ's sake. And I knew they were killers, or at least working for killers. Hell, I saw what happened to Kenny and McCartney."

"You helped to bury them."

"So if I make these two angry I'm only going to get more of a beating, and they might use a gun instead of a fist, and they might even get carried away and shoot me. But I didn't have time to think it through. All I could do was react. And, as I said, I got lucky."

"I'd have paid to see it."

"You wouldn't want to pay too much. It was over in less time than it took me to tell about it. The adrenaline gives you a rush, I'll say that. When I was standing there watching one of them hurrying away on his bad foot while the other rolled around hugging his liver, I felt like Superman's big brother."

"You had the right."

"And I thought, well, the hell with you assholes. I was off the case, I was done with it, but fuck the two of you, and I'm back on it." I took a breath. "But I realized that wasn't so about the time the adrenaline wore off. What happened didn't change anything."

"No."

"I walked half a block and had to hang on to a lamppost while I threw up. I haven't puked on the street since I stopped drinking, and that's a few years now."

"Beyond the sore stomach," he said, "how do you feel now?"

"I'm all right."

"I'd say you could do with a drink, but you wouldn't take one, would you?"

"Not tonight."

"And doesn't your crowd ever recognize special circumstances? What manner of man would begrudge you a drink on a night like this?"

"It doesn't matter what anybody else would do," I said. "I'm the only man who can give me permission."

"And you won't."

"Suppose I decided it was all right to drink when I got punched in the stomach. What do you think would happen?"

He grinned. "You'd soon have a sore midsection."

"I would, because I'd make sure I got hit a lot. Mick, a drink wouldn't help me any. All it would do me is harm."

"Ah, I know that."

"And I don't really want one, anyway. All I want is to give you some of your money back, and then to go home and get in a hot tub."

"The last's a good idea. The heat will draw the pain and make the morning easier. But I'll not take money from you."

"I had to rent a car," I said, "and I put in an afternoon's work, and TJ spent a few hours riding the phone and the computer. I figure I earned about half of the thousand you gave me."

"You took a beating," he said, "and risked a bullet. For the love of God, man, keep the fucking money."

"I'D HAVE ARGUED with him," I told Elaine, "but I'd fought enough for one night. So I kept the money and treated myself to a cab home. I felt silly, riding that short a distance on a nice night like this, but I didn't really figure I needed the exercise."

"And you didn't want to run into them again."

"I never even thought about it," I said, "but maybe that was in the back of my mind. Not the idea of meeting up with them specifically, but the sense that the streets weren't a safe place all of a sudden."

I hadn't planned on saying anything to her, not right away. But when I walked into the apartment she took one look at me and knew something was wrong.

"So you're done working for Mick," she said now.

"I was done anyway. In the movies the best way to keep a detective on the job is to try scaring him off, but that's not how it works in the real world. Not this time, anyway. Mick wouldn't let me give the money back, but he didn't try to talk me out of resigning, either. He knew I'd done what I set out to do."

"Do they know that, honey?"

"The two heavies? I told them so, and I think they believed me. Punching me out was part of their deal, so the guy took his best shot, but that didn't mean he didn't believe me."

"And now?"

"You think he changed his mind?"

"In his mind," she said, "you were quitting the job because he'd managed to intimidate you."

"And that was partly the case. Although it would be more accurate to say he'd reinforced a decision I'd already made."

"But then you fought back," she said. "And won."

"It was a lucky punch."

"Whatever it was, it worked. You sent one scampering and left the other writhing in agony. What's so funny?"

" 'Writhing in agony.' "

"Rolling around and trying to put his liver back together? That sounds to me like writhing in agony."

"I suppose."

"What I'm getting at is you weren't acting intimidated. Though I suppose you must have been afraid."

"Not while it was going on. You're too much in the moment to have any room left for fear. Afterward, walking across Fifty-third Street, I started sweating like the guy in *Broadcast News*."

"The guy in . . . oh, Albert Brooks. That was a funny movie."

"And then of course I had to stop and vomit. In the gutter, of course, because I'm a gentleman. So I guess we can say I was scared, once it was over and there was nothing to be scared of. But for a few critical seconds there I was Mister Cool."

"My hero," she said. "Baby, they didn't see you afterward, did they? They missed the shakes and the flop sweat. All they ever saw was Mister Cool."

"You're concerned they're going to turn up again."

"Well, aren't you?"

"I can't rule out the possibility. But why should they? They'll see for themselves I'm not chasing out to Jersey or hanging out at Grogan's. I went there tonight, but I won't be going there again until all of this blows over."

"And you don't think they'll want to get even?"

"Again, it's possible. They're pros, but even a pro can let his ego get caught up in his work. I'll keep my eyes open the next couple of weeks, and I'll stay out of dark alleys."

"That's never a bad idea."

"And you know what else I think I'll do? I'll carry a gun."

"That one?"

I'd put it on the coffee table. I picked it up now and felt the weight of it on my palm. It was a revolver, a .38-caliber Smith, with hollow-point shells in five of the cylinder's six chambers.

"I carried one a lot like this," I said, "when I was on the job. They always weigh more than you think they're going to, even a stubby one like this. It's got a one-inch barrel. The piece I mostly carried had a two-inch."

"When you came up to my apartment," she said, "the first thing you would do was take off your gun and set it aside."

"As I remember it, the first thing I would do was kiss you."

"The second thing, then. You made a ritual of it."

"Did I?"

"Uh-huh. Maybe it was a way of showing you felt safe with me."

"Maybe."

When we met, I was a married cop and she was a sweet and innocent young call girl. Ages ago, that was. Another lifetime, two other lifetimes.

I said, "A few years ago they realized the cops were outgunned by the bad guys, especially the drug dealers. So they called in the revolvers and gave everybody nines. Nine-millimeter automatics. More rounds in the clip than you can load into one of these, and more stopping power. But I think this is as much gun as I'll need."

"I hope you won't need any gun at all, but I agree it's not a bad idea for you to carry it. But is it legal?"

"I have a carry permit. This gun's not registered, or if it is it's not registered to me. So in that sense it's a violation for me to carry it, but I'm not going to worry about it."

"Then I won't worry, either."

"If I have to use it, the fact that it's unregistered is the least of my problems. And if there's an incident that I'd just as soon not report, the lack of paper could be a plus."

"You mean if you shoot someone and walk away from it."

"Something like that." I put the gun on the table and yawned. "What I'd like to do is go straight to bed," I said, "but I'm going to soak in a hot tub first. Come morning I'll be glad I did."

I DIDN'T DOZE off in the tub, but I came close. I stayed in it until the water wasn't hot anymore. I toweled dry and headed for the bedroom, and when I got there the lights were dim and there was soft music playing, a John Pizzarelli album we both liked. She was standing beside the bed, wearing perfume and a smile, and she came over to me and unfastened the towel from around my waist.

"You've got something in mind," I said.

"See what happens when a girl marries a detective? He doesn't miss a thing. Now why don't you get in the middle of the bed and lie on your back with your eyes closed?"

"I'll fall asleep."

"We'll see about that," she said.

AFTERWARD SHE SAID, "Maybe it's an affirmation of the life force. Or maybe I just got horny at the thought of you stretching those two goons. But that was nice, wasn't it? And it didn't hurt your sore tummy or anything else because you didn't have to move a muscle. Well, maybe one muscle.

"And I love you so much, you old bear. It makes me crazy to think of anybody trying to hurt you, and all I want to do is hunt them down and kill them. But I'm a girl and that means I'm stuck with the traditional female role of providing aid and succor. Especially succor.

"And all you want to do is sleep, you poor bear, and this crazy broad won't leave you alone. You had your succor—don't you love that word?—and now you're drifting off. Oh, sleep tight, my darling. Sweet dreams. I love you."

I AWOKE KNOWING I'd had some unusually vivid dreams but unable to recall them. I showered and shaved and went into the kitchen. Elaine had gone off to a yoga class and left a note telling me as much, and that coffee was made. I poured myself a cup and drank it at the living room window.

My stomach was predictably sore from the blow I'd taken, and there was some equally predictable discoloration. It would be worse tomorrow, in all likelihood, and then it would start getting better.

Both my hands were a little stiff and sore, too, from the right that had glanced off the side of his head and the left that had gone where it was supposed to. I had other muscular aches here and there, in the arms and shoulders, in the calf of one leg, and in my upper back. I'd used various muscles in ways I didn't often use them, and there was a price to pay. There always is.

I took a couple of aspirin and dialed a phone number I didn't have to look up. "I almost called you last night," I told Jim Faber, after I'd filled him in on what he'd missed after we'd parted company.

"You could have."

"I thought about it. But it was pretty late. If Elaine hadn't been here I wouldn't have hesitated, it was no time for me to be alone, but she was here and I was all right."

"And you don't keep booze around the house."

"No, and I didn't want a drink."

"Still, going straight to a ginmill right after a street fight . . ."

"I paused at the threshold," I said, "and decided I was all right. I had a message to deliver, and I delivered it, and then I got the hell out of there and came home."

"How do you feel now?"

"Old."

"Really? I'd think you'd be feeling like a young lion. How old were the guys you beat up?"

"I wouldn't say I beat them up. I surprised them and I lucked out. How old? I don't know. Say thirty-five."

"Kids."

"Not exactly."

"Still, that's got to feel good, Matt. Two young fellows and you knock them on their asses? Even if luck had a little to do with it—"

"More than a little."

"—it still goes in the books as a win."

We talked some more, and he steered the conversation to our Sunday dinner date, suggesting we meet at the Chinese vegetarian place across from the Coliseum. "Months since we ate there," he said, "and I'm in the mood for some of that famous ersatz eel of theirs."

"Out of business," I said.

"You're kidding. Since when?"

"I don't know, but I saw the sign in their window sometime early last week. 'Restaurant Close. Go Somewhere Else. Thanks You.' Not quite the way they'd put it in the English as a Second Language class, but the message was crystal clear."

"Elaine must be distraught."

"Try inconsolable. We found a vegetarian place in Chinatown, there are a few of them down there now, but the one on Fifty-eighth was a favorite of hers and it was right around the corner. It's going to leave a hole in her life."

"It'll leave a small one in mine. Where else am I gonna find eel made from soybeans? I don't care for real eel, only the phony kind."

"You want to try the place in Chinatown?"

"Well, I'd like to have that eel dish one more time before I die, but that's a long way to go for it."

"I'm not even sure they've got eel on the menu. The joint on Fifty-eighth's the only place I've ever seen it."

"In other words we could drag our asses all the way downtown and I'd wind up having abalone made out of gluten?"

"It's a risk you'd be running."

"Or lamb chops made out of library paste. Eel aside, I'd just as soon stick to real food, so let's forget about Chinatown. God knows there are enough Chinese places in the neighborhood."

"Pick one."

"Hmmm," he said. "Where haven't we been in a while? How about the little place on Eighth and Fifty-third? You know the one I'm thinking of? The northeast corner, except it's not right *at* the corner, it's one or two doors up the avenue."

"I know the one you mean. The Something Panda. I want to say Golden, but that's not right."

"Pandas are generally black and white."

"Thanks. You're right, though, we haven't been there in ages. And as I recall it was pretty good."

"They're all pretty good. Six-thirty?"

"Perfect."

"And can I trust you to stay out of fistfights between now and then? And ginmills?"

"It's a deal," I said.

THERE'S A GUN shop on Centre Market Place, around the block from the old Centre Street police headquarters. They've been there forever, and they carry a wide range of weapons, along with a full stock of police gear and training manuals. I went there to buy a shoulder holster, and as an afterthought I picked up a box of shells, the same hollow-point ammunition as the five in the Smith. Anybody can buy a holster, but I had to show a permit to buy the shells. I'd brought mine, and showed it, and signed the register.

They had Kevlar vests, too, but I already owned one. In fact I was wearing it, I'd put it on before I left the house.

It was a warm day to be wearing a bulletproof vest, with the humidity a few percentage points beyond the comfort range. I didn't need a jacket on a day like that, but I was wearing my navy blazer. I had the little Smith jammed under my belt, and I needed the jacket to keep it from showing, even as I'd need it to conceal the shoulder holster.

They gave me the shells and the holster in a paper bag, and I walked around carrying it, looking for a place to have lunch. I passed up a slew of Asian restaurants and wound up on Mulberry Street, on the two-block stretch that's about all that's left of Little Italy. I sat in the rear garden at Luna and ordered a plate of linguini with red clam sauce. While they were fixing it I locked myself in the men's room. I shucked my jacket and put on the holster, adjusted the straps, then drew the gun from my waistband and tucked it in place. I checked the mirror, and it seemed to me that the bulge of the holster would be visible clear across the room. It was more comfortable, though, than walking around with the gun in my belt, especially with my middle as sore as it was.

On the way back to my table I had the feeling that everybody in the restaurant, if not everyone in the neighborhood, knew I was armed.

I ate my lunch and went home.

WHEN TJ CALLED I was watching Notre Dame beat up on Miami. I'd slung my blazer over the back of a chair and I was sitting around in my shirtsleeves, with the holster in place and the gun in it. I put on the blazer and went across the street to the Morning Star.

We usually sat at one of the window tables, and he was there when I arrived, sipping orange juice through a straw. I moved us to a table near the kitchen, far away from the windows, and sat where I could keep an eye on the entrance.

TJ noted all this without comment. After I'd ordered coffee he said, "Heard all about you. How you the baddest dude in the 'hood, kickin' ass and takin' names."

"At my age," I said, "it's more a matter of kicking ass and forgetting names. What did you hear and where did you hear it?"

"Already said what I heard, and where you think I heard it? I was over at Elaine's shop. Oh, did I hear it on the street? No, but if you tryin' to build yourself a rep, I be happy to spread the word."

"Don't do me any favors."

"You all dressed for success. Where we goin', Owen?"

"Nowhere that I know of."

"Elaine says you be all done investigatin' what went down in Jersey, but I was thinkin' maybe you just told her that to put her at ease."

"I wouldn't do that. I was done anyway, before the incident last night, and all it did was confirm what you and I already determined."

"We ain't workin', must be you dressed up just to come here for coffee." He cocked his head, eyed the bulge on the left side of my chest. "That what I think it is?"

"How would I know?"

" 'Cause how you know what I thinkin'? 'Cept you do know, an' I know, too, 'cause she already said how you takin' precautions. That the piece you took off of the dude?"

"The very same. It's not hard to spot, is it?"

"Not when you lookin' for it, but it ain't like you wearin' a sign. You was to go around like that all the time, you'd want to get your jacket tailored so it don't bulge."

"I used to carry night and day," I said. "On duty or off. There was a departmental regulation that said you had to. I wonder if it's still on the books. With all the drunken off-duty cops who've shot themselves and each other over the years, the brass might have decided to rethink that particular rule."

"Cops'd carry anyway, wouldn't they? Reg or no reg?"

"Probably. I lived out on Long Island for years, and the regulation was only in force within the five boroughs, but I carried all the time. Of course there was another regulation requiring a New York City police officer to reside within the five boroughs, but it was never hard to find a way around that one."

He sucked up the last of the orange juice and the straw made a gurgling noise. He said, "Don't know who thought up orange juice, but the man was a genius. Tastes so good it's near impossible to believe it's good for you. But it is. Unless they lyin', Brian?"

"As far as I know, they're telling the truth."

"Restores my faith," he said. " 'Member the time I bought a gun on the street for you? Gave it to you in a Kangaroo, same as the seller gave it to me."

"So you did. It was a blue one."

"Blue, right. Sort of a lame color, if I remember right."

"If you say so."

"You still got it?"

I'd obtained the gun for a friend who was dying of pancreatic cancer. She wanted a quick way out if it got too bad to be borne. It got very bad indeed before it finally killed her, but she'd somehow been able to live with it until she died of it, and she'd never had to use the gun.

I didn't know what became of the gun. I suppose it sat on a shelf in her closet, snug in the blue Kangaroo fanny pack in which I'd delivered it. I suppose somebody found it when they went through her effects, and I had not the slightest idea what might have become of it since.

"They ain't hard to find," he went on. "All those Korean dudes, got them little stores, tables out front full of sunglasses and baseball caps? They all got Kangaroos. Set you back ten, fifteen dollars, few dollars more if you go for all leather. How much you have to pay for that shoulder rig?"

"More than ten or fifteen dollars."

"Kangaroo wouldn't spoil the line of your jacket. Wouldn't need to be wearin' a jacket, far as that goes."

"I probably won't need the gun at all," I said. "But if I do I won't want to screw around with a zipper."

"You sayin' that's not how Quick Draw McGraw does it."

"Right."

"What a lot of the dudes do is leave the zipper open. That looks sort of cool anyway."

"Like wearing sneakers with the laces untied."

"Sort of like that, 'cept you ain't likely to trip over your Kangaroos. Things turn tense, you just reach in your hand and there you are." He rolled his eyes. "But I be wastin' my breath, Beth, on account of you ain't about to get no Kangaroo, are you?"

"I guess not," I said. "I guess I'm just not a Kangaroo kind of guy."

I WENT BACK and watched some more football, changing channels whenever they went to a commercial and not really keeping track of any of the games. A little before six I turned off the TV and walked down to Elaine's shop. ELAINE MARDELL, the sign above the window says, and the shop within is a good reflection of the proprietor—folk art and antiques, paintings she's salvaged from thrift shops and rummage sales, and the oils and drawings of a few contemporary artists she's discovered. She has an artist's eye, and spotted the gun instantly.

"Oho," she said. "Is that what I think it is? Or are you just glad to see me?"

"Both."

She reached to unbutton the jacket. "It's less obvious that way," she said.

"Until it opens up and becomes a lot more obvious."

"Oh, right. I didn't think of that."

"TJ was pushing hard for a Kangaroo."

"Just your style."

"That's what I told him."

"This is a nice surprise," she said. "I was just getting ready to close up."

"And I was hoping to take you out to dinner."

"Hmmm. I want to go home and wash up first."

"I figured you might."

"And change clothes."

"That too."

Heading up Ninth, she said, "Since we're going home anyway, why don't I cook something?"

"In this heat?"

"It's not that hot, and it'll be a cool evening. In fact it might rain."

"It doesn't feel like rain."

"The radio said it might. Anyway, it's not hot in our apartment. I kind of feel like pasta and a salad."

"You'd be surprised how many restaurants can fix that for you."

"No better than I can fix it myself."

"Well, if you insist," I said. "But I was leaning toward Armstrong's or Paris Green, and afterward we could go down to the Village and hear some music."

"Oh."

"Now there's enthusiasm."

"Well, what *I* was thinking," she said, "was pasta and a salad at home, to be followed by a double feature on the VCR." She patted her handbag. "*Michael Collins* and *The English Patient*. Romance and violence, in whichever order we decide."

"A quiet evening at home," I said.

"He said, barely able to contain his excitement. What's wrong with a quiet evening at home?"

"Nothing."

"And we missed both of these movies, and we've been promising ourselves we'd see them."

"True enough," I said.

We left it at that until we hit the lobby of our building. Then I said, "We're both overreacting, aren't we? You don't want me to leave the house."

"And you want to prove the bastards can't keep you from doing anything you want to do."

"Whether or not I really want to do it. One thing you forgot to mention is it's Saturday night, and anyplace we go is likely to be crowded and noisy. If I weren't such a stubborn son of a bitch, a quiet evening at home would probably strike me as a terrific idea."

"You don't sound like such a stubborn son of a bitch."

"I did a few minutes ago."

"But you're starting to come around," she said. "Will this tip the balance? I stocked up on Scotch bonnet peppers the other day. The sauce for the pasta will loosen your scalp, and that's a promise."

"Dinner first," I said, "and then *Michael Collins*. That way if I fall asleep in front of the set all I'll miss is *The English Patient*."

"You drive a hard bargain, mister."

"Well, I married a Jewish girl," I said. "She taught me well."

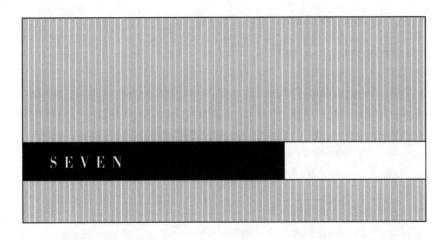

SEVEN

SUNDAY MORNING I looked at my middle and half the colors in the rainbow looked back at me. It felt a little better even though it looked a good deal worse, and it seemed to me my other aches and pains had receded some.

I got dressed and went into the kitchen for a bagel and a cup of coffee. Elaine asked how I felt and I told her. "A few years ago," I said, "I'd have come back a lot faster from a punch like that. I wouldn't have had to check every morning to see how I felt."

"And maintenance keeps taking more time and effort," she said. "Who the hell had to bother with exercise? Speaking of which, I think I'll get over to the gym for an hour."

"I'm almost desperate enough to join you."

"Why don't you? There's every machine you could possibly want, and plenty of free weights if you want to be a Luddite about it. And tons of women in Spandex to look at, and the whirlpool afterward for your aching muscles. And the look on your face tells me you're not coming."

"Not today," I said. "I used up too much energy just hearing about the machines. You know what I really feel like? Nothing so energetic as a gym workout, but a nice long walk. Down to the Village and back, or up to Ninety-sixth Street and back."

"Well, you could do that if you want to."

"But you don't think I should."

"Just dress warm, huh? Wear your vest and your shoulder holster."

"Maybe I'll hang around the house today."

"Why don't you, sweetie? You can do some very gentle partial sit-ups if you want to mend quicker. But why not give those jerks another day to lose interest in you?"

"It makes sense."

"Plus you've got the Sunday *Times* to read, and just lifting it is more exercise than people in the rest of the country get in a month. And there must be plenty of sports on television."

"I think I'll have another bagel," I said. "It sounds as though I'm going to need the energy."

I READ THE paper and watched the Giants game. When it ended I switched back and forth between the Jets and Bills on NBC and a seniors golf tournament. I didn't much care who won the football game—they didn't either, from the way they were playing—and the golf wasn't even interesting, although there was something curiously hypnotic about it.

It had the same effect on Elaine, who brought me a cup of coffee and wound up staring transfixed at the set until they broke the spell with a Midas Muffler commercial. "Why was I watching that?" she demanded. "What do I care about golf?"

"I know."

"And what do I care about Midas Mufflers? When I buy a muffler it'll be the brand George Foreman advertises."

"Meineke."

"Whatever."

"Since we don't have a car . . ."

"You're right. When I buy a muffler it'll be cashmere."

She left the room and I went back to watching the golf, and, while some fellow in too-bright clothing lined up his birdie putt, I found myself thinking of Lisa Holtzmann. What I was thinking was that it was just the right sort of lazy afternoon to spend at her apartment.

Just a passing thought, even as I'll still have the thought of a drink, even in the absence of any real desire for one. I'd smelled all that bourbon the other night, and the bouquet had gone straight to the memory banks, but it hadn't made me want a drink. I'd smelled it again the next day, along with smells of blood and death and gunfire, fainter a day later but still very much there to be noted. I hadn't wanted a drink then, either.

And I didn't want Lisa now, but evidently I wanted to be out of the space I was in, not the physical space of our apartment but the mental space, the chamber of self I occupied. That's what she'd always been, more than a source of pleasure, more than a conquest, more than good company. She was a way to get out, and I was a person who would always want to get out. No matter how comfortable my life was, no matter how well suited I was to it and it to me, I would always want to slip away and hide for a while.

Part of who I am.

Just seeing her there, just catching her eye, just watching her holding hands with Florian, had served to put her in mind. I wasn't going to see her. I wasn't even going to call her. But it was something I could talk about later with Jim, and something I wasn't going to bother thinking about anymore for now.

Meanwhile, I'd watch the fellows play golf.

"YOU LOOK NICE," Elaine said. She reached to touch the front of my windbreaker and felt the gun through it. "Very nice. The way it billows out, the holster's completely hidden. And if you keep it zipped halfway like that, you can get it in a hurry, can't you?"

I demonstrated, drawing the gun, putting it back.

"And your red polo shirt," she said, and reached to undo a button. "Oh, I see, you had it buttoned so the vest wouldn't show. But it looks better open, and so what if the vest shows? You can't tell what it is. It could be an undershirt."

"Under a polo shirt?"

"Or a tattoo," she said. "You look good. There's just enough contrast between the windbreaker and your khakis so it doesn't look like a uniform."

"I'm glad," I said, "because I was really concerned about that."

"Well, you should be. Suppose some dame pulls up and asks you to check her oil? How would you feel?"

"I don't think I'm going to answer that."

"You're a wise man," she said. "Gimme a kiss. Mmmm. Have fun. Be careful. Give my love to Jim."

I went outside. It felt like rain, and we could use it. The air was thick and heavy, and needed the rinsing a good downpour would provide. But my guess was it was going to hold off awhile longer, as it had been holding off for several days now.

I walked the long crosstown block to Eighth Avenue and a few blocks downtown to the restaurant, which turned out to be the Lucky Panda. There was a panda depicted on the sign, conventionally black and white, and smiling as if he'd just won the lottery.

Jim Faber was already there, and he was easy to spot in a restaurant that was mostly empty. The table he'd chosen was one I'd have picked myself, against a side wall in the rear. He was reading the magazine section of the *Times*, and he put it aside at my approach and got to his feet.

"Ike and Mike," he said.

We shook hands, and I said, "Come again?"

He pointed at me, then at himself. " 'Ike and Mike, they look alike.' You never heard that expression?"

"Not recently."

"I had twin cousins three years older than myself. I ever mention them?"

"I don't think so. Their names were Ike and Mike?"

"No, of course not. Their names were Paul and Philip, but everybody called Philip Buzzy. God knows why. But I had this uncle, not the twins' father but another uncle, and every time he saw them he said the same thing."

" 'Hello, boys.' "

" 'Ike and Mike, they look alike.' Every goddamn time, which meant every family event, and there were plenty of those. For a family full of people who didn't much like one another, we got together a lot. 'Ike and Mike, they look alike.' Must have driven them up the fucking wall, but they never complained. But then you didn't complain in my family. You learned not to."

" 'Quit your crying or I'll give you something to cry about.' "

"Jesus, yes. Your father used to say that?"

"No, never. But I had an uncle who was always saying that to his kids. And I gather it wasn't just talk."

"I heard it a lot myself growing up, and it wasn't just talk in our house, either. Anyway, that's the sorrowful saga of Ike and Mike."

We were both wearing tan windbreakers over red polo shirts and khaki slacks. "We're not quite twins," I said. "I'm wearing a bulletproof vest."

"Thanks for telling me. Now I'll know to duck behind you when the lead starts flying."

"When you do," I said, "I'll be blazing away at the bastards."

"Oh? You're packing heat?"

"In a shoulder rig," I said, and slid the zipper down far enough to show it, then zipped it up again.

"I'll sleep better," he said, "knowing my dinner companion is armed and dangerous. Change seats with me."

"Huh?"

"C'mon," he said. "Change seats with me. That way you can have a view of the entrance."

"If anybody tries anything," I said, "it'll be on the street. The only thing I have to worry about in here is the mu shu pork."

He laughed at that, but all the same he came around the table, and I shrugged and took the seat he'd vacated. "There," he said. "I've done my part. I suppose you have to keep your jacket on, unless you want the whole world to see that you're strapped. What's the matter?"

" 'Packing heat,' " I said. " 'Strapped.' "

"Hey, I stay current on the lingo. I watch TV." He grinned. "I'm keeping my jacket on, too, but not out of solidarity. I swear the last time I was in here it was in the middle of a heat wave and it was hotter in here than it was outside. Today's a nice autumn day and they've got the air conditioner going full blast. Did you have air conditioning at home when you were a kid?"

"Are you kidding? We were lucky we had air."

"Same here," he said. "We had a fan, and everybody would huddle together in front of it, and it would blow hot air on us."

"But you didn't complain."

"No, heat was different," he said. "Heat you could complain about. Here's our guy. You want to order?"

"I haven't even looked at the menu," I said. "And I want to wash up first. If you want you can go ahead and order for both of us."

He shook his head. "No hurry," he said, and told the waiter we'd need a few minutes.

I found the men's room and used it. The usual sign advised me that employees were required to wash their hands, and I washed mine, even though I was unemployed at the moment. They had one of those hot-air dryers instead of paper towels, and if I'd noticed it ahead of time I might not have been so quick to wash my hands. I hate the damned things, they take forever and my hands never feel dry when I'm done. But I'd washed them, and now I stood there and dried them, and while it took its time I thought how I'd report all this to Jim in a few minutes.

I looked at myself in the mirror and fussed with my shirt collar, trying to hide the vest without buttoning the top button. Not that anyone could really see it, or know what they were seeing. Not that it mattered. Still, if I took hold of it and tugged it down a little in front—

That's what I was doing when I heard the shots.

I COULD HAVE failed to notice them. They weren't that loud. Or I could have taken them for something else. A truck backfiring, a waiter dropping a tray. Anything at all.

But for some reason I knew instantly what I was hearing and realized just what it meant. I burst out of the men's room and raced the length of the hallway and into the dining room. I took in the scene there at a glance—Jim, an openmouthed waiter, a pair of customers trying to shrink into the woodwork, a thin blond woman on the verge of hysteria, another woman trying to calm her. I ran past all of them and out the door, but the shooter was nowhere to be seen. He'd vanished around a corner or jumped into a waiting car. Or disappeared in a puff of smoke, but whatever he'd done he was gone.

I went back inside. Nothing had changed. No one had moved. Jim was at our table, his back to the entrance. He had resumed reading while I was in the men's room, and the magazine section was on the table, open to an article about parents who kept their children out of school and educated them at home. I'd known a few people over the years who'd talked about wanting to do that, but nobody who'd actually done it.

He must have been reading when the killer approached, and he probably never saw it coming. He'd been shot twice in the side of the head with a small-caliber pistol, a .22, as it turned out. There was a time when such weapons were ridiculed as toys or ladies' guns, but they'd since become the ordnance of choice for professional killers. I'm not entirely sure why. I'm told that a lighter bullet tends to carom around inside the skull, greatly increasing the likelihood that a head shot will prove fatal. Maybe it's that, or maybe it's an ego thing. If you're really good at your trade you don't need a cannon, you can do fine with a scalpel.

He'd been shot twice, as I said, once in the temple, once in the ear. Not much more than an inch separated the two bullet holes. The killer got in close—I could see the powder burns, I could smell scorched hair and flesh—and he'd dropped the gun when he was done using it, leaving it behind along with the ejected casings.

I didn't touch the gun or move to examine it. I didn't know then that it was in fact a .22, I didn't recognize the maker or model, but that's what it looked like, and that's what the wounds looked like.

He'd slumped forward, the unwounded side of his face pressed against the magazine open on the table in front of him. Blood had trickled down his cheek and some of it had pooled on the magazine.

Not a lot of blood, though. You pretty much stop bleeding once you're dead, and he must have been dead before the killer cleared the threshold, perhaps even before the gun hit the floor.

How old was he? Sixty-one, sixty-two? Something like that. A middle-aged man in a red polo shirt and khakis, wearing an unzipped tan windbreaker. He still had most of his hair, though it had crept back some from his forehead and was thinning at the crown. He'd shaved that morning, nicking himself lightly on the chin. I couldn't see the place now but I'd noticed it earlier, before I went to the men's room. He did that a lot, cut himself shaving. Used to do that a lot.

Ike, of Ike and Mike.

I stood there. People were saying things and they may have been saying some of them to me, but nothing was registering. My eyes were focused on a sentence from the article on home schooling, but that wasn't registering either. I just stood there, and eventually I heard a siren, and eventually the cops showed up.

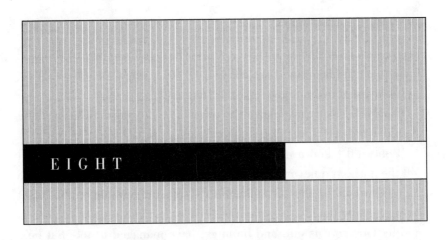

IF ONLY.

If only I'd canceled dinner. We'd seen a lot of each other in the past several weeks. Let's skip a week, I could have suggested. He wouldn't have objected. Odds are he'd have been secretly relieved.

If only we'd gone down to Chinatown. The vegetarian place down there was on Pell Street, up a long flight of narrow stairs. A pro would never hit anybody in a place like that, leaving himself with a tricky escape route.

If only I'd put on different clothes. I've never paid much attention to what I'm wearing, I generally grab the top shirt off the stack. This time the shirt happened to be red, and so did his.

Whoever tagged me from the Parc Vendôme to the Lucky Panda was following a man in a red polo shirt and khaki slacks and a tan windbreaker. And when he (or whoever he called) entered the restaurant himself, he saw a man in those very clothes sitting alone at a table, the only person around who came close to fitting the description. He didn't need to ask to see some ID. He did what he'd come to do and dropped the gun on the floor and took off.

If only he'd taken a good look at Jim first.

If only I'd worn my blazer. So what if it bulged a little over the shoulder holster? I wasn't posing for a layout in *GQ*.

If only I'd taken a minute to empty my goddamn bladder before I left the house. I'd never have left the table, I'd have been sitting across from Jim when the shooter walked in. Son of a bitch would have thought he was seeing double. He might well have decided to shoot both of us and let God sort us out, and he might have managed it, too, but he'd have had a moment's confusion, a few seconds while he paused and figured it out, and maybe that would have been time enough for me to spot him and go for my own gun.

If only I'd resisted his suggestion to change seats. Jim might have seen the guy walk in, might have had a chance to react. And the shooter, seeing his face instead of the back of his head, might have realized he had the wrong man.

If only I'd skipped washing my hands. Or wiped them on my pants instead of wasting time at the hot-air dryer. I'd have been emerging from the men's room right around the time the shooter was approaching Jim's table. I could have called out a warning, could have drawn my own gun, could have dropped the bastard before he shot my friend.

If only . . .

If only I'd stood there and taken my beating like a man the other night. It wouldn't have killed me, and that would have been the end of it. I'd have learned my lesson, or seemed to, and they'd have left me alone. But no, I had to be a hero, I had to show off and fight back.

If only I'd been wearing sneakers that night. I was wearing them now. Why couldn't I have been wearing them then? When I stomped the foot of the guy behind me, he'd have grunted and held on, and I'd have earned an extra wallop for my troubles.

If only I'd followed through. If I insisted on fighting back and if I was lucky enough to come out ahead, why couldn't I have finished the job? If only I'd acted on my impulse and kicked the slugger in the head, and kicked him again, and kept at it until I kicked his fucking head in. And put a bullet in the other one's chest while I was at it, and pressed the gun into his buddy's fist. Let the cops figure that one out. With a couple of lowlife skells like that, they wouldn't kill themselves trying.

Oh, hell. If only I'd passed on the case in the first place. Told Mick I didn't want to get involved. I'd wound up telling him that anyway just a day later.

Story of my life, always a day late and a dollar short.

IF ONLY I'D fired him as a sponsor. I'd been sober for years, I'd evidently long since mastered the subtle art of not drinking a day at a time, so what did I need with a sponsor? Why prolong the relationship, and why maintain the silly tradition of Chinese Sunday night dinners?

Elaine could have reminded me that I was a married man, that I ought to be having dinner every Sunday with my wife. She'd never do that, it wasn't like her at all, but if only she had.

If only I'd never picked him as a sponsor in the first place. He'd been the obvious choice, the only person who paid any real attention to me when I started coming to meetings at St. Paul's. I was still drinking on and off at first, not at all sure I wanted to be there and apparently incapable of declaring myself an alcoholic, or indeed of saying anything more than I absolutely had to. When it was my inescapable turn to speak, I'd say, *My name is Matt, and I think I'll just listen tonight.* I didn't think anyone noticed me, and it was months later before I learned that I'd had an AA sobriquet for a little while there. People referred to me as Matt the Listener.

But he took an interest, always said hello, always passed the time of day. Invited me to join a couple of them for coffee after the meeting. Listened respectfully when I spouted nonsense in the manner of the newly sober. Offered the occasional suggestion, so gently put that I rarely realized I hadn't thought of it myself.

I keep hearing I ought to get a sponsor, I said offhandedly one night. Said it after having rehearsed it for two days. What do you think? I said.

It's probably not a bad idea, he said.

No, I said, about you being my sponsor. What do you think about that?

I think I probably already am, he said. But, he said, if you'd like to make it formal, I'd say it sounds okay to me.

He was just this guy in an old army jacket. For a long time I didn't know what he did for a living, or what life he had outside the AA rooms. Then he led a meeting and I heard his story. And then we got to know each other, and drank gallons of coffee at meetings and after meetings, and sat across the table from each other on hundreds of Sunday nights.

If only I'd picked someone else to be my sponsor, or no one at all. If only I'd looked around that basement room and said thanks but no thanks and gone back out for a drink.

HE'D NEVER LET me get away with crap like that. You must have one hell of an ego, he told me more than once, to be that hard on yourself. Where do you get off setting yourself such impossibly high standards? Who do you think you are, anyway? The piece of shit the world revolves around?

I said, You mean I'm not?

You're just a man, he said. You're just another alcoholic.

That's all?

That's enough, he said.

IF ONLY THE past were subject to change.

When TJ has second thoughts at the computer, he can press certain keys and undo the previous action. But, as a pinball addict told me years ago, the trouble with life is there's no RESET button.

What's done can never be undone. It's set in concrete, carved in stone.

Omar Khayyam wrote it ages ago, and put it so well that even I can remember the lines:

The Moving Finger writes; and, having writ,
Moves on, nor all your Piety nor Wit
Shall lure it back to cancel half a Line,
Nor all your Tears wash out a Word of it.

If only that were not so.
If only . . .

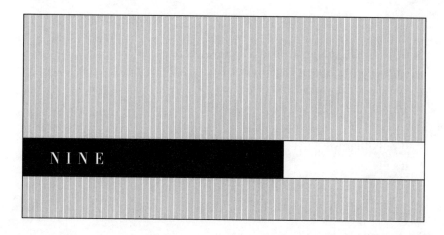

I WAS QUESTIONED at length at the crime scene, first by the uniforms who responded to the 911 call, then by somebody in plainclothes. It's impossible to remember the questions and answers because I was only dimly aware of the procedure while it was going on. A portion of my mind was struggling to pay attention, taking in what was being said by others within earshot, monitoring the questions I was asked and the answers I gave. The rest of me was somewhere else, wandering aimlessly through corridors of the past, sending out forays into an alternate future. An if-only future, a future in which, because I'd done something differently, Jim was still alive.

When I was eleven or twelve I got hit in the forehead with a baseball and walked around all day with a concussion. This was like that. As if I'd been swathed in cotton wool, enveloped in fog. I wasn't really taking anything in, and it would all imprint on my memory like dream time, soft and hazy and out of focus, with pieces missing.

It was a quarter to ten when the fog cleared, or lifted, or whatever it does. I noted the time on the wall clock in the squad room upstairs at Midtown North, where I dimly recall being taken in the back of a blue and white police cruiser. We could have walked; the station house was on Fifty-fourth west of Eighth, literally a stone's throw from the Lucky Panda.

I suppose the whole precinct house knew the restaurant. Cops have a legendary appetite for doughnuts, but they also put away a lot of Chinese food, and some of Midtown North's Finest were likely to be at least occasional patrons of the Lucky Panda. That gave me one more entry in the If-Only sweepstakes. Why couldn't there have been a couple of uniforms at a front table? The shooter would have taken one look and gone home.

A quarter to ten. I hadn't even noticed the time until now. I'd met Jim around six-thirty. We talked for a minute or two. I went to the lavatory, I used the lavatory, I came rushing out of the lavatory . . .

Three hours gone since then, and gone in no time at all. I must have spent a lot of it sitting or standing around, waiting for something to happen, waiting for somebody to tell me what to do. I must have been in a very tractable state. Unaware as I was of the passage of time, I hadn't grown bored or impatient.

"Matt? Here, whyntcha have a seat? We'll go over this one more time and then you can go home and get some rest."

"Sure," I said.

This detective's name was George Wister. He was lean and angular, with a sharp nose and chin and a carefully trimmed little mustache. His beard was dark and heavy, and I suppose he'd shaved when he got up that morning but he needed to shave again and knew it. He had a habit of touching his cheek or chin, running a finger against the grain of his whiskers, as if to check just how urgent was his need for a shave.

He was around forty, 5'10", dark brown hair, deep-set dark brown eyes. I registered all this and wondered why. Nobody would be asking me to describe the investigating officer. What they'd have liked from me was a description of the killer, and I couldn't help them with that.

"I'm sorry to have kept you so long," Wister was saying. "But you know how these things work. You were on the job yourself."

"Years ago."

"And it seems to me I've seen you around the house. You're tight with Joe Durkin, aren't you?"

"We've known each other awhile."

"And now you're working private." I dug out my wallet and started to show him my license. "No, that's all right," he said. "You showed me before."

"It's hard to keep it straight. What I showed and who I showed it to."

"Yeah, and everybody wants to go over the same ground, and the whole experience takes it out of you to begin with. You must be dead on your feet."

Was I? I didn't even know.

"And anxious to get home." He touched his chin, his cheek. "Deceased is James Martin Faber," he read off a clipboard, and went on to read Jim's address and the name and address of his place of business, looking at me each time for confirmation.

I said, "His wife is—"

"Mrs. Beverly Faber, same address. She's being notified, in fact they've probably been over to see her by now. Get her to make a formal ID."

"I'll have to see her myself."

"You want to get some rest first, Matt. You're in shock yourself right now."

I could have told him it was wearing off. I was myself again, whatever that amounted to. But all I did was nod.

"Faber was a friend of yours."

"My sponsor." The word puzzled him, and I was sorry I'd used it because now I had to explain it. Not that there was any reason not to explain. There's a tradition against breaking the anonymity of another AA member, but it's a courtesy extended only to the living. "My AA sponsor," I said.

"That'd be Alcoholics Anonymous?"

"That's right."

"I thought anybody could join. I didn't know you had to be sponsored."

"You don't," I said. "A sponsor's something you get after you've joined, more a combination friend and adviser. Sort of like a rabbi on the job."

"A more experienced guy? Pulls strings for you, helps you keep your nose clean?"

"It's a little different," I said, "in that there are no promotions in AA, and the only way you can get in trouble is by picking up a drink. A sponsor is someone you can talk to, someone who'll help you stay sober."

"Not a problem I've got," he said, "but a lot of cops do, and no wonder. The stress you got to deal with day in and day out."

Every job's stressful when you need a drink.

"So the two of you met for dinner. You have something special on your mind, something you needed to talk about?"

"No."

"You're married, he's married, but the two of you left your wives home on a Sunday night and went out for Chinese."

"Every Sunday night," I said.

"That so?"

"With rare exceptions, yes."

"So it was a regular thing. Is that standard procedure in AA?"

"Nothing's standard in AA," I said, "except not drinking, and even that's not as standard as you might think. Our Sunday dinners started as part of the sponsorial relationship, a way to get to know each other. Over the years it became just a part of our friendship."

" 'Over the years.' He was your sponsor for a long time?"

"Sixteen years."

"You're kidding. Sixteen years? And you haven't had a drink in all that time?"

"Not so far."

"And you still go to the meetings?"

"I do."

"What about him?"

"He did."

"Meaning he stopped?"

I was trying to figure out how I was supposed to answer that when he got the point and his face flushed. "Sorry," he said. "Been a long day." He looked down at the clipboard. "Every Sunday night. Always the same restaurant?"

"Always Chinese," I said. "Different restaurants."

"Why Chinese? Any particular reason?"

"Just a habit we got into."

"Well, you could pick a new Chinese restaurant every week and it'd be awhile before you ran out. What I'm getting at, who knew the two of you were going to be there tonight?"

"Nobody."

"I take it you didn't make a reservation."

"At the Lucky Panda?"

"Yeah, I wonder did anybody ever make a reservation there. At lunch, maybe, because they'll fill up noontime during the week, but on nights and weekends you can shoot deer in there."

"Or people," I said.

He looked at me, unsure how to respond. He drew a breath and asked me who picked the restaurant.

"I'm not sure," I said. "Let me think. He'd suggested a place on Fifty-eighth, but they'd gone out of business. Then I suggested Chinatown and he said that was too much trouble, and I think he was the one who thought of the Lucky Panda."

"And when was this?"

"Yesterday, it must have been. We talked on the phone."

"And picked the time and the place to meet." He wrote something down. "And the last time you actually saw him was . . ."

"Friday night at the meeting."

"That'd be an AA meeting, right? And you spoke on the phone yesterday and met for dinner tonight as arranged."

"That's right."

"Did you mention to anybody where you'd be having dinner?"

"I may have said something to my wife. I don't even know."

"But nobody else."

"No."

"And he'd have told his wife?"

"Possibly. He'd probably have told her he was having dinner with me, but I don't know that he'd have bothered telling her where."

"You know his wife?"

"To say hello to. I doubt I've seen her twenty times in sixteen years."

"You didn't get along?"

"He and I were friends, that's all. Elaine and I had dinner with Jim and Beverly a couple of times, but that's literally all it was. Two or three times."

"Elaine being your wife."

"Right."

"How were they getting along?"

"Jim and his wife?"

"Uh-huh. He ever talk about that?"

"Not lately."

"So as far as you know . . ."

"As far as I know, they were getting along fine."

"He'd have said if they weren't?"

"I think so."

"Who can you think of that he wasn't getting along with?"

"Jim got along with everybody," I said. "He was a very easygoing guy."

"Didn't have an enemy in the world."

He sounded skeptical, the way cops do. "If he did," I said, "I didn't know about it."

"How about his business?"

"His business?"

"Uh-huh. He was a printer, right? Had a printshop here in the neighborhood?"

I got out one of my business cards. "He printed these for me," I said.

He ran his thumb across the raised lettering. Maybe he wanted to see if it needed a shave. "Nice work," he said. "Okay if I keep this?"

"Sure."

"Know anything about his business?"

"It didn't come up in conversation a lot. A couple of years ago he was talking about packing it in."

"Getting out of the business?"

"He was tired of it and I guess business was slow enough to be discouraging. For a while he was looking into buying a coffee bar franchise. This was back when there was a new one opening every time you turned around."

"My brother-in-law bought one," Wister said. "It's been a pretty good thing for him, but they're working every minute, him and my sister both."

"Anyway, he decided against it and stayed with the printshop. Sometimes he talked about retiring, but I never got the impression he was ready to do it."

"It says here he was sixty-three."

"That sounds about right."

"He in a position to retire?"

"I have no idea."

"He didn't talk about investments or debts, anything like that?"

"No."

He probed his chin stubble. "Anything about a criminal element?"

"A criminal element?"

"Trying to muscle in on his business, say."

"If anyone tried," I said, "he'd have handed them the keys and wished them the best of luck. He squeezed a living out of the business, but it's not something you get rich at, not something a gangster would want to take over."

"He do any work for them?"

"For gangsters?"

"For organized crime."

"Jesus," I said.

"It's not as farfetched as it sounds, Matt. Criminal enterprises need the same kinds of goods and services as everybody else. They need letterhead and invoice forms and order blanks and, yes, business cards, and God knows what else. They own a lot of restaurants, so they're always getting menus printed. No reason your friend couldn't have done some of their printing. He wouldn't necessarily have known who he was doing it for."

"I suppose it's possible, but—"

"It's also possible they'd have asked him to print up something that wasn't kosher. To duplicate government forms or somebody else's purchase order blanks, something dubious like that. Maybe he went along, maybe he refused to go along, maybe he learned something along the way he was better off not knowing."

"What's your point?"

"What's my point? My point is your friend Faber was the victim of what looks like a very professional hit. Those guys don't shoot you just to keep in practice. If he was mobbed up in any kind of way, innocent or otherwise, you're doing him no favor by keeping it a secret."

"Believe me, I'm not keeping any secrets."

"Can you think of anybody who'd want to see him dead?"

"No."

"Anyone associated with him who might have paid to have him killed? Or anyone in the criminal world who might have had any kind of a grudge against him?"

"Same answer."

"You arrived at the restaurant, you sat down at the table. What was his state of mind?"

"Same as always. Calm, serene."

"Nothing bothering him, far as you could tell?"

"Nothing that showed."

"What did you talk about?"

"Anything and everything. Oh, you mean tonight?"

"You were with him a minute or two before you went to the john. What did the two of you talk about?"

I had to think. Ike and Mike, and then what?

"Air conditioning," I said.

"Air conditioning?"

"Air conditioning. They had theirs turned up so it was like an icebox in there, and we talked about that."

"Small talk, in other words."

"Too small to remember."

He took another tack, asked me if I'd got even the slightest glimpse of the shooter. I said what I'd been saying all along, that he was out the door and gone before I got back from the men's room.

"Now memory's a funny thing," he said. "Different things affect it. Your mind doesn't want to let a piece of information in, it walls off a section of memory and won't give you access to it."

"I could give you examples," I said, "but that's not what happened here. I was in the john when I heard the gunshots. I came running, I saw what had happened, and I chased out into the street hoping to get a look at him."

"And you never saw him."

"Never."

"So you don't know if he was tall or short, fat or thin, black or white . . ."

"I understand the witnesses said he was black."

"But you didn't see him yourself."

"No."

"Or any black man in the restaurant."

"I didn't pay much attention to the other customers, before or after the shooting. But the place was close to empty, and no, I don't believe any of the other people in it were black."

"How about seeing a car pulling away, which you didn't happen to take note of at the time?"

"I'd have taken notice, because that's what I was looking for, either a man on foot or a car pulling away."

"But you didn't see either one."

"No."

"Or a cab or . . ."

"No."

"And now you can't come up with anyone with a reason to want James Faber dead."

I shook my head. "Not to say no such person exists," I said, "but I can't think of him, and I've got no reason to believe in his existence."

"Except for what happened tonight."

"Except for that."

"How about yourself, Matt?"

I stared hard at him. "I must be missing something here," I said levelly. "Are you really suggesting I set him up and ducked into the bathroom so some gunman I'd hired could come in and start blasting?"

"Take it easy. . . ."

"Because that's so far off base I didn't even know how to react to it."

"Easy," he said. "Sit down, Matt. That's not at all what I was getting at."

"It's not?"

"Not at all."

"That's what it sounded like."

"Well, then, that's my fault, because it's not what I intended. I said 'How about you?' meaning is there anybody with a reason to have *you* hit."

"Oh."

"But you thought . . ."

"I know what I thought. I'm sorry I went off like that."

"Well, you didn't yell and scream, but your face got so dark I was afraid you were going to stroke out on me."

"I guess I'm more exhausted than I realized," I said. "You're saying the shooter could have got the wrong man?"

"It's always possible when the shooter doesn't know the vic personally. Faber was what, a couple of years older?"

"I'm taller by a few inches, and he was heavier, and thicker in the middle. I don't think we looked much alike. Nobody ever called me Jim by mistake, I'll tell you that much."

"You have any old enemies? From when you were on the job, say?"

"That's over twenty years ago, George. I'm off the job longer than I was ever on it."

"Well, what enemies have you made lately? You're a PI. You working on any mob-related cases?"

"No."

"Anything at all where you might have rubbed some hard case the wrong way?"

"Nothing," I said. "These days I work mostly for lawyers, checking out witnesses in personal injury and product liability lawsuits. I got a kid with a computer who does most of the heavy lifting for me."

"So you can't think of a thing."

"No."

"Well, why don't you run on home, then? Sleep on it, see what comes to you overnight. You know how it's probably going to turn out, don't you?"

"How?"

"Mistaken identity. I got a feeling what happened, and God knows it wouldn't be the first time. Somebody saw your friend, mistook him for a mope who burned him in a drug deal, or dicked his wife, some damned fool thing. Or, and I've known of cases, there's a contract out on some guy, some poor bastard looked nothing like your friend, and somebody spots him and drops a dime on him, and the guy who gets the call goes to the wrong fucking Chinese restaurant. He shows up at the Lucky Panda on Eighth instead of the Golden Rabbit on Seventh or the Hoo Flung Poo on Ninth."

"Maybe."

"The moon's full, you know."

"I didn't notice."

"Well, it's overcast. You can't see it, but it's on the calendar. To-morrow night, actually, but that's close enough. That's when weird shit happens."

I remembered the moon Wednesday night, the gibbous moon. And now it was full.

"So go on home. There's uniforms chasing down witnesses now, tak-ing testimony from people who were on the street when it went down, or maybe looking out their windows, wondering is it ever gonna rain. You know how it works. We'll check everything out, we'll see what our snitches have to tell us, and if we get lucky we'll come up with the shitbag who pulled the trigger." He worried his chin. "It won't bring him back, your friend," he said, "but it's what we do. It's all we can do."

I WALKED HOME on Ninth Avenue. I passed a few bars along the way, and each time I felt my heart race just the least little bit at the sight of them. It was an appropriate response. I couldn't stand the movie that was playing in my head, and booze was a sure bet to drown the sound track and fade the image to black.

Here's looking at you, Jim. Down the hatch. Bombs away. Mud in your eye, fella.

Thanks for helping me stay sober for the past sixteen years. Who's to say I could have done it without you? And now I'll honor your memory by forgetting everything you taught me.

No, I don't think so.

Jim stopped watching *NYPD Blue* when Sipowicz drank after his son's death. What a jerk, he said. What a fucking asshole.

He can't help it, I said. He's just a character, all he can do is what it says in the script.

I'm talking about the writer, he said.

So I wasn't going to pick up a drink, but I couldn't pretend the desire wasn't there. My eyes took note of each gin joint, each winking neon beer sign. My mouth may have watered a little. But my feet kept on walking.

I looked for the moon, the full moon, but couldn't see it.

Anxiety grabbed me as I walked into the lobby of our building, and in the elevator I had a sudden vision of what I was going to find on the fourteenth floor. The door kicked in, furniture overturned, pictures slashed.

And worse . . .

The door was shut and locked. I rang the bell before I used my key, and Elaine was on the other side of the door when I got it open. She started to say something and stopped when she got a look at my face.

"Jim's dead," I said. "I got him killed."

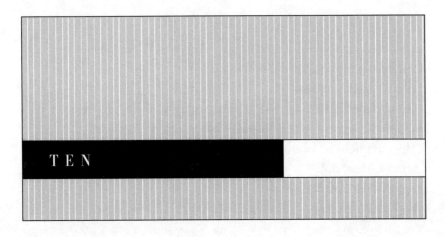

TEN

"SUPPOSE I was in shock," I said, "and I suppose I still am, to some extent. But no matter how thick the fog got, I never lost sight of my commitment to the obstruction of justice."

"Because you didn't tell them everything?"

"Because I deliberately misled them and withheld information I knew to be pertinent. I sat there parrying questions about Jim's printing business when it was crystal clear to me why he was killed. The shooter made a mistake, all right, and it had nothing to do with phases of the moon. He was supposed to shoot a middle-aged guy in khakis and a windbreaker and a red polo shirt, and that's what he did."

"Why couldn't you tell them that?"

"Because it would tie me to Mick Ballou and drop both of us in the middle of a full-scale homicide investigation. They'd want to know where all the bodies were buried, and that's not a figure of speech. I'd be on the spot for failing to report the murders of Kenny and McCartney, and for in fact actively covering up their deaths. We broke a lot of laws the night we dug up Mick's back yard."

"You'd lose your license."

"That's the least of it. I could face criminal charges."

"I didn't think of that."

"It seems to me I committed a couple of felonies," I said, "and we crossed a state line with a trunkful of corpses, so there might be a federal charge involved as well. Even so, I might have taken my chances if I'd thought leveling with Wister would do any good."

"It won't bring Jim back."

"No, but neither will anything else. It won't catch his killer, either. Jim was an innocent bystander who walked into the middle of a gang war."

"Is that what it is? Gang warfare?"

"That's what it looks like. That's what it looked like in the storage room in Jersey. If I'd had any sense I'd have bowed out then and there."

"I wish you would stop blaming yourself."

I let that pass. She'd said it more than once, and I still didn't have a response to it. I said, "There are things the cops are good at, but solving gang-related homicides isn't one of them. Even when they get lucky and learn who gave the order and who pulled the trigger, they can't put together a case that'll hold up in court."

"I guess they're helpless against organized crime."

"Not exactly helpless. The RICO laws gave them broad powers, and in the past few years they've made some major cases and put away a lot of mob guys. They'll get somebody to wear a wire, they'll get some-body else to roll over on his boss, and next thing you know there's one more guy in the federal joint at Marion, complaining that nobody there can make a decent marinara sauce. That works, and so do some of the local stings they run, like renting a storefront and receiving stolen goods, then locking up all the people who walked in the door with minks and TV sets."

"They get a lot of press when they do that."

"And I'm sure that's one of the things they like about it. But it's good police work just the same. Some of my contemporaries might disagree, but I think the NYPD's better than when I was a part of it. They're doing a superior job. But that doesn't mean they're going to come up with the guy who shot Jim."

"Still," she said, "it bothers you that you held out on them."

"I think it would bother me more if I hadn't. I'd have had fun explaining a lot of things, including the gun I was carrying."

"I was wondering about that. Nobody spotted it?"

"I wasn't a suspect and nobody had any reason to pat me down. I kept my windbreaker zipped up. It was chilly in the restaurant and on the street, but it was warm and stuffy in the squad room at Midtown North. I kept waiting for Wister to tell me to take off my jacket and get comfortable, but he never did."

"But if you'd told them you were the intended victim . . ."

"Then they'd have asked me a few hundred questions, and everything would have had to come out, including the gun. 'This? Well, you've already got the murder weapon, and anyway this is a .38, not a .22, and you can see it hasn't been fired recently. I haven't registered it yet because I just acquired it the other day from this guy who was pounding on my stomach.' "

"How is your stomach, by the way?"

"It's fine."

"But it must be empty. You didn't get dinner, you haven't had anything since lunch."

"I don't want anything."

"If you say so."

"Why the look?"

"I was just thinking what Jim would say about letting yourself get too hungry."

"He'd say not to," I said. "But I'm not hungry. Right now the thought of food turns my stomach."

"If you change your mind . . ."

"I'll let you know. Say, is there any coffee? I could stand a cup of coffee."

.   .   .

"WHAT BOTHERS ME," I said, "is that I held out without thinking twice. It was second nature."

We were at the kitchen table, with coffee for me and herbal tea for her. I had taken off the windbreaker, and the gun and holster. I'd taken off the polo shirt, shucked the Kevlar vest, and put the shirt back on again. The vest was draped over the back of a chair now, and the gun and holster were on the kitchen counter.

I said, "I was a cop for a lot of years, and then for a long time I worked private without a license. I finally got one because it was an inconvenience not to have it, and it was costing me work. But there was another reason. I had it in the back of my mind that it would make me respectable."

"You never said that before."

"No."

"When you and I got married," she said, "I told you something. Do you remember what it was?"

"I was just thinking about it the other day. You said it didn't have to change anything."

"Because we were already committed to each other, so how could a piece of paper change things? And you were already respectable."

"Maybe that's the wrong word. Maybe I was looking for the license to make me more legitimate, more a part of the establishment."

"And did it?"

"That's the thing," I said. "It didn't. You know, I lost most of my illusions about the system during my years as a cop. They say working in a meat-packing plant ruins your appetite for sausage, and something similar happens on the job. You're essentially taught to break the rules. I learned to cut corners, learned to stand up in court and lie under oath. I also took bribes and robbed the dead, but that was something else, that was more about the erosion of my own morals. It may have been job-related, but it didn't arise directly out of how I'd learned to regard the system.

"Then I put in my papers and quit," I went on, "and you know about that. It was abrupt, one day I was a cop and one day I wasn't, but in another sense it was a more gradual process. I was still a cop at heart.

All I lacked was a badge and a paycheck. I still saw the world the same way. I knew guys working in houses all over the five boroughs, and I pulled strings and called in favors when I was working my own cases. Or I bought favors, paying cops for information as if they were my snitches."

"I remember."

"Well, the years went by," I said, "and everybody I knew died or retired. Joe Durkin's my only real friend on the job, and I never even knew him back then. I'd been working private for years before he and I got acquainted. And now he's always talking about retiring himself, and one of these days he'll do it."

"Suppose it had been him instead of Wister asking you questions tonight."

"Would I have told the same lies? Probably. I don't see what else I could have done. I might have been a little less comfortable lying to Joe, and he might have sensed I was holding out. As far as that goes, Wister may have sensed as much himself."

"It's complicated, isn't it?"

"Very. It's hard to know what I am. 'My name is Matt and I'm an alcoholic.' I've said that so many times I'm beginning to believe it, but beyond that point it gets a little fuzzy. For years I've been cutting corners and making my own rules. I learned how on the job and I never learned how not to. I've deliberately subverted the law, and now and then I've taken it into my own hands. I've played judge and jury. Sometimes I guess I've played God."

"You always had a reason."

"Everybody can always find a reason. The point is I've done illegal acts, and I've worked for and with criminals, but I've never thought of myself as a criminal."

"Well, of course not. You're not a criminal."

"I'm not sure what I am. I tell myself I try to do what's right, but I don't know how I make that determination. The phrase that comes to mind is 'moral compass,' but I'm not sure I know exactly what a moral compass is, or if I have one."

"Of course you do, honey. But the needle keeps spinning around, doesn't it?"

"The only rule I've got to live by," I said, "is 'Don't drink and go to meetings.' Jim says if I do that much everything else'll work out the way it's supposed to."

"So you do and it does."

"Oh, it works out. That's another thing he told me, things always work out. And God's will always gets done. That's how you find out God's will. You wait and see what happens."

"You've quoted that line before."

"I've always liked it," I said. "I guess it was God's will for Jim to die tonight, and for me to live. Otherwise it wouldn't have happened, right?"

"Right."

"Sometimes," I said, "it's hard to figure out what God has in mind. Sometimes you have to wonder if He's paying attention."

WE TALKED FOR a long time. Ages ago, in another lifetime, when she was a hooker and I was a cop married to somebody else, part of what drew me to her was that she was so easy to talk to. In a sense I suppose that was part of the job description in her chosen field. A call girl, after all, ought to put men at ease. But it seemed to go beyond that for us. I sensed that I could be entirely myself in her presence, that it was me she liked, not the man I pretended to be, not the man I thought the world wanted me to be.

Maybe that, too, was part of the job description.

I drank coffee and she sipped her herb tea and I talked about Jim. I told stories from early sobriety, before she and I had found each other again after having been out of touch for years. "At first I figured he was a nice enough fellow," I told her, "but I wished to God he would leave me alone, because I knew I wasn't going to stay sober and he was just one more person to disappoint. Then I started to look forward to seeing him at meetings. As far as I was concerned he was Mister AA himself, the voice of sobriety. As a matter of fact he came into the program less than two years before I did. I was in my first ninety days when I heard him speak on his second anniversary. I look back now, and what's two years? A person with two years is just beginning to clear the cobwebs out of his head. So he was actually pretty new himself, but from my perspective he was dry enough to be a fire hazard."

"What would he tell you now?"

"What would he tell me? He'll never tell me anything again."

"But if he could."

I sighed. " 'Don't drink. And go to meetings.' "

"Do you want to go to a meeting now?"

"It's too late for the midnight meeting on Houston Street. They've got another one at two A.M., but that's too late for me. So no, I don't want to go, but I don't want to drink, either, so I guess it evens out."

"What else would he tell you?"

"I can't read his mind."

"No, but you can use your imagination. What would he say?"

Grudgingly I said, " 'Get on with your life.' "

"And?"

"And what?"

"And are you going to?"

"Get on with my life? I don't really have a choice, do I? But it's not that easy."

"Why not?"

"I told those two bozos the other night that I was done working for Ballou, and I told Mick the same thing. And that was that."

"But?"

"But I must have known it wasn't going to be that easy," I said, "or I wouldn't have gone straight to Jovine's for a shoulder rig. I told myself if I stayed away from Mick and kept close to home they'd find it easy to forget about me. But obviously they'd already made a decision to kill me, and tonight was the first chance they got, and they took it." I frowned. "It shouldn't change anything. Oh, I'm raging inside over Jim's death. Most of my anger's at myself for getting him killed, but—"

"You didn't get him killed."

"I put him in harm's way. Blame or no blame, that's hard to argue with. He was killed because someone mistook him for me, and that happened because I met him for dinner. And because I'd given some-one cause to want me dead."

"I could argue with you, but I won't."

"Good. As I was saying, most of my anger's with myself. But there's some left over for the shooter, and for whoever sicced him on me."

"Two different people?"

"Two minimum. Somebody made the decision, either the slugger with the slicked-down hair or the guy who gave him his orders. Somebody else staked out our building and followed me from here to the Chinese restaurant. He could have been the slugger or his chum—they'd both recognize me without trouble—or there could have been a third person, someone who wouldn't have to worry that I might recognize him."

"If so, maybe he doubled as the shooter."

"Maybe, but I'd bet against it. I think he followed me to the restaurant, then posted himself across the street, making a quick call on his cell phone. . . ."

"I guess they've all got cell phones these days."

"Everybody but you and me, it seems like. Even Mick's got one, if you can believe that. He used it the other night to call ahead to the farm and say we were on our way."

" 'Leave a light burning, and a shovel on the back steps.' "

"The tail calls the shooter, who gets in his car and hurries to the scene. They meet on the street and the tail points to the Lucky Panda. 'Red shirt, tan jacket, Gap khakis, sneakers,' he says. 'You can't miss him.'

"Then he gets behind the wheel, unless there's already a driver in addition to the shooter. Whoever's doing the driving puts the car someplace handy and keeps the motor running, and the shooter goes in with a gun and comes out without it, and he jumps in the car and they're gone."

"And a man's dead," she said.

"And a man's dead."

"It could have been you."

"It was supposed to be me."

"But God had other ideas."

That was one way to look at it. I said, "Two men on Ninth Avenue the night before last. A third who ordered the hit. A fourth man to trail me to the Lucky Panda, and a fifth to walk in and pull the trigger. And maybe a sixth man to drive the car." I looked at her. "That's a lot of people to get even with."

"Is that what you want to do?"

"You can't help wanting to," I said. "The urge is pretty basic, and I suppose it's instinctive, even cellular. 'They did it to us, we're gonna do it to them.' Look at human history."

"Look at Bosnia," she said.

"But it's five or six people, as I said, and I don't even know who they are. And I can't make myself believe Jim's spirit is crying out for vengeance. If there's a part of you that survives, I'm inclined to believe it's not the part that takes things personally. Didn't you ask what Jim would tell me now? Well, what he wouldn't tell me is to get out there and kill one for the Gipper."

"No, that doesn't sound like Jim."

"I hate the idea of sitting back and letting them get away with it," I said, "but I'm not sure anybody ever really gets away with anything, and I think I've largely outgrown the notion that the world can't get along without my help."

"It's a pretty common delusion," she said, "and the more religious a person is, the more he'll subscribe to it. If there's one thing the fundamentalists of the world have in common it's the conviction that God's work won't get done unless they pitch in and do it. Their God's all-powerful, but He's screwed unless they help Him out."

I drank some coffee. I said, "It's not my job to punish them. I'm not appointing myself judge and jury, and I'm not volunteering for the firing squad, either. I told them I was off the case, and I told Mick the same thing, and Jim's death doesn't change that. I still want to walk away from it."

"Thank God for that."

"But there's a problem. See, I don't think I can."

"Why not?"

"I walked away from it two nights ago," I said, "and it didn't do me any good. Their response was to send somebody to kill me. As far as they were concerned I was still on the case. Or maybe they didn't care. On or off, I was the son of a bitch who kicked their asses, and maybe that's all you have to do around here to get Madame Defarge to knit your name in the shawl. Because one way or another I got my name on the Death List, and Jim's dying isn't going to get me off it."

"So even if you don't do a thing . . ."

"I'm still marked for death. By now they probably know they killed the wrong guy, and if not they'll know by morning. I may be inclined to think of Jim as having died for my sins, but that won't make them accept his death as a substitute for mine."

"Your name's still in the shawl."

"I'm afraid so."

She looked at me. "So? What do we do?"

WHAT WE TRIED to do was make love, but that didn't really work, so we just held each other. I told a few stories about Jim, some she'd heard before, others that were new to her. A couple of them were funny, and we laughed.

She said, "I probably shouldn't say this, but it's rattling around in my head and making me crazy. I'm terribly sorry for what happened to Jim. I'm sorry for him and I'm sorry for Beverly, and of course I'm sorry for you.

"But sorry isn't all I feel. I'm glad it was him and not you."

I didn't say anything.

"It's something I find myself thinking all the time," she said. "It's what the voice in my head says every time I read the obituaries, and sometimes I think that's *why* I read the obituaries. So I can say 'Better her than me' whenever some dame my age dies of breast cancer. 'Better him than Matt' when some poor guy drops dead on the golf course. 'Better them than us' whenever there's an earthquake or a flood or a plague or a plane crash. Whoever they were, whatever happened to them, better them than us."

"It's a pretty natural response."

"But for a change it really resonates, doesn't it? Because it was pretty much a case of one or the other. If Jim went to the bathroom and you stayed at the table . . ."

"It might have turned out differently. I'd have been facing the door when he walked in. And I had a gun."

"And would you have gone for it in time?"

If I'd looked up when the door opened, I'd have seen a stranger, a black man who looked not at all like the pair of white guys who jumped me. And that's if I looked up. I might well have been engrossed in the menu, or reading Jim's magazine.

"Maybe," I said. "But probably not."

"So better him than you is what I say. My heart aches for Beverly, it makes me sick to think of what she's going through right now, but better her than me. These aren't noble sentiments, are they?"

"I don't suppose they are."

"But God knows they're heartfelt. And you have to feel the same way, baby. Because you can tell yourself it should have been you there, slumped in your own blood, but it wasn't you and in your heart you're glad of it. I'm right, aren't I?"

"Yes," I said after a moment. "I guess you are. I almost wish it weren't so, but it is."

"All that means is you're glad to be alive, sweetie."

"I guess so."

"That's not necessarily a bad thing."

"I guess not."

"You know," she said, "it probably wouldn't hurt you to cry."

She may have been right about that, too, but we weren't going to find out. The last time I remember crying was at an early AA meeting, when I spoke up for the first time to identify myself as an alcoholic. The tears that followed took me completely by surprise. My eyes have stayed dry ever since, except for the occasional movie, and I don't think that counts. Those aren't real tears, any more than the fear that grips you at a horror film is genuine fear.

So I couldn't cry and I couldn't make love, and it turned out I couldn't sleep, either. I almost drifted off and then I didn't, and finally I gave up and got out of bed and got dressed. I put the vest on under my shirt, and the holster over it. I zipped the windbreaker just far enough to conceal the gun.

Then I went into the other room and made a phone call.

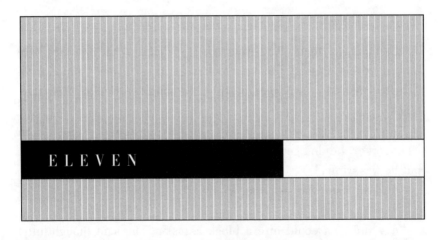

"**A** BLACK MAN," Mick said, looking across the table at me.

"According to the witnesses."

"But you never saw him yourself."

"No, and I didn't get to question the witnesses, either, but I understand they all agreed the shooter was black. Medium height, medium build, twenties or thirties or forties—"

"Narrows it down."

"And he had a beard or a mustache."

"One or the other?"

"Or both," I said. "Or neither, I suppose. He was in and out in less time than it takes to tell about it, and nobody had any reason to look at him before the shooting started, and then all they wanted to do was keep from getting shot themselves."

"But he was black," Mick said. "On that point they're in rare agreement."

"Yes."

"Is it niggers then? And what am I to them, or they to me?" He picked up his glass of whiskey, looked at it, set it down untouched. "The two men who gave you a beating," he said, "or tried to. Were they black?"

"They were both white. The one with the gun sounded like a born New Yorker. I didn't get a good look at the other one, or hear him talk, but he was white."

"And the man who shot your friend . . ."

"Was black."

"A white man could hire a black assassin," he said thoughtfully. "But would this man bring in someone from outside? Wouldn't he use one of his own?"

"Who is he?"

"I don't know."

"But someone's trying to . . ."

"Take it all away," he said. "And I don't know who he is, or why it's me he's after."

I DIDN'T REALLY think there'd be anyone staked out at the Parc Vendôme, but I'd just had my horse stolen and I wasn't about to leave the barn door unlocked. I went down to the basement and slipped out of the building by the rear service entrance. On my way to Grogan's I looked over my shoulder a lot. Nobody tailed me, and no one popped up out of the shadows in front of me.

Mick had said he'd make a pot of coffee, and he was at a table when I got there, with a bottle and glass in front of him and a stoneware coffee mug across from him. I scanned the room from the doorway. It was getting on for closing, but there were a fair number of people who didn't want the weekend to end, pairs and singles at the bar, a few couples at the tables. I spotted Andy Buckley and Tom Heaney way in back at the dartboard, Burke behind the bar, and old Eamonn Dougherty on the other side of it. Mick had pointed him out once as a legendary IRA gunman. He was killing men before you were born, he'd said.

There were a couple of other familiar faces, too.

I walked to where Mick was sitting, picked up my coffee mug, and carried it to a table along the wall. His eyes widened at this, but when I motioned for him he joined me, bringing his bottle and glass.

"You didn't care for the other table?"

"Too close to those folks," I said. "I didn't want to listen to their conversation, or for them to be listening to ours."

"I already heard enough of theirs," he said, amusement in his eyes. "It's a serious discussion of their relationship that they're having."

"I thought it might be," I said, and then I told him about my visit to the Lucky Panda, and his eyes hardened and his face turned serious.

And now he said, "I was wrong to get you involved."

"I could have turned you down."

"And would have, had you known what you were getting into. I'd no idea myself I'd be putting you in danger. But you're in it now, man."

"I know it."

"They didn't believe you'd heed their warning. Or didn't care. You embarrassed them, made them look bad. That's more than my two did, for Jesus' sake."

"Kenny and McCartney."

"Executed, the poor lads."

Two tables away, the fellow got up and went to the bar for fresh drinks. The woman looked sidelong at me, the trace of a smile on her lips. Then she lowered her eyes.

"And Peter Rooney," Mick said.

"That's a familiar name. Do I know him?"

"You might have met him here. Let me see, how would you know him? Well, now, he had the tattoo of a ship's anchor on the back of his left hand, just below the wrist."

I nodded. "Long, narrow face, balding in front."

"That's the man."

"He had the look of a sailor, too."

"And what sort of look is that? Ah, never mind. The ferry to Staten Island is all the sailing he ever did. Or will do."

"Why's that?"

He regarded his glass of whiskey. He said, "You know I always have some money on the street. The Jews taught me that. It's like bread upon the water, isn't it? You put your money on the street and it comes back to you multiplied. Peter worked for me, at the job sites and the union halls. Making loans, you know, and receiving payments. He did none of the heavy work, you understand, as he was not cut out for it. A strong warning was as far as he'd go. After that I'd have to send someone else. Or go myself, as likely as not."

"What happened to him?"

"They found him stuffed head first into a trash bin in an alley off Eleventh Avenue. He'd been beaten so that his own mother wouldn't know him, were she alive to see him, which thanks be to God she's not. Beaten half to death, and then stabbed dead in the bargain."

"When did this happen?"

"I couldn't say when it happened. It was midmorning he was found, and early this evening by the time I learned of it." He picked up his glass and drank it down like water. "Did I know this friend of yours?"

"I don't think so."

"You never brought him here, then?"

"He stopped going to bars awhile ago."

"Ah, one of that lot. Not the one you were talking about the other night, was he? That went on retreat with the Buddhists?"

"That was him, as a matter of fact."

"Ah, Jesus. It's a curious thing. I've had that conversation in mind, do you know, and I was thinking that's a man I'd like to know. And now I'll never have the chance. Tell me his name again."

"Jim Faber."

"Jim Faber. I'd raise a glass to his memory, but perhaps he wouldn't care for that."

"I don't think he'd mind."

He poured a short drink. "Jim Faber," he said, and drank.

I took a sip of coffee and wondered what the two of them would have made of each other. I wouldn't have expected them to hit it off, but who's to say? Maybe they'd have found some common ground, maybe Jim had sought the same thing sitting in the zendo that Mick looked for at the Butchers' Mass.

Well, we'd never know.

He said, "They'll try for you again, you know."

"I know."

"By dawn they'll know their mistake, if they don't know it now. What are you going to do?"

"I don't know. All I've done so far is lie to the cops."

"Do you recall the time I went to Ireland? I was avoiding a subpoena, but 'twould be as good a place to dodge a bullet. You could fly out tomorrow and come back when they sound the all-clear."

"I suppose I could."

"You and herself. I know you've never been there, but has she?"

"No."

"Ah, you'd love it, the two of you."

"You could come along," I said. "Show us around, give us the grand tour."

"Just walk away and let them take what they want," he mused. "Do you know, I've thought of it. It's not my way, but is it my way to fight something I can't see? Let them take it, let them have it all."

"Why not?"

He fell silent, considering the question. Over his big shoulder I saw Andy Buckley lean forward to waft a dart. He lost his balance, and Tom Heaney reached out to set him right. Tom, another Belfast native, worked the bar days, and hardly said a word. He came along when Mick and I had that business in Maspeth. Tom took a bullet that night, and the four of us rode clear out to Mick's farm with Andy at the wheel. Mick got a doctor to patch him up, and Tom hardly said a word throughout the ordeal, and was just as closemouthed afterward.

Someone at the bar was laughing—not, surely, the ever-silent Mr. Dougherty—and at the table near us the man was telling the woman that it was no easier for him than it was for her.

"Maybe it's not supposed to be easy," she said.

I looked across at Mick, wondering if he'd heard what she said. He was forming a response to my question, and then his face changed as he caught sight of something behind me. Before I could turn to see what he was looking at, he was in motion, swatting the little table and sending it flying, cup and saucer and bottle and all, then heaving himself at me across the space where the table had been.

There was a ragged burst of gunfire. Mick hurtled into me and I flew over backward, my chair breaking up into kindling beneath me. I landed on it and he landed on top of me. He had a gun in his fist and he was firing it, snapping off spaced single shots in answer to the bursts of automatic-weapon fire from the doorway.

I caught sight of something sailing overhead. Then there was a loud noise, with shock waves rolling, rolling like the sea. And then there was nothing at all.

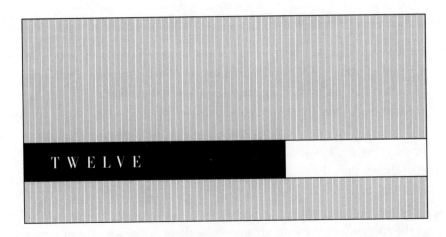

I COULDN'T HAVE been out for very long. I don't remember coming to, but the next thing I knew I was on my feet, with Mick urging me on. He had one big arm around my waist, the hand clutching a battered leather satchel. He'd gone and fetched it from his office, so I must have been unconscious for at least as long as it had taken him to do that. But not much longer than that.

He had a pistol in his other hand, an army-issue .45 with the front sight filed down. I managed a look around but couldn't take in what I was seeing. Chairs and tables were overturned, some of them smashed to splinters. Barstools lay on the tile floor like corpses. The backbar mirror had disappeared, all but a few stray shards still left in the frame. The air was thick with the residue of battle, and my eyes stung from smoke and the fumes of gunpowder and spilled whiskey.

There were bodies scattered around, looking like dolls tossed aside by a thoughtless child. The man and woman who'd been discussing their relationship were together in death, sprawled alongside their overturned table. He was flat on his back with most of his face gone. She lay curled on her side, bent like a fishhook, with the top of her head open and her brains spilling from her shattered skull.

"Come on, man!"

I suppose he was shouting, but his voice didn't sound very loud to me. I guess the bomb blast had left me partially deaf. Everything was slightly muffled, the way it is in an airport when you're fresh off a plane and your ears haven't popped yet.

I heard him and the words registered, but I stayed where I was, rooted to the spot, unable to draw my eyes from them. This is no easier for me than it is for you, he'd told her.

Famous last words . . .

"They're fucking dead," Mick said, his tone at once brutal and gentle.

"I knew her," I said.

"Ah," he said. "Well, there's fuck-all you can do for her now, and no time to waste trying."

I swallowed, trying to clear my ears. It was like getting off a plane in the middle of a war zone, I thought. Smelling the cordite and the death, and stepping over bodies on the way to the baggage claim.

One such body lay in the doorway, a small man with delicate Asian features. He was wearing black pants and a lime green shirt, and at first I took it for one of those Hawaiian shirts with tropical flowers on it. But it was a solid-color shirt and the flowers were three bullet holes and his blood supplied the petals.

Resting in the crook of his arm was the automatic rifle with which he'd sprayed the room.

Mick stopped long enough to snatch up the gun, then gave the dead man a solid boot in the side of the head. "Go straight to hell, you fucker," he said.

A car stood at the curb, a big old Chevy Caprice, the body badly pitted with rust. Andy Buckley was behind the wheel and Tom Heaney was standing alongside the open door, a gun in his hand, covering our exit.

We dashed across the sidewalk. Mick shoved me into the back seat, piled in after me. Tom got in front next to Andy. The car was moving before the doors were shut.

I could hear sirens. Imperfectly, as I heard everything, but I could hear them. Sirens, coming our way.

"YOU'RE ALL RIGHT, ANDY?"

"I'm fine, Mick."

"Tom?"

"No harm, sir."

"Good job you were both in the back. What hell they made of Grogan's, eh? The fuckers."

We'd headed north on the West Side Drive, then cut over to the Deegan at some point. Andy offered more than once to drop me and Mick wherever we wanted to go, but that wasn't what Mick wanted. He said he wasn't sure yet where he'd be staying, and wanted a car.

"Well, this here's a step down from the Caddy," Andy said. "But it was just down the block, and a lot quicker than getting yours out of the garage."

"It'll do me fine," Mick said. "And I'll take good care of it."

"This piece of shit? You treat it nice, it'll die of shock." He slapped the steering wheel. "She runs good, though. And the body damage is a plus, far as I'm concerned. You can park it on the street and know it's gonna be there when you come back for it."

We drove through the Bronx, a part of town I know hardly at all. I lived there briefly as a child, upstairs of the little shoe store my father opened—and closed, whereupon we moved to Brooklyn. The building where we lived is gone, the whole block bulldozed for an addition to the Cross-Bronx Expressway, and my recollection of the neighborhood is gone with it.

So I couldn't really keep track of where we were, and I might have been equally lost in more familiar terrain, my hearing still imperfect and my whole inner self numb and befogged. There wasn't much conversation, but I missed a portion of what there was, tuning in and out.

Tom said he'd walk from Andy's house, there was no need to take him to his door, and Andy said it was easy enough to run him home, that it wasn't far at all. Mick said near or far we'd drop Tom at his home, for God's sake.

Andy said, "You're in the same place, Tom? Perry Avenue?" and Tom nodded. We drove there through unfamiliar streets and Tom got out in front of a little box of a house clad in asphalt siding. Mick said he'd be in touch, and Tom nodded and trotted to the door and stuck his key in the lock, and Andy turned the car around.

At a red light he said, "Mick, are you sure I can't run you back to the city? You can keep this car and I'll get a subway home."

"Don't be silly."

"Or you can pick up the Caddy. Or I'll get the Caddy, whatever you say."

"Drive yourself home, Andy."

Andy lived on Bainbridge Avenue, on the other side of the Mosholu Parkway from Tom. He pulled up in front of his house and got out of the car. Mick leaned out the window and motioned him over, and Andy walked around the car and leaned against it with his hand on the roof. "My best to your mother," Mick said.

"She'll be sleeping now, Mick."

"By Jesus, I should hope so."

"But I'll tell her when she wakes up. She asks about you all the time."

"Ah, she's a good woman," Mick said. "You'll be all right now? You'll have no trouble getting your hands on a car?"

"My cousin Denny'll let me take his. Or somebody else will. Or I'll grab one off the street."

"Be careful, Andy."

"Always, Mick."

"They're hunting us down like rats in a sewer, the bastards. And who are they? Niggers and Chinamen."

"Looked more like Vietnamese, Mick. Or Thai, could be."

"They're all one to me," he said, "and what am I to them? What's their quarrel with me? Or poor Burke, for Jesus' sake, or any of the boys?"

"They just wanted to kill everybody."

"Everybody. Even the customers. Old men drinking their pints. Decent people from the neighborhood having a last jar before bed. Ah, 'twas a last jar for some of them, right enough."

Andy stepped back and Mick got out of the car himself and looked around, then shook himself like a dog shaking off water. He walked around the car and got behind the wheel, and I got out myself and got in front next to him. Andy stood on the sidewalk and watched us drive off.

NEITHER OF US said anything on the way back, and I guess I must have faded out. By the time I checked in again we were back in Manhattan, somewhere down in Chelsea. I could tell because I recognized a Cuban-Chinese restaurant and got a sudden sense memory of their coffee, thick and dark and strong, and remembered the waiter who'd brought it to the table, a slow-moving old fellow who walked as though his feet had been bothering him for years.

Funny what you remember, funny what you don't.

On Twenty-fourth Street off Sixth Avenue, at the edge of the Flower District, Mick braked to a stop in front of a narrow brick building eight stories tall. There was a steel roll-up door like the kind at E-Z Storage, but narrower, only a little wider than a car, with a pair of windowless doors on either side of it. The door on the right had a column of buzzers at its side, suggesting that it led to the offices or apartments above. The door on the left showed two rows of stenciled lettering, black edged in silver on the red door. McGINLEY & CALDECOTT, it proclaimed. ARCHITECTURAL SALVAGE.

Mick unlocked and rolled up the metal door, revealing a small street-level garage. Once he'd kicked a couple of cartons out of the way there was just enough room to park a full-size car or a small van. He motioned, and I slid behind the wheel and maneuvered the Chevy into the space.

I got out and joined him on the sidewalk, and he lowered the door and locked it, then unlocked the red door with the lettering on it. We stepped inside and he drew the door shut, leaving us in darkness until he found a light switch. We were at the head of a flight of stairs, and he led me down them to the basement.

We wound up in a huge room, with narrow aisles threaded among dense rows packed with bureaus and tables and chests of drawers and boxes stacked to shoulder height. It was, as promised, an architectural salvage firm, and the full basement constituted the showroom and stockroom all in one.

Ever since the Dutch bought the place, Manhattan's been a town where they throw buildings up only to knock them down again. Demolition is an industry in itself, construction's twin, and, if its main goal is an empty lot, I was looking at its by-products. Drawers and boxes spilled over with every sort of hardware you could strip from a structure before you took a wrecking ball to it. There were cartons full of nothing but doorknobs, brass ones and glass ones and nickel-plated ones. There were boxes of escutcheon plates and hinges and locks and things I recognized but didn't know the names of, and there were other things I couldn't identify at all.

Carved wooden columns stood here and there, looking for a ceiling to hold up. One section was crammed with ornamental stone and cement work from the outsides of buildings—gargoyles with their tongues protruding, real and imaginary animals, some sharply detailed, others as hard to make out as the inscriptions on old gravestones, weathered by time and acid rain.

A year or two ago Elaine and I spent a weekend in Washington, and in the course of it we dragged ourselves through the Holocaust Museum. It was wrenching, of course—it's supposed to be—but what hit us the hardest was a room full of shoes. Just shoes, an endless heap of shoes. Neither of us could quite explain the room's ghastly impact, but I gather our response was not atypical.

I can't say the plastic milk crates overflowing with doorknobs elicited a similar emotional reaction. My gut didn't churn at the thought of what had happened to all the doors to which those knobs had once been fitted, or the long-vanished rooms behind those doors. But somehow the endless array of hardware, sifted and sorted with Teutonic thoroughness, did call to mind that room full of shoes.

"Where buildings go to die," Mick said.

"Just what I was thinking."

"It's a good old business. Who could guess what you can strip off an old building before you knock her down? You pull the plumbing, of course, and the boiler, and sell all that for scrap, but there are people who find a use for all the old hardware and ornamentation. If you were restoring an old brownstone, say, you'd want all the details authentic. You'd come here and go home with replacement crystals for the chandelier, or a better chandelier entirely. And door hinges, and a marble mantel for the fireplace. It's all here, whatever you might want and much you wouldn't."

"So I see."

"And did you know there are those that collect bits of ornamentation? Caldecott has one customer with a passion for gargoyles. There was one he bought too heavy to carry, and your man delivered it and saw his collection. Two small rooms in Christopher Street was all he had, and there's shelves all round stuffed with dozens of fucking gargoyles of all sizes, all of them making horrible faces, and one uglier than the next. From the description it must have been as cluttered as this place, but that's how it is when you're a collector. You must be forever getting more of whatever it is you fancy."

"Do you own this place, Mick?"

"I've an interest in it. You might say I'm a silent partner." He picked up a tarnished brass hinge, turned it in his hand, put it back where he'd found it. " 'Tis a good business for a man. You sell for cash, and you've no purchase records because you don't purchase your stock, you salvage it. So you've cash coming in and cash going out, and that's a useful sort of business in this day and age."

"I imagine it is."

"And I'm a useful partner for the lads. I've connections in the construction and demolition trade, labor and management both, and that's a help in securing salvage rights to a building. Oh, it works out well for all concerned."

"And I don't suppose your name's on the paperwork."

"You know my thoughts on the subject. What you don't own can't be taken from you. I've a set of keys, and the use of the office when I want it, and a place to park a car where it can't be seen. They keep their van there, they use that bay for loading and unloading, but Brian McGinley takes the van home at the day's end. And that reminds me."

He dug the cell phone out of his pocket, then changed his mind and put it back. We walked the length of one aisle to an office in the back, where he sat at the gray metal desk and looked up a number and made a call. The phone had a rotary dial, and might have been salvage itself.

He said, "Mr. McGinley, please. . . . I know it is, and I'd not call at this hour but out of necessity. . . . I'm afraid you'll have to wake him. Just tell him it's the big fellow."

He covered the mouthpiece and rolled his eyes. "Ah, Brian," he said. "Good man. Do you know, I think you and Caldecott are closed for the week. No one's to come in until you hear from me. . . . That's the idea. And my apologies to your wife for the lateness of the hour. Why don't you make it up to her and take her to Puerto Rico for a few days? . . . Well, Cancún then, if she likes it better. . . . And you'll phone Caldecott? And anyone else that ought to be told? Good man."

He hung up. " 'The big fellow,' " he said. "It's presumption, hanging that tag on myself. That's what they called Collins."

"And De Valera didn't like it."

"A sanctimonious bastard, wasn't he? Tell me something. Where the hell's Cancún?"

"The Yucatán Peninsula."

"That's Mexico, isn't it? Mrs. McGinley likes it there, likes it better than phone calls in the middle of the night. 'I can't wake him, he's sleeping.' Well, if he wasn't sleeping, you wouldn't *need* to wake him, you silly cow." He sighed, leaned back in the oak desk chair. "How the hell do you know Dev didn't like it? You never went to the movie."

"Elaine rented it," I said, "and we watched it on the VCR. Jesus Christ."

"What?"

"That was last night we saw it. It doesn't seem possible. It feels more like a week."

"It's a full day you had, isn't it?"

"So much death," I said.

"The two we buried at the farm, and that was what, four nights ago?

Then Peter Rooney, but you only know of him from my telling you. And then your friend, the Buddhist. I drank to his memory, and the next minute they were making a charnel house of Grogan's, killing people left and right. Burke was killed, you know."

"I didn't know."

"I looked for him and found him on the floorboards behind the bar, covered with glass from the mirror and with a terrible hole in his chest. Dead at his post, like a captain going down with the ship. I'd say that's the end of that bar. Next time you see it some Korean'll have it, selling fruits and vegetables around the clock."

He fell silent, and after a long moment I said, "I knew her, Mick."

"I thought you did."

"You know who I meant?"

"Of course I do. Herself as was sitting nearby, that you didn't want to be hearing their conversation. I had a feeling right then."

"Did you?"

"I did. Do you know, moving to the next table probably saved our lives. It put us off to the side and gave us that extra fraction of time to hit the floor before the bullets reached us." He cocked his head, looked at something on the wall. "Unless it's all worked out in advance," he said, "and you die when your time comes and not before."

"I wonder."

"Ah, that's man's lot, isn't it? To wonder." He opened desk drawers until he found the one with the bottle of Jameson in it. He cracked the seal and drank from the bottle. He said, "Was she the one, then?"

"The one?"

"Your bit on the side."

"I guess that's as good a phrase as any. We stopped seeing each other awhile ago."

"Did you love her?"

"No."

"Ah."

"I cared for her, though."

"That's rare enough," he said, and took another drink. "I never loved anyone. Aside from my mother and my brothers, but that's a different matter, isn't it?"

"Yes."

"Of women, I loved none and cared for few."

"I love Elaine," I said. "I don't think I've ever loved anyone else."

"You were married before."

"A long time ago."

"Did you love her?"

"There was a time when I thought I did."

"Ah. What was this one's name?"

"Lisa."

"She was a fine-looking woman."

My mind filled with a picture of her as I saw her last, her skull shattered. I blinked it away and saw her in her apartment, wearing jeans and a sweater, standing in front of a window with a view of the setting sun. That was better.

"Yes," I said. "She was."

"It was sudden, you know. I doubt she ever knew what hit her."

"But she's gone."

"That she is," he said.

HE HAD THE old leather satchel on top of the desk and was poking around in it. "Cash from the safe," he said. "Some papers. All the guns I could grab up. The police can get a court order and torch the safe, or they'll do it without a court order. What they can't use as evidence against me they'll shove in their pockets. So I didn't want to leave them too much."

"No."

"And anything they left would be useless to me, as I couldn't go back for it. They'll have it sealed off, once they've finished with their photographs and measurements, all the scientific things they do. You'd know more about that than I."

"The crime scene routine's changed since my day," I said. "It seems to me they shoot a lot of videotape these days. And they keep getting more scientific."

"Though what's the need for science in this? One man sprays a room with bullets and another hurls a bomb. I wonder have they finished carrying out the dead yet. I wonder how many dead there were, and others dying."

"We'll hear it on the news."

"Too many, whatever the number. A whole row drinking their pints at the bar, and a stream of bullets to knock them off their stools. Not Eamonn Dougherty, though. Never a scratch on him. Did I not once tell you he'd outlive us all?"

"I believe you did."

"The murderous wee bastard. I wonder how old he is. Jesus, he was in Tom Barry's flying column. He has to be ninety, and he could be ninety-five. A long life to live when you've all that blood on your hands. Or do you suppose the blood washes off after so many years?"

"I don't know."

"I wonder," he said, and looked down at his own hands. "You saw the gunman. Vietnamese, Andy thought. Or Thai, or God knows what else. Did you get a look at the one that threw the bomb?"

"No."

"He got away, and I scarcely saw him myself. There was his big face, looming over the other's shoulder, and then he threw the bomb and after that I never saw him again. It seems to me he was a very pale washed-out sort of white."

"And partnered with an Asian."

"It's the entire United fucking Nations arrayed against me," he said. "It's no more than luck they weren't trying to kill me."

"You mean all that was just to get your attention?"

"Oh, they came to do murder, and it was murder they did. But I'd say the man who sent them never expected to find me there, or yourself either. He sent those two to destroy the place and kill as many people as they could." He hefted the weapon he'd taken from the dead Asian. "If I hadn't shot the fucker," he said, "he'd have gone on firing until he killed everyone in the room."

And if he hadn't been quick as a cat, knocking me down even as he drew the gun . . .

"A big moon face pale as death. Does that sound like anyone you know?"

"A cop said the moon's full tonight."

"Then maybe that was himself. The man in the moon, come down to pay his respects. What about the two who waylaid you the other night?"

I described them as well as I could and he just shook his head. They could be anybody, he said. Anybody at all.

"And it was a black man did the shooting at the Chinese restaurant. It makes a man long for the old days, when the only people I had to worry about were the Eyetalians. And they may have been bad bastards but you could reason with them. Now it's the Rainbow Coalition, with all the races of man uniting against me. What's next, do you suppose? Cats and dogs?"

"Are you safe here, Mick?"

"Safe enough, for as long as I'll be here. I didn't want to go to any of my apartments. There's people who know about them. Only a few people, and they're people I trust, but how do I know who's to be trusted? Andy Buckley's almost a son to me, but who's to say what he'll do if some bastard puts a gun to his head?"

"That's why you wouldn't let him drop us off."

"No, I wanted a car handy, and a less noticeable car than the Cadillac. But he's no need to know where I am. He can't reveal what's been kept from him."

"Couldn't you go to the farm?"

He shook his head. "There's altogether too many know of the farm. And it's too far away from everything." He took a drink. "If I wanted to be away from it all," he said, "I could stay with the brothers."

That puzzled me for a moment. Then I said, "Oh. The monastery."

"The Thessalonians, of course. What were you thinking?"

"You said the brothers, and we were talking about the shooter being black and the Rainbow Coalition, and . . ."

"Ah, that's rich," he said. "No, it's the brothers on Staten Island, not the brothers on Lenox Avenue." He looked at his hands again. "I'm a terrible Catholic," he said. "Ages since my last confession, and a soul well blackened with sins. But I could go there, to the brothers, and they'd take me in and ask me no questions. Whoever he is, he'd never think to hunt me there. He'd not be sending his black and brown shooters, or his pale white bomb throwers, either."

"Maybe that's not a bad idea, Mick."

"It's no idea at all," he said, "because I can't do it."

"Why not? Suppose you just walk away from it all."

He shook his head. "There's nothing to walk away from. I don't know who he is or what he wants, the man who's set all this in motion, but it can't be anything I have. Am I a crime boss with a great territory? I'm nothing of the sort. I own a few pieces of property, I have some business interests, but that's not what he wants. Don't you see? It's personal with him. He wants to destroy me." He uncapped the bottle, took a drink. "And all I can do," he said, "is try to get him first."

"Before he gets you."

"Is there another way? You're the policeman."

"Years ago."

"But you can still think like one. Give me a policeman's advice. Shall I go swear out a complaint? Against person or persons unknown?"

"No."

"Or ask for police protection? They couldn't protect me if they wanted to, and whyever should they want to? Haven't I lived my whole life on the other side of the law? And now it's kill or be killed, and how can I be hoisting a white flag and asking them to change the rules?"

A DOOR AT the left rear corner of the basement opened onto a flight of steps leading up to the air shaft. Mick unbolted the door and asked me again if I didn't want to catch a few hours' sleep before I went home. I could have the couch, he said. He was drinking, he'd just sit in the chair and sip whiskey until he dozed off.

I told him I didn't want Elaine to wake up before I got home. She'd turn on the news and hear what had happened at Grogan's.

" 'Twill be everyone's lead story," he said. "I'd put on the radio to learn the number of dead, but I'll know soon enough." He gripped my shoulder. "Go on home. And keep your eyes open, will you?"

"I will."

"And pack your bags and take herself off to Ireland or Italy or wherever she wants to go. Just so you get the hell away from here. Will you do that?"

"I'll let you know."

"That's what I want to hear from you, that you're at the airport waiting for your flight to board."

"How will I call you? What's the phone number here?"

"Wait a minute," he said, and scribbled on a piece of paper, straightened up and handed it to me. "The cellular phone. I never give out the number because I don't want a fucking telephone ringing in my pocket. I just bought the creature because you can never find a pay phone that works, or if you do you've no quarters for it. I don't know how much time I'll spend here, and I don't want to answer the store phone anyway, with people calling to inquire about doorknobs and strap hinges. Call me from the airport, eh? Will you do that?"

He didn't wait for an answer, just gave me a pat on the back and a shove out the door. I headed up the dark stairs and heard the door close, heard the lock turn.

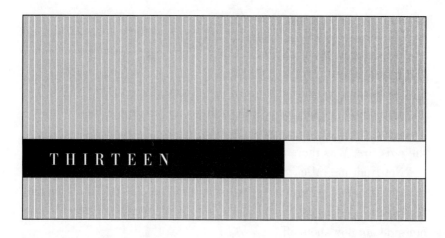

THIRTEEN

"**H**E SAVED MY LIFE," I said. "No question. The one guy was spraying the room with bullets, trying to kill everything with a pulse. There was a couple two tables away having a low-voltage lovers' quarrel. Killed, both of them. Same thing would have happened to me if I'd stayed in my chair."

"But not if you'd stayed in bed."

"I'd have been fine," I said. "Until the next time I walked out the door."

She'd been sleeping when I got home, but not deeply. The sound of my key in the lock was enough to wake her. She got up, rubbing sleep out of her eyes, put on a robe and followed me into the kitchen. I made the coffee for a change, and while it dripped through I told her every-thing that had happened.

She said, "Bombs and bullets. I'd say it sounds like *The Godfather, Part Four*, except it doesn't, not really. It sounds like a war."

"That's what it feels like."

"Welcome to Sarajevo. Or isn't there a bar in the East Village called Downtown Beirut?"

"On Second Avenue, if it's still in business."

"Two people go out for a beer so they can talk about their relationship, and the next thing you know they're wearing toe tags. Caught in the crossfire. Was there any crossfire?"

"Not from me. Mick emptied his gun at him. He was the one who shot the shooter. My gun never made it out of the holster, and Tom and Andy were all the way in the back, so I don't think anybody else on our side got any shots off."

" 'Our side.' " She sipped her coffee and made a face. It was too strong. When I make the coffee it always comes out too strong.

She said, "He was saving his own life, you know."

"He covered me with his body. Flopped on top of me, deliberately shielded me."

"But it must have been reflexive, don't you think? Something happened and he simply reacted."

"So?"

"So he didn't consciously think, *Matt's in danger and I have to knock him down and shield him from bullets.* He just did it."

"Would the act have scored higher on the nobility charts if he'd thought it over first? If he'd stopped to think we'd both be dead."

"You're right," she said. "You see what I'm doing, don't you? I'm trying to minimize what he did so you won't feel obligated to him. You almost got killed twice in one night. I want you to quit the game before your luck runs out."

"I don't think I can do that."

"Why not? How does what happened change anything? If Mick saved your life it was because he wants you to live, not so you can stand shoulder to shoulder with him on the battlefield. Didn't he tell you to take me to Ireland?"

"That's what he said."

"I've never been there. And I get the feeling we're not going."

"Not right now."

"Want to tell me why?"

"Because it really is a war," I said, "and nobody's going to let me be Switzerland. What were we saying before? My name's in the shawl. The only way I could stay neutral at this point is to pack up and leave the country."

"So? Your passport's in order."

I shook my head. "I can't sit on a stone fence in County Kerry, hoping my problem will solve itself."

"So you're going to be involved."

"That's got to be better than sitting around with my thumb up my ass waiting for something to happen."

"Besides, the man saved your life."

"That's a factor."

"And a man's gotta do what a man's gotta do. Does that get factored in, too?"

"It's probably part of the equation," I admitted. "I may think most of that guy stuff is bullshit, but that doesn't render me immune to it. And it's not all crap. If I'm going to live in this town I can't let people scare me out of it. And I have to live in this town."

"Why? We could live anywhere."

"We could, but we don't. We live here."

"I know," she said. "This is home." She tried her coffee again, then gave up and carried her cup to the sink. "It's a shame," she said. "I don't know about sitting on stone fences, but it would have been fun to go to Ireland."

"You can still go."

"When? Oh, you mean now? No thanks."

"Or Paris, or anywhere you want."

"Where I'll be out of harm's way."

"That's right."

"So you won't have to worry about me."

"So?"

"So forget about it. If I'm gonna sit around waiting for the phone to ring, I'd just as soon stay where it's a local call. Don't try to talk me around, okay? Because it won't work. I may not be a Taurus but I'm just as stubborn as you are. If you won't go, neither will I."

"It's your call. Will you close the shop?"

"That I'll do. I'll even hang a sign that says I'm off on a buying trip until the first of October. Will this be over and done with by the end of the month?"

"One way or another."

"I wish you hadn't put it that way."

I said, "That couple I mentioned? At Grogan's?"

"The low-level lovers' quarrel? What about them?"

"She's someone we used to know."

"Oh?"

"Lisa Holtzmann."

The two women had met in an art history class at Hunter. That's how I came to know her husband, and how she came to call me after he was killed.

"My God," she said. "And she was killed?"

"Instantly, from the look of things."

"That poor girl. What a life and what a death. Where was it we saw her?"

"Armstrong's, and it was awhile ago."

"And we didn't bother saying hello. Who knew we'd never see her again?" She frowned. "What was she doing at Grogan's? I know what she was doing, but you wouldn't think that would be her kind of place, would you?"

"As far as I know, that's the first time she ever went there. No, that's not true, because they were there the other night."

"The night before last?"

"No, the night the whole thing started. Wednesday, it would have been. Before we went over to the storage place in Jersey. She was there with the same guy, and it may have been the same table. And it wasn't his kind of place, either."

"Who was he?"

"His name was Florian."

"Florian? First name or last?"

"First, I assume. 'Matt, this is Florian. Florian, this is Matt.' "

"Snappy dialogue. Florian. Did he have long hair and play a Gypsy violin?"

"He had a wedding ring."

"He did and she didn't."

"Right."

"So he was married and she wasn't, and maybe that's why they were in a low-down boozer instead of some more gentrified establishment." She put her hand on mine. "First Jim and then Lisa. This has been quite a night for you, hasn't it?"

"There were a lot of others killed at Grogan's, too."

"You mentioned the bartender. Burke?"

"And people I knew by sight, and others I didn't know at all. So much death."

"I'm reeling from it myself and I wasn't even there. You were there both times."

"It doesn't feel real."

"Of course not. It's too much to take in. And you must be exhausted. Did you get any sleep at all before you went out to get shot at?"

"That's not why I went out. And no, I couldn't even keep my eyes closed."

"I bet you could now."

"I think you're right," I said, and got to my feet. "You know, I used to be able to miss a night's sleep now and then and just keep going. Of course I had an engine back then that burned alcohol for fuel."

"Your engine didn't have quite so many miles on it then, either."

"You think that's got something to do with it?"

"Of course not," she said. "You haven't lost a step. Get some sleep, slugger. Now."

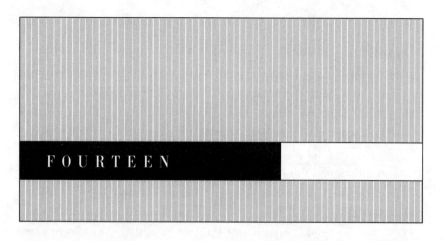

FOURTEEN

DROPPED OFF right away, and I don't think I so much as changed position until my eyes snapped open a little past noon. I hadn't awakened that abruptly in years. It wasn't like waking up, it was like coming out of a blackout.

When I'd showered and shaved, Elaine met me with a cup of coffee and told me the phone had been ringing all morning. "I let the machine pick up," she said. "A lot of people who wanted to know about Jim, or who wanted to tell you about Jim. And other people, too. Names I didn't recognize and some I did. Joe Durkin, and that other cop, the one from last night."

"George Wister?"

"That's the one. He called twice. The second time I thought he could see me. 'Please pick up the phone if you're listening to this.' Very stern, very parent-to-child, and just the sort of thing guaranteed to elicit a strong fuck-you response from *moi*. Needless to say, I did not pick up."

"What a surprise."

"I didn't even pick up when it was for me. It was Monica, and I wasn't in the mood to hear about her latest married boyfriend. The one time I did pick up, though, was when TJ called. He'd seen the news and he wanted to make sure you were all right. I told him you were, and I also told him not to open up today. In fact I had him put a sign in the window."

" 'We Be Closed for the Month So's We Can Be Buyin' Some New Stock, Jock.' "

"I also called Beverly Faber. You can imagine how much I wanted to make that call, but I figured I had to. She sounded sedated, or maybe she was just groggy from shock and lack of sleep. The cops had her up until all hours answering questions. The impression they left her with, or maybe it's the one she wanted to be left with, is that Jim's murder was a case of mistaken identity."

"Well, it was."

"Right now she seems to see it as the workings of random fate. Do you remember when that actress dropped something out a window? I think it was a flower pot."

"God, that was ages ago. I was a cop when it happened. In fact I was still in Brooklyn, I hadn't transferred to the Sixth. That's how long ago it was."

"The flower pot fell something like sixteen stories and killed a guy walking home from dinner. Wasn't that it?"

"Something like that. The question at the time was how the flower pot got out the window. Not that she was aiming at the poor jerk, but did it really just happen to fall or did she pick it up and throw it at somebody?"

"And he ducked and it went out the window?"

"Maybe. Whatever it was, it was a hell of a long time ago."

"Well, Beverly remembers it like it was yesterday. Her Jim was like the guy who got hit with the flower pot, just minding his business until God's thumb came down and squashed him like a bug." She made a face. "You know," she said, "I never liked Beverly. But I certainly felt for her, and I really wanted to like her for the duration of the phone call."

"I know what you mean."

"She's not an easy woman to like. I think it's her voice, she sounds like she's whining even when she's not. Listen, are you hungry?"

"Starving."

"Well, thank God, because I was afraid I was going to have to tie you down and force-feed you. Go listen to your messages while I fix you something."

I played the messages and jotted down names and numbers, even though I didn't much want to return any of the calls, especially the ones from either of the cops. Wister's second message was as Elaine had described it, and drew much the same response from me as it had from her. Joe Durkin's call, logged in just half an hour before I'd opened my eyes, sounded at once urgent and irritated, and didn't make me eager to get him on the phone.

I deleted the messages—you can't really erase them, it's digital, so there's no tape to erase. I went into the kitchen and ate everything Elaine put in front of me, and when the phone rang again I let the machine screen it. The caller hung up without leaving a message.

"There were a lot of those," she said. "Hangups."

"There always are. A lot of the time it's telemarketers."

"God, do you remember my brief career as a telemarketer? What a washout I was."

"That wasn't telemarketing."

"Of course it was."

"It was phone sex," I said.

"Well, it's the same thing. Either way you're jerking people off over the phone. God, that was funny, wasn't it?"

"You didn't think so at the time."

"I thought it was something I could do, and it turned out it wasn't. That was around the time I met Lisa."

"Right."

"Before you and I moved in together, and before I opened the shop. I'd stopped seeing clients and I couldn't figure out what to do with the rest of my life."

"I remember."

"Matt?"

"What?"

"Oh, nothing."

I rinsed my plate at the sink, put it in the rack to dry.

She said, "You'll want to call TJ."

"In a little while."

"And did you want to catch the TV news? New York One had a lot of crime scene footage."

"It'll keep."

She was silent for a moment, gathering her thoughts. Then she said, "You and Lisa were close, weren't you?"

"Close?"

"Look, do me a favor, okay? Tell me to shut up and mind my own business."

"I'm not going to tell you that."

"I wish you would."

"Ask your question."

"Was she the one you were sleeping with? God, I can't believe I said that."

"The answer's yes."

"I know the answer's yes. It ended awhile ago, didn't it?"

"Quite a while ago. I hadn't seen her since before the two of us saw her at Armstrong's."

"That's what I thought. I knew you were seeing somebody. That's what I meant when I said . . ."

"I know."

"That marriage didn't have to change anything. And I meant it. Did you think I was being noble? Because I wasn't."

"I figured you meant it."

"And I did, and I was not for one minute being noble. I was being realistic. Men and women are different, and one of the ways they're different is sex. They can throw me out of the Sisterhood for saying so, but I don't care. It's true. And I ought to know, right?"

"Right."

"Men screw around, and for years I made a very nice living being somebody they screwed around with. And most of them were married, and none of it had anything to do with their marriages. They screwed around for a lot of reasons, but all of them added up to one reason: Men are like that."

She picked up my hand, turned my wedding ring around and around.

She said, "I think it's probably biological. Other animals are the same way, and don't tell me they're all neurotic or responding to peer pressure. So why should I expect you to be different, or why should I even *want* you to be different? The only thing to worry about is if you found somebody else you liked better than me, and I didn't think that would happen."

"It never will."

"That's what I decided, because I know what we've got. Did you fall in love with her?"

"No."

"It was never a threat, was it? To us."

"Not for a minute."

"Look at me," she said. "I've got tears in my eyes. Can you believe it?"

"I can believe it."

"The wife crying over the death of the mistress. You'd think they'd be tears of joy, wouldn't you?"

"Not from you."

"And 'mistress' is the wrong word for her. You'd have to be paying her rent, and seeing her every afternoon from five to seven. Isn't that how the French manage these things?"

"You're asking the wrong person."

"*Cinq à sept,* that's what they call it. What'll we call her? How about the Designated Girlfriend?"

"That's not bad."

"I just feel so *sad.* Oh, yes, hold me. That's better. You know how I feel, baby? Like we lost a member of the family. Isn't that ridiculous? Isn't that nuts?"

ONE OF THE first calls I returned was from Ray Gruliow. "I need your professional services," he said, "and for a change I've got a client with reasonably deep pockets, which means you can bill at your full hourly rate."

"I don't suppose he can wait a couple of weeks."

"I wouldn't even want to wait a couple days on this one. Don't tell me you're booked up."

"That's what I just told another member of your profession. I'll be a little more candid with you."

"In light of our warm personal and professional relationship."

"That's the idea. I've got some personal business, Ray, and I can't even think about work for the time being."

"Personal business."

"Right."

"Some would call that oxymoronic, don't you think? If it's personal, how can it be business?"

"How indeed?"

"Wait a minute. This wouldn't have anything to do with something that happened last night in your part of town, would it?"

"Like what?"

"You see the headline in the *Post*? 'Slaughter on Tenth Avenue,' they called it, with the originality for which they're famous."

"I haven't seen the papers yet."

"Or the TV?"

"No."

"Then you don't know what I'm talking about?"

"I didn't say that."

"I see," he said. "Very interesting."

I was silent for a moment. Then I said, "I think I need legal advice."

"Well, young man, today's your lucky day. I just happen to be an attorney."

"I was there last night."

"Are we talking about Tenth Avenue?"

"Yes."

"And you were there when the excrement hit the ventilating system?"

"Yes."

"Jesus Christ. You know the body count? The last I heard it stood at twelve dead and seven wounded, and at least one of the wounded is circling the drain. One of the morning news shows had an interior shot of the bar, and it looked a lot like Rotterdam after the Luftwaffe paid a call."

"It looked pretty bad when I saw it last."

"But you're all right?"

"I'm fine," I said.

"And you got out before the cops turned up."

"Yes," I said. "Earlier in the evening I had dinner with a friend at a Chinese restaurant."

"And in Beijing I understand everybody's favorite place is Mc-Donald's. Go figure, huh?"

"I guess it didn't make the news."

"You guess what didn't make the— This is a restaurant in the same neighborhood as the other place?"

"More or less. Eighth Avenue."

"It made the news, all right, probably *because* it was in the same neighborhood. Lone gunman shoots a lone diner for no reason at all. He ran a copy shop in the neighborhood, if I remember correctly."

"Well, a printshop."

"Close enough. So?"

"You met the guy."

"I met him?"

"You heard him qualify six months ago at St. Luke's," I said. "He had seventeen years. Jim F."

"Your sponsor."

"Right."

"He's the guy you have dinner with every Sunday. They said he was a lone diner, but I guess he wasn't."

"He was alone when it happened. I was washing my hands. Ray, the two things are related and I'm the link. I held out on the cops last night, and then I got the hell out of Grogan's before they arrived on the scene. They've been leaving messages on my machine and I don't want to talk to them."

"So don't talk to them. You're under no obligation to do so."

"I'm a licensed private investigator."

"Oh, that's a point. That does obligate you in certain ways, doesn't it? On the other hand, if you're working for an attorney, you're shielded to a degree by lawyer-client privilege."

"You want to hire me?"

"No, this time around I'm going to be your lawyer. Is your friend still ably represented by the resourceful Mark Rosenstein?"

"I believe so."

"Have him call Mark," he said, "and have him tell Mark to hire you to investigate various matters in connection with pending legal action. Can you remember all this?"

"I'm writing it down. The only thing is, my guy could be hard to reach."

"I'll call Mark. it's not as though he has to do anything. Meanwhile, you might want to read the papers and look at the television."

"I suppose I'll have to."

"New York One profiled your friend in the course of a stand-up in front of what's left of his place of business. They made him sound like Al Capone out of Damon Runyon. Bloodthirsty but somehow engaging."

"That's fair enough."

"That great piece of theater with the bowling ball. Did that really happen?"

"I wasn't there," I said. "And you never get a straight answer from him on the subject."

"If it didn't happen," he said, "it damn well should have. Remember, don't tell them a thing. And call me if you need me."

I CALLED TJ, and he picked up the papers and brought them over. We sat in front of the TV and he channel-surfed while I saw what the tabloids had to say. They both gave it the front page—the *News* just slugged it HELL'S KITCHEN—but it had broken too late to get the full treatment inside, and must have missed the early editions altogether. The columnists and feature writers would be all over it tomorrow morning, but for now there were just the bare facts. The body count varied, the *Post* had one more dead than the *News*, and names were withheld pending notification of kin.

The TV reporters didn't have a whole lot more hard news, aside from more recent numbers for the casualties. But they had names and photos of some of the dead. Some of the photos looked familiar, but otherwise none were of people I knew. They evidently hadn't identified Lisa or her friend yet, or hadn't managed to notify family members.

The interior shots of Grogan's were as described, and as I remembered the place when Mick was dragging me out of it. And the exteriors were what you'd expect, with one reporter after another doing a stand-up in front of the sweet old saloon, its windows swathed in sheets of plywood now, the sidewalk in front still carpeted with debris and broken glass.

TV's edge was in sidebars and backgrounders, in interviews with survivors and neighborhood residents, in profiles of Michael "The Butcher" Ballou, Grogan's legendary unofficial proprietor, and heir to a long-standing tradition of savage Hell's Kitchen barkeeps. They trotted out the old stories, some truer than others, and of course they didn't fail to include the one about the bowling ball.

"That happen?" TJ wanted to know.

According to all versions of the tale, Mick Ballou had had a serious difference of opinion with another neighborhood character named Paddy Farrelly, who disappeared one day and was never seen again. The day after Farrelly was last sighted, Mick allegedly made the rounds of the neighborhood ginmills (including Grogan's, no doubt, which had not yet come into his hands) carrying the sort of bag in which a bowler carries his ball.

What he did in the various saloons, aside from having a glass of whiskey, depended on which version of the story you were hearing. In some he simply made a show of setting the bag significantly on top of the bar, then asking after the absent Farrelly and drinking his health "wherever the dear lad may be."

In other renditions he opened the bag, offering a look within to those who wanted it. And in one over-the-top version he went door to door, saloon to saloon, each time yanking the severed head of Paddy Farrelly out by the hair and showing it around. "Doesn't he look grand?" he said. "When did he ever look so fine?" And then he invited people to buy old Paddy a drink.

"I don't know what happened," I told TJ. "I was over in Brooklyn, still in uniform, and I'd never heard of Paddy Farrelly or of Mick, either. If I had to guess, I'd say he did make the rounds and he did have a bowling bag with him, but I don't believe he opened it. He might have, if he was wild and drunk enough, but I don't think he did."

"And if he had? Where I'm goin', what you figure was in the bag?"

"He could have had the head in there," I said. "I don't doubt for a minute that he killed Farrelly. I understand they really hated each other, and if he got the chance he probably killed him with a cleaver, and wore his father's apron while he did it. He might well have dismembered the body for disposal, and that would have involved cutting the head off, so yes, he could very well have had the head in the bag."

"Never found the body, did they?"

"No."

"Or the head, I guess."

"Or the head."

He considered this. "You ever been bowlin'?"

"Bowling? Not in years and years. There was a cops' league in Suffolk County when I lived in Syosset. I was on a team for a few months."

"Yeah? You have one of those shirts, got your name on the pocket?"

"I don't remember."

" 'I don't remember.' That means you did, Sid, and you don't want to admit it."

"No, it means I don't remember. We ordered shirts for everybody, but I had to quit the team when I got a gold shield and my hours changed."

"And you didn't bowl no more after that?"

"Once that I remember. I was off the police force and living at the hotel, and a friend of mine named Skip Devoe was always organizing things." I turned to Elaine. "Did you ever meet Skip?"

"No, but you've talked about him."

"He was an owner of a joint on Ninth and a hell of a fellow. He'd get a bee in his bonnet, and the next thing you knew we'd all be traipsing out to Belmont for the racing, or to Randall's Island for an outdoor jazz concert. There used to be a bowling alley on the west side of Eighth two or three doors up from Fifty-seventh, and he got it in his head we had to go bowling, and the next thing you knew half a dozen drunks descended upon the place."

"And you just went the once?"

"Just the one time. But we talked about it for weeks after."

"What became of him?"

"Skip? He died a couple of years later. Acute pancreatitis, but then they never put on the death certificate that the deceased died of a broken heart. The story's too long to tell right now. Besides, Elaine's already heard it."

"And the bowlin' alley's gone."

"Long gone, along with the building it was in."

"I bowled once," he said. "Felt like a fool. Looked so easy, and then I couldn't do it."

"You get the hang of it."

"I can see how you would, and then you just be tryin' to do the same thing over and over again. I see 'em sometimes on television, and those dudes are really good at it, and I keep waitin' for 'em to nod off in the middle of the game. How'd we get on this subject?"

"You brought it up."

"The bag. They never found the head, I was wonderin' did they ever find the bag. Don't matter if they did or didn't. Point is, that's a nice friend you got."

"You've met him."

"Yeah."

"He's who he is," I said. "He can be very charming, but he's a lifelong criminal and he's got a lot of blood on his hands."

"Times I met him," he said, "was when I was with you, an' we fell by that place of his that got trashed."

"Grogan's."

"Didn't see a lot of black folks there."

"No."

"Not workin' there, not havin' a drink there."

"No."

"Dude was polite to me an' all, but all the time I was there I was real conscious of what color I was."

"I can see how you would be," I said. "Mick's an Irish kid from a bad neighborhood, and those were the people who hanged black men from lampposts during the Civil War draft riots. He's not likely to decorate the windows for Martin Luther King Day."

"Probably uses the N word a lot."

"He does."

"Nigger nigger nigger," he said.

"Sounds silly when you say it over and over."

"Most any word does. What you say, he's who he is. We's all of us that."

"But you might not care to work for him."

"Not in his bar, Lamar. But then it don't look like it gone be open for business anytime soon. But that ain't the way you mean."

"No."

"We was workin' for him a couple days ago, wasn't we? He much more of a racist now than he was then?"

"Probably not."

"So why would I all of a sudden not want to be workin' for the man?"

"Because it's dangerous and illegal," Elaine said. "You could have some major trouble with the police, and you could even get killed."

He grinned. "Well, all that's cool," he said, "but I just know there's gotta be a downside."

"You think that's funny, don't you?"

"So do you, or you wouldn't be tryin' so hard to keep from laughin'." To me he said, "What we gonna do, exactly? Grab some guns and head for the OK Corral?"

I shook my head. "I don't think either of us is cut out for that," I said. "There will probably come a time for that, and it'll be up to somebody else to do it. Right now, though, nobody knows where the OK Corral is, or who's holed up there."

"Was the Clantons, way I remember it."

"This time around the Clantons don't have names or faces. What's called for is some detective work."

"An' we the detectives," he said. He scratched his head. "We didn't get too far with E-Z Storage. Fact, we took it as far as we could and signed off the case."

"We haven't got much more now than we did then, but there are a few things."

"Dude who shot your friend."

"That's one. Right now the main thing we know about him is he's black."

"Narrows it down."

"It does, as a matter of fact, because we also know he's a professional. And he screwed up, he shot the wrong person."

"Word might get around."

"It might," I agreed. "Second, there's the gunman at Grogan's."

"Asian dude."

"Southeast Asian, from the looks of him."

"That's right, you saw the man. I was thinkin' they didn't show his face on the TV, but you got to see him up close."

"Closer than I'd have liked. They haven't released his name or anything about him, but that doesn't mean they don't know it."

"Get his name, trace him back, see who he used to hang out with."

"That's the idea. Our third opening's the two guys who jumped me a few blocks from here."

"Pounded on you, till you went and pounded on them."

"I got a good look at one of them," I said. "I'd recognize him again."

"You figure he lives in New York?"

"He'd pretty much have to. Why?"

" 'Cause that's how we'll do it, Hewitt. Just drive around lookin' at people, an' pick him out of the eight million faces we see."

"Well, that's one way."

"But you can think of another."

"I can," I said. "The trouble is, it's not a whole lot better than your way."

"Well, we flexible," he said. "We try your way, an' if it don't work we try mine."

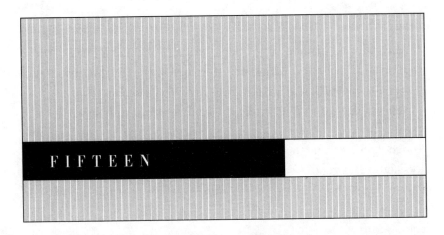

FIFTEEN

"**G**EORGE WISTER'S NOT a bad guy," Joe Durkin said. "A good cop and a bright fellow. He doesn't know what to make of you. You want to know something? I'm not so sure I know what to make of you myself."

"What do you mean?"

"You were having dinner with your friend last night. You went to the can and he got shot. And you couldn't think of a reason on earth why somebody'd want to kill good old Jim."

"I still can't."

"Bullshit," he said. "That the same jacket you were wearing last night?"

"So?"

"Same as your friend had on. Don't jerk me around, will you? You were the intended vic. Only reason you're here now is you picked the right time to take a leak."

We were in a Greek coffee shop on Eighth, just a block down from the Lucky Panda. I'd have preferred a different meeting place, but I'd already rejected his first suggestion, the squad room at Midtown North, and he hadn't liked my idea of getting out of the neighborhood altogether and meeting somewhere down in Chelsea or the Village.

When I'd got there he was at a back booth, drinking coffee and halfway through a piece of cherry cheesecake. He said it was good and I ought to have some, but I told the waiter I'd just have a cup of coffee. Joe said it was good we'd stayed in the neighborhood, that it was going to rain. I said they kept predicting rain and it kept not raining. He said they'd be right sooner or later, and the guy brought my coffee and we got down to it.

Now I said, "I guess that's true. I was evidently the shooter's actual target."

"It took you until today to figure that out?"

"Wister suggested as much last night. In an offhand way, after he'd gotten through floating the idea that Jim had been printing up green cards and bearer bonds for the Five Families. I took it about as seriously."

"When did you change your mind?"

"When I talked to Mick Ballou."

"Your friend,"

"He's a friend of mine, yes. You know that."

"And you know what I think about it. A lot of guys on the job have made themselves grief that way, having friends like that. Buddies from the old neighborhood, guys who went one way while they went another."

"I'm not on the job anymore, Joe."

"No, you're not."

"And Ballou and I don't go back that far. I put in my papers years before I met him."

"And the two of you just hit it off, huh?"

"Since when do I have to explain my friendships to you? You're a friend of mine, and I don't get a grilling from Ballou on the subject."

"Is that a fact? I guess he's more broad-minded than I am. Where were we? You were saying you changed your mind when you talked to your good friend the murderer. When was this?"

"After I finished with Wister. I stopped at his place on my way home."

"Not exactly on your way. You walked over to Ninth and turned left instead of right. I don't suppose you dropped in for a drink."

"I'd just lost one friend and felt the need to say hello to another," I said. "And when I got there he told me how he'd been having problems."

"Oh?"

"There was a fellow who did some odds and ends for him who wound up in a garbage can on Eleventh Avenue."

"Peter Rooney, and the odds and ends had to do with Ballou's shylocking operation. What'd he do, hold out a few dollars and Ballou put him in the Dumpster?"

"He didn't know who'd killed Rooney, but I gather there had been other incidents as well, and the implication was somebody was trying to muscle in on him. His take on Jim's shooting was that I'd been the target, and it was because I was a friend of his."

"That's what he told you."

"Yes."

"And I don't suppose he mentioned who was putting the screws to him."

"He said he didn't know."

"Like getting roses from a secret admirer? Except instead of roses it's death threats?"

"Maybe he knew and didn't say."

"Yeah, and maybe he said and it's you that doesn't want to say. And then what happened?"

"What happened?"

"Yeah. What did you do next?"

"I went home. I can't say I took it all that seriously. Why should a friendship make me the target of a presumably professional hit?" I shrugged. "I couldn't sleep. I was up late, drinking coffee in the kitchen and grieving for my friend."

"That's your friend Jimmy."

"Jim. Nobody ever called him Jimmy."

"Your friend Jim, then. As opposed to your friend Mick."

I let that go. "Then Elaine woke me around noon," I said, "after she heard about the incident at Grogan's."

"The incident."

"The bombing, although I gather it was more than that. There was gunfire as well, wasn't there?"

"You tell me."

"How's that?"

He picked up his empty coffee cup and tapped it against the edge of the saucer. "The way I hear it," he said, "you were there."

"I just got through telling you I was there. Then I went home, and it must have been two hours later that the shit hit the fan."

"Two hours later."

"Maybe three."

"Not the way I heard it."

"You heard I was there when it happened?"

"That's right, Matt," he said, looking straight at me. "That's exactly what I heard."

"Who's saying that?"

"Information received. You want to rethink your story?"

"My story? I haven't got a story. I told you what happened."

"And you were nowhere to be seen when the crap was flying."

"No."

He frowned. "I blame it on all those years on the job," he said. "If there's one thing a cop learns it's how to tell a lie and stick with it. And it's like riding a bicycle, right? You never forget how."

"You think I lied to you?"

"What gives you that idea?"

"Well, I think you lied to me. 'Information received.' You never heard I was at Grogan's. You were on a fishing trip."

He spread his hands. "We had a description, couple of guys seen leaving the scene. One was Ballou and the other could have been you."

"What did they say, it was a white male with two arms and two legs?"

"All right, point taken. The description we had could fit half the precinct. If they'd thrown in pain in the ass, then I'd have no doubts. Maybe I was fishing, but that doesn't make me wrong. Goddamn it, I still think you were there."

"Well, it's a free country. You can think whatever you like."

"I'm glad I've got your permission. While you're at it, you want to give me your word you weren't there when it all went down?"

"What for? You just got through telling me my word's not worth shit."

"I guess it's still worth something," he said, "Or you wouldn't be reluctant to give it. I'm not sure what kind of a game you're playing, my friend, but I don't think I like it. What are you trying to do, do you even fucking know?"

"I'm not sure I understand the question."

"Maybe all you're trying to do is stay alive, and in that case I can't say I blame you. Here's a question you can answer straight. Have you been over there this afternoon?"

"Where, Grogan's?"

"Uh-huh. You happen to walk by, have a look-see?"

I shook my head. "I came straight over here. From what I saw on the TV, there's nothing to see but plywood at this point."

"It's a shame you didn't get to see it the way I did. I was there this morning right after my shift started. They'd removed the bodies by then, but I had pictures to look at."

"I don't envy you that."

"And I don't envy the poor bastards who were first on the scene, far as that goes. What a fucking nightmare." He cocked his head. "If it was you looking at the pictures, there might have been one you recognized."

"What do you mean?"

"Does the name Lisa Holtzmann mean anything to you?"

"Of course," I said without hesitation. "From a few years ago. She was a client, her husband got shot making a phone call."

"Killed by mistake, as it turned out. Like your friend last night."

"What about Lisa? She was at Grogan's last night?"

"You didn't know?"

"I didn't hear her name on the news."

"She was there," he said. "And come to think of it, maybe you wouldn't have recognized her from the picture. What I saw was strictly closed casket."

"I've seen her around the neighborhood a few times over the years. Never at Grogan's, as far as I can recall."

"She wasn't there when you dropped by earlier?"

"It's possible, I suppose. If she was I didn't see her."

"If she was, she should have gone home when you did. You could have walked her home."

"What are you getting at?"

"I don't even know. Matt, if you're holding out information that could help clear the case, you're not doing anybody any good. Straight answers for a minute, okay? Do you know who shot your friend Faber?"

"No. I heard it was a black man, but I can't even say that out of my own knowledge."

"Guy was a pro, way it sounds to me. You don't know who might have hired him?"

"No."

"Or who was behind the mess at Grogan's?"

"No, but I'm willing to believe it was the same person who hired the other shooter."

"And you don't know who that might be, and neither does Ballou."

"Not unless he's holding out on me."

"And you don't think he is?"

"I can't see why he would. Did they say on the news the shooter at Grogan's was Asian?"

"One of them was. We've got zip on the second man."

"I didn't know there was a second man."

"The bomb chucker. Unless there was just the one guy, did the shooting *and* threw the bomb, but that seems a little unlikely. The eyewitness testimony suggests a second man, but it's not conclusive."

"But the shooter was Asian."

"Vietnamese, as a matter of fact. Wasn't that on the news?"

"If it was I missed it. All I heard was Asian."

"Maybe they didn't release it yet. Don't ask me his name, but it's on file, along with his fingerprints and his pictures, full face and profile. Been on file a few years now."

"You've got a sheet on him?"

"He was a troubled youth," he said. "Remember Born To Kill? Slope gang based downtown, got a lot of press a few years ago for being more homicidal than the Viet Cong?"

"Weren't they the ones who shot up a wedding party in Jersey?"

"Was it a wedding or a funeral? Whatever it was, it had all the old Mafia guys shaking their heads, wondering what the world was coming to. BTK was mostly running protection gangs in Chinatown, giving the tongs some grief, the usual first-generation crap. Reason you don't hear about them anymore is they mostly wound up dead or in jail. Or both, like our friend from last night. He did three years upstate for robbery and assault, and then last night he was dead at the scene." He leaned forward. "Somebody shot his lights out. Maybe you, with what you got right there inside your jacket."

"It's a .38," I said. "Is that what you dug out of Mr. Dead at the Scene?"

"We left that little chore to the medical examiner. But no, he got punched out with three shots from a .45. When did you start carrying a gun?"

"When I saw the news this morning. I've got a carry permit, if that's been worrying you."

"Yeah, it's a load off my mind."

"What was his name?"

"Who, the dead shooter? They've all got the same name."

"That must be handy," I said. "You call out one name and they all come running."

"You know what I mean. They all got names like you'd order in a restaurant if you could just figure out how to pronounce it. This one, his name started with *NG*, so even if I remembered it I wouldn't know how to say it."

"If you get sick of being a cop, you can always go to work for the UN."

"Or the State Department, teaching 'em how to be diplomatic. What the hell do you care about the name of some dead slope?"

"It was just an idle question."

"Only it didn't sound that idle. What are you holding out?"

"Not a thing."

"Am I supposed to believe that?"

"Believe what you want."

"You know," he said, "you're licensed by the state of New York. You can't withhold evidence."

"I don't have any evidence to withhold. Any suspicions or theories I might have aren't evidence, and I'm under no obligation to pass them on."

"If you were there last night, what you saw is evidence."

"I was in the bathroom," I said deliberately, "and what I saw was my own face in the mirror, and I already told Wister—"

"I'm talking about Grogan's. You son of a bitch, you *knew* I was talking about Grogan's."

"I already told you I left before there was anything to see."

"You were home in your own kitchen."

"That's right."

"Drinking coffee. That what you do when you can't sleep? Drink coffee?"

"If only I'd checked in with you, you could have told me to make it warm milk instead."

"You're making a joke, but it's the best thing in the world before you go to bed. Even better, sweeten it with a stiff shot of scotch. But I guess you'd leave the scotch out, wouldn't you?"

"Probably."

"Or maybe not. Maybe you chip around. Is that why you like hanging out with your gangster friend? Do you sneak drinks from time to time?"

"So far I haven't."

"Well, give yourself time. What did your other friend think of you hanging out in ginmills with cheap crooks? Your friend Jim. I bet he thought it was a great idea."

"Is there a point to all this?"

"The point is I think you were there last night."

"No matter what I say."

"No matter what. You were at Grogan's when the shit hit the fan, and you must have been standing right in front of it, which is why you're so full of it right now. You know what he wants to do? George Wister? He wants to put out an order and have you picked up."

"I suppose he can do that if he wants."

"Nice of you to give him permission."

"But he's not going to learn anything he doesn't already know."

"Matt, Matt, Matt," he said. "I thought we were friends."

"So did I."

"Except they say a cop can only be friends with another cop, and that's not what you are anymore, is it?"

"I'm the same thing I've been for as long as we've known each other."

"Seems to me you've changed. But maybe not." He sat back in his seat. "Let's wrap this up, okay? I don't know how deep you're into all of this, but the main reason I'm here now is to warn you off. Stay the hell away from Ballou."

I didn't say anything.

"Because he's finished, Matt. Somebody came real close to doing the world a favor last night. He dodged the bullet, but he may not be that lucky next time. And you know there's gonna be a next time."

"Unless first-rate police work leads to the quick arrest of those responsible."

"And how can we miss, with the cooperation we're getting from the public? Not the point. Which is that he's going down. He's the focus of a major departmental investigation. If the next bomb or bullet doesn't get him, all that means is he'll do time."

"He hasn't yet."

"He's led a charmed life. Charmed lives don't last forever."

Neither did the other kind. I said, "He's a friend in need, so I should drop him."

"Like a hot rock. What he is is a friend in deep shit, and he earned every ounce of it, and you'll go down with him if you stand too close. Jesus Christ, Matt, are you too thick to get that I'm trying to do you a favor? Am I wasting my breath here or what?"

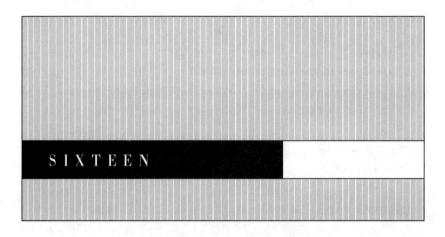

SIXTEEN

I WENT HOME, entering as I'd left, via the service entrance. There were two new messages on the machine. One was from Ray Gruliow, saying that he'd spoken to Mark Rosenstein, and I was now officially engaged to investigate in the interests of Rosenstein's client, one Michael Francis Ballou. The other was from Denis Hamill at the *Daily News*, hoping I could say something quotable for a column he was doing on the death of a great saloon. I called him back and told him Grogan's wasn't dead, it was only sleeping.

I called Ray Galindez at home after trying and failing to reach him at work. His wife, Bitsy, answered, and asked after Elaine, and brought me up to date on their kids. Then she said, "I suppose you want to talk to the boss," and I held until Ray picked up.

"I need your professional services," I said, "but it has to be off the record."

"No problem. Who'll I be working with?"

"Just me. I saw a guy the other day, and I wish I had a picture of him."

"That'll be great," he said. "You're easy to work with. Some people are just too eager to please you. 'Yeah, that's good, that looks like him'—except it doesn't, but they don't want to hurt your feelings. When do you want to do this? I'd say tonight, but we got this evening planned with Bitsy's sister and her dork of a husband. Do me a favor and tell me it's so urgent I've got to cancel."

"It's not that urgent."

"I'm sorry to hear it. In that case, is tomorrow okay? These days they've got me in Bushwick."

"I know, I tried you there first."

"Yeah, ordinarily I'd be working but I took a personal day. My older boy had a soccer game and I wanted to be there. I'll tell you, watching him play, I think he'll have to be an artist like his old man."

"There's worse things."

"I guess. You want me to come by your place tomorrow? I'm off at four and the station house is right next to the subway. I could be there easy by five."

"Maybe it would be better if I came to you."

"You sure? Because that's great as far as I'm concerned. Saves me a train ride. You want to come by the job? I got more time on my hands there than I know what to do with."

"It might be a little too public."

"Right, you wanted this off the record. So maybe that's not such a hot idea. That was quite a thing happened in your part of town last night."

"Terrible," I agreed. "Look, would it be an intrusion if I came to your house? You're off at four, so say five o'clock? Would that be all right?"

"That'd be fine. I know Bitsy'd love to see you. In fact why don't you bring Elaine with you? I've got some new work I've been trying to get up the nerve to bring in and show to her. Come around five and you'll stay and have dinner with us."

"I think it'll just be me," I said, "and I don't think I'll have time for dinner."

.　.　.

I TRIED TJ across the street, and when he didn't answer I called his beeper number. I had the TV on when he called back, and I muted it while the machine picked up and told him to leave his message at the tone. "I know you there," he said, "on account of you just beeped me, so—"

"So you must be a detective," I said, "to figure that out. Where are you?"

"You a detective too. Can't you tell?"

He must have held the phone toward the crowd, because the background noise picked up in volume. "O'Hare Airport," I said.

"Morning Star restaurant."

"Well, I was close."

"An' I was slow callin' back, 'count of I had to wait on a lady to get off the phone. She had me goin' for a minute. What she did, she put in her quarter and dialed her number and then she just didn't say anything. Just stood there with the phone to her ear. I wanted to tell her, like, if they ain't answered by now ain't nobody home. How many times you gonna let it ring?"

"She was listening to her messages."

"Yeah, well, I doped that out, but it took me a minute. What I been doin', I thought I might learn something on the street but they just sayin' the same shit they sayin' on the TV news. You been over to Grogan's?"

"No."

"Well, don't be wastin' your time. Ain't nothin' to see. It's the same as we saw on TV, with the plywood panels up. And there's yellow crime scene tape over the plywood and on the doors, and notices posted sayin' to keep away."

"Which might not be a bad idea."

"Fine with me. Ain't nothin' there worth a second look. All I did was ask a few questions. I wore a button-down shirt and carried a clipboard, so they figured I had the right."

"From here on in," I said, "maybe you should stick to the kind of questions you can ask electronically."

"Like cyber questions? There still be things got to be done the old way. You got to ask a street question to get a street answer."

"I asked some coffee shop questions myself," I said. "The shooter at Grogan's was Vietnamese out of Born To Kill. He did time on a robbery and assault charge, and his name starts with *NG*."

"If that don't stand for No Good, it's probably Nguyen."

"It could be," I said, "or it could be something else. I don't know if it's his first name or his last name, and I'm not a hundred percent sure of the *NG*."

"Lot you don't know."

"Seems to be more every day."

"Far as first name or last, Asian names is hard to figure that way. Like the last name'll come first. Like Mao Zedong, Mao's his family name. But if you was on first-name terms with the dude, which'd be hard even if he wasn't dead, you'd call him Mao."

"That's fascinating."

"But it might be different for Vietnamese. And two letters is all we got of his name, first *or* last."

"A little social engineering might get you the rest of it."

"Might."

"And then if there was a way to find out where he went to prison, and who he met there . . ."

"Hard to do at your desk," he said. "Prisons and government agencies and like that, they got secure systems. Hard to hack your way in, and if you do you leave a trail and they can trace it back and see who came callin'. You say he was in Born To Kill?"

"So I'm told."

"Means I best be changin' my clothes, Mose. Blue button-down's too lame and too tame for where I be goin'."

"Be careful."

"Got to," he said. "What the dude said, ain't it?"

"What dude would that be?"

"One lived in the woods and didn't pay his taxes. Musta been before Lyme disease, when you could still get by with that shit. You know the dude I talkin' about. Said to watch out for jobs you got to dress up for."

"Thoreau."

"Yeah, that's him. I be dressin' down, not up, but it comes to the same."

I said, "You know, it's not video games out there. They use real bullets."

"You mean the players don't come back to life when you put in another quarter?"

"And I promised Elaine I wouldn't get you killed."

"You did? You promised her that?"

"Why is that so funny?"

"Well, see," he said, "she made me promise I wouldn't let nothin' happen to you. How we both supposed to keep our word?"

WE ATE AT home. Elaine makes a mushroom-and-tofu Stroganoff that we both like, and she served it with a big green salad. After dinner I went into the other room and called Beverly Faber. I'd tried her a couple of hours earlier but hung up gratefully when the line was busy. This time she answered, and I hung in there and got through the phone call. By the time I returned to the kitchen to tell Elaine I'd called, I had already forgotten both sides of the conversation, what I'd said and what she'd said. Something about a private funeral for family members only, to be followed by a memorial service in a couple of weeks.

"He's at peace now," Elaine said.

"He was at peace all along," I said. "He was a pretty peaceful guy. He wasn't happy all the time, for that you pretty much have to be a moron, but he was good at taking things in stride. You were right before. She's a hard woman to like, our Beverly."

"I think she loved him."

"And he loved her. It wasn't always smooth sailing for the two of them, but they made it work. I think I'll go to a meeting."

I put on a sport jacket, a Harris tweed with elbow patches she'd picked out for me. I'd tried it on earlier, and it was a better fit over the holster than the blazer.

"Heavier than your windbreaker," she said, rubbing the sleeve, "but it doesn't zip up. Will you be warm enough?"

"I'll be fine."

"Take an umbrella. It's not raining yet but it will before the night is over."

I opened my mouth to argue, then shut it and took the umbrella. "I may not be back till late," I said.

"I won't wait up," she said. "But call anytime. I'll let the machine screen the calls, so stay on the line and give me time to answer."

"I will."

She squeezed my arm. "And don't you dare get killed," she said.

THERE'S A MEETING every weeknight at my home group at St. Paul the Apostle. A home group is like family, and I wanted to be there, but it was too soon to face a lot of shared memories of Jim and questions about what exactly had happened to him. In a small town I'd have had a problem, but I was in New York and had dozens of meetings to choose from.

I caught the IRT at Columbus Circle and got off at Ninety-sixth and Broadway. The meeting was in the church basement—they very often are—and I got there a few minutes early and helped myself to a cup of coffee. I didn't know anybody there, and I was just as glad. I wanted to be in a meeting, but I didn't want to talk to anybody.

At eight o'clock the chairman opened the meeting. He had somebody read the preamble and then introduced the speaker, a woman who looked like a young suburban matron with two kids and a golden retriever. She told a harrowing story, mostly drugs but with plenty of booze in it, told of rapes at knifepoint while trying to score smack in Harlem, told of trading blow jobs for hits on the crack pipe in Alphabet City hellholes. She was two years sober now and she had her life back. She also had HIV, and a T-cell count that was not so hot, but so far she was otherwise asymptomatic and she had high hopes.

"Anyway," she said, "I've got today."

During the break I put a dollar in the basket and had another cup of coffee and a stale oatmeal cookie. There were some announcements—the annual dinner dance six weeks away, some openings on the outgoing speakers' list, a member in the hospital who'd appreciate calls. Then the meeting reopened for a round robin.

If I'd known it was going to be a round robin I probably would have gone somewhere else. I grew oddly tense as my turn approached. I suppose I knew I ought to say something, and knew too that I didn't want to.

"My name is Matt," I said, "and I'm an alcoholic. Thanks for your qualification. It was very powerful. I think I'll just listen tonight."

Matt the Listener.

SEVENTEEN

"**MATTHEW SCUDDER,**" Danny Boy said. "First I heard you were dead. Then I heard you weren't. Logic told me that both of these reports could not be true."

"Where would we be without logic?"

He smiled and pointed to a chair, and I pulled it back and sat down. When the meeting ended I'd walked downtown on Amsterdam and looked for him at Mother Blue's. When I didn't find him there I walked the rest of the way to Poogan's Pub, on West Seventy-second. He was at his usual table, with a bottle of iced vodka in a hamper next to him and an unconvincing transsexual in the seat opposite him. She used her hands a lot while she talked, and what she said had Danny Boy laughing.

I drank a Perrier at the bar while she talked and gestured and Danny Boy laughed and listened. I didn't think he'd noticed me, but at one point he looked my way and caught my eye. A little later the TS stood up—she was tall enough for basketball—and extended a hand. It was a bigger hand than any woman ever sported, with long nails painted a bright blue. Danny Boy took her huge hand in his small one and pressed it to his lips. She whooped gaily and flounced away, and then it was my turn.

Seven nights a week he's at one place or the other, sitting at the table they reserve for him, listening to music (live at Mother Blue's, recorded at Poogan's), chatting up the Girlfriend of the Month, and brokering information. After the bars close—and both of his places stay open as late as the law allows—he's apt to hit an after-hours club uptown.

But he gets home before the sun comes up, and stays put until it goes down. Danny Boy Bell is African-American, and the cumbersome phrase fits him better than black, because in point of fact he's whiter than white, an albino with white hair and pink eyes and pale, almost translucent skin. Sunlight's dangerous to him, and any strong light bothers him. What the whole world needs, he has often said, is a dimmer switch.

I sat where the TS had been sitting, and Danny Boy picked up his glass of iced vodka and told me he was glad I was alive.

"So am I," I said. "Exactly what did you hear?"

"What I said. First the word came that you'd been gunned down in a restaurant. Then the bush telegraph ran a correction. It wasn't you after all. It was somebody else."

"A friend of mine. I left the table and the shooter made a mistake."

"And didn't know it until later," he said. "Because he must have reported a successful mission in order for your name to be in the first word that hit the street. Who was your friend?"

"Nobody you would have heard of."

"A square john?"

"A fellow Perrier drinker."

"Oh, and that's how you knew him? A close friend?"

"Very."

"I'm sorry to hear it. On the other hand, Matthew, I'm glad you're not on my list."

"What list is that?"

"Just an expression."

"It's a new one on me. What kind of list?"

He shrugged. "It's just something I did awhile back. I sat down and started writing down a list of everybody I could think of who was dead."

"Jesus Christ."

"Well, he might or might not belong on the list, depending on who you talk to. Same goes for Elvis. But this particular list was limited to people I'd known personally."

"And you wrote down their names."

"It sounds stupid," he said, "and I think it probably was, but once I got started I couldn't seem to stop. I got pretty compulsive about it. I'd think of a name and I'd have to write it down. It was sort of like the Vietnam Memorial in Washington, except those guys got a wall, not some pages in a notebook. And they had something in common. They all died in the same war."

"And the others were all friends of yours."

"Not even that. Some of them I couldn't stand and others were people I just knew to say hello to. But it was a trip, Matthew. One name would lead to another, and it was like dominoes tumbling over in your memory. I found myself remembering people I hadn't thought of in years. Neighbors from when I was growing up. My pediatrician. A kid across the street who died of leukemia, and a girl in my fifth-grade class who got hit by a car. You know what I realized?"

"What?"

"Most of the people I know are dead. I guess that happens when you've been around long enough. I once heard George Burns say something like that. 'When you're my age, most of your friends are dead.' Or words to that effect. The audience laughed, and I've never been able to figure out why. What's funny about it? Does it seem funny to you?"

"Maybe it was the way he said it."

"Maybe. And now he's dead. George Burns. But I never met him, so he's not on my list. And neither are you, because your heart's still beating, and I'm glad to know it."

"So am I," I said, "but somebody wants to put me on the list."

"Who?"

"I wish I knew," I said, and filled him in.

"I heard it got nasty at Ballou's joint," he said. "It's all over the papers. It must have been a bloodbath."

"It was."

"I can believe it. I didn't know you were there."

"A couple of hours ago I told a cop I wasn't."

"Well, I'll never say different. Ballou really doesn't know who's sticking it to him?"

"No."

"Got to be the same person that ordered you hit."

"I would think so."

"Whoever he is, he's an equal opportunity employer. Hires killers in every available color. Black, white, and yellow."

"A few white guys, if you count the pair who braced me on the street."

"And you didn't recognize anybody?"

"There was only one guy I got a really good look at. And no, I'd never seen him before. Next time I see you I'll show you his picture. In the meantime, I'd like to know what you know."

"Less than you do, I'd have to say. The big news was that you were dead, and then the not-so-big news was that the big news was bogus."

"The fact that I was alive was less newsworthy?"

"What do you expect? Look at the *Times*. They print corrections all the time, but they don't stick them on the front page." He frowned. "The other big item is that somebody's going to war with Mick Ballou, and I have to say I know a lot more about that from TV than I hear through the grapevine."

"Somebody's got to know something."

"Absolutely. The question is where do you start, and I'm thinking the shooter."

"There were two shooters."

"The black one, because the yellow one's not talking, whereas the black one must be talking a blue streak, to add one more color to the palette. Incidentally, speaking of blue, how did you like Ramona's fingernails?"

"I was meaning to ask about those. Does she paint them or is that their natural color?"

"Matthew, if you asked her she'd think you were serious. She honestly believes she's got the world fooled. She doesn't think anybody can tell."

"Can tell what? That she paints her nails?"

"That she wasn't born with a pussy. That she didn't get those cantaloupe tits from a surgeon."

"She's what, Danny? Six-four?"

"In her nylons. And big hands and feet, and an Adam's apple, although that's in line for a paring as soon as she gets the money together. All that and she's still convinced the whole world thinks she's the real deal. And before you even ask, you prying son of a bitch, the answer is no, I haven't." He poured some vodka, held it aloft, looked at the world through it. "Not that I haven't thought about it," he said, and drank it down.

"You could hardly help thinking about it."

"She's a nice kid," he said. "She makes me laugh, which gets harder and harder to do. And the size, you know. That's an attraction in itself. The contrast."

"Whether it was God or the medical profession," I said, "somebody sure made a lot of her."

"Well, God made a lot of Texas, too, but that's no reason to go there. But she's attractive. Wouldn't you say she's attractive?"

"No question."

"And of course she's nuts. She is genuinely out there, and, you know, I've never regarded that as a fault in a woman."

"No, I've noticed that."

"So I'm tempted," he said, "but I've essentially decided to wait until she's had her Adam's apple done. You know, with the height difference and all, that Adam's apple would be hard for me to overlook." He frowned. "Talk about losing the thread of a conversation. Where were we?"

"The black shooter."

"Right, and here's what I was thinking. The word got around that you were dead. Now that word could only have come from the man who thought he shot you—before he learned otherwise. So he's a talker, and now he's got something new to talk about. It shouldn't be too hard to get a line on him. Sometimes you can backtrack a piece of information and see where it came from. Other times you sort of circle around it."

"Whatever works."

"Keep in touch, Matthew. And one other thing. The guy knows he missed, and whoever sent him knows he missed. Either he'll try again or somebody else will."

"I thought of that."

"Of course you did. That's why you've got a bulge under your jacket. Nice jacket, by the way, bulge or no bulge."

"Thanks."

"Anyway, be careful, will you? And stay off my list."

IT WAS RAINING by the time I left Poogan's. That reminded me, and I went back for my umbrella, which I'd left at Danny Boy's table. The miracle was that I hadn't left it at the meeting.

Cabs disappear when it rains, and I guess it had been coming down long enough to thin their ranks. I'd just about decided to walk the fifteen blocks when a cab pulled up and let out a fat black man who looked a lot like Al Roker, the jolly TV weatherman, but who was actually a pimp named Bad Dog Dunstan. If he was jolly, he'd kept the word from getting out.

He had two girls with him, and weighed as much as the two of them together. They hurried into Poogan's, trying to keep their hair from getting wet, while he dug a roll out of his pocket to pay the driver and I held the door so the cab wouldn't take off without me.

Dunstan's eyes went wide at the sight of me, and I sensed that he'd heard the big news and missed the retraction. We knew each other only by sight and had never spoken, but I didn't stand on ceremony. A passed-along cab on a rainy night seemed to me enough of an introduction.

"False alarm," I said. "I'm not dead yet."

He smiled broadly, but the effect was somehow more savage than jolly. "Glad to hear it," he boomed. "We all dead soon enough. No need to rush the season."

He went into Poogan's. I got in the cab and went home.

ELAINE WAS WATCHING a *Law & Order* rerun on A&E, one of the earlier shows with Michael Moriarty and Dann Florek. We'd both seen the episode before, but that never seems to matter.

"I miss Michael Moriarty," Elaine said. "Not that there's anything wrong with Sam Waterston."

"They always get good people."

"But with Michael Moriarty, you can see the character thinking. You can just about see the thoughts."

And a little later she said, "Why does the judge *always* suppress the confession and the vital evidence?"

"Because it's true to life," I said.

It was one of the darker shows in the series; the Colombian enforcer gets acquitted and the prosecution's chief witness gets whacked after the verdict, along with what's left of his family. Elaine said, "Well, doesn't that just make you feel good all over?" and turned off the set and went into the other room. I picked up the phone and dialed the number Ballou had given me.

He answered on the third ring. "I hope you're at the airport," he said.

"How did you know it was me?"

"Nobody else has the number. It's only the second time I heard it ring, and the first time was when I called myself from another phone, just to make sure the fucker worked. It's a curious thing, having a phone go off in your pocket. I was a minute thinking what it was. What time's your flight?"

"I'm not at the airport."

"I was afraid of that. Are you at home?"

"I am, but why?"

"I'll call you back on the other phone," he said, and broke the connection. I hung up myself, and the phone rang almost immediately, and it was him.

"That's better," he said. "That's an awful little thing for a man to be talking into, and you never know who might be listening to you. Some fucker could pick us up on his car radio, or the fillings in his teeth. I talked to Rosenstein and he told me I'd hired you. That was days ago, says I, and how did you even hear of it? It seems your lawyer called him. You'd think one of us was getting ready to sue the other."

"I hope not."

"I'd say it was unlikely. I'm glad for your help, but I have to say I wish you were in Ireland."

"I may wish it myself before this is over."

"What are you doing now? I'll take the car out and pick you up, we can go for a ride."

"I think I'm going to make it an early night."

"I don't blame you, but I've the urge to be doing something. I didn't do a fucking thing all day."

"When I first got sober, my sponsor told me it was a successful day if I got through it without picking up a drink."

"Then I had a most unsuccessful day," he said, "for first I drank myself drunk and then I drank myself sober. Your sponsor. That's the Buddhist, the one who was killed?"

"That's right. And what he told me was perfectly true. If I didn't drink it was a successful day for me. And it's a successful day for you if you're still alive at the end of it."

"Ah. I take your meaning."

"You want to fight back, but first you have to know what you're up against. And that's where I come in."

"It's detective work, is it?"

"Yes."

"But you've nothing to work with. Are you getting anywhere?"

"It's hard to tell. But I'm working a couple of different angles, and if one of them doesn't work then another one will."

"Jaysus, that's the first good news I've had all day."

"It's not even news. I'm just getting started."

"You'll bring it off," he said. "Ah, I wish you were in Ireland but I'm fucking glad you're not. We'll find out who he is, this dirty bastard, and we'll get him. And we'll kill him."

"Yes," I said. "We'll kill him."

EIGHTEEN

Gborge Wister had called while I was at Poogan's, and he called again Tuesday morning and told the machine he wanted to talk to me. He sounded as though he meant it. He left his home number and said to call him there up until noon, and at Midtown North after that.

I had breakfast and read the paper. A few minutes before eleven I called him at the precinct and whoever caught the call told me he hadn't come in yet. I left my name and said I was returning his call. "He has my number," I said, "but I'll be out all day. I'll try him again later."

I went and sat at the window and watched the rain. Around twelve-thirty I called his home. The area code was 914, which would put him north of the city, most likely in Westchester or Orange County. A woman answered and said I'd just missed him. I left my name and said I'd try him at work.

. . .

LATER ON I called TJ to see if he wanted to take a run out to Williamsburg with me. He wasn't in his room across the street, so I called his beeper number. I hung around for fifteen minutes, then gave up. I put on my windbreaker and remembered to take an umbrella. Elaine caught me at the door and asked if I'd be home for dinner. I said I'd catch something on the run, and if TJ called to tell him it was nothing important, I just wanted company.

I rode the A train to Fourteenth Street and transferred to the L. My father died on the L train. He was riding between two cars, and he fell, and the train ran over him. I suppose he ducked out for a smoke, although it was no more legal to smoke on the platform between the cars than in the cars themselves. For that matter, you weren't allowed to ride between the cars like that, smoking or not. He was probably liquored up at the time, which may have had something to do with his decision to slip out for a cigarette, and with his falling, too.

I never ride the L train without thinking of that. I'd probably get over it if I rode it on a regular basis, but it's the line that runs across Fourteenth Street and under the East River, then through north Brooklyn until it ends up in Canarsie. I haven't been on it often enough over the years for my mind to tire of reminding me each time of how my old man died.

Not as though it were the L train's fault. I couldn't blame the train, and I couldn't really blame him, either. Shit happens.

Forty years ago, that was. More, closer to forty-five.

"A LITTLE DIFFERENT from the last time you saw it," Ray Galindez said. "We pulled off all the asphalt siding. I'll tell you, there must have been one hell of a siding salesman came through Brooklyn back in the early fifties. When me and Bitsy bought this place, I don't think there were two houses on the block didn't have some kind of siding covering up the brick. Now that green monstrosity across the street is the lone holdout. I don't know why anybody ever thought that crap was a good idea."

"Isn't it supposed to cut your heating bills?"

"That's what we've got global warming for. But it was some job, pulling it off and repointing the brick. I had help working on the brick, but me and Bitsy did the rest of the work ourselves."

"I guess that's where your summer went."

"Spring and summer both, but it's worth it, you know. And real satisfying. Which is more than you can say for the job these days. Come on in, and what can I get you to drink? There's coffee, but it's like superstrong. Except you like real strong coffee, don't you? You sure you're not Puerto Rican, Matt?"

"Me llamo Matteo," I said.

We sat in the kitchen. They'd bought a narrow two-story row house on Bedford Avenue, midway between the subway stop and McCarren Park. The neighborhood, Northside, was turning increasingly artsy, as were nearby Greenpoint and much of the rest of Williamsburg. Industrial buildings were being converted to artists' lofts, far more affordable than those across the river in SoHo and TriBeCa, and little houses like Ray and Bitsy's were shedding their siding like butterflies emerging from cocoons.

It was an unusual neighborhood for a cop to choose but a natural one for an artist, and Ray was both. A police sketch artist, he had an uncanny ability to render in black and white the images summoned up from a witness's memory. And there was a further dimension, a genuine artistry that had led Elaine to request a drawing he'd done of a chilling sociopath as my Christmas gift to her. Then she'd engaged him to draw her long-dead father, working not from photos but extracting the man's features from her memory. She'd since given Ray a show in her shop, and steered some commissions his way. Someday I wanted him to do a real portrait of her, but right now I needed him to do that same thing the city paid him to do.

"Two goons jumped me a few nights ago," I told him, "and I got a good look at one of them. But I didn't report it, and it's almost certainly connected to some other matters where I'm playing a lone hand."

"So the department's not supposed to know about this. I've got no problem with that, Matt."

"You're sure?"

"No problem at all. I'll tell you something, I'm sitting on the fence.

I'd put in my papers tomorrow if money wasn't an issue." He waved a hand, brushing the whole subject aside. "Tell me about this mutt that wanted a piece of you," he said, pencil in hand. "What did you happen to notice about him?"

We had done this before, though not recently, and we worked well together. In this instance our task was an easy one, because I could close my eyes and bring the image into sharp focus. I could picture the face of the man who'd held a gun on me, could see the expression he'd shown when he set himself to take a swing at my middle.

"That's it," I said, when the pencil lines on the pad matched the face I remembered. "You know, no matter how many times we do this it never ceases to amaze me. It's like a Polaroid camera, the film pops out and turns into a picture before your eyes."

"Sometimes they'll catch the guy and you'd swear I drew him from life, it's that close. And I have to tell you that feels good."

"I can imagine."

"And other times they get the guy, and I see his photo, and I look back and forth between the photo and my drawing, and I swear there's no resemblance whatsoever. Like they could be members of different species."

"Well, that's the witness's fault, Ray."

"It's both our fault."

"He's the one who remembered the guy wrong."

"And I'm the one didn't dig out the right memory, which is part of what I do."

"Well, yeah, I see what you mean. But you can never expect to be a hundred percent."

"Oh, I know that. It's frustrating, that's all."

"And you're not crazy about the job these days."

"I'm marking time, Matt."

"How old are you and how close are you to your twenty?"

"I'm thirty-three and I've got eleven years in."

"So you're more than halfway there."

"I know, and I hate to give it up. And it's not just the pension, it's the benefits. I could quit now and cover the basics, paying the mortgage and putting food on the table, but what about medical insurance?"

I asked why the job was getting to him.

"I'm obsolete," he said. "When they had the Identi-Kits I thought, well, hell, it's Mr. Potato Head for cops. Paste on a mustache, paste on a different hairline, you know how it goes."

"Sure."

"I could run rings around that thing, and I knew it. Then they developed a computer program that did the same thing but was a lot more sophisticated about it, and now they got it so you can take an image and morph it. You know, stretching a feature, shrinking it, whatever."

"I can't believe it's better than you at getting a likeness."

"I have to say I agree with you. But the thing is anybody can do it. All they do is train you and you can do it. Maybe you can't draw a straight line with a ruler, but you can be a police artist all the same. And there's more. See, they like the way the computer likenesses present."

"How do you mean, present?"

"To the public. I do a drawing, people look at it, they say to themselves, oh, an artist did this, so it's just an approximation. But they can make that computer likeness come out looking like a photograph, and you see it and it seems authentic. It's got credibility. It may not look like the perpetrator, but it sure shows up nice on TV."

I tapped the sketch he'd done. "This one's never going to be seen on TV," I said, "and it looks just like the son of a bitch."

"Well, thanks, Matt. Now how about the other one?"

"The other goon? I told you, I didn't get a good enough look at him."

"Maybe you saw more than you think you did."

"The light was bad," I said. "The streetlamp was shining in my eyes and his face was in shadow. And he was only in front of me for a second or two anyway. It's not a question of memory."

"I understand," he said. "All the same, I've had some luck in similar situations."

"Oh?"

"What I think happens," he said, "is that the memory doesn't get suppressed, but it barely registers in the first place. You see something, and the image hits the retina, but your mind's on something else and you never know you see it. But it's there all the same." He spread his hands. "I don't know, but if you're not in a hurry . . ."

"I'm certainly willing to try."

"Okay, so just get comfortable and let yourself relax. Start with your feet and just let them go completely limp. This isn't hypnosis, by the way, which is to my mind a great way to get people to remember things they never saw in the first place. This is just to relax you. Now your lower legs, letting them relax completely. . . ."

I didn't have a problem with the relaxation technique, having gone through something similar at a workshop Elaine dragged me to once. He led me through it, and he had me envision a canvas hanging on a wall, all in a gilded frame. Then he instructed me to see the face painted on the canvas.

I was all set to tell him it wasn't working, and then damned if there wasn't a face looking back at me on the framed canvas I'd constructed in my mind's eye. It didn't look as if it had been pieced together with an Identi-Kit, either, or morphed on a computer. It was a real human face with a real expression on it. And I knew it, by God. I'd seen it before.

"Shit," I said.

"You're not getting anything? Give it time."

I sat up, opened my eyes. "I got a face," I said, "and I was all excited, because it was like magic the way it appeared."

"I know, that's what it's like. Like magic."

"But it was the wrong face."

"How do you know?"

"Because the face I just saw belongs to somebody else. A few days prior to the incident I was in a bar, and I caught a glimpse of a guy. You know how you'll see a person and you know him but you don't know how you know him?"

"Sure."

"That's what happened. Our eyes met, and I knew him and he knew me, or seemed to. But I can't think how, and the fact of the matter is I probably saw him once on the subway and his face imprinted itself in my memory. New York's like that. You'll see more people in a day than the entire population of a small town. Except it's in passing. You don't really see them."

"But you saw this face."

"Yes, and now I can't get it out of my mind."

"What's it look like?"

"What's the difference, Ray? It's just a face."

"It's just a face?"

"You know what I mean."

"Why not describe it a little?"

"You want to sketch the guy? Why?"

"To clear the slate. Right now you try to picture a face and that's the face that comes up. So if we get that face on paper we'll be getting it out of your mind." He shrugged. "Hey, it's only a theory. I got the time, and I always enjoy working with you, but if you're in a big hurry . . ."

"There's no hurry," I said.

And the face seemed eager to be drawn. I watched it emerge as we worked together, the head very wide at the top and tapering sharply like an upside-down triangle, the exaggerated eyebrows, the long narrow nose, the Cupid's bow mouth.

"Whoever he is," I said, "that's him."

"Well, it's an easy face to draw," Ray said. "A caricaturist would have a ball with him. In fact this here comes out looking like caricature, because the features are so prominent."

"Maybe that's why I remembered it."

"That's what I was thinking. It stays with you, if it was a meal you'd say it sticks to your ribs. It'd be a hard face to forget."

BITSY CAME HOME while we were working, but she stayed out of the kitchen until we were done. Then she joined us and I had another cup of coffee and a piece of carrot cake. I left the house with the two sketches, sprayed with fixative and tucked between two sheets of cardboard inside a padded mailer. Elaine would want the originals. She'd frame them and hang them in the shop, and sooner or later somebody would buy them.

I gave Ray $300, and I had trouble getting him to take it. "I feel like a thief," he said. "You come to my house and I get more enjoyment than I've had in the last two months on the job, and on your way out the door I pick your pocket." I told him I had a client and he could afford it. "Well, I won't pretend I can't find a use for it," he said, "but it still doesn't seem right to me. And I collect again when Elaine sells the originals. How can that be right?"

"She collects, too. She's not a charity."

"Even so," he said.

I walked through the rain to the subway and got downstairs just as a train was pulling out. I sat there while three outbound trains came and went before I caught one back to the city. I could have transferred at either Sixth or Eighth to a train that would take me to Columbus Circle, but what I did was get off the train at Union Square and walk over to the Kinko's at Twelfth and University. I made a dozen copies of the sketch of the guy who'd punched me in the stomach. I didn't have any use for copies of the other sketch, but I made a couple anyway while I was at it.

Some years ago I'd spoken at a group called Village Open Discussion, and I seemed to remember that they met on Tuesday evenings at a Presbyterian church just a block west of the copy shop. It was a big meeting, a young crowd. There was a show of hands after the speaker, and there were always plenty of hands in the air. Matt the Listener sat back and listened.

It was still raining when I left, so I passed up the outdoor pay phones for one in a coffee shop on Sixth Avenue. I dialed my own number, waiting for the machine, and Elaine picked it up on the first ring."

"That's a surprise," I said. "I thought we were screening our calls."

"Oh, hi, Monica," she said. "I was just thinking about you."

I felt a chill, and tensed my stomach muscles as if in anticipation of a blow. I said, "Are you all right?"

"Oh, never better," she said. "I could do without the rain, but other than that I've got no complaints."

I relaxed, but not entirely. "Who's there with you?"

"I was going to call," she said apologetically, "but then these two friends of Matt's dropped by. Did you ever meet Joe Durkin? Well, he's married, so forget it."

"You're good at this," I said. "But that's not the Monica I know. She's only interested if they're married."

"Yeah, he's kind of cute," she said. "Hang on and I'll ask him. . . . My friend wants to know your name and if you're married."

"Don't get too cute or he's gonna want to talk to me."

"He says his name is George, and the other is classified information. But there's a ring on his finger, if that means anything." She laughed. "You'll love this. He says he's working undercover and it's part of a disguise."

"Yeah, I love it," I said. "How long are they likely to hang around, do you have any idea?"

"Oh, gee," she said. "I really couldn't say."

"Anybody call?"

"Yes."

"But you don't want to say the names, so just answer yes or no. Did Mick call?"

"No."

"TJ?"

"Uh-huh, a little while ago. You know, you really ought to get back to them."

"I'll call him."

"There was something else I had to tell you, but I can't think what it was."

"Somebody else called?"

"Yes."

"Feed me the initials."

"Absolutely, baby."

"AB?"

"Uh-huh. That's right."

"Andy Buckley?"

"I knew you'd understand."

"Did he leave a number?"

"Sure, for all the good it does."

"Because he left it on the machine and you don't have it handy.

Never mind, I can get it. If those two get on your nerves, tell them to get the hell out."

"My sentiments exactly," she said. "Look, sweetie, I have to go now. And I'll tell Matt what you said."

"You do that," I said.

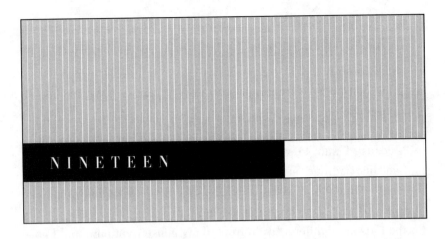

NINETEEN

I KNEW MICK would know Andy's number, so I tried him first on his cell phone. When it went unanswered I tried it again in case I'd dialed wrong, and after six rings I gave up.

Bronx Information didn't have a listing for an A or Andrew Buckley, but I'd figured the phone was probably in his mother's name, and there were two Buckleys listed on Bainbridge Avenue. I wrote down both numbers, and when I called the first a youngster said, "Naw, that's the other one. Next block up and 'cross the street."

I called the second number and a woman answered. I said, "Mrs. Buckley? Is Andy there?"

He picked up and said, "Yeah, Mick?"

"No, it's Matt Scudder, Andy."

He laughed. "Fooled me," he said. "She said, 'A gentleman for you,' and that's what she always says when it's the big fellow. Just about anybody else, she goes, 'It's one of your friends.' "

"The woman knows quality when she hears it."

"She's a pistol," he said. "Listen, have you talked to Mick lately?"

"No, I haven't."

"I thought I'd hear from him but I haven't. Where's he staying, do you happen to know?"

"I don't."

"Because I want to switch cars with him. What I did, I went down and got his Cadillac out of the garage, and I don't want to park it on the street. That's fine with the bucket of bolts I drive, but a car like that parked out in the open is what the fathers call an occasion of sin for the kids around here. It's in front of my house right now, and I gave a kid from down the block twenty bucks to watch it, and you want to know what I'm doing? I'm sitting in the window watching him."

"I think Mick wants to hang on to your car," I said. "He said his is too visible."

"Oh, yeah? Fine with me, only I thought we were supposed to switch. You got his cell phone number?"

"He doesn't seem to give it out."

"I know, he just uses it when he can't find a pay phone. You want to know, what I think is he lost the number of his own phone and doesn't know how to find it out. Hey, don't tell him I said that."

"I won't."

"Let's you and I stay in touch, huh? I'll call you if he calls me, and you do the same. I mean, I'm sitting tight here and that's cool, but I wish I knew what was going on."

"I know what you mean."

"You up for anything? You want me to drive you anywhere?"

"You should have asked me sooner. I just got back from Williamsburg."

"You don't mean Williamsbridge, do you?"

"No, I mean Williamsburg in Brooklyn."

" 'Cause the Williamsbridge neighborhood's just the other side of the Bronx River Parkway, though I can't think why you'd want to go there. And neither could you, obviously, because you didn't. Why Williamsburg, and what did you do, take the Williamsburg Bridge? They been fixing that thing forever."

"I took the L train."

"You should have called me. You know what I think I'll do? I think I'll put Mick's car back in the garage before my twenty bucks runs out and it gets swiped by the kid I hired to watch it. But I'm serious, you want a ride, gimme a call. There's always a car I can take."

"I'll keep it in mind."

"And keep in touch," he said. "What happened the other night . . ."

"I know."

"Yeah, you were there, weren't you? Stay close, Matt. We got to watch each other's back, next little while."

I CAUGHT TJ in his room and met him at the Starbucks on Broadway and Eighty-seventh. He was already there when I arrived, sitting at a table with an iced mochaccino, wearing black jeans and a black shirt with a pink necktie an inch wide, all topped off with a Raiders warm-up jacket and a black beret.

"Had to stop and change clothes," he said, "an' I still beat you here."

"You're greased lightning," I said. "What did you change out of that was less appropriate than what you've got on?"

"You don't think this here's appropriate? For where we goin'?"

"It's fine."

"It's as appropriate as that sad old zip-up jacket of yours. What I had on earlier was camo pants and my flak jacket, and that was very appropriate for where I was at, but not for Mother Blue's."

"And where was that?"

"Flushing. See a girl I know."

"Oh."

"What you mean, 'Oh'? I was on the clock, Brock. I was gettin' the job done."

"How so?"

"Girl's got a black daddy, Vietnamese mama. Her face tends to break out. Wasn't for that, she could be a model. Girl is seriously fine lookin'."

"Vietnamese . . ."

"You got it. She had a brother was in Born To Kill, an' she used to know all those dudes. Guy who shot up the bar Sunday was Nguyen Tran Bao. Very violent cat, what she said, but we already knew that."

"I don't know," I said. "He seemed like such a nice quiet boy."

"He did his robbery and assault bit at Attica, an' when he came back he wasn't exactly rehabilitated. Matter of fact, he was hangin' out with a white dude he got to know upstate, and the general impression was the two of them was doin' bad things."

"A white dude."

"Very white, and what you call moon-faced."

"The bomb thrower."

"What I was thinkin', Lincoln."

"Did she happen to know his name?"

He shook his head. "Only way she knew what Goo been up to since prison is she made some phone calls. She pretty much lost touch with BTK when she moved out of Chinatown."

"Goo? Is that what they call Nguyen?"

"What *I* call him, 'cause it a whole lot easier to say. Anyway, I be callin' her tomorrow, see if she found anybody could come up with a name to go with his face. Even if she can't, we got Goo's full name an' we know where he went to college."

"Maybe the dean will give us a transcript of his record," I said. "You did good work."

"Just part of the service," he said, and lowered his head and sucked up the rest of his mochaccino. "Now what? We gonna hear some old people's music?"

THE GROUP ON the small stage was a quartet, an alto sax and a rhythm section, and they were as white as I was and almost as white as Danny Boy. They all wore black suit jackets and white dress shirts and faded jeans, and I somehow knew they were European, though I'm not sure how I could tell. Their haircuts, maybe, or something in their faces. They finished the set and the audience, about three-quarters black, was generous with its applause.

They were Polish, Danny Boy told me. "I have this mental picture," he said. "This kid's sitting in his mother's kitchen in Warsaw, listening to this tinny little radio. And it's Bird and Dizzy playing 'Night in

Tunisia,' and the kid's foot starts tapping, and right then and there he knows what he wants to do with his life."

"I guess that's how it happens."

"Who knows how it happens? But I have to say they can play." He glanced across the table at TJ. "But I suppose you're more a fan of rap and hip-hop."

"Mostly," TJ said, "Ah likes to go down by de river an' sing dem good ol' Negro spirituals."

Danny Boy's eyes brightened. "Matthew," he said, "this young man will go far. Unless, of course, someone shoots him." He helped himself to a little vodka. "I made some inquiries. The person who caused that unpleasantness in the Chinese restaurant the other night is a disillusioned and bitterly disappointed young man."

"How's that?"

"It seems he got half his money in advance," he said, "upon acceptance of the assignment, with the balance due on completion. As far as he's concerned, he completed the job. He went where he was told to go and did what he was supposed to do. How was he to know there were two gentlemen in the restaurant fitting the same description? There was in fact only one such gentleman to be seen when he entered, and he dealt with the man accordingly."

"And they don't want to pay him the rest of his money?"

"Not only that, but they've had the effrontery to ask for a refund of their initial payment. Not, I shouldn't think, with any realistic expectation of receiving it, but as a sort of counter to his demand for payment in full."

TJ nodded. "Somebody ask you for money, you turn around an' ask *him* for money. An' maybe he go away."

"That seems the theory," Danny Boy said. "*I* think they should have paid the man."

"Keep him from runnin' his mouth."

"Exactly. But they didn't and he did."

"What do they owe him?"

"Two thousand dollars," Danny Boy said.

"Two thousand still owing? Out of four?"

"Guess you ain't worth much," TJ said.

"You get what you pay for," Danny Boy said. He took a sheet of paper from his wallet, put on reading glasses and squinted through them. "Chilton Purvis," he read. "My guess is they call him Chili, but maybe not. He's living at 117 Tapscott, third floor rear. I never heard of Tapscott Street myself, but it's supposed to be in Brooklyn."

"It is," I said. "Right around where Crown Heights butts up against Brownsville." His eyebrows rose, and I said I'd worked there years ago. "Not in the same precinct, but close enough. I don't remember a thing about Tapscott Street specifically, and I suppose it's changed since then anyway."

"What hasn't? A lot of Haitians in the area these days, and Guyanese, and folks from Ghana and Senegal."

"All looking to make a better life for themselves," TJ said, "in this land of opportunity for all."

"He's afraid the police are coming for him," Danny Boy said, "or that his employers will show up to seal his lips with a bullet. So he stays in his room all the time. Except when he gets the urge to party and smoke crack and run his mouth."

"Suppose he could pick up the two thou he's got coming just by fingering the man who stiffed him. You think he'd go for that?"

"He'd be a fool not to."

"We already know he a fool," TJ said. "Killin' folks for chump change."

"I'll want to show him a sketch," I said. "But first let me show you, Danny Boy." I opened the envelope, got out one of the copies of Ray's drawing of the slugger. He studied it through his reading glasses, then took them off and held it at arm's length.

"Nasty," he decided, "and not too bright."

"And nobody you know?"

"Unfortunately not, but I wouldn't be surprised if he and I have friends in common. May I keep this, Matthew?"

"I can let you have a couple of extras," I said. I counted out three or four for him, and passed one to TJ, who was edging over for a look.

"Don't know him," he said without hesitation. "Who the other dude?"

"What other dude?" Danny Boy wanted to know.

I produced the second sketch. "Just an exercise," I said, and explained how Ray Galindez had drawn it to clear my mind. But it hadn't worked, I said, in that I'd still been unable to summon up the face of the second mugger.

Danny Boy looked at the second sketch, shook his head, passed it back. TJ said, "I's seen him."

"You have? Where?"

"Round the neighborhood. Can't say where or when, but he got one of those faces sticks in your mind."

"That must be it," I said. "I caught a glimpse of him last week in Grogan's, and I thought he looked familiar, and it's probably because I'd seen him the same as you did. And you're right, he's definitely got one of those faces."

"All those strong features," Danny Boy said, "and you don't expect to find them all on the same face, do you? That nose shouldn't go with that mouth."

I gave TJ a sketch of the slugger and folded one and tucked it in my wallet. As an afterthought I added a copy of the second sketch as well. I put everything else back in the padded mailing envelope.

I looked at my watch, and Danny Boy said, "The band'll be back in a couple of minutes. You want to catch the next set?"

"I was thinking I might go over to Brooklyn."

"To see our friend? You might find him in."

"And if not I could wait for him."

"Keep you company," TJ said. "He ain't in, you can tell me stories to pass the time, an' I can pretend I ain't heard 'em before."

"Past your bedtime," I said.

"You need someone to watch your back, Jack, 'specially when you's the wrong skin tone for the neighborhood. An' if you's to brace this dude Chili, you got to know two's better than one." At the concern in my face, he said, "Hey, I'll be safe. You armed and dangerous, man. You'll protect me."

"Just stay away from parked cars," Danny Boy said, and we both stared at him. "Oh, from when I was a kid," he said. "I told you about my list, right? Well, when I was growing up there were always a few kids every year who got run over by cars, and the cops sent someone around every spring and every fall to tell the schoolkids about traffic safety. You ever pull that detail, Matthew?"

"I was spared."

"There'd be this slide show, and an explanation of how each victim bought it. 'Mary Louise, age seven. Ran from between parked cars.' And half the time or more, that was it, running out from between parked cars. Because the motorist didn't see you coming."

"So?"

"So in my young mind, it was the parked cars that were dangerous. I'd sort of slink past them on the street, like they were crouched and ready to spring. Wasn't until later I realized that the cars that were parked were essentially benign. It was the moving ones that would kill you."

"Parked cars," I said.

"That's it. A fucking menace."

I thought for a moment, then turned to TJ. "If you really want to tag along to Brooklyn," I said, "why don't you do me a favor? Go to the men's room and stow this under your shirt."

He took the padded envelope, weighed it in his hand. "Don't seem fair," he said. "You got your state-of-the-art Kevlar vest, an' I got cardboard. You think this'll stop a bullet?"

"It's so you'll have your hands free," I said, "although I'm not sure that's an advantage. And put it in back, not in front, so that it doesn't spoil the lines of your shirt."

"Already planning on it," he said.

When he was out of earshot, I said, "I've been thinking about your list, Danny Boy."

"Just so you stay off it."

"How's your health?"

He gave me a look. "What did you hear?"

"Not a thing."

"Then what's the matter? Don't I look good?"

"You look fine. The question is Elaine's, as a matter of fact. It was her first reaction when I told her about your little list."

"She was always a perceptive woman," he said. "She's the real detective in the family, you know."

"I know."

"Well," he said, and folded his hands on the table. "I had this little operation."

"Oh?"

"Colon cancer," he said, "and they got it all. Caught it early and got it all."

"That's good news."

"It is," he agreed. "The surgery got it before it could spread, and they wanted to do chemo afterward just in case, and I let them. I mean, who's gonna roll the dice on that one, right?"

"Right."

"But it was the kind of chemo where you get to keep your hair, so it wasn't all that bad. The worst part was the colostomy bag, but there was a second operation to reattach the colon—Jesus, you don't want to hear this, do you?"

"No, go on."

"That's it, really. I felt a lot better about life after the second operation. A colostomy bag puts a crimp in a man's love life. There may be girls who are turned on by that sort of thing, but I hope I never meet one."

"I never heard a word, Danny Boy."

"Nobody did."

"You didn't want visitors?"

"Or cards in the mail, or phone calls, or any of that shit. Funny, because information's my life, but I wanted a lid on this. I trust you'll keep it quiet. You'll tell Elaine but that's all."

"Absolutely."

"There's always a chance of a recurrence," he said, "but they assure me it's slim. No reason I can't live to be a hundred. 'You'll die on someone else's specialty,' the doc tells me. I thought it was a nice way to put it." He poured himself some more vodka and left the glass on the table in front of him. "But it gets your attention," he said.

"It must."

"It does. That's when I started making the list. I knew all along that nobody lives forever, but I guess I didn't quite believe that it applied to me. And then I did."

"So you started writing down names."

"I suppose every name I put down was one more person I'd outlasted. I don't know what I thought that would prove. No matter how long your list gets, sooner or later you get to be the final entry on it."

"If I made a list," I said, "it'd be a long one."

"They all keep getting longer," he said, "until they don't. Here comes TJ, so we'll talk about something else. He's a good boy. Keep his name off the list, will you? And your own, too."

THE RAIN HAD quit, at least for the time being. There were cabs cruising on Amsterdam and I hailed one. "Waste of time," TJ said. "He ain't about to go to Brooklyn."

I told the driver Ninth and Fifty-seventh. TJ said, "Why we goin' there, Claire?"

"Because I don't happen to have two grand on me," I said, "and Chilton Purvis might want a look at it."

" 'Show me the money!' Mean to say we actually gonna pay him that much?"

"We're going to say so."

"Oh," he said, and thought it over. "You keep that kind of money 'round your house? I'da knowed that, I'da stuck you up."

We got out of the cab on the northeast corner and walked to the hotel entrance. "Let's go up for a minute," I said. "I want to use the phone to make sure I haven't got cops in the living room. And you can get that envelope for me. I'll leave it across the street."

Upstairs in his room he said, "If you was all along meanin' to leave the envelope at your house, why'd I have to stick it up under my shirt?"

"To make sure you wouldn't leave it in the cab."

"You wanted to talk private with Danny Boy."

"Go to the head of the class."

"I been at the head of the class all along, so ain't no need for me to go there. Wha'd you an' him talk about?"

"If I'd wanted to share it with you," I said, "I wouldn't have sent you to the men's room."

I called across the street, and talked to the machine until Elaine picked up and said the coast was clear. TJ and I went downstairs, and he waited at the hotel entrance while I crossed the street and entered the Parc Vendôme lobby. I went upstairs, got twenty hundred-dollar bills from our emergency stash, and told Elaine not to wait up.

Three cabbies in a row passed up the added incentive of a twenty-dollar tip for a ride to Brooklyn. There's a regulation, they have to take you anywhere in the five boroughs, but what are you going to do if they won't?

"That dude just now," TJ said. "He was tempted. He wouldn't do it for twenty, but he'da done it for fifty."

"The city'll do it for a buck and a half each," I said, and we walked over to Eighth and caught the subway.

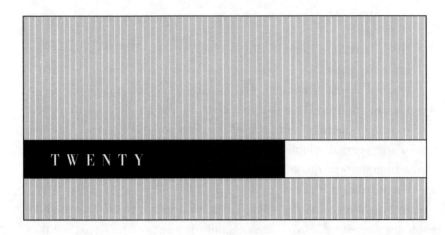

TWENTY

THERE MAY HAVE been a closer subway stop than the one where we got off. We wound up walking eight or ten blocks on East New York Avenue. It wasn't the best neighborhood in town, nor was this the best time to be in it—well after midnight when we left the subway station, and close to one by the time we found Tapscott Avenue.

Number 117 was a brick-and-frame house three stories tall. The siding salesman had evidently missed this part of town, and his efforts might have helped. As it was, the structure and the ones on either side of it looked abandoned, the ground-floor windows covered with plywood, some of the other windows broken, and a sour air of neglect that hovered like fog.

"Nice," TJ said.

The front door was open, the lock missing. The hall lights were out, but it wasn't pitch black inside. A little light filtered in from the street. I could see from the buzzers and mailboxes that there were two apartments on each of the three floors. Third-floor rear shouldn't be all that hard to find.

We gave our eyes time to get accustomed to the dim light, then found the stairs and climbed the two flights. The building may have been abandoned but that didn't mean it was empty. Light seeped from under the front and rear doors on the second floor, and someone had either cooked an Italian meal or ordered in a pizza. The smell was there, along with the smells of mice and urine. There was also what I took at first for conversation, but then they cut to a commercial and I realized it was a radio or TV set.

There was more light on the top floor. The front apartment was dark and silent, but the door of the rear apartment was ajar, and light poured through the inch-wide gap. There was music playing at low volume, too, something with an insistent beat.

"Reggae," TJ murmured. "He supposed to be from the islands?"

I approached the door, listened, and heard nothing but the music. I weighed my options, then knocked on the door. No answer. I knocked again, a little louder.

"Yes, come on in," a man said. "You can see it is open."

I pushed the door open and walked in, TJ right behind me. A slender dark-skinned man rose to his feet from a broken-down easy chair. He had an egg-shaped head topped with short hair and a button nose over a pencil-line mustache. He was wearing a Georgetown University sweatshirt and powder-blue double-pleated slacks.

"I fell asleep," he explained, "listening to the music. Who the hell are you? What are you doing in my house?"

He came across as more curious than outraged. The accent may have had something to do with it. He would have sounded West Indian even without the background music.

I said, "If you're Chilton Purvis, then I'm the man you've been hoping to see."

"Tell me more," he said. "And tell me who is your darker companion. Can he be your shadow?"

"He's a witness," I said. "He's here to make sure I do what I'm supposed to do."

"And what are you supposed to do, mon?"

"I'm supposed to give you two thousand dollars."

His face lit up, his teeth gleaming in the light from a battery-operated lantern. "Then you are indeed the mon I hope to see! Close the door, sit down, make yourselves comfortable."

That was easier said than done. The room was squalid, with crackled plaster and water-stained walls. There was a mattress on the floor, with a couple of red plastic milk crates stacked beside it. The only chair was the one he'd recently vacated. TJ did draw the door shut, or as close to shut as it went, but we stayed on our feet.

"So they saw the rightness of my position," Chilton Purvis said. "And quite proper, too! I went where I was supposed to go, I did what I was supposed to do. Did I leave the mon alive? No. Did I leave a trail? No. How am I supposed to know there is another mon? Nobody tells me. There is one mon in the restaurant who fits the description. I do my job. I put him down. And they do not wish to pay me?"

"But you're going to get paid," I said.

"Yes! And that is excellent news, the most excellent news. Give me the money and we will smoke some herb, if that is to your liking. But the money, before anything else."

"First you'll have to tell me who hired you."

He looked at me, and it was like what Elaine said about Michael Moriarty. You could see him think.

"If you do not know," he began, and stopped, and thought some more.

"They wouldn't pay you," I said. "But I will."

"You are the mon."

"I'm not the police, if that's what you mean."

"I *know* you are not the police," he said, as if that much was obvious. For the longest time people looked at me and knew I was a policeman. Now this one looked at me and knew I was not. "You," he said, "are the mon I was supposed to kill." His smile was sudden, and very wide. "And now you bring me money!"

"The world is a curious place."

"The world is strange, mon, and every day more strange. You pay me the money to point my finger at the mon who paid me to kill you. I say that is very strange!"

"But it's not a bad deal," I said. "You get your money."

"Then I would say it is a good deal. A fine deal."

"Just tell me who hired you," I said, "and where I can find him, and you'll get paid."

"You have brought the money?"

"I've brought the money."

"Ah," he said. "I can give you this mon's name. Would that be good?"

"Yes."

"I wrote it down," he said. "On a slip of paper, along with his address. You want that as well? His address?"

"That would be useful."

"Also a phone number. Just let me see where I put that slip of paper." He fumbled in the topmost milk crate alongside the bed, his back to me, then spun around suddenly, a gun in his hand. The first two shots he snapped off went wide but the third and fourth hit me, one in the center of the chest, the other a few inches below and to the right.

I'd had my jacket unzipped, and I guess I must have sensed something, because I had my gun in my hand by the time he started shooting and I was squeezing the trigger and returning fire about the same time I got hit. I was wearing the Kevlar vest, of course, and its manufacturer would have been proud of it. The slugs didn't penetrate. This is not to say they bounced off like spitballs off an elephant. The effect was like getting punched with considerable force by someone with tiny hands. It didn't feel good, but knowing that it had worked, that the vest had stopped the bullets, felt wonderful.

He wasn't wearing a vest. I fired twice and both bullets went home, one high on the right side of his chest, the other in the solar plexus two inches north of his navel. He threw up his hands when the bullets hit him and the gun went flying. He staggered, doing the little dance they do when they score a touchdown, and then his feet went out from under him and he sat down hard.

"You shot me," he said.

I caught my breath and went over and knelt next to him. "You shot me," I said.

"It did me no good. Bulletproof vest, yes? A .22 will not penetrate.

Head shots! That is what one must have. But when you are forced to hurry your shot . . ."

"Why shoot me in the first place?"

"But that was my job!" He might have been explaining it to a child. "I try, I fail. Not my fault, but still. Then you come in my door and I have another chance. If I kill you they will pay me my two thousand dollars!"

"But I was going to give you the two thousand."

"Be serious, mon. How I know you will give me the money? All I got to do is shoot you. That way I make sure. I take the money off your corpse, *and* I collect the money that they owe me." He winced as pain gripped him, and blood seeped from his wounds. "Besides, you think I know their names? You hire a killer, you do not tell him your name. Not unless you are a crazy mon!"

"And you didn't have a phone number for them?"

"What you think?" He winced again and his eyes rolled. "I'm shot bad, mon. You got to get me to a hospital."

I got the sketches from my wallet, unfolded them, showed him the one of the slugger. "Take a look," I said. "Have you seen this man before? Is he one of them?"

"Yes, he is one. Him I know, but not his name. Now you must get me to the hospital."

I wondered if he'd even looked at the sketch. I showed him the other one. "And this man?"

"Yes! Him too! Both of them, they are the men who hired me, said come shoot this mon when we tell you."

"You're useless," I told him. "If I showed you a hundred-dollar bill you'd swear Ben Franklin hired you."

I put the sketches away. He said, "I am hurting bad, mon. Now you take me to the hospital?"

I looked at him for a moment, and then I got to my feet. "No," I said.

"No! What are you telling me, mon?"

"You son of a bitch," I said. "You just tried to kill me and now you expect me to save your life? You killed a friend of mine, you son of a bitch."

"What are you going to do with me?"

"I'm going to leave you here in your blood."

"But I will *die!*"

"Good," I said. "You can be on the list."

"You would leave me to die?"

"Why not?"

"Fuck you, mon! You hear what I'm saying to you? Fuck your mother and fuck you!"

"Well, fuck you too."

"*Fuck* you! I hope you die!"

"Everybody dies," I said. "So fuck you."

I turned at a sound. Like a cough, but not a cough.

TJ was down, his back against the wall. His skin was gray, his face twisted in pain. He had both hands pressed to his left thigh, and blood, nearly black in that light, seeped between his splayed fingers.

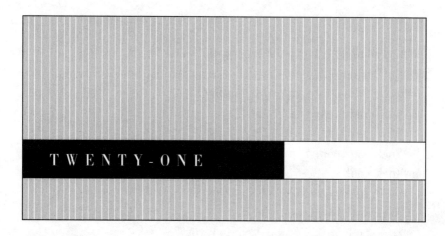

TWENTY-ONE

"DIRECT PRESSURE ON the wound," I said. I'd torn the pocket off my shirt, and now I placed his fingers on the wad I'd made of it. "Can you hold it there good and tight?"

"Think so."

"You're not gushing blood," I said. "It didn't hit an artery. How do you feel?"

"Hurts."

"Try to hang on," I said. "Try to keep pressure on the wound."

" 'Kay."

I took a quick tour around the room, running the sleeve of my jacket over any surfaces where we might have left prints. It didn't seem to me we'd touched anything. The squalid little room didn't invite touching.

Chilton Purvis lay where he'd fallen. There was a pink froth bubbling out of the corner of his mouth, and I guessed that one bullet had hit a lung. His eyes stared accusingly at me and his lips worked but no words got past them.

His gun had caromed off a wall and landed on top of his mattress. I thought, That's the gun that killed Jim. But of course it wasn't, he'd dropped that one at the scene. I left this one where it lay, left the little portable radio playing reggae, left everything where it was, including Chilton Purvis. I knelt down, got one hand under TJ's legs and the other beneath the small of his back, and got him up over my shoulder in a fireman's carry.

"Keep the pressure on the wound," I said.

"We goin'?"

"Unless you like it here."

"We just leavin' him?"

"One's all I can carry," I said.

I MADE IT down the stairs and onto the street. Light still showed under the doors of some of the other apartments, but none of the doors flew open, and no one rushed out to see what all the shooting was about. I guess you learn to keep a damper on your curiosity when you're living in an abandoned building.

We weren't going to find a cab cruising on Tapscott Street. I headed for East New York Avenue, a block and a half away, but at the corner of Sutter I caught sight of a gypsy cab and hollered at it.

The car was an old Ford, the driver a Bangladeshi. TJ was at my side when the cab pulled up to us, keeping all his weight on the un-injured leg, maintaining pressure on the wound. I had an arm around him to steady him as I reached for the cab door with the other hand.

"What is the matter with that man?" the driver demanded. "Is he sick?"

"I have to get him to a doctor," I said, and lifted TJ into the back seat and crawled in after him. "I want to go to Manhattan, to Fifty-seventh Street and Ninth Avenue. The best way to go—"

"But look at him! He is injured. Look! He is bleeding!"

"Yes, and you're wasting time."

"This is impossible," he said. "I cannot have this man bleeding in my cab. It will stain the upholstery. It is impossible."

"I'll give you a hundred dollars to drive us to Manhattan," I said. I showed him the gun. "Or I'll shoot you in the head and drive us there myself. You decide."

I guess he believed I'd do it, and for all I know he was right. He put the car in gear and pulled away from the curb. I told him to take the Manhattan Bridge.

.We were on Flatbush Avenue crossing Atlantic when he said, "How did he hurt himself, your friend?"

"He cut himself shaving."

"I think he was shot, yes?"

"And if he was?"

"He should be in a hospital."

"That's where we're going."

"There is a hospital there?"

Roosevelt is at Tenth and Fifty-eighth, but that wasn't where we were going. "A private hospital," I said.

"Sir, there are hospitals in Brooklyn. There is Methodist Hospital quite near here, there is Brooklyn Jewish."

"Just go where I said."

"Yes, sir. Sir, you will try to keep the blood to a minimum? The cab is my wife's brother's, it does not belong to me."

I got out a hundred-dollar bill and passed it to him. "Just so you know you're getting this," I said.

"Oh, thank you, sir. Some people, they say they will pay extra, you know, and then they do not. Thank you, sir."

"If there is any blood on the seat, that should pay for cleaning it."

"Most certainly, sir."

I had my fingers on top of TJ's and kept pressure on the wound. I felt his grip slacken as I took over. He was in shock, and that can be as dangerous as the wound itself. I tried to remember what you did for shock victims. Elevate the feet, I seemed to recall, and keep the patient warm. I didn't see how I could manage either of those things for the time being.

The driver was right, he belonged in a hospital, and I wondered if I had the right to keep him away from them. Bellevue was probably tops for gunshot trauma, and we were on the bridge approach now. Easy enough to redirect the driver to First Avenue and Twenty-fifth.

For that matter, Roosevelt's ER was first-rate, and closer to home. And I could delay the decision until we got uptown.

I managed to delay it all the way to the Parc Vendôme. When the cab pulled up in front of our entrance I gave him a second $100. "This is so you can forget all about us," I told him.

"You are very generous, sir. I assure you, I have no memory at all. Can I help you with your friend?"

"I've got him. Just hold the door."

"Certainly. And sir?" I turned. "My card. Call me anytime, any hour, day or night. Anytime, sir!"

THE DOCTOR WAS a spare, trim gentleman with perfect posture. His hair and mustache were white but his eyebrows were still dark. He came out of the bedroom carrying his disposable Pliofilm gloves and some other sickroom debris, and Elaine pointed him to a wastebasket.

"Wait now," he said, and fished around in the basket. He straightened up, holding a chunk of lead between his thumb and forefinger. "The young man may want this," he said. "For a souvenir."

Elaine took it, weighed it on her palm. "It's not very big," she said.

"No, and he can be grateful for that. A larger bullet would have done more damage. If you're going to get shot, always go for small caliber and low muzzle velocity. A BB from an air rifle would be best, but they always seem to find their way into children's eyes."

Elaine had known whom to call, as I'd guessed she would. What we needed was a doctor who wouldn't insist on moving TJ to a hospital, a doctor prepared to ignore the regulation requiring him to report all gunshot wounds to the authorities. I knew that Mick had a tame physician, if he was still alive since he patched up Tom Heaney a few years back, and if a few more years on the booze had left him with hands still capable of keeping a grip on his forceps and scalpel. But Mick's doctor was upstate. I needed somebody here in the city.

Elaine had called Dr. Jerome Froelich, who I gathered had performed more than his share of abortions in the pre–*Roe v. Wade* days, even as he'd written more than his share of morphine and Dexedrine prescriptions. It was around two in the morning when she called him, and he grumbled but he came.

She asked him how bad it was.

"He's resting comfortably," he said. "I sedated him and dressed the wound. He probably ought to be in a hospital. On the other hand, maybe he's lucky he's not. He's lost some blood, and they'd most likely give him a unit or two of whole blood, and you know what? If it was me, I'd just as soon not have some stranger's blood dripping into my veins, thank you just the same."

"Because of HIV?"

"Because of any number of goddamn things, including ones they can't test for because nobody knows what they are. I just don't have a lot of faith in the blood supply these days. Sometimes you've got no choice, but if all you are is down a pint or so, I'd rather give the body a chance to make its own. You know what I want you to do?"

"What?"

"Go out and get a juicer. Then—"

"We've already got one," she told him.

"I'm not talking about citrus, I mean a vegetable juicer. You got one of those?"

"Yes."

"Well, good for you," he said.

"We don't use it much, but—"

"You should. Things are worth their weight in gold. What you do, buy beets and carrots. Organically grown's best, but if you haven't got a source—"

"I know where I can get them."

"Beet juice is a blood builder, but don't give it to him straight. Mix it half and half with carrot, and prepare it fresh each time before you give it to him. It's not as quick as a transfusion, but nobody ever got hepatitis from it."

"I knew beet juice was supposed to be a blood builder," she said, "but I don't know if I would have thought of it. And I never expected to hear it recommended by a doctor."

"Most doctors never heard of it, and wouldn't want to hear of it. But I'm not like most doctors, my dear."

"No, you're not."

"Most doctors don't take care of themselves the way I do. Most doctors don't look or feel this good at my age. I'm seventy-eight. Assure me I don't look it."

"You know you don't."

"You should see me after I've had an uninterrupted night's sleep. I'm even more gorgeous then. I'm expensive, though, day or night. This is going to cost you two thousand dollars."

"All right."

"Look at her, she doesn't bat an eye. It's a ridiculous price, but here's something even more ridiculous. If you'd taken the young fellow to a hospital it would have wound up costing you that and more by the time you got out of there."

I didn't have to hunt for the money. I'd taken it along in case I had to show it to Purvis, and now I counted it out and handed it to Dr. Froelich.

"Thank you," he said. "I won't give you a receipt, and neither will I report it, to the police or to the IRS. The price includes aftercare, incidentally. I'll drop around sometime late afternoon to check on him and change the dressing. Check his temperature every couple of hours, give him aspirin when he needs it for pain, and call me if his fever spikes. If it does, but I don't think it will. And don't forget the beet juice. Beet and carrot, equal parts, all you can get into him. It's good to see you, Elaine. I've often thought of you, wondered what became of you. You're as beautiful as ever."

"More," I said.

He cocked his head, looked at her. "You know," he said, "I believe you're right."

"I DON'T KNOW," I said after he'd left. "Maybe I should have taken him straight to a hospital."

"You heard what Jerry said. He's probably better off here, and drinking beet juice instead of getting a transfusion."

"That's good to know," I said. "But the thing is I didn't know it at the time. I could see the bleeding wasn't too severe, and I didn't think he was in any immediate danger. If a doctor looked at him and saw that hospitalization was necessary, there'd be time to get him to an ER then."

"That makes sense."

"Gunshot wounds have to be reported," I said, "and I didn't want that. He's a young black male without a police record, and that's the sort of distinction you don't want to give up for no good reason."

"I know he'll be glad he wasn't hospitalized."

"I was probably thinking of myself as well. The slug Froelich took out of him may make a nice souvenir, but if they'd dug it out at Bellevue or Roosevelt or Brooklyn Jewish they wouldn't have let him keep it. They'd have turned it over to the cops, and a ballistics check might show an interesting matchup."

"With the bullets that killed Jim Faber?"

"No, because he left the gun at the scene. But with a gun found in an apartment in Brooklyn, along with a dead body with a couple of other bullets in it. Bullets from a .38 revolver, and that reminds me. I'm going to have to get rid of this gun."

"Because it leads straight to the dead man in Brooklyn. You want me to take it out and drop it down a storm drain?"

"Not until I find a replacement for it. I thought about leaving it at the scene and taking his gun, but what do I want with a dinky little .22?"

"Mah man wants a man's gun," she drawled. "I'll tell you one thing you can get rid of right now, and that's the shirt you're wearing. It's got bullet holes in it. Well, not holes, because the bullets didn't go through, but bullet marks. How about the jacket? No, he missed that, but it's got bloodstains, and so do your slacks. Why don't you take a shower while I run all your clothes through the washing machine? Or is it a waste of time? I can get the stains out, but are there still traces that show up in a test?"

"There may be," I said, "but if the stains are invisible to the naked eye I'd say that's enough. If we get to the point where they do spectroscopic tests on everything in my closet, it won't matter what they find. TJ left some blood on the floor at Tapscott Street, and they can tie him to it with a DNA match, so I'm not going to worry about blood traces that nobody can see."

I took a shower, then put on clean clothes and had a look at TJ. He was sleeping soundly and his color looked better. I put a hand on his forehead. It felt warm, but not dangerously so.

In the living room, Elaine told me I shouldn't have bothered getting dressed. "Because you have to sleep," she said. "You can catch a few hours on the couch. I'll sit up with him, and then you can take over when the stores are open, and I'll go buy beets and carrots. I almost fell over when Jerry started telling me about beet juice." She took a moment, then said, "He performed one of my abortions, but before that he was a client."

"I wasn't going to ask."

"I know, but why should you have to wonder? Speaking of having to wonder, do you think he's dead? The man in Brooklyn?"

"He was well on his way when I left. I'd say he's probably dead by now."

"Unless someone phoned for an ambulance."

"That seems unlikely. Even if they did, my guess is he'd be dead at the scene or DOA at the hospital."

"Does it bother you?"

"That he's dead?"

"And that you didn't try to save him."

"No," I said. "I don't think so. He killed Jim, you know."

"I know."

"You'd think that would have filled me with rage when I stood there in front of him, but it didn't. He was just a problem to solve. He had some information I wanted. Or at least I thought he did at the time. It turned out he didn't know anything. He identified one sketch and got my hopes up, but then I showed him one Ray and I did as an exercise, someone completely out of the frame, and he ID'd him, too. I could have shown him a picture of the Dalai Lama and he'd have sworn that was the guy who set me up."

"He just wanted to get to the hospital."

"That's it. But the point is I didn't walk in with vengeance in mind.

I fully intended to stiff him on the two grand, but I wasn't planning to shoot him. If he hadn't started firing, my gun would never have left the holster."

"But he did."

"But he did, and I shot the son of a bitch, and then he expected me to get him patched up. Well, the hell with that. I don't think I could have if I'd wanted to, but why even make the effort? I hadn't been willing to kill him, but I was willing to let him die."

"He had it coming."

"You could probably say that about most people. Still, the guy's a poster child for the death penalty. He struck me as a pretty pure sociopath. He'd kill anybody, just so you paid him. God knows how many people he killed in his life, and Jim wouldn't have been the last. He wouldn't even have been the last this week if I hadn't been wearing the vest."

"I was thinking that," she said, "but I decided I'm not going to allow myself any thoughts that start with *if*. There are too many of them and they're too upsetting. You're alive, thank God, and TJ's alive. That's enough for now."

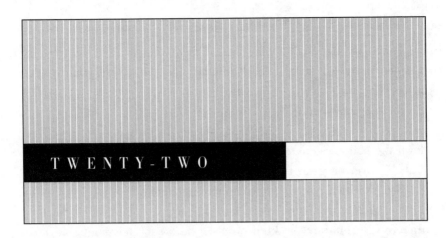

TWENTY-TWO

GOT A few hours on the couch. They were fitful, with a lot of dreams that dispersed like smoke when I opened my eyes. TJ was alone in the bedroom, his features relaxed in sleep. For a moment he looked about twelve years old.

Elaine was in the kitchen watching the news. "Nothing about a dead man in Brownsville," she said.

"There wouldn't be. A black man dead of gunshot wounds in an abandoned building? Not the kind of item that makes a news director holler for a film crew."

"They'll investigate it, though."

"The police? Of course they will. You get any kind of a homicide, you try to clear it. This one's easy to read. Dead man on the floor, shot twice in the chest with a .38. Another gun nearby, a .22, recently fired, and several slugs from it there in the apartment."

"Oh?"

"The two that the Kevlar vest stopped, plus one that missed both of us. They can dig it out of the wall if they want to take the trouble. Blood—the dead man's, and another person's, presumably the shooter."

"But we know better."

"And a blood trail, I'd have to assume, leading out the door and down the stairs. Scenario's got to be that two men had an argument, probably over drugs or women—"

"Because what else do grown men argue about."

"—and they shot each other, and the survivor decided not to stick around. It's certainly the kind of case you try to clear, but you don't knock yourself out. You wait until somebody says, 'Listen, what for you want to hassle me about ten dime bags of product when I'm the man can give you the dude shot that Cayman dude over on Tapscott Street?' And you make your deal and pick up your perp."

"Cayman? Purvis was from the Cayman Islands?"

"Just a guess. He was wearing a Georgetown University sweatshirt."

"So? That's in DC."

"Keep going."

"Georgetown is the capital of the Caymans," she said, after some thought. "So if that's where you're from, a Georgetown University sweat-shirt would be a hip thing to wear."

"Stands to reason."

"Of course it's also the capital of Guyana."

"It is?"

"Uh-huh. So maybe he's Guyanese."

"Maybe," I said. "Then again, maybe he stole the shirt."

"I used to like the Caymans," she said, "back when a suntan was considered sexy, instead of precancerous. He's been sleeping pretty soundly. He woke up one time when I was taking his temperature and I got him to drink some water, and then he went right back to sleep. He's running a slight fever, a little over a degree."

"I think that's to be expected."

"Yes, I'd say so. One of us has to go buy beets and carrots."

I said I'd go. The place she sent me was on Ninth Avenue near Forty-fourth. It was an oversized health food store with a big produce section and no end of herbs and vitamins. There was probably something on the shelves that would have him healed overnight without even a scar, but I didn't have a clue what it was or where to look for it. I bought enough beets and carrots to fill two shopping bags and took a cab home.

She had the juicer set up by the time I got there, and I watched as she washed beets and carrots and cut them up and ran them through the thing. The result may have been half carrot but all you could see was the beet, dark and purplish as blood from a vein.

She went into the bedroom with a big glass of the stuff and I tagged along to see how much of a fight he put up. "This is beet juice," she said, "mixed with carrot. The doctor said you have to drink it to replace the blood you lost."

He looked at her. "Like a transfusion?"

"But without the needles and tubes."

"Doc said so? Same one as was here before?" She said yes, and he took the glass from her and drank it off in two swallows. "It ain't bad," he said, sounding surprised. "Kind of sweet. What you say it was? Beet and carrot?"

"That's right. Could you drink some more?"

"I believe I could," he said. "Got a powerful thirst."

While she prepared it I helped him to the bathroom, then back to bed. He couldn't believe how weak he was, or how much the few steps to the john and back exhausted him. "It's just a flesh wound," he said. "Ain't that what they say? Then they up and runnin' like nothin' ever happened."

"That's in the movies."

"Anyway," he said, "they all flesh wounds, 'cause that's what folks is made out of. Wha'd the doc give me, you happen to know? A person could do okay sellin' it on the street."

"Don't tell the doc," I said. "He might try it."

WE NURSED HIM through the day. Elaine napped on the couch and I took a turn watching him sleep and talking with him when he was awake. His fever rose during the afternoon, and when it hit 102° Elaine called

Froelich. He said he'd be over in two hours, but to call him again if it reached 104° before then. But it broke, and when the doctor arrived and took his temperature it was normal.

Froelich changed the dressing, said the wound was healing nicely, and told TJ he should consider himself lucky. "If it had hit the artery," he said, "you could have bled out. If it hit the bone, you could be laid up for a month."

"If it missed me completely," TJ said, "I could be out playin' basketball."

"You're too short," Froelich told him. "These days they're all giants. Keep doing what you've been doing, and stay with the beet juice. Incidentally, it'll color your urine."

"Yeah, well, I found that out. Thought I was bleedin' to death, Beth, and then it came to me where I seen that color before. I'd been drinkin' it by the quart."

He dozed off after the doctor left, and I wound up taking an unpremeditated nap of my own in front of the TV set. When I woke up Elaine reported that he was starting to complain a little, and she took it for a sign of recovery. "He says if he was in his own place, meaning across the street, he could check his e-mail and keep up with some message boards, whatever they are."

"It's a computer thing," I said. "You wouldn't understand."

WE SPENT A quiet evening at home. TJ had an appetite, and finished a second portion of the lasagna. He also had the idea he could get to and from the bathroom on his own, and asked if Elaine still had the cane she'd used in the spring when she sprained her ankle. She found it and he took a couple of hesitant steps with it and saw it wasn't going to work. His wound was too raw for him to put any weight at all on that leg.

The phone rang intermittently. We let the machine pick up, and half the time the caller rang off without leaving a message. Maybe it was some phone sales rep who wanted to talk us into switching long-distance carriers, or maybe it was someone reluctant to issue death threats to an answering machine. I didn't waste a lot of time worrying about it.

Then right around midnight it rang, and after the recorded message and the tone there was a pause that seemed eternal, but was probably only five or six seconds. Then a voice I knew said, "Ah, 'tis I. Are you there then?"

I picked up and talked to him, put down the receiver and found Elaine. "It's Mick," I said. "He's in his car, driving around. He wants to come by and pick me up."

"Did you tell him yes?"

"I haven't told him anything yet."

"TJ's much better," she said. "I can manage here. And it's not over yet, is it? TJ was shot, and the man who shot Jim is dead, but it's not over till it's over. Isn't that what they say?"

"That's what they say. And no, it's not over."

"Then you'd better go," she said.

TWENTY-THREE

I WAITED IN the lobby and watched the street while the midnight-to-eight doorman shared his views on global warming. I can't remember the thread of his argument, but he saw it as a direct result of the collapse of world communism.

Then Andy Buckley's battered Caprice pulled up at the curb, and started rolling again as soon as I was inside it. The night was clear and cool and I caught a glimpse of the moon. It was gibbous, and just about the same shape as it had been the night we dug the grave. It had been waxing then and now it was on the wane.

"Andy was trying to reach you," I remembered to tell him. "He wanted your number, but I let him think I didn't have it."

"When was this?"

"Yesterday, early evening. Have you talked to him since?"

"Yesterday and today as well. He had the Cadillac and wanted to trade cars."

"So he said."

"I told him he had the better of the deal, but he was afraid to park the thing for fear some harm would come to it. Least of my worries, I said, but he would have none of it. He put it back in the garage and now he's driving some old wreck of his cousin's."

"That's what he said he was going to do."

We'd turned on Broadway and were heading downtown. "Now where'll we go?" he wondered. "Just so we're going somewhere and doing something. It's the inactivity drives a man mad. Knowing the other side is up to something, whoever they are, and not knowing what, and doing not a thing about it. I sat up all last night with a bottle and a glass. I don't mind drinking and I don't mind drinking alone, but I wasn't doing it for the pleasure of it. It was out of boredom, and that class of drinking is deadening to the soul."

"I know what you mean."

"You did some of the same in your day, did you? And lived to tell the tale. What luck have you had with the detecting? Are we any closer to knowing what we're up against?"

"We know more than we did," I said. "TJ found out a few things about the Vietnamese who shot up the bar, and we've got a line out for something on his partner."

"The bomb thrower, that would be."

"That's right. And I've got a sketch of one of the two men who mugged me."

"They were the ones mugged, by the time it was over."

I let that go. "I've got a sketch," I said, "but so far no one's recognized it. There were a lot of things I might have done today, but I had to spend it at home taking care of TJ."

"Why, for the love of God? Hasn't he managed for years taking care of himself?"

"Oh, of course, we haven't talked since then. How could you know?"

"How could I know what?"

"He was shot last night," I said.

"Fucking Jesus," he said, and hit the brake pedal. A car behind us braked hard, and the driver leaned on his horn. "Aaah, fuck yourself," Mick told him, and demanded to know what had happened.

I told him the whole story. I broke it off when we got to McGinley

& Caldecott, resumed the narration after we'd stowed the car in its parking space and made our way down the stairs and through the narrow aisle to the office. He poured himself a drink, and from a table-model refrigerator he produced a can of Perrier.

"They didn't have bottles," he said. "Only the cans. It should be all right, don't you think?"

"I'm sure it'll be fine. I've been known to drink tap water in a pinch, as far as that goes."

"Nasty stuff," he said. "You don't know where it's been. Get on with it, man. You left him for dead, the black bastard?"

"He was on his way out. He couldn't have lasted long. It was black comedy, now that I think about it. The two of us stood there snarling 'fuck you' at each other. I can't swear to it, but I think those were his last words."

"I wouldn't doubt they're the last words of more than a few of us."

I told him how TJ'd been shot, and how I got him home. "I put a gun to the cabdriver's head," I said, "and at the end of the ride he gave me his card and said to call him anytime, any hour of the day or night. I love New York."

"There's no place can touch it for people."

When I was finished he sat back in his chair and looked at the drink in his hand. "It must have gone hard when you turned to the boy and saw he'd been shot."

"It was strange," I said. "I'd just been shot twice myself and watched the bullets bounce off. And I'd shot back and my bullets didn't bounce off, and I felt as though I was in charge of the world. Then I turned around and the bottom fell out, because while I'd been feeling like the master of the universe TJ's blood was oozing out between his fingers, and I didn't even know what was going on."

"He's a son to you, isn't he?"

"Is he? I don't know. I've already got sons, two of them. I wasn't around much when they were growing up and I don't see much of them now. Michael's out in California and Andy's in a different place every time I hear from him. I don't know that I've installed TJ in their place, but I suppose he's a sort of surrogate son. To Elaine, certainly. She mothers him, and he doesn't seem to mind."

"Why should he?"

"I don't know that I act like a father to him. More like a crusty old uncle. Our relationship's fairly ritualized. We joke around a lot, trade good-natured insults."

"He loves you."

"I suppose he does."

"And you love him."

"I suppose I do."

"I never had a son. There was a time I got a girl in trouble and she went off and had the baby and put it up for adoption. I never heard if it was a boy or girl she had. I never cared." He drank some whiskey. "I was young. What did I care about children? I wanted only to be left alone, and she went off and had the child and gave it away, and I heard no more about it. Which was as much as I cared to hear."

"It was probably best for the child."

"Oh, of course it was, and for the girl, and for myself as well. But every now and then I'll find myself wondering. Not what might have been, but just wondering how the wee one turned out, and what sort of a life it had. Night thoughts, you know. Nobody has such thoughts in the light of day."

"You're right about that."

"For all I know for certain," he said, "it may not have been my child at all. She was an aisy sort of a girl, if you know the word."

"Same as easy?"

"I'd say it's the same word, but there's a softer sense to it when you say it the Irish way. An aisy girl. She swore it was me put her in the club, but how could she be sure? And how could I?" He looked at my can of Perrier and asked me if I wanted a glass for it. "You can't drink water straight out of a can," he said, and found a clean tumbler in a cupboard, and poured the water into it for me, and assured me it was better that way.

"Thanks," I said.

"Years later," he said, "there was another one I got in the family way, and I never heard about it until she told me she'd got rid of it. Had an abortion, you know. Jesus, that's a sin, I told her. I don't believe that, says she, and if it is then the sin's on me. Why didn't you tell me, says I. Mickey, says she, to what end? You weren't about to marry me. Well, she was right about that. You'd only have tried to talk me out of it, says she, and I'd already made up my mind. Then why tell me at all, says I. Well, says she, I thought you'd want to know. I'll tell you, man, women are the strangest creatures God ever put on the earth."

"Amen," I said.

"There's a saying, or mayhaps it's the words of a song. It holds there are three things a man must do in the course of a lifetime. Plant a tree, marry a woman, and father a son. Well, I've planted trees. In the orchard, and then I put in a great windbreak of hemlock, and I planted horse chestnut trees along the drive. I don't know how many trees I've planted, but I'd call it a fair number." He lowered his eyes. "I never found a woman I cared to marry. And never fathered a child. Even if it was my baby she had, it takes more than that to make a true father of a man. So I'll have to be content with my trees."

"Then again, your life's not over yet."

"No," he said. "Not yet."

A LITTLE LATER he said, "You killed the man who killed your friend. Good for you."

"I don't know if it was good for me. It was better for me than it was for him, I'll say that much."

"I wouldn't have left him breathing, myself. Even if it was his last breaths he was taking. I'd have put one more bullet into him to make sure."

"It never occurred to me. I wasn't planning on killing him."

"How could you not? He killed your friend."

"Well, I've killed him now, and Jim's still dead. So what difference did it make?"

"It made a difference."

"I wonder."

"What the hell were you going to do? Pay him two thousand dollars and shake his bloody hand?"

"I wasn't going to shake hands with him. And I wasn't going to pay him the money. I was going to stiff him."

"And then turn your back on him and walk out the door? How did you expect him to take it?"

I was silent for a moment, thinking long thoughts. Then I said, "You know, maybe I set it up, and set myself up in the bargain. I didn't consciously intend to kill him. When I walked in there and saw him I couldn't even manage to hate him. It'd be like hating a scorpion for stinging you. It's what they do, so what else can you expect from him?"

"Still, you'd grind that scorpion under your heel."

"Maybe it's not a good analogy. Or maybe it is, I don't know. But I wonder if I knew all along that I was going to kill him, and if I stage-managed things to give myself an excuse. Once he drew on me, I had permission. I wasn't murdering him, I wasn't executing him. It was self-defense."

"And it was."

"Not if I made him draw."

"You didn't make him draw, for Jesus' sake! You offered him money."

"I told him I had the money on me, and I let him know I was the man he was supposed to kill. Isn't that baiting the trap? If I wanted to keep him from drawing on me, all I had to do was walk in there with a gun in my hand. I had every chance in the world to get the drop on him and I didn't take it."

"You didn't expect him to try anything."

"But I should have. What else could he be expected to do? And the fact of the matter is I *did* expect it. I must have, because I was already reaching for my gun by the time he came up with his. Somehow or other I anticipated his response or I could never have responded so quickly myself. He opened fire, and that was my excuse, and I gunned him down."

"I hear what you're saying."

"And?"

"And whoever knows the reasons why we do what we do? I'll say this much. If you blame yourself for killing the bastard, you're off your head."

"I blame myself for getting TJ shot."

"Ah, I never took that into account. Still, who's to say it's not for the best?" I looked at him, puzzled. "What the soldiers call a million-dollar wound," he explained. "For he's out of it now, isn't he? And should live to tell the tale."

A LITTLE LATER he said, " 'Twas the vest saved you, was it?"

"The shirt I was wearing was ruined," I said. "But the vest stopped both rounds."

"They say it won't stop a knife thrust."

"So I understand. It's a kind of fabric, and evidently a knife blade can pierce it. I suppose the same thing would be true of an ice pick."

"Is it heavy? Like wearing a coat of mail?"

"It's not featherweight." I unbuttoned my shirt and let him examine the vest, then buttoned it up again. "It's an extra layer," I said, "and might be welcome on a cold day. On a warm day, you're tempted to leave it at home."

"It's a great thing, science. They make a vest that can stop a bullet, and next they make a bullet that can pierce a vest. It's the same as armies are forever doing, but on a more personal level. A good thing you were wearing one last night."

"Do you want one? Because they're easy enough to buy, and nobody has to teach you how to use it. You just put it on."

"Where would you get one?"

"The cop shops have them. I went downtown, but there's one on Second Avenue near the academy, and others in the other boroughs. What's the matter?"

"I'm just seeing myself walking into a cop shop. They'd never let me walk out again."

"I'd pick one up for you, if you want."

"Would they ever have my size?"

"I'm sure they would."

He thought about it, then let out a sigh. "I wouldn't wear it," he said.

"Why not?"

"Because I never would. Because I'm a fool, I suppose, but it's the way I am. I'd have it in mind that I was trying to get the best of the

Lord, and that He'd show me who's boss by making sure I got shot in the head, or done with a knife or an ice pick."

"Like Achilles."

"Just so. The heel was the only vulnerable part of him. And so he was shot in the heel, and died of it."

"That's superstition though, isn't it?"

"Didn't I say I was a fool? And a superstitious one in the bargain. Ah, there's differences between us, man. When you get in a car you always fasten your seat belt."

"And a good thing, too, when you stop short the way you did tonight."

"Didn't you give me a turn, though, saying the boy was shot? But the point is that you always wear a seat belt and I never do. I can't bear the feeling of being confined that way."

"A vest wouldn't confine you any more than a shirt does. It would just keep bullets out."

"I'm not explaining it well."

"No, I guess I understand."

"I just don't want to do what I should," he said. "I'm a contrary bastard. That's all."

"THERE'S JUST THE four of us," he said. "Tom and Andy and yourself and myself."

"Don't you have anybody else?"

"I've people who work for me, or do the odd job. They'll head for the hills now there's a war on, and why shouldn't they? They're not soldiers at all, they're what you could call civilian employees. So that's four of us, and who knows how many there are of them?"

"Fewer than there used to be."

"We each did for one, didn't we? Though the one you shot was hired help, and the same could be true of the Vietnamese. Wasn't he the murderous little bastard?" He shook his head. "I wonder how many that leaves. More than four, I'd guess."

"You're probably right."

"So we're outnumbered, and outgunned as well if that automatic rifle of his is anything to go by."

"Except you took it, didn't you? So it's ours now."

"And small use to us, with the clip close to empty. I should have seen if he had a spare in his pocket. Although as I recall we were in a bit of a hurry."

"You saved my life that night."

"Ah, go on with you."

"Just stating a fact."

"What did we say when we were kids? 'I saved your life the other day, I killed a shit-eating dog.' I'm glad childhood comes early in life because I'd hate to go through it now. Tell me something. What did you think of that movie?"

"To change the subject."

"It could do with changing. Did you care for it?"

"What movie was that?"

"*Michael Collins*. Didn't you tell me you rented the video?"

"I thought it was good."

"Did you? It was all true, you know."

"I was wondering about that."

"They took the odd liberty. The scene in Croke Park, when the British rake the crowd with gunfire? In fact they used a machine gun, not the revolving gun in the armored car. It was an image sticks in your mind, the way they did it, but what happened was terrible enough."

"It's hard to believe it happened at all."

"Oh, it happened well enough. The other thing they did, they had his friend Harry Boland die in the fighting at the Four Courts. Collins's friend, he dives into the Liffey and a soldier shoots him?"

"I remember."

" 'Twas years later he died, long after Collins was buried. He lived to be a minister in Dev's government. He was a sanctimonious bastard, Dev. Your man who played him had him just right. Even looked like him." He took a drink. "He was the best of them. Collins, I mean. He was a fucking genius."

"When he wiped out the British agents," I said. "Was that part accurate? Killing them all the same day?"

"That was the genius of it! He had his spy in Dublin Castle, yes, but then he gathered his information and bided his time. And killed all of the fuckers of a Sunday morning. It was over before they knew it had begun." He shook his head. "Listen to me, will you? You'd think I knew him. He was dead and in his grave fifteen years before I was born. But I've studied him, you know. I've heard the old men's stories and I've read books. You start off with a lot of heroes, you know, and then you learn a bit about them and they're heroes no more. But I've never ceased to admire Collins. I wish . . . no, you'll think it too queer."

"What?"

"I wish I could have been him."

"Elaine's answer to that would be that maybe you were."

"In a past life, do you mean? Ah, it makes a nice story, but it's hard to believe in it, isn't it now?"

"This from a man who has no trouble with transubstantiation?"

"But that's different," he protested. "If the nuns had drilled reincarnation into my head I'd believe that, too." He looked away. " 'Twould be pleasant to believe I was the Big Fella once. But what a fucking comedown for himself, eh? To be Michael Collins in one lifetime, and to come back as Mick Ballou."

HE SAID, "We were talking of guns before. Are you still carrying the same one?"

I nodded. He held out a hand and I gave it to him. He turned it over in his hand, lowered his head and sniffed it.

"Cleaned it since you fired it," he said.

"Yes, and reloaded it. At least the cop who takes it off me won't know it's been fired recently. But I ought to get rid of it altogether."

"Ballistics."

"Yes. They wouldn't make the match unless they looked for it, but they might look for it. I'd have tossed it by now but I didn't want to walk around unarmed."

"No, you can't do that. But I can help you out." He opened the satchel he'd brought from Grogan's, pulled out guns and set them on the desk. "These automatics are good," he said. "Or are you partial to revolvers?"

"That's what I'm used to. And don't automatics tend to jam?"

"So they say, but I've never had it happen to me. Either of these would give you more firepower than what you've been carrying."

"I don't know if they'd fit in the holster." I tried one, and it didn't. I put it back and picked up a revolver not unlike the one I'd been using. It was another Smith, but chambered for magnum loads. I tried it in the holster and it was a perfect fit.

"I've no extra rounds for it," he said. "There'd be a box in the safe, and there they'll stay. Have you had a look at the old place?"

"The bar, you mean? Only on television."

"I drove past it. Sad to see it like that." He shook off the memory. "I ought to be able to get hold of some shells to fit this thing."

"I'll buy a box tomorrow."

"Jesus, that's right. You've a permit, they'll sell you whatever you want."

"Well, they won't sell me a bazooka."

"I wish they would. I'd buy one, if I knew where to point it. It's hard to fight what you can't see. Take this, in the meantime."

He handed me a little nickel-plated automatic that lay in the palm of his hand like a toy.

"Here," he said. "Put it in your pocket, it weighs next to nothing. There's only the clip that's in it, but it's not the sort of thing you'd be likely to reload."

"Where did you get it?"

"I took it away from a man years ago, and I can tell you he'll have no further use for it. Go ahead, put it in your pocket."

"Two-Gun Scudder," I said.

IT WAS LIKE one of our long nights at Grogan's, with the door locked and only the two of us left. There were people dead and the world going to hell around us, but for all that it was an easy night, or even an aisy one. The conversation flowed, and when it ran out from time to time there would be a long silence.

"When you die," he said thoughtfully, " 'tis said you see your whole life. But you don't see it minute by minute, like a speeded-up film. It's like everything you ever did in all your days was a brushstroke, and now you see the whole painting all at once."

"It's hard to imagine."

"It is. What a picture that would be! 'Twould be worse than the dying, to have to look at it."

THERE WAS SOMETHING I'd forgotten. I was wondering what it was and thinking I ought to get on home when Mick said, "So he was no help at all to you."

"Who are we talking about?"

"The man you left for dead. Did you ever tell me his name? I can't recall."

"Chilton Purvis."

"Ah, you told me. I remember now. He had nothing to tell you?"

"They never told him a name, or gave him a number to call."

"Or if they did he wouldn't tell it."

"He'd have told me anything at that point," I said. "All he cared about was getting to the hospital. When I showed him the sketch, he ID'd the thing before I got it unfolded. He'd have sworn that was the guy who shot JFK if he thought that's what I wanted."

"You mentioned a sketch," he said. "Just before you told me that the boy was shot."

"Which was right around the time you stood up on the brake pedal and gave the guy behind us a heart attack."

"Aaah, he should learn how to fucking drive. But this sketch. You never said your man in Brooklyn saw it."

"I don't know that he really saw it. 'Yes, mon, that's him'—but he barely looked at it. I showed him another sketch by the same artist, someone he couldn't possibly have seen, and yes, mon, that was him, too. Which one, I asked him. Both of them, he said. And anyone else I wanted to throw in the hopper, just so I hauled his ass to the ER."

"He's looked at another picture now," he said. "His whole life laid out before him. He'll identify that straight enough. Do you have that sketch on you?"

"Oh, for Christ's sake."

"No harm if you don't. Next time'll do."

"I've got it," I said, "and I meant to show it to you hours ago. He's hired help, but my guess is he's a lot closer to the top man than Chilton Purvis or the Vietnamese. Maybe you'll know him."

I got out my wallet, found the sketch of the man who'd hit me, showed it to him. It was well drawn, he observed. You got a real sense of the man. But it was no one he recognized.

"Now the other one," he said.

"It's just a face," I said. "Somebody *I* thought I recognized, but couldn't place. I couldn't get the face out of my mind, so my artist friend drew it."

He took the sketch and the color drained from his face. He looked at me and his green eyes were fierce. "Is this a joke?" he demanded. "Is this a fucking joke?"

"I don't know what you're talking about."

"You've seen this man, have you?"

"At Grogan's, the night we buried Kenny and McCartney. I just had a quick glimpse of him but he's got a memorable face."

"Indeed he does. I'll never forget it."

"You know him?"

He ignored the question. "And you recognized him."

"He looked familiar to me but I couldn't place him. TJ says he thinks he's seen him around the neighborhood."

"And is that where you've seen him? Around the neighborhood?"

"I don't know. I almost think . . ."

"Aye?"

"That it's a face from the past. That I saw it years and years ago, if I ever saw it at all."

"Years and years."

"But who is he? You know him, obviously, but I never saw you react like that. It's almost as if . . ."

"As if I'd seen a ghost." He stuck out his finger, touched the sketch. "And what do you think that is? What's that if it's not a ghost?"

"You've lost me."

"I've lost it all," he said, "for how am I to contend with a ghost? What chance have I against a man who's thirty years dead?"

"Thirty years?"

"Thirty years and more." He took the sheet of paper in both hands, brought it closer, held it at arm's length. "Just the head," he said. "All you'd put in a drawing, isn't it? And it's how I saw him last, and how I see him in my mind. Just the head."

He threw down the sketch, turned to me. "Don't you see it, man? It's Paddy Fucking Farrelly."

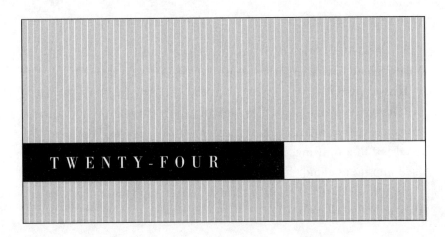

TWENTY-FOUR

"HOW OLD WAS he, this man you saw?"

"I don't know. Somewhere in his thirties."

"That was Farrelly's age when he died. I killed him, you know."

"That's what I always understood."

"By God, I have to say he had it coming. He was a bad bastard, that one. I had my troubles with him in school days. A few years older than myself, and a bully he was, a terrible bully. That ended when I got my size and gave as good as I got. He didn't care for that, the dirty bastard.

" 'Tis a vast city, New York, but the old Kitchen's not so big, and the pool we swam in wasn't large at all. We were forever in each other's way, forever coming head to head with each other, and everybody knew how it had to end. By God, I thought, if someone's after getting killed it needn't be myself, and I laid for the bastard, and I did for him.

"You've heard the stories, and there's a mix of the true and the false in them. This much is true: I took his great ugly head off his shoulders.

Do that, I thought, and your troubles with a man are at an end, for the best doctors in the world won't sew him together again.

"I never thought to run a stake through his heart."

"LET'S FIGURE THIS OUT," I said.

"It's a mystery," he said. "If you'd been brought up in the Church you'd know that mysteries can't be figured out. They can only be contemplated."

We were in an all-night diner he knew in Brooklyn, way the hell out in Howard Beach not far from JFK. He'd wanted to get away from McGinley & Caldecott, as if Paddy Farrelly's ghost had itself taken up residence there. I don't know how he managed to find the diner, or how he knew of it to begin with, but I figured we were safe there. The place was as remote as Montana.

For a man who'd just seen a ghost he had a good appetite. He put away a big plate of bacon and eggs and home fries. I had the same, and it was good. I could probably be a vegetarian like Elaine, but only if bacon was declared a vegetable.

"A mystery," I said. "Well, I didn't have the advantage of a Catholic education. I think of a mystery as something to be solved. Can we agree that it's not a ghost I saw?"

"Then it's a resurrection," he said, "and Paddy's an odd candidate for it."

"I think it would have to be his son."

"He never married."

"Did he like the ladies?"

"Too well," he said. "He'd have his way with them if they liked it or not."

"Rape, you mean?"

"Words change their meaning," he said. "Over time. When we were young it was scarcely rape if they knew each other. Unless it was a grown man with a child, or someone forcing himself upon a married woman. But if a girl was out with a man, well, what did she think she was getting into?"

"Now they call it date rape."

"They do," he said, "and quite right. Well, if a girl was with Paddy, she ought to know what she was in for. There was one was going to press charges, but Paddy talked to her brother and her brother talked her out of it. No doubt he threatened to kill the whole family, and no doubt the brother believed him."

"Nice fellow."

"If I go to hell," he said, "as I likely will, it won't be his blood on my hands that puts me there. But, you know, there were enough he didn't need to force. Some women are drawn to men like him, and the worse the man the greater the attraction."

"I know."

"Violence draws them. I had some drawn to me that way, but they were never the sort of woman I cared for." He thought about that for a moment. Then he said, "If he had a son, he'd have no love for me."

"When did Paddy die?"

"Ah, Jesus, it's hard to remember. I can't be sure of the year. 'Twas after Kennedy was shot, I remember that much. But not long after. The following year, I'd say."

"1964."

" 'Twas in the summer."

"Thirty-three years ago."

"Ah, you've a great head for mathematics."

"That would fit, you know. The man I saw was somewhere in his thirties."

"There was never any talk of Paddy having a son."

"Maybe she kept it quiet, whoever she was."

"And told the boy."

"Told the boy who his father was. And maybe told him who killed him."

"So that he grew up hating me. Well, don't they grow up in Belfast hating the English? And don't the Proddy kids grow up hating the Holy Father? 'Fuck the Queen!' 'Nah, nah, fuck the Pope!' Fuck 'em both, I say, or let 'em fuck each other." He drew out his pocket flask and sweetened his coffee. "They grow into good haters if you teach them early enough. But where the hell has he been all these years? He's spit and image of his father. If I'd ever laid eyes on him I'd have known him in an instant."

"I saw how you reacted to the sketch."

"I knew him at a glance, and I'd have known him as quick in the flesh. Anyone who knew the father would recognize the son."

"Maybe he grew up outside of the city."

"And nursed his hatred all these years? Why would he leave it so long?"

"I don't know."

"I could imagine him coming for me in his young manhood," he said. " 'When boyhood's fire was in my blood'—you know that song?"

"It sounds familiar."

"That's when you'd think he'd have done it, when boyhood's fire was in his blood. But he's well past thirty, he'd have to be, and boyhood's fire is nothing but dying embers. Where the hell's he been?"

"I've some ideas."

"Have you really?"

"A few," I said. "I'll see where I can get with it tomorrow." I looked at my watch. "Well, later today."

"Detective work, is it?"

"Of a sort," I said. "It's a lot like searching a coal mine for a black cat that isn't there. But I can't think what else to do."

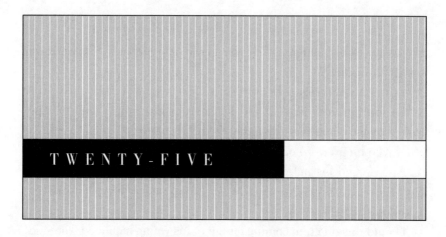

T W E N T Y - F I V E

I WAS HOME and in bed before sunrise, up and showered and shaved before noon. TJ had had a good night, and was sitting up in front of the television set, wearing navy blue chinos and a light blue denim shirt. He'd told Elaine he had clean clothes in his room, but she'd insisted on buying him an outfit at the Gap. "Said she didn't want to invade my privacy," he said, rolling his eyes.

I brought him up to speed and let him have another look at the man I'd come to think of as Paddy Jr., whatever his name might turn out to be. I was hoping there was a computerized shortcut to the task at hand.

"The Kongs could probably do it," he said, "if we knew where they at, an' if they still into that hackin' shit. *An'* if the records you talkin' about's computerized."

"They're city records," I said, "and they're over thirty years old."

"Be the thing for them to do. Have some people sit down an' input all their files. Be a real space saver, 'cause you can fit a whole filing cabinet on a floppy."

"It sounds like too much to hope for," I said. "But if Vital Statistics has all their old files on computer, I wouldn't even have to hack into their system. There's an easier way."

"Bribery?"

"If you want to be a tightass about it," I said. "I prefer to think of it as going out of your way to be nice to people, and having them be nice in return."

THE CLERK I found was a motherly woman named Elinor Horvath. She was nice to begin with and got even nicer when I palmed her a couple of bills. If only the records in question had been in computerized files, she could have found them for me in nothing flat. As TJ had explained it to me, all she would have to do was sort each pertinent database by Name of Father. Then you could just shuffle through the F's and see exactly who had been sired by someone named Farrelly.

"All our new records are computerized," she told me, "and we're working our way backward, but it's going very slowly. In fact it's not really going at all, not after the last round of budget cuts. I'm afraid we're not a high-priority division, and the old records aren't high priority for us."

That meant it had to be done the old-fashioned way, and it was going to require more time than Mrs. Horvath could possibly devote to it, no matter how nice a guy I was. The money I gave her got me ensconced in a back room where she brought me file drawers full of birth certificates filed in the City of New York starting January 1, 1957. I couldn't believe he was over forty, not from the glimpse I'd had of him, nor could I imagine he'd been more than seven years old when Paddy got the chop. According to what I knew about the father, by then the son would have had enough neglect or abuse or both to have been spared a passion for revenge.

That gave me my starting date, and I'd decided I'd go all the way to June 30, 1965. The killing of Paddy Farrelly, which Mick recalled as having taken place during the summer, might have occurred as late as the end of September, and the darling boy himself might have been conceived that very day, for all I knew. It all seemed unlikely, but you could say that about the whole enterprise.

It was slow work, and if you sped up out of boredom you ran the risk of missing what you were looking for. The records were in chronological order, and that was the sole organizational scheme. I had to scan each one, looking first at the child's name on the top line, then at the father's name about halfway down. I was looking for Farrelly in either place.

I was fortunate, I suppose, in that it wasn't a common name. Had the putative father been, say, Robert Smith or William Wilson, I'd have had a harder time of it. On the other hand, every time I hit some inapplicable Smith or Wilson I'd have at least had the illusion that I was coming close. I didn't hit any Farrellys, neither father nor child, and that made me question what I was doing.

It was mindless work. A retarded person could have performed it as well as I, and possibly better. My mind tended to wander, it almost had to, and that can lead to a sort of mental snow-blindedness, where you cease to see what you're looking at.

One thing that struck me, wading through this sea of names, was the substantial proportion of children who had different last names from their fathers, or no father listed at all. I wondered what it meant when the mother left the line blank. Was she reluctant to put the man's name down? Or didn't she know which name to choose?

I was close to losing heart, and then Mrs. Horvath turned up with a cup of coffee and a small plate of Nutter Butter cookies, and the next file drawer. She was out the door before I could thank her. I drank the coffee and ate the cookies, and an hour later I found what I was looking for.

The child's name was Gary Allen Dowling, and he'd been born at ten minutes after four in the morning on May 17, 1960, to Elizabeth Ann Dowling, of 1104 Valentine Avenue in the Bronx.

The father's name was Patrick Farrelly. No middle name. Either he didn't have one or she didn't know it.

IN MYTHS AND fairy tales, just knowing an adversary's name is in itself empowering. Look at Rumpelstiltskin.

So I felt I was getting somewhere when I hit the street with Gary Allen Dowling's birth certificate copied in my notebook, but all I really had was the first clue in a treasure hunt. I was better off than when I started, but I was a long way from home.

I bought a Hagstrom map of the Bronx at a newsstand two blocks from the Municipal Building and studied it at a lunch counter over a cup of coffee, wishing I had a few more of those Nutter Butter cookies to go with it. I found Valentine Avenue, and it was up in the Fordham Road section, and not far from Bainbridge Avenue.

I thought I might be able to save myself a trip, so I invested a quarter in a call to Andy Buckley. His mother answered and said he was out, and I thanked her and hung up without leaving a name. I was annoyed for a minute or two, because now I was stuck with a long subway ride and rush hour was already in its preliminary stages. But suppose he'd been in? I could send him to Valentine Avenue, and he could establish in a few minutes what I was already reasonably certain of—i.e., that Elizabeth Ann Dowling no longer lived there, if in fact she ever had, and neither did her troublesome son. But he wouldn't ask the questions I would ask, wouldn't knock on doors and try to find someone with a long memory and a loose tongue.

The house was still standing, as I thought it probably would be. This wasn't a part of the Bronx that had burned or been abandoned during the sixties and seventies, nor was it one where there'd been a lot of tearing-down and rebuilding. 1107 Valentine turned out to be a narrow six-story apartment house with four apartments to the floor. The names on the mailboxes were mostly Irish, with a few Hispanic. I didn't see Dowling or Farrelly, and would have been astonished if I had.

One of the ground-floor apartments housed the super, a Mrs. Carey. She had short iron-gray hair and clear unflinching blue eyes. I could read several things in them and cooperation wasn't one of them.

"I don't want to get off on the wrong foot with you," I said. "So let me start by saying I'm a private investigator. I've got nothing to do with the INS and very little respect for them, and the only tenants of yours I'm interested in lived here thirty-some years ago."

"Before my time," she said, "but not by much. And you're right,

INS was my first thought, and as little love as you may have for them I assure you it's more than my own. Who would it be you're asking after?"

"Elizabeth Ann Dowling. And she may have used the name Farrelly."

"Betty Ann Dowling. She was still here when I came. Her and that brat of a boy, but don't ask me his name."

"Gary," I said.

"Was that it? My memory's not what it was, though why I should remember them at all I couldn't say."

"Do you remember when they left?"

"Not offhand. I started here in the spring of 1968. God help us, that's almost thirty years."

I said something about not knowing where the time goes. Wherever it went, she said, it took your whole life with it.

"But I raised a daughter," she said, "on my own after my Joe died. I got the apartment and a little besides for managing this place, and I had the insurance money. And now she's living in a beautiful home in Yonkers and married to a man who makes good money, although I don't like the tone he takes with her. But that's none of my business." She collected herself, looked at me. "And none of yours either, is it? Oh, come on in. You might as well have a cup of tea."

Her apartment was clean and cheery and neat as a pin. No surprise there. Over tea she said, "She was a widow too, to hear her tell it. I held my tongue, but I know she was never married. It's the sort of thing you can tell. And she had these fanciful stories about her husband. How he was with the CIA, and was killed because he was going to reveal the real story of what happened in Dallas. You know, when Kennedy was shot."

"Yes."

"Filling the boy's ears with stories about his father. Now how long was it she was here? Is it important?"

"It could be."

"The Riordans took her apartment when she moved out. No, wait a minute, they did not. There was an older man moved in and died there, poor soul, and you may guess who had the luck to discover the body."

She closed her eyes at the memory. "An awful thing, to die alone, but that'll be my lot, won't it? Unless I last long enough to wind up in a home, and God grant that I don't. Mr. Riordan's still upstairs, his wife passed three years ago in January. But he never so much as met Betty Ann."

"When did he move in?"

"Because you'd know she was out by then, wouldn't you?" She thought a moment, then surprised me by saying, "Let's ask him," and snatching up the phone. She looked up the number in a little leather-bound book, dialed, glared in exasperation at the ceiling until he answered, and then spoke loudly and with exaggerated clarity.

"You have to shout at the poor man," she said, "but he hears better on the phone than face to face. He says he and his wife lived here since 1973. Now the old man who died, McMenamin was his name, it's an old Donegal name, if I'm not mistaken. Mr. McMenamin might have been here a year but he wasn't here two. It was vacant between tenants, but it wasn't vacant long either time, flats in this house are never vacant long. So my guess is your Betty Ann and her son left here in 1971. That would mean I had her in my house for three years, and I'd say that would be about right."

"And about enough, I gather."

"And you'd be right. I wasn't sorry to see the back of her, or the boy either."

"Do you know why she left?"

"She didn't offer and I didn't ask. To go with some man would be my guess. Another CIA man, no doubt. She left no forwarding address, and if she had I'd have long since tossed it out." I asked if anyone else in the building was still here from those days. "Janet Higgins," she said without hesitation. "Up in 4-C. But I doubt you'll get anything useful out of her. She barely knows her own name."

She was right. I didn't get anything useful from Janet Higgins, or in the house on either side, or across the street. I could have knocked on a few more doors, but I wasn't going to find Betty Ann Dowling on the other side of them, or her son either. I gave up and went home.

.   .   .

BY THE TIME I got home, Dr. Froelich had come and gone, changing TJ's dressing and pronouncing him fit for travel. He'd told him to keep the leg elevated as much as possible. "But not when you're walking," he said, "because it's awkward as hell, and it looks silly. So what's the answer? Stay off the leg. Give it a chance to mend."

Elaine had picked up a second cane, and he used both of them to get across the street to the hotel. I went with him, and sat in the armchair while he got on-line and checked his e-mail. He'd accumulated dozens of messages in the time he'd been gone. Most of them were Spam, he said, bulk e-mailers trying to sell him porn photos or enroll him in unlikely financial ventures. But he had correspondents all over the world as well, people he traded jokes and quips with in a half-dozen different countries.

It didn't take him long to catch up, and then I told him what I knew about Gary Dowling and his mom. The last address I had for them was twenty-five years old, and they could be using Farrelly as a last name.

"That F-A-R-L-E-Y?" I shook my head and spelled it for him, and he made a face. "Leave the *Y* off an' you got Farrell, rhymes with barrel. Put the *Y* on an' it's Farrelly, rhymes with Charlie. Don't make no sense."

"Few things do."

"If she got a listed phone, I can find her. Take awhile, is all. There's a site, got all the phone listings by state. You figure New York?"

"I suppose you have to try it first."

There was an Elizabeth Dowling in Syracuse, and a number of E Dowlings, including one in the Bronx. That was far too simple and obvious, of course, and it turned out to be Edward, and he'd never heard of an Elizabeth or a Betty Dowling and didn't sound as though he appreciated my call.

We tried New Jersey next, and then Connecticut. After that we skipped to California and Florida because they're states that people tend to go to. I got quite expert at my part of the program, dialing the numbers from the lists TJ printed out, saying, "Hello, I'm trying to reach an Elizabeth Dowling who resided on Valentine Avenue in the Bronx in the 1960s." It only took a sentence or two to determine that they couldn't help me, and I would get off the line in a hurry and move on to the next listing.

"Good we get to make our toll calls free," TJ said, "or we be runnin' up a powerful tab."

He got way ahead of me—the computer could find Dowlings faster than I could call them—and that gave him a chance to hobble over to the bed and elevate his leg. When I was between calls he said, "Meant to tell you, I phoned that girl this afternoon."

"And which girl would that be?"

"Sweetheart of BTK? Black father, Viet mama? She say she wonderin' why she didn't hear from me."

"So you told her you took a bullet in a shoot-out."

"Told her I had the flu. Vitamin C, she said. Yes, ma'am, I said, an' did you find out about the dude with the face like the moon? Found out his street name is all. You want to take a guess, Bess?"

"Moon," I said.

"Moon. Friend of Goo's from Attica, an' that be all anybody knows about him. Said thanks a lot, an' call me when them pimples clear up."

"You didn't say that."

"Course not." He cocked his head, looked at me. "You sick of makin' phone calls, ain't you? You got somethin' else to do, I can work the phone. I can even elevate my damn leg while I do it."

I LEFT AND started walking uptown. I hadn't eaten anything since Mrs. Horvath's Nutter Butter cookies, and I stopped in front of a Chinese restaurant on Broadway, a block or two beyond Lincoln Center. I hadn't eaten Chinese food since my last dinner with Jim ten days ago. I would never be having dinner with him again, and maybe I'd never be in the mood for Chinese, either.

Oh, get over it, a voice said, and it was Jim's voice, but it wasn't a mystical experience, it was my imagination, supplying the response I could expect from him. And he was right, of course. It wasn't the food or the restaurant, it was the guy who walked in with a gun, and he wasn't going to be doing that anymore.

Still, I couldn't eat a Chinese dinner without thinking about Jim. I had hot and sour soup and beef with broccoli, and I remembered how he'd told me he wanted to have that vegetarian eel dish one more time before he died.

The food was all right. Not great, but not terrible, either. I knocked off a pot of tea with the meal, and afterward I ate the orange wedges and cracked open the fortune cookie.

There is travel in your future, it advised me. I paid the check, left a tip, and traveled the rest of the way to Poogan's.

"THE GUY WHO hit you was Donnie Scalzo," Danny Boy said. "I thought I was going to come up empty, Matthew, and then one fellow turned up who looked at the picture and knew him in a heartbeat. He's a Brooklyn boy and I guess he never got across the bridge much, but this fellow grew up in Bensonhurst right near Scalzo. I think they got thrown out of the same grammar school."

"I hope it wasn't before they learned to diagram sentences."

"Do they still teach that? I remember my eighth-grade teacher standing at the blackboard drawing lines, taking sentences apart and putting them back together. Here's a subordinate clause angling off this way, and there goes a prepositional something-or-other slanting up toward the ceiling. Did you get that in school?"

"Yes, and I never knew what the hell they were doing."

"Neither did I, but I bet they don't do it anymore. It's another lost art. It would have been useful knowledge for Donnie, because he just recently got out of the joint. His sentence was five-to-ten, and he could have had fun diagramming that. Aggravated assault, so I guess you weren't the first guy he ever took a swing at."

"You don't happen to know where he served it, do you?"

"Tip of my tongue. Upstate, but not Dannemora, not Green Haven. Help me out here."

"Attica?"

"That's it. Attica."

.   .   .

I WENT HOME and called TJ. "Attica," he said. "We gettin' a lot of hits on that site. Too late to call, though."

"A call won't really do it," I said. "I think I'll have to go up there and talk to somebody."

"Attica," he said again, rolling the word on his tongue this time, as if looking for a name that rhymed with it. "How you get there, anyway?"

"Easiest thing in the world," I said. "Just hold up a liquor store."

MICK CALLED, WANTING to know if I'd heard anything from Tom Heaney, whom he'd been unable to reach. I said I hadn't, but that anybody who'd called would have had to talk to the machine. Tom, I pointed out, barely talked to people. I told him what I'd learned—about Moon, about Donnie Scalzo, and about Gary Allen Dowling.

I made it an early night, and I was at Phyllis Bingham's travel agency at nine on the dot. She was already at her desk. I told her I wanted to go to Buffalo, and while she brought up what she needed on her computer she asked how Elaine was doing on her buying trip. Of course she would have seen the sign in the shop window, it was just up the street, but for a minute I didn't know what she was talking about. I said it was going fine, and she said she could get me on a 10:00 A.M. Continental flight out of Newark, but that wouldn't give me any time to pack. Nothing to pack, I said. She booked me on the flight and on a return flight at 3:30 the same afternoon. If I missed it there'd be another two hours later.

"I guess you won't get to look at the Falls," she said.

I went out and got a cab right away, and I didn't even have to talk the driver into making the trip to Newark. He was delighted. I made my plane with a few minutes to spare and landed an hour later in Buffalo. I rented a car and drove to Attica, and that took another hour because I missed a turn and had to double back. I was there by noon and I was out of there by two, which put me way ahead of Gary Allen Dowling, not to mention Goo and Moon and Donny. It only took me forty minutes to get back to the Buffalo airport, where I had plenty of time to turn in the rental car and grab a meal before they called my return flight.

There was a long line for cabs at Newark, so I saved a few dollars and took a bus to Penn Station and the subway home. I walked in the door and Elaine said, "You said you'd be home for dinner and I didn't believe you. But you may not be able to stay."

George Wister had turned up, she told me, but this time she'd said I was out and refused to let him in. He came back with a partner and a warrant, but she'd spoken to Ray Gruliow, who was waiting with her when Wister showed up. She let them in, and after Wister had satisfied himself that I wasn't there he traded threats with Ray and then left.

"They were looking for a gun," she said, "and I knew you wouldn't have tried to take yours through a metal detector. I looked all over before I found it in your sock drawer. I took it to the basement and locked it in our storage bin, and after they left I went down and retrieved it, holster and all. It's back with your socks."

"There's another gun," I said. "A little one, it must be in the pocket of the jacket I was wearing the other night."

I looked in the closet, and it was still there. I put it in my pocket, and got the magnum from my sock drawer and donned the holster. I'd felt oddly vulnerable all day, walking around unarmed, which was odd in light of the fact that, up until less than a week ago, I went unarmed all the time.

She said the charge on the warrant was hindering prosecution, which Ray said was bullshit, and just meant that Wister had a tame judge on hand. He was planning to squash it, or quash it, or something.

I said I'd call him, and took a step toward the phone, but she caught my arm. "Don't call anybody yet," she said. "First there's a message you should hear."

We went in and she played it. A voice I'd never heard before said, "Scudder? Look, I got no quarrel with you. Just back out of this thing and you got nothing more to worry about."

She played it a second time, and I listened to it. "The call came in around three-thirty," she said. "After I heard it I took the phone off the hook."

"To keep him from calling back."

"No, so you could call him back. If you hit star-69—"

"It calls back the last person who called. You wanted to make sure he was the last person."

I picked up the receiver, pressed the disconnect button, and hit *69. The phone rang twelve times before I gave up and broke the connection.

"Shit," she said.

I hit REDIAL and let it ring another twelve times. "It's ringing its brains out," I said. "Now if only there was some way to find out where."

"Isn't there? Aren't all calls logged automatically?"

"Only the completed ones."

"How about the call we received? That was completed."

"And if I had a good friend at the phone company I could get at the data. The Kongs managed something similar once, but I don't have them on tap and the phone company computers are harder to hack than they used to be. And you know how it would turn out, don't you?"

"How?"

"It'll be a pay phone that they called from, and what help is that?"

"Rats," she said. "I thought I did good."

"What you did was good. It just didn't lead anywhere. But it still might. We can try it again later."

"And leave the phone off the hook until then?"

"No, we just won't make any calls out. That way anytime you hit REDIAL you'll get that number again. And if you really have to make a call, do it and don't worry about it, because I don't have high hopes that we're going to get him this way."

"Rats." She pressed a button, played the message another time. "You know what?" she said. "He's lying."

"I know."

"He wants you to stop pressing, which is a good sign, isn't it? It means you're getting close. And he wants to make you lower your guard. But he still intends to kill you."

"Tough," I said.

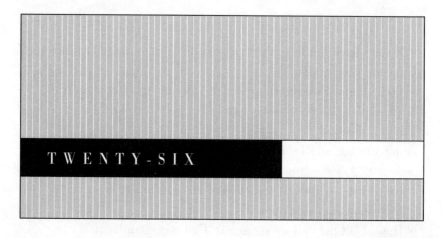

TWENTY-SIX

I DIDN'T WANT to stay for dinner. I'd just eaten in Buffalo, and I didn't want to hang around if Wister decided to come over again, with or without his chickenshit warrant. Elaine wondered if they'd have our building staked out. I didn't think they'd waste the manpower, but I'd continue to use the service entrance. I'd come in that way just now, probably out of habit, and it was a habit I'd stay with.

I had a cup of coffee, and told her what I'd learned in the small town of Attica, where the state penitentiary was the principal industry. Gary Allen Dowling, who had in fact used the names Gary Farrelly and Pat Farrelly as occasional aliases, had been released in early June after having served just over twelve years of a twenty-to-life sentence for second-degree murder. He and an accomplice had held up a convenience store in Irondequoit, a suburb of Rochester. According to the accomplice, who rolled over on Dowling and pleaded to a lesser charge of robbery and manslaughter, it had been Dowling who herded two employees and a customer into a back room, made them lie face down on the floor, and executed them all with two rounds each to the head.

I remembered the case. I hadn't paid much attention to it at the time because it happened a couple of hundred miles away upstate, and the city has always provided crime enough to keep my mind occupied. But I'd read about it, and it had been fodder for the pols in Albany who'd been trying to get a death penalty bill through the governor's office. It turned out to be easier to get a new governor.

Dowling had been twenty-four when he shot those people, twenty-five when he went away. He'd be thirty-seven now.

He went to Attica, and his traitorous partner in crime was sent to Sing Sing, in Ossining. Within a matter of months the partner turned up dead in the exercise yard. He was doing bench presses, and the bar he was supposed to be lifting had over five hundred pounds of iron on it. His chest was crushed, and nobody seemed to know how it had happened, or who might have had a hand in it.

Dowling let all of Attica know he'd arranged it. Revenge was sweet, he said. It would have been even sweeter if he could have been there to see it go down, but it was sweet all the same.

Later the same year an inmate he'd had words with was knifed to death, and it was like so many murders inside the walls, you knew who did it but you couldn't hope to prove it. Dowling did his first bit in solitary as a result. You didn't need evidence to put a man in the hole.

His mother was the only person who visited him, and she drove down from Rochester once a month to see him. Her visits were less frequent in recent years because she was ill, and got so she needed to get someone to drive her. It was cancer, and she died of it during the final winter of his confinement. He might have been released to attend her funeral, but he was in solitary at the time. It was funny, he'd learned to behave himself in prison, but he lost it when he learned of her death and choked a guard half to death before they pulled him off. You wanted to make allowances for someone who'd just had that kind of news, but it was the kind of incident you couldn't overlook, and he was in the hole while his mother went in a hole of her own.

June 5 they'd let him out. No question, really, with the good time he'd accumulated. He'd have been odds-on for the death penalty if it had been on the books at the time, but even without it you'd expect someone who'd done what he'd done to serve straight life without parole. Not how it worked, though.

The official I talked to didn't have much faith in the system he served. It didn't seem to him that there was a whole lot of rehabilitation going on. You had some men who never did a bad thing until the night they got drunk and killed their wife or their best friend, and most of them would probably be all right after their release, but he wasn't sure the prison system could take the credit. And there were the sex offenders, and you'd be better believing in the tooth fairy than in the possibility of straightening out those monsters. When it came to your hardened criminals, well, some got old and just couldn't cut it anymore, but could you call that rehabilitation? All you did was warehouse 'em until they were past their expiration date.

One thing he was sure of, he told me. Gary Allen Dowling would be back. If not in Attica, then in some other joint. He was positive of that.

I hoped he was wrong.

THAT'S WHAT I learned in Attica. I don't think I could have told her all of it, not then, over one cup of coffee. I told her the greater portion of it, though, and I told the rest to Mick a little later.

The phone rang while I was trying to decide if I wanted a second cup. I went to listen to the machine and picked up when I heard Mick's voice. "By Jesus," he said, "have you spent the whole evening on the telephone?"

"The evening's young," I said. "And I haven't been on the phone at all. Elaine took it off the hook, and I'll tell you why some other time."

"I've been going half mad," he said. "I can't reach anybody. Have you heard from Andy or Tom?"

"No, but the phone's been off the hook, so—"

"So they couldn't call you if they wanted to, nor could they call me as they haven't the number. Twice I've called Andy and twice his mother's told me he's out and she doesn't know where. And there's no one at all answering at Tom's house."

"Maybe they're out having a beer somewhere."

"Maybe they are," he said. "Have you any plans yourself?"

It was Friday. I always went to the step meeting at St. Paul's on Friday night. Then I always had coffee afterward with Jim. I'd thought I might do the first, even if I couldn't do the second.

But I had a lot to tell him. I'd found out quite a bit since I'd talked to him last.

"No plans," I said.

"I'll come by for you. Fifteen minutes?"

"Make it twenty," I said, "and don't come around the front. In fact why don't you pull up in front of Ralph's Restaurant at Fifty-sixth and Ninth?"

I kissed Elaine and told her I didn't know when I'd be back. "And go ahead and make phone calls if you want," I said.

"I was thinking," she said. "If I make outgoing calls from another extension, it won't change the redial mechanism on that phone. Or am I forgetting something?"

"No," I said, "I think you're right, and I should have thought of that."

"Then you wouldn't need me."

"Yes I would. But I think I'll try it once more before I go."

I punched REDIAL, and *69 appeared in the little window, and after a moment someone's phone rang. I was wondering how long to give it, and then in the middle of the fourth or fifth ring it was picked up. There was silence at first, and then a soft voice, a man's, said, "Hello?"

The voice was curiously familiar. I willed it to say more, but when it spoke again the words were much fainter, as if he was talking to someone else and not into the phone. "There's no one there," he said, and there was another silence, and then the connection was broken.

"Bingo," I told Elaine.

"It worked, huh?"

"Like a charm. That was brilliant, taking the phone off the hook. You're a genius."

"That's what my father always said," she said. "And my mother always told him he was crazy."

I made a note of the time. In the morning I'd have to find someone at the phone company who could pull the LUDS on my phone, and I could find out who it was I'd just called. Because I didn't think that was a pay phone. And if I could find out where it was located, I could find them when they thought they couldn't be found.

I think a subscriber's entitled to a record of his own calls, if you can find the right person to ask. I know a cop can get that kind of information in a hurry, and if I couldn't find a cop who'd help me out I could always impersonate one myself. That's against the law, but lately it seemed as though everything I did was against the law.

I rode down to the basement and went out the service entrance. Wister could have two teams watching the building, one in back and one in front, but I didn't think he even had one. I took a look around, just to make sure, and then I went over and stood in a darkened doorway alongside of Ralph's. He didn't keep me waiting long.

TWENTY-SEVEN

"**A** SON TO avenge him," Mick said. "That's more than the likes of Paddy Farrelly ever deserved."

"He's a son who hasn't exactly covered himself with glory in the course of his young life."

"A true son of the father, then. Say the mother's name again."

"Elizabeth Dowling."

"I've known a share of Dowlings over the years, but I don't recall an Elizabeth."

"The woman in the Bronx called her Betty Ann. She was living there when the baby was born, and she may have been living there or nearby all along."

"I wonder how Paddy met her. It could have been at a dance. That was how you used to meet Irish girls, at a dance on a Saturday night." He had a faraway look in his eye. "I never knew her, and I doubt she ever knew me. But she must have known *of* me, and known it was myself put Paddy out of her life and his own. If the cow'd had any sense she'd have thanked God for the favor I did her. Instead she made a hero out of him and a villain out of me, and brought the boy up to kill me."

"I guess he always liked killing," I said. "He had no practical reason to kill those people in the store. All that did was turn up the heat. It pretty much guaranteed he'd get caught and do substantial time. He killed them because he wanted to."

"The same with Kenny and McCartney."

"And the same when the Vietnamese he met in prison sprayed bullets all over your bar, and his other prison buddy tossed a bomb. Moon's name is Virgil Gafter, incidentally, suspected of a couple of felony-related homicides, but it was an assault charge that put him in Attica."

"You learned a lot in that prison."

"Everybody does," I said. "Some of them learn to live within the laws, and the rest learn to be better at breaking them."

"I THINK THE cops know Chilton Purvis did the shooting at the Chinese restaurant," I said. "They'd have found out the same way I did. Word got around, and somebody with a badge heard it from one of his snitches. And I think they went looking for Purvis and found him dead in his room on Tapscott Street, unless he'd already been picked up and they found him in the morgue."

"And that's why they came looking for you?"

"That's why," I said. "If they don't know Purvis was the shooter, his death is just another homicide, presumably black-on-black, presumably drug related. Two men shoot each other and one walks away from it. But now they've got someone with a motive to kill Purvis."

"Namely yourself."

"They also found a blood trail," I said, "so the reasoning would be that Purvis and I shot each other and I fled the scene. I'll bet they checked hospitals, and I'll bet when Wister showed up with his warrant he expected to find me in bed and bandaged up. Failing that, he'd have liked to find a .38 that would match the bullets they dug out of Purvis."

"What happens when they catch up with you?"

"I can't worry about that now. The funny thing is the blood might clear me. Because I didn't get so much as a scratch when Purvis and I traded shots, and there's no way they'll get a DNA match between my blood and TJ's. If they try to match the blood to him, well, that's a different story, but they'd have to think of it, and I'm not sure they will."

"I GATHER WE'RE going to the Bronx."

"That's less remarkable than some of your feats of detection," he said, "as we're nearly there."

"Where are we going?"

"Perry Avenue."

"Where Tom lives."

He nodded. "You'll remember we dropped him there, after the trouble at Grogan's."

Trouble in the Irish sense. In America, trouble is something a kid has learning algebra. In Ireland it can be a bit more dramatic.

I said, "Because you couldn't reach him on the phone?"

"He's a lodger in an old woman's house. Has a room and kitchen privileges, and can watch television in the parlor of an evening. Takes his meals there, breakfast and dinner, if he's there to eat them."

"So?"

"The phone is hers," he said, "and she's always home to answer it. And today it rang unanswered every time I called."

"She couldn't have stepped out?"

"She never does. She has the arthritis, and it's a bad case of it. It keeps her at home."

"And when she needs something from the market . . ."

"She calls the corner store and they deliver. Or Tom goes for her."

"There's probably an explanation."

"I fear there is," he said, "and I fear I know what it is."

I didn't say anything. He stopped for a red light, looked both ways, and drove on through it. I tried not to imagine what might happen if a cop pulled us over.

He said, "I've a feeling."

"I gathered as much."

"I've surely told you what my mother said."

"That you've got a sixth sense."

"Second sight is what she called it, but I'd say it amounts to the same thing, a sixth sense or the second sight. 'Twas herself I got it from. When my brother Dennis went to Vietnam, we both knew we'd seen him alive for the last time."

"And that's the second sight?"

"I hadn't finished."

"I'm sorry."

"One day she calls me over. Mickey, says she, I saw your baby brother last night, and all robed in white he was. And I turned white myself, for hadn't I heard Dennis's voice in my ear that morning. I'm all right, Mickey, says he. You needn't worry about me, says he. And not that day but the day after she got the telegram."

I felt a chill. I get hunches and feelings, and I've learned to trust them in my work, though I don't let them keep me from getting out and knocking on doors. I believe in intuition, and in ways of knowing the mind knows nothing of. Still, stories like that give me a chill.

"I had a feeling before I called his house. Before the first time that it rang and went unanswered."

"And I gather the feeling persisted."

"It did."

"But you waited until you reached me before heading up here."

"You or Andy. You were the first I reached. But you'd be wondering why I didn't go on my own." He was silent for a moment. "It's an answer does me no credit," he said. "It's for fear of what I might find, of what I know I'll find. I don't want to come upon it alone."

"YOU'VE GOT YOUR GUN?"

"You gave me two," I said, "and I've got them both."

"Good job she hid the one where the cops wouldn't find it. In the basement, was it?"

"In our storage bin down there. Even if they'd known it existed, I don't think their warrant would have covered it."

"Ah, she's a smart one," he said. "That was quick thinking."

"You don't know the half of it," I said, and told him about her trick with *69.

"So that's why she took the phone off the hook. And he left you a message? Was it Paddy's boy himself?"

"I don't think so. The voice sounded familiar, and I think it was the fellow I took the gun away from. Donnie Scalzo, that would be."

"From Bensonhurst, wasn't it? Another nationality heard from."

"But I may have heard Dowling's voice," I said, and told him of the last phone call before I left the apartment, with a soft voice saying hello, and then telling someone else that there was no one there.

"You wouldn't think he'd have a soft voice."

"You wouldn't. And his voice seemed familiar to me, and I don't know why it would."

"When would you have heard him before?"

"I don't think I ever did, and I wish this voice had had more to say, because there was something familiar about it and I can't say what or why. Unless it was just that it sounded Irish."

"Irish," he said.

"There was a hint of brogue."

"Well, Farrelly and Dowling, that's Irish on both sides. You could say he came by it honestly. Paddy had nothing you'd call a brogue. I've the Irish way of talking, but that's my mother's doing. Some lose it and some don't, and I never did." His eyes narrowed. "A hint of brogue. A familiar voice, a hint of brogue."

"I'll trace the call tomorrow," I said, "and clear up some of the mystery."

THE HOUSE ON Perry Avenue was self-standing, a little two-story box on a small lot. The lawn in front was brown in spots, but neatly mowed. I suppose a neighborhood kid took care of it for the old woman, or maybe Tom ran a mower over it once or twice a week. It wouldn't take him long. Then he'd go in and have a beer, and she'd thank him for doing such a nice job.

We parked two doors away, right next to a fire hydrant. I pointed it out, and Mick said nobody'd be around to ticket us at that hour, much less to tow the car. And we wouldn't be on the premises for long, anyway.

Nor were we. We went up the walk to the front door and knocked and rang the bell. The door was wood, set with a window divided into four mullioned panes, and he didn't wait long at all before drawing the gun from his belt and using the butt of it to break out one of the panes. He reached through the opening, turned the knob, and let us in.

I'd smelled death through the broken window and walked in the door to see it close up. The old woman, her gray hair thinning and her legs hugely swollen, sat in her wheelchair in the front room, her head hanging to one side, her throat cut. The whole front of her was soaked with her blood, and there were flies buzzing in it.

Mick let out an awful groan at the sight of her, and crossed himself. I hadn't seen him do that before.

We found Tom Heaney in the kitchen, lying on the floor, with gunshot wounds in the chest and temple. There was a heel mark on his face, as if he'd been kicked or stepped on. His eyes were wide open.

So was the refrigerator door. I could picture Tom standing at the open refrigerator, helping himself to a beer or the makings of a sandwich. Or maybe the hard work of murder had built an appetite in one of the killers, and he'd stopped for a snack on the way out.

Mick bent over and closed Tom's eyes. He straightened up and closed his own for a moment. Then he nodded shortly to me and we got out of there.

TWENTY-EIGHT

"AH, TIS I again, Mrs. Buckley, disturbing you one more time. Has he returned yet, do you know? Ah, that's good." He covered the cell phone mouthpiece with his hand. "She's getting him," he said.

We were in the car, parked on the opposite side of Bainbridge Avenue from the Buckley house. We'd taken a roundabout route to get here, with Mick turning up one street and down another almost at random, the big Caprice making its way through the Bronx like an elephant lumbering through high grass. Neither of us talked while he drove, and the silence was heavy in the roomy old car, heavy and thick. There'd been too many deaths and it felt as though they were in there with us, all those mean acts of murder, the bodies heaped in the back seat, the souls displacing the air itself.

Now he said, "Andy, good man. Your own car's right across the street from you and us inside it waiting for you."

He folded the phone, put it back in his pocket. "He'll be a minute," he said. "It's a relief to find him at home."

"Yes."

"I'll tell you," he said, "it was relief enough when she answered. His mother. Now that the bastards are after killing old ladies."

I watched the door across the street, and in a matter of minutes Andy came through it, wearing a plaid shirt and blue jeans with the cuffs folded up and carrying his leather jacket. At the curb he stopped long enough to put the jacket on, then trotted on across the street. Mick got out and Andy sat behind the wheel. I got out as well and sat in back, and Mick walked around the car and got in front next to Andy.

"Crazy day," Andy said. "I couldn't reach anybody. I tried what numbers I had for you, Mick, and I called a couple of bars looking for you. I didn't really think you'd be there but I didn't know how to get in touch with you."

"I tried you and could never find you in."

"I know, my old lady said you called. I was out all day, I took my cousin's car and drove around. I was going stir crazy, you know? I even went into Manhattan and drove past the bar. You probably already seen what it looks like, all plywood and yellow tape."

"I drove past it myself the other evening."

"And I called you, Matt, but I hung up when the machine answered. And then I called a couple of times and the line was busy. I figured the two of you were talking to each other and that was why I couldn't get through to either of you."

He put the car in gear, and when the traffic thinned he pulled away from the curb. He asked if he should head anywhere in particular. Mick told him to drive where he liked, as one place was no worse than another.

He drove around, coming to full stops at stop signs, keeping well under the speed limit. After a few blocks he asked if either of us had spoken to Tom. "Because I was trying to reach him, too, and nobody answered, and you know the woman he lives with never leaves the house. All I could think of was he took pity on her and took her to a movie, or she had a stroke or something and he took her to the hospital. Or there was something wrong with the phone, so I went over there and leaned on the doorbell."

"When was that?" Mick wondered.

"I don't know, I didn't notice the time. Maybe an hour ago? I rang the bell and knocked on the door, and then I went around and rang the back doorbell and knocked on that door, and when I saw nothing was happening I got back in my car. You want to give him a call? Or even go over there, because I'll admit it, I'm spooked."

"We've just come from there," Mick said, and told him what we'd found.

"Jesus," Andy said. He hit the brake, but not as abruptly as Mick had done when he learned TJ had been shot. He checked the mirror first and braked to a smooth stop, pulled over and parked. "I got to take this in," he said evenly. "Give me a minute, huh?"

"All the time you want, lad."

"Both dead? Tom and the old woman?"

"They shot him dead and cut her throat."

"Jesus Christ. All I can think, that could have just as easy been our house, and me and my mother. Just as easy."

"I was glad just now when she said you were home," Mick said, "but before that I was glad just to hear her voice. For I had the same thought myself."

Andy sat there, nodding to himself. Then he said, "Well, this just adds to it, doesn't it? Reinforces it."

"How's that?"

"Why I was trying to get in touch," he said. "Something I was thinking."

"About what?"

"About them coming after us the way they're doing. Picking us off one by one. I had an idea."

"Let's hear it."

"There's just the three of us left. I think we got to stick together. And I think we got to pick someplace that's safe. I'm out here in the Bronx, and anyone comes for me, all they got to do is kick the door in. Matt, you're in a doorman building, maybe it's a different story, but you can't stay inside with the door locked all the time. And even if you do, what's to stop them from shooting the doorman like they been shooting everybody else, and then going up and kicking your door in?"

"Nothing," I said.

"And Mick, you're holed up and not telling anybody where, and that's smart, but all you got to do is move around like you're moving around right now, riding around in a car, and you're a pretty identifiable guy. All you need is one person to see you and the wrong person to get wind of it, you know what I mean?"

"And what's your answer, then?"

"The farm."

"The farm," Mick said, and thought about it. At length he said, "I told Matt he ought to go to Ireland. He said I should come along and show him the country. Isn't this the same thing?"

"Not exactly."

"Either way I'm running from them."

"You wouldn't be running away, Mick. That's the whole point. You'd be taking a position and waiting for them to come to you."

"Now you've got my interest," Mick said.

"We go there tonight and settle in. Right away, without giving the bastards another shot at us. We set up our defenses. There's just the one entrance, isn't there? The long drive we took the last time we were there?"

"With the horse chestnut trees."

"If you say so. All I know is Christmas trees and the other kind. They come up that drive when we know they're coming, be like fish in a barrel, wouldn't it?"

"Keep talking."

"I don't even know who knows the farm exists outside of the three of us. But there's probably some that do. But what I was thinking, and you got to remember I had all day long with nothing to do but think about this . . ."

"You're doing fine, man."

"Well, see, we settle in. And then we get the word to someone with a big mouth. One thing we know about these guys is they've got good sources of information. If the word's on the street they're gonna hear it. And the word'll be that the three of us are holed up where we're sure nobody could ever know about it, and we're drinking like fish and running broads in and out of the place, just partying it up day and night. Do I have to spell it out? You can take it from there, Mick."

"They'd expect to have it easy. But we'd be waiting for them."

"And trap the lot of them, Mick."

"All on the farm," he said. "It'd mean digging, wouldn't it? And we'd need a bigger hole than last time." The corners of his mouth lifted. "But I'll not mind the work. I'd say we can use the exercise."

WE'D GO RIGHT away, we decided. We didn't need anything. There was food enough on the farm to last the winter, between what was growing in the garden and what Mrs. O'Gara had put up in jars. There was a store in Ellenville, and if we were there long enough to need a change of clothing we could buy what we needed there.

And Mick's leather satchel was in the back seat, with guns and ammunition and cash. He even had his father's apron in there, and the old man's cleaver. And there were extra firearms out at the farm, O'Gara's twelve-gauge shotgun and a deer rifle with a scope sight.

"Just one thing," Andy said. "I want to go by my house, tell my mother she won't see me for a few days."

"Call her," Mick said. "Use my cell phone or wait and call her from the farm."

"I'd rather tell her in person," he said. "I've got another box of shells in my room for the gun I'm carrying. I'd just as soon bring them along. And it'll give me a chance to smoke a cigarette. It's a long way out to the farm without a cigarette."

"It's your car you'll be driving," Mick said. "I guess you can smoke in your own car if you have a mind to."

"Makes it hard on a couple of nonsmokers," Andy said. "It's close quarters in a closed car, or even with a window open. I'll just smoke a cigarette at the house before we go. And there's another thing. I'm going to tell her to go visit my uncle Connie north of Boston. She's been saying she hasn't seen her brother in a long time, and what better time for her to go? Because they could come looking for me, Mick, and it might not matter if I was there or not, and I wouldn't want anything to happen to her."

"God, no."

"Who knows if she'll even go, but it won't hurt to suggest it to her. And when I think about Tom and the old lady . . ."

"Enough said."

It didn't take long before we were back on Bainbridge Avenue and parked in front of Andy's house. He got out of the car and trotted up the walk, used his key, and disappeared inside the house. After a moment Mick got out his cell phone and dialed a number, then almost immediately snapped the thing shut. "I thought I'd call O'Gara," he said, "but I don't want to call on this thing. My luck the wrong person would pick it up."

"On the fillings in his teeth. We can find a pay phone."

"We can just go out there," he said. "It's not that late, and he needn't have advance warning." He was silent for a moment, then sighed heavily. "Change seats with me," he said. "I'll get in back where I can put my feet up. I might even close my eyes and get a little sleep on the drive out."

I got out of the car and we changed seats. He walked around the car and got into the back seat behind the driver, turning so that he could put his legs up on the seat.

A few minutes later Andy emerged. He had a cigarette going, and stopped on the sidewalk to take a long drag on it. He took a final drag as he stood beside the open car door, then flicked the butt out into the street. Sparks danced when it hit the pavement.

He got in the car, turned the key, gunned the motor. He grinned, tapped the steering wheel twice. "We're off," he said. "Everybody watch out."

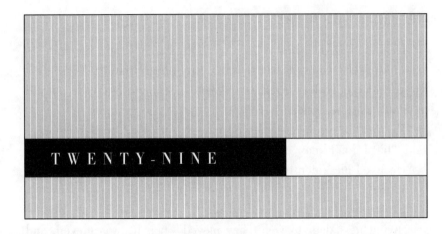

TWENTY-NINE

ANDY TOOK THE Grand Concourse to the Cross-Bronx, then drove straight west. We crossed the George Washington Bridge into New Jersey and picked up the Palisades Parkway. Mick had been silent until then, and I thought he might have nodded off back there, but now he said, "I've been thinking. This is a grand idea of yours, Andy."

"Well, I had time on my hands, and no dartboard handy to take my mind off of things."

"You're a strategist," Mick said. "You're another Michael Collins."

"Oh, come on now."

"You are indeed."

"I'm his Russian cousin," Andy said. "Vodka Collins."

"We'll lure 'em into a trap," Mick said, "and draw the ends tight, and there they'll be. Ah, I'll want to see the look on his face when he knows I've done for him. He's a Bronx boy, Andy. Did you know that?"

"No."

"He's the long-lost bastard son of Paddy Farrelly, and I'm going to send him to the same place I sent his dirty bastard father. Yes, he's a Bronx boy, though he moved away years ago. Where was it he moved to, Matt? Upstate, was it?"

"He was ten or eleven when he moved from Valentine Avenue," I said, "but I don't know exactly when that was."

"He lived on Valentine Avenue? That's like two blocks over from Bainbridge."

"He was in the eleven hundred block," I said, "so it's not like he was living next door to you. They moved when he was eleven, and he was living in Rochester when he committed the crime he went to prison for, but I don't know what interim moves his mother might have made."

" 'Twas in the Bronx he spent his formative years," Mick said, rolling the phrase on his tongue. "His formative years. So we may safely call him a Bronx boy. Well, set a Bronx boy to catch a Bronx boy, eh? While we drove around I found myself thinking what a splendid borough the Bronx is. It became a joke for a while there, didn't it? But there's beautiful parts to it."

"I was thinking that myself."

"Matt lived in the Bronx himself. Or am I misremembering?"

"There's nothing wrong with your memory. But we only lived there for a short time."

"So we can't call you a Bronx boy."

"I don't think so."

"Your father had a store," Mick said. "He sold children's shoes."

"Jesus, how did you remember that?"

"I don't know," he said. "How do we remember some things and forget others? It's certainly not a matter of what's useful to remember and what's not. There's no end of useful things I can't recall to save myself, and yet I remember your father's shoe store."

A LITTLE LATER he said, "Is your mother well, Andy?"

"She is, Mick. Thanks be to God."

"Thanks be to God," he echoed. "When you went to talk to her just now I suppose you found her in the kitchen."

"Matter of fact, she was parked in front of the TV."

"Watching a program, was she?"

"And looking at the paper at the same time. Why, Mick?"

"Ah, just wondering. Looking at the paper. The *Irish Echo*, was it?"

"I didn't even notice. It could have been the *Echo*."

"Do you ever read it yourself, Andy?"

"More for the older people, isn't it? Or the greenhorns fresh off the boat."

"Off the plane, these days. Well, your people are a great old family, you know. The Buckleys, I'm talking about. Some were what you'd call Castle Irish. Do you know the term? It means they were in with the lot at Dublin Castle, the British crown's representatives in Ireland. But there were other Buckleys that were very republican. Which were yours, I wonder?"

Andy laughed. "I get people asking if I'm related to that guy, you know who I mean, uses all the big words on television? But you're the first person ever asked me what side my people were on back in the old country."

"Has your mother ever gone back?"

"No, she was just a girl when she came over. She's got no interest in going back. It's hard enough to get her to visit her brother in Massachusetts."

"Your uncle Connie, that would be."

"Right."

"And how about yourself? Have you ever been over to the old country?"

"Are you kidding? I've never been anywhere, Mick."

"Ah, you should go. There's nothing like travel for broadening a man. Though I've done little enough of it myself. Ireland, of course, and France. Matt's been to France. And to Italy as well, have you not?"

"Just briefly," I said.

"I've not been there myself. But then the last time I was in Ireland

I went over to England as well, just to see if they were the devils I learned them to be at my mother's knee."

"And were they?"

"Not at all," he said. "They couldn't have been nicer. I was treated decently everywhere I went. For all the problems they've had with the Irish, they always made me feel welcome."

"Maybe they didn't know you were Irish," Andy suggested.

"You're entirely right," Mick said. "Most likely they took me for a Chinaman."

AS WE TURNED onto 209 he said, "It's a good scheme, Andy. I've been thinking about it these last few miles. The only hard part will be getting the word to them so they don't suspect the source of it. It would help if we knew who's been helping them all along. Have you any ideas yourself, lad?"

Andy considered, shook his head. "There's a lot of guys hang out at Grogan's," he said.

"Not now there's not."

"Well, used to be. People who'd run an errand for you, or lend a hand on the big jobs. I had to guess, I'd say somebody took one of them aside and got a few drinks into him, got him talking."

"You think that's it, do you?"

"Be my guess."

"There's a great Irish tradition of hating the informer," Mick said. "There's that movie, and I can remember about your father's shoe store, Matt, so why can I not recall the name of that actor? I can see his face but can't summon up his name."

"Victor McLaglen," I supplied.

"The very man. Oh, the most hated man in Ireland was the man who bore tales. 'The Patriot's Mother.' Do you know that song?"

Neither of us did. In a surprisingly soft voice he sang:

Alana, alana, the shadow of shame
Has never yet fallen on one of your name

And oh, may the food from my bosom you drew
In your veins turn to poison ere you turn untrue

"It's the mother singing," he explained, "and she's urging her boy to die on the gallows rather than inform on his fellows."

Alana machree, oh, alana machree
Sure, a stag and a traitor you never shall be

"Ah, 'tis a terrible old song, but it gives you an idea how our people felt on the subject. A great tradition of hating the informer. And of course you know what that means."

"What?"

"A great tradition of informing," he said. "For how could you have the one without the other?"

THE CAPRICE DIDN'T offer as smooth a ride as the Cadillac. It wasn't as whisper-quiet, either, with more road noise audible and a rattle somewhere in the rear end. But it was comfortable all the same, with Andy and me in front and Mick stretched out in the back and the headlights cutting the darkness in front of us. I half wished we could ride on like that forever.

We'd turned onto the unnumbered road, and Mick said, " 'Twas along here we saw the deer."

"I remember," Andy said. "I almost hit him."

"You did not. You stopped in plenty of time."

"A good thing, too. He was a big one. If I'd thought, I'd have counted the points."

"The points?"

"On his antlers, Mick. That's how the hunters rate the bucks, by the number of points on their antlers. He was a big one, but don't ask me how many points he ran to, because I wasn't paying attention."

"Hunters. O'Gara posts the property, keeps the hunters off of it. I don't want the trespassing, you know. And I don't want deer shot on my land. They're terrible predators, you can't keep them out of the orchard, but I won't have men shooting them. I wonder why that is."

"You're getting soft in your old age."

"I must be," he agreed. "Slow down a bit, why don't you?"

"Slow down?"

"There's deer all through here. The big buck was standing in the middle of the road, but sometimes you've no warning at all and they leap out right in front of you."

I thought of Danny Boy and his list, and pictured the deer dashing out from between parked cars.

Andy eased up on the gas and the car slowed some.

"In fact," Mick said, "why don't you pull over altogether?"

"Pull over?"

"Sure, what's our rush? We'll all stretch our legs and you can smoke a cigarette."

"I'd just as soon wait, to tell you the truth. We're almost there."

"Pull over," Mick said.

"Yeah, sure," Andy said, "only I got to find a spot with some room on the shoulder. Should be a place coming up soon."

Mick drew a breath, then leaned forward and hooked an arm around Andy's throat. He said, "Matt, take hold of the wheel, that's a good man. Andy, ease the brake on, and do it gently, boy, or I swear I'll throttle you. Guide us off the road, Matt, that's lovely, and now turn off the ignition. And take his gun, the one in his waistband, and see if he's got another on him."

"This is crazy," Andy said. "Mick, don't do this."

There were two guns, one under his belt in front, the other at the small of his back. I got them both, and Mick motioned for me to set them on the dashboard.

"Out of the car," Mick said. "Come on now. Here's our spy, Matt. Here's our informer. Stand still, Andy. And don't even think about running. You wouldn't make ten yards. I'd shoot the legs out from under you, you know I would."

"I'm not going anywhere," Andy said. "You've got this all wrong. Matt, tell him, will you? He's got this all wrong."

"I'm not so sure of that," I said.

To me Mick said, "You knew, didn't you?"

"Not as early as you did. I had a sense of where you were going but I thought you were just fishing. But then I caught on when he said his mother was watching television."

"And reading the newspaper."

"Right."

"Are you guys both nuts? I'm a spy because my ma's watching the TV?"

"That call you made," I said, "a minute or two after Andy went into the house. You passed it off as a call to O'Gara and hung up before he could answer. But you didn't call the farm, did you? You called Andy's number."

"I did."

"And you got a busy signal," I said. "So you knew he was on the phone, calling Dowling and letting him know we were on our way."

Andy said, "Let me get this straight. You called my house, Mick? While I was in there talking to my mother?"

"But you weren't talking to her," Mick said. "You were talking to Paddy Farrelly's son. A pity you didn't talk to her instead. She might have sung you a verse or two of that song. 'The Patriot's Mother,' and I trust you can remember it as I haven't the heart to sing it again for you."

"The line was busy," Andy said. "That's what this is all about? The line was busy?"

"It was."

"Jesus, I was in the john. Maybe she made a call while I was taking a leak. Why don't you call her right now and ask her?"

Mick let out a sigh, then reached to lay a hand on Andy's shoulder. "Andy," he said gently, "why do you think people have been going to Confession for all these centuries? They feel better afterward. And don't tell me you've nothing to confess. Andy, look at me. Andy, I know it's you."

"Aaah, Jesus, Mick."

"Suggesting we go to the farm, all of us, and lay a trap for them. That set the alarm bells ringing. You'd have done better to let me come up with the idea myself, with maybe the least bit of a hint from yourself to steer me in that direction.

"And you'd no way of knowing I'd be wary the instant the farm was mentioned. You see, your murderous friend fell into a wee trap himself. He called Matt's house, and Matt pressed the numbers you press to call the person back. The person who answered didn't say much. But didn't you say he sounded Irish? And had a soft voice?"

I nodded.

"O'Gara, it must have been. They kept him alive in case I called, so that he could answer the phone. 'There's no one there,' he told them, and they broke the connection. Do you suppose he and his wife are still alive, Andy? Or have they killed them already, now that you called to say we were on our way?"

"Jesus, Mick."

"Were you there when they killed Tom, Andy? And the old woman in the wheelchair?"

"They never said they were going to do that."

"And what did you think they were going to do with her? Put her on a bus to Atlantic City, with a bag of quarters for the slot machines?"

"Oh, God," he said. He had his face in his hands, and his shoulders were heaving.

Gently Mick said, "How did he get to you, Andy? Did he remember you from school?"

"He was a year behind me at St. Ignatius."

"And you knew him well, did you?"

"Not well at all, but when he turned up I knew him right away. He had the same face when he was a kid."

"And he turned you. Turned you against me."

Andy's arms hung at his sides. His jaw was slack and his eyes glassy. He said, "I don't know what happened, I swear I don't. I guess it was the carrot and the stick both at once. He said I got table scraps from you, that there'd be a lot of money if I threw in with him. And he said I'd be dead if I didn't. And her with me."

"Your mother."

"Yes."

"You should have come straight to me, Andy."

"I know. God, I know. I never thought . . ."

"What?"

"I don't know," he said. "I don't know what I thought. What difference does it make? You're gonna kill me. Well, hell, go ahead. I can't say I don't deserve it."

"Ah, Andy," he said. "Why would I kill you?"

"We both know why. God knows I gave you cause."

"Didn't I tell you we've a great national tradition of informing? You made your bed, but why lie in it if you can make it again?"

"What do you mean?"

Mick clapped him on the shoulder. "You changed sides," he said, "and now you'll change 'em again and come back where you belong. They've set a trap for us, have they? We'll have at them, the three of us, and see them caught in their own trap."

"You'd let me come back?"

"And why not? Jesus, you've been with me for years and against me for days. We need each other, Andy."

"Mick, I'm a bastard. You're a good man and I'm nothing but a bastard."

"Forget that for now."

"Mick, we can do it. They're expecting us to drive in like we own the place. Then I park the car where I always park it and I hang back and smoke a cigarette while you and Matt go up to the house. And they come out of the house with guns in their hands."

"It was a good plan. Would they have a sentry posted, do you think? Someone to spot us when we turn into the drive?"

"They might."

"I would," he said, "in their place. I'd put someone where he could see the headlights. What about O'Gara? Have they killed him yet?"

"I don't know. They didn't tell me much. Tom Heaney's landlady, that took me by surprise. I didn't think they would do that, I really didn't."

"And it bothers you, but is it worse than killing poor Tom? Ah, let it go. Talk won't bring him back, or any of the others. John Kenny and Barry McCartney. You knew they were going to the storage place. You went along with Dowling, didn't you?"

"I stayed outside," he said. "So they wouldn't see me. It was supposed to be a straight hijack, and I was going to drive the truck. Then

I heard the shots." He took a breath. "I didn't know there was going to be any killing, Mick. It started out as a way to steal from you. They were going to grab the liquor and sell it and I was going to get a cut."

"And no one was going to get hurt."

"Not the way I heard it. And then Barry and John were dead and I was in the middle of it. And then it just fucking grew."

"Out of control," Mick said. "Like wildfire."

"Worse."

"Worse. Peter Rooney, and Burke, and all those that died at Grogan's. And Matt's friend, that went to retreat with the Zen Buddhists. And myself saved for last. Didn't they try to get you to do it, Andy? It would have been easy for you. A bullet in the back of the head when I was looking the other way. Easier than setting up at the farm and luring me there."

"I could never do it, Mick."

"No, I didn't think you could."

"And he wants to do it himself. He hates you."

"He does."

"He says you killed his father. I don't know if he ever saw the man, and what's it matter anyway? It's ancient fucking history, for Christ's sake."

"So's the Battle of the Boyne," Mick said, "and yet there's some that never got over it. Ah, Andy. It had to be you or Tom, and once I saw Tom dead that left only yourself. It broke my heart, knowing that."

"Mick . . ."

"But you're back, and that's what counts. It's good to have you back, Andy."

"Jesus, Mick. You'll never have to worry about me again. I swear to God, Mick."

"Ah, don't I know it?" he said, and rested a cupped hand at the back of Andy's head, and put his other hand beneath Andy's chin, and moved both hands, and broke Andy Buckley's neck.

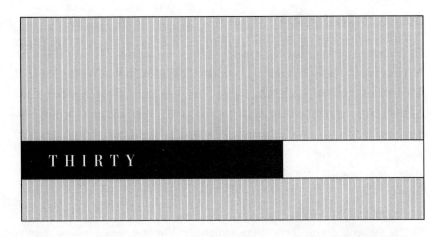

THIRTY

"WHAT CHOICE DID I have? What else could I do?"

I didn't have an answer. He got the keys from the ignition, walked around to the trunk, unlocked it. He came back and picked up Andy's corpse without any apparent effort and carried him on his shoulder, then laid him gently in the trunk and slammed the lid. The noise when it swung shut was sharp and sudden on that dark and silent country road.

"No choice at all," he said, "and I swear I didn't want to do it."

"I didn't think you were going to," I said. "Not then, at any rate. You took me by surprise."

"And him as well, I shouldn't wonder. I wanted to give him a bit of hope, you know, and put him at his ease. It's fear that's hardest on a man, and I wanted to spare him that. As it was, there must have been an instant when he knew what was happening, and then it was over. Ah, Christ, it's a bad old world."

"It's that, all right."

"A hard life in a bad old world. He was as close as I'll ever come to having a son. Paddy Farrelly got himself a son, as like as not by forcing himself on the Dowling bitch, and his boy's painting the city with blood to avenge his father's memory. And my son's helping him do it." He steadied himself, drew a breath. "Except he's not my son and never was. Just a decent lad who never added up to much. A good steady hand, with a dart or a steering wheel. Do you think I should have let him live?"

"I can't answer that."

"What would you have done yourself? You can answer that, can't you?"

"You could never trust him," I said.

"No."

"Or rest easy, knowing what he'd done. All those people, all that blood. Being the man you are, I don't see how you could have acted differently."

"Being the man I am."

"Well, you've never been one to forgive and forget."

"No," he said. "I never have. And too old to learn new tricks, I'd have to say." He bent down, picked up a pack of Marlboros Andy had dropped. "A clue," he said ironically, "and now it's got my prints on it. And who gives a fuck, anyway?" He flung the pack across the road, bent down again and came up with Andy's Zippo lighter. I thought he was going to throw that as well, but he frowned at it and stuck it in his pocket. Then he reached to scoop up a handful of gravel and hurled that after the cigarettes.

I waited while he leaned against the side of the car and let the fury drain out of him. Then in an entirely different tone of voice he said, "What they don't know is there's another way onto the property. It backs up against state land, you know. And there's a back road goes into the state land, and then you can walk through a few acres of woods and you're on my land out behind the old orchard. They'll only know to watch the driveway, and they'll be waiting for three men in a car, not two men on foot."

"That gives us a little bit of an edge."

"And we'll need it, as there's two of us and who knows how many of them. I should have asked him how many they had, but would he even have known?"

"There were the two who mugged me. Donnie Scalzo and the one whose face I never did see. The Vietnamese is dead, but his partner Moon Gafter's still around, and he'll probably be on hand for the finale. That's three, and Dowling makes four, but there could be one or two others we don't know about."

"Four at a minimum," he said. "Very likely five, and possibly six. All arrayed against the two of us. They're defending and we're on the attack, which is to their advantage, but we know the ground better than they do. We've a bit of the home field advantage."

"And the element of surprise."

"And that," he agreed. "But, you know, I'm presuming something, and I've no right to. Because you don't have to be a part of the rest of it. You can go home."

I just shook my head. "It's too late for that," I said. "Unless we both go home. They set a trap and you figured it out and walked away from it, and took out the man who set it. You could walk away and let them figure out what to do next."

"I'd rather deal with them now, while I've got them all bottled up in there."

"I agree. And I'll be there with you."

We got in the car. He started it up. I found myself trying to determine if the car felt any lighter now that we didn't have Andy with us anymore, and then I remembered that the weight was the same. He'd been behind the wheel before, and now he was in the trunk.

"I HAD A feeling, you know."

"About Andy."

"From early on, it must have been. After the trouble at the bar, I made sure I dropped him off and kept the car. I didn't want him to know where I was staying. And I didn't let him have the cell phone number."

"I don't know about the second sight," I said, "but I'd say you have good instincts."

"And that may be all it is," he said, "but I don't know. Let me concentrate now, we've got our turn coming up and it's an easy one to miss. Ah, will you look at that!"

Ahead of us, a whole herd of deer bounded one after another across the narrow road. I counted eight of them, and I may have missed one.

"They're hard on crops and shrubbery," he said, "and a fucking menace on the highway, but what a beautiful sight they are. Why the hell would anybody want to shoot them?"

"I've got a friend in Ohio, a cop named Havlicek, who's always trying to get me to go out there and hunt deer with him. He can't understand why I'm not interested, and I can't understand why he is."

"It's enough of a strain killing people," he said. "I've no time to waste on deer."

He found the back road he was looking for and we made our turn. Half a mile in there was a chain across the road with a sign on it announcing that access was forbidden except to authorized personnel. I got out and unhooked the chain. He drove through and I replaced the chain and got back in the car.

We followed the one-lane road through the woods. I couldn't say how far we drove. We crept along slowly, rarely going over ten miles an hour. I kept waiting for more deer to explode out of cover in front of us, and God knows the woods were full of them, but we didn't see any others.

Eventually the road ran out in a small clearing. There was a little cabin there, and a canvas-topped 4WD utility vehicle parked not far from it. Mick reached into the back of the Chevy and went through the leather satchel, selecting some of its contents and adding them to a dun-gray canvas sack. He took mostly guns and extra ammunition, and left behind the money and papers from the safe. He'd already grabbed up a red plastic flashlight from the glove box, and on a hunch I checked the utility vehicle. It was unlocked, as I'd figured it would be, and it had a flashlight mounted on a clamp above the passenger door, encased in hard black rubber and twice as bright as the one from the Caprice.

"Good man," Mick said.

I didn't see any way out but the way we'd come in, but Mick struck off to the left, and the beam of his flashlight revealed a path. He had the canvas sack in one hand and the flashlight in the other, and I was carrying the second flashlight and had my other hand free. I had the revolver he'd given me in my shoulder holster, and the little .22 automatic in my pocket. And I'd kept one of the guns I'd taken from Andy, another automatic, this one a 9mm. I was carrying it as he'd carried it, under my waistband in the small of my back.

The air was cool, and I was glad of the Kevlar vest if only for the warmth it provided. The ground was soft underfoot, the path narrow. Our own footfalls were the only sound I could hear, and it seemed to me we were making a lot of noise, although I couldn't see how it mattered. We were well out of earshot of anybody at the farm.

After a long silence he said, "He didn't have a priest. I wonder if it matters. We used to think it did, but there's much that's changed with the years. I doubt he cared whether he had a priest or not. Priest or no priest, he'll be seeing it now."

"Seeing . . ."

"The picture of his life. If that's what happens. But who knows what happens? Though I suspect I'll find out soon enough."

"We both may."

"No," he said. "You'll be all right."

"Is that a promise?"

"It's the next thing to it," he said. "You'll be home soon enough, sitting in your kitchen drinking coffee with your good woman. I've a strong feeling about that."

"Another feeling."

"And there's a twin feeling alongside of it," he said. "About myself."

I didn't say anything.

" 'You've the second sight,' my mother said, 'and right now it's a wonder to you, Mickey, but you'll find it's as much a curse as ever it was a blessing, for it will show you things you'd sooner not see.' There were things she was wrong about, by God, but that was never one of them. I don't think I'll live to see the sun up, man."

"If you really believe that," I said, "why don't we turn around and go home?"

"We'll go on."

"Why?"

"Because we must. Because I'd have it no other way. Because if I'm not afraid of the men and their guns, whyever should I be fearful of my own thoughts? And I have to tell you this. I don't mind dying."

"Oh?"

"Whoever would have thought I'd last this long? You'd think someone would have killed me by now, or I'd have died of my own recklessness. Oh, I had a good old run of it. There's things I did and wish I hadn't, and there's others I wished I'd done and never will, but I wouldn't change the whole of it if I could. And just as well, because you never can, can you?"

Nor all your tears wash out a word of it . . .

"No," I said. "You never can."

"I'm lucky to have had what I've had, and if it's over then it's over. And I've seen too many men die to fear the act of dying. If there's pain, well, there's pain enough in life. I'm not afraid of it."

"When you were in Ireland that time," I remembered, "I had to trade a suitcase full of money for a kidnapped child, and I had to walk right up to a couple of guns in order to do it. The men with the guns were unstable, and one of them was crazy as a shithouse rat. I figured there was a very good chance I'd die then and there. But I honestly wasn't afraid. I know I must have told you that, but did I ever tell you why?"

"Tell me."

"It was a thought I had. I realized I'd lived too long to die young. And I don't know why the hell I found that reassuring, but I did. And I wasn't afraid."

"And that was a few years ago," he said, "and I'm a couple of years older than yourself." He cleared his throat. "I won't have a priest myself," he said. "You know, I have to say that bothers me."

"Does it?"

"Not the lack of some whey-faced lad in a dog collar to touch me on the forehead and send me fluttering off to Jesus," he said. "I don't care about that. But I always had it in the back of my mind that I'd get a chance to make a full confession before I died. I thought I'd die easier with the weight of the sins off me."

"I see."

"Do you? You probably don't, not being brought up in the Faith. It's hard to explain Confession to someone who's not Catholic. What it is, and what it does for you."

"We have something like it in AA."

"Do you?" He stopped dead in his tracks. "But I never heard that. You have a sacrament of Confession? You go to priests and bare your souls?"

"Not exactly," I said, "but I think it amounts to essentially the same thing. There's a program of suggested steps."

"Twelve of them, isn't it?"

"That's right. Not everybody pays attention to them, especially at first, when it's hard enough just staying away from the first drink. But people who work the steps seem to have a better chance of staying sober in the long run, so most people get to them sooner or later."

"And confession's a part of it?"

"The fifth step," I said. "The precise language of it—but do you really want to hear all this?"

"Indeed I do."

"What you're supposed to do is admit to God, to yourself, and to another human being the exact nature of your wrongs."

"Your sins," he said. "But how do you decide what's a sin?"

"You figure it out for yourself," I said. "There's no authority in AA. Nobody's in charge."

"The lunatics are running the asylum."

"That's about it. And how you approach the step is open to interpretation. The advice I got was to write down everything I ever did in my life that bothered me."

"By God, wouldn't your hand be cramped up by the time you were done?"

"That's exactly what happened. Then I sat down with my notes in front of me and talked it all out with another person."

"A priest?"

"Some people do it with a clergyman. In the early days that was the usual way. Nowadays most people take the step with their sponsor."

"Is that what you did?"

"Yes."

"And that was the Buddhist fellow? Why can I never remember the poor man's name?"

"Jim Faber."

"And you told him every bad thing you ever did."

"Pretty much. There were a few things that I didn't think of until later on, but I told him everything I could remember at the time."

"And then what? He gave you absolution?"

"No, he just listened."

"Ah."

"And then he said, 'Well, that's it. How do you feel now?' And I said I thought I felt about the same. And he said why don't we go get some coffee, and we did, and that was that. But later I felt . . ."

"Relieved?"

"I think so, yes."

He nodded. "I'd no idea your lot did any of that," he said. "It's a good bit like Confession, but there's more ritual and formality our way. No surprise, eh? There's more ritual and formality to everything we do. You've never done it our way, have you?"

"No, of course not."

" 'No, of course not.' There's no 'of course' about it with you, is there? You've been to Mass with me. More than that, you took Holy Communion. Do ye even remember that?"

"I wouldn't be likely to forget it."

"Nor I myself! By God, what a strange fucking time that was. The two of us fresh from Maspeth with blood on our hands, and there we were at St. Bernard's at the Butchers' Mass, staying put as we always did while the others went up to take the wafer. And all of a sudden there you are, on your feet and on your way to the altar rail, and I a step behind you. I with decades of sins unconfessed, and you an unbaptized heathen altogether, and we took Communion!"

"I don't know why I did it."

"And I never knew why I followed you! And yet I felt wonderful afterwards. I couldn't tell you why, but I did."

"So did I. I never did anything like that again."

"I should hope not," he said. "Neither did I, you may rest assured of that."

We walked a little ways in silence, and then he said, "Ritual and formality, as I was saying. 'Bless me, Father, for I have sinned,' is what I'd say as a way of starting. 'It has been forty years and more since my last confession.' Sweet Jesus, forty years!"

I didn't say anything.

"And then I don't know what I'd say. I don't think there's a commandment I've not broken. Oh, I've kept my hands off the altar boys, and that's more I guess than some of the priests can say for themselves, but I can take no credit for that as it's been lack of inclination that's spared them. I suppose I could go through the list, commandment by commandment."

"Some people do the Fifth Step by going through the list of deadly sins. You know, pride, greed, anger, gluttony . . ."

"It might be easier. There's seven sins, and that's three fewer than the commandments. I like your way, though. Just saying the sins that are weighing on your soul. Well, I've enough of those. I've lived a bad life and done bad things."

A twig snapped underfoot, and I heard something scurry in the brush, some small animal we'd startled. Off in the distance I heard what must have been the hooting of an owl. I don't think I ever heard one before. He stopped walking, leaned his back against a tree.

"One time," he said, "I was trying to get this man to talk. He had money hidden and he wouldn't say where it was. Hurting him only seemed to strengthen his will. And so I reached in and took his eye out, plucked it right out of his head, and I held it in the palm of my hand and showed it to him. 'Your eye is looking at you,' I said, 'and it can see right into your soul. Now shall I take the other one as well?' And he talked, and we got the money, and I put the barrel of my gun to his empty eye socket and blew out his brains."

He fell silent, and his words hung in the air around us, until the breeze could waft them away.

"And then there was another time," he said. . . .

.   .   .

I'VE FORGOTTEN ALMOST everything he said.

I can't explain how that happened. It's not as though I wasn't paying attention. How could I have done otherwise? The wedding guest could have more easily ignored the Ancient Mariner.

Even so, the words he spoke passed through my consciousness and flew off somewhere. It was as if I was a channel, a conduit for his confession. Maybe that's how it is for priests and psychiatrists, who hear such revelations regularly. Or maybe not. I couldn't say.

We walked and he talked, sometimes at great length, sometimes quite tersely. There was a point when we reached a clearing and sat on the ground, and he went on talking and I went on listening.

And then there was a point when he was done.

"A LONGER WALK than I remembered it," he said. "It's slower going at night, and we stopped now and then along the way, didn't we? The stream's my property line. It's just a dry ditch in the heat of summer, and a regular torrent when the snows melt in the spring. Let's find a place to cross it where we won't get our feet wet."

And we managed, stepping on a couple of rocks.

"After he heard you out, your Buddhist friend," he began, and caught himself. "Jim Faber, that is to say."

"You remembered his name."

"There's hope for me yet. After he heard you out, was that the end of it? He didn't absolve you of your sins. Did he at least give you any penance? Any Aves to say? Any Our Fathers?"

"No."

"He just left it at that?"

"The rest was up to me. The way we do it, we have to forgive ourselves."

"How, for God's sake?"

"Well, there are other steps. It's not penance, exactly, but maybe it works the same way. Making amends for the harm you've done."

"However would a man know where to begin?"

"And self-acceptance," I said. "That's a big part of it, and don't ask me how you do it. It's not exactly my own area of expertise."

He thought about it and nodded slowly. The corners of his mouth turned up the slightest bit. "So you won't grant me absolution," he said.

"I would if I could."

"Ah, what kind of a priest are you? The wrong kind entirely. Knowing you, you'd probably change wine into water."

"The miracle of Insubstantiation," I said.

"Wine into Perrier," he said. "With all the tiny bubbles."

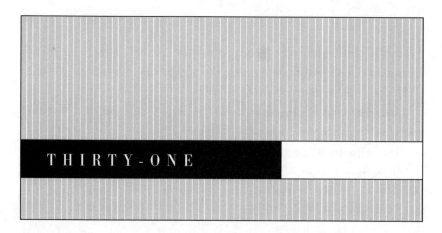

THIRTY-ONE

WE WERE ON his land from the moment we'd forded the little stream, and we had another five minutes in the woods before we came to a cleared patch of ground. At the high ground on the other side of the clearing was the orchard, to the side of which we'd buried Kenny and McCartney. Beyond the orchard were the gardens and the hogpen and the hen coop, and a ways past that was the old farmhouse.

"Now we'd best be quiet," he murmured, "for voices carry. They'd never hear us this far off, but the animals might. In fact 'twill be the devil's own trick getting past the hog lot without the beasts knowing it. Even if we're dead quiet they'll catch our scent, though how they can smell anything at all beyond their own raw stench is a great puzzle to me."

And there were a few guinea fowl penned in with his hens, he said. Pretty creatures, that roosted in the trees and made a racket when you went near them. O'Gara liked having them, liked the way they looked, and assured him they were a delicacy and much prized on the fanciest table, but he found them stringier than chicken and not as tasty. They were splendid for raising an alarm, though, true watchdogs with wings, and there'd be a little noise from them, a little grunting from the hogs, no matter how carefully we got by them. But these were city boys we were coming after, and what would they make of a bit of cawing and oinking from the livestock?

We switched off our flashlights. There was enough moonlight for us to make our way over cleared ground. We walked slowly, picked up our feet deliberately and set them down softly. When we cleared the orchard I could see lights on in the farmhouse. The only sound I could hear was my own breathing.

We walked on. There was a graveled path but we kept to the side of it, where the grass and weeds made a quieter surface underfoot than the loose gravel. A lighted window in the farmhouse kept drawing my eyes. I could picture them in there, sitting around a table, eating and drinking things from the big old refrigerator, opening Ball jars and spooning out preserves that Mrs. O'Gara had put up. I didn't want to imagine all this, I wanted to concentrate on what I was doing, but the images filled my head anyway.

He stopped in his tracks, caught my arm.

"Listen," he whispered.

"To what?"

"That's it," he said. "As close as we are, we should hear them."

"In the house?"

"The animals," he said. "They can hear us. They should be stirring, and we should be hearing them."

"I can't hear them," I whispered back, "but I can certainly smell them."

He nodded and sniffed the air, sniffed it again. "I don't care for it," he said.

"Would anybody?"

He frowned. He was picking up something on the night air that I couldn't make out. I guess he was used to smelling his hogs and chickens, and knew when something didn't smell as it should.

He touched a finger to his lips, then led the way. The smell got stronger as we neared the fenced hogpen. He went right up next to the fence, leaned his forearms on the topmost rail. Not a sound came from within, and now I smelled it, too, a stale top note to the usual reek of the animals' waste.

He switched on his flashlight, played it around the pen, stopped the beam when it lit up a dead hog. The animal lay on its side in its own blood, its great white flank stitched with bullet holes. He moved the light here and there, and I could make out others.

He switched off the light, nodded to himself, and started walking to the hen coop. It was the same story there, but a little more vivid, with blood and feathers everywhere. He stood there and looked at the carnage and breathed deeply, in and out, in and out. Then he switched off his light and turned on his heel and began walking back the way we'd come.

My first thought was that he was going to walk away from it, from all of it, that we'd go back across the stream and through the woods to where we'd left the Chevy. But I knew that couldn't be, and realized he was heading for the little toolshed, the one that looked like an outhouse. I knew there was a shovel in there, and another inane thought came unbidden, that he was going to bury the slain animals. But that couldn't be, either.

He said, "When a mink or a weasel gets into a henhouse, why, it will kill like that. You'll find every hen dead and none of them eaten. Wanton savagery you'd call it, but, don't you see, the weasel has a reason. It wants the blood. It drinks the blood from each of them, and leaves the flesh. So if you said it was bloodthirsty, why, you'd only be saying the simple truth. It's thirsty for the blood."

He turned to me. "What *they* wanted," he said, "was target practice. A chance to test their guns and show off for each other. And the joy of shooting the animal and watching it stagger around, blood spouting from it, and then shooting it again. And again."

I thought about what he'd said. I nodded.

"In a way," he said, "it makes it easier."

"How do you mean?"

"I was trying to think how to get the O'Garas out of there. On the small chance that they were still alive. But I know now there's no chance at all. Was it O'Gara answered the phone when you called?"

"I couldn't swear to it. But I think it probably was, yes."

"That's what they kept him alive for," he said. "Not for you to call, for they'd never have thought that might happen. But in case I called. I might have called before I came out, and they'd have had him there to answer, with a gun to his head and a gun to his wife's, and no way for him to do anything but whatever they told him to do."

"Couldn't they still be alive?"

"No," he said, "and you can blame me for that, if you've a mind to. 'Twas Andy's call that killed them. If I'd stopped him from going back into his house, he'd have had no chance to make that call. And they'd have kept O'Gara alive, him and his wife both, and they'd still be alive now. I thought of that, you see, but I thought of it too late. I thought of it when I called Andy's number and got the busy signal. Now they'll know we're on our way, I thought, and then it struck me what the immediate consequences of knowing would be, and I saw my mistake."

"You can't blame yourself for that."

"I could," he said, "but I won't waste a great lot of feeling on it. Call or no call, they might have killed them anyway by now. Out of boredom, for lack of anything else to kill. And even if they were alive now there's little enough chance they'd still be breathing an hour from now. We've a hard enough task ahead of us without having to get two people out of that house alive." He sighed. "It's a blameless life they led, both of them. They got to heaven a few hours early, that's all. They're up there now, wouldn't you say? While we're down here in hell."

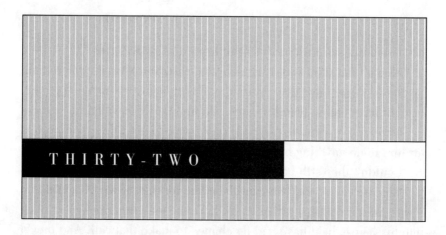

THIRTY-TWO

"**WE'VE ANOTHER GREAT ADVANTAGE**," he said. "They're stupid."

He was half in and half out of the little toolshed, making his preparations, filling jars and bottles from a five-gallon can, stuffing rags into their mouths as stoppers. I squatted nearby, holding the light for him. The toolshed was way in back near the orchard, not far from where we'd dug the two-man grave. The ground had settled some since we mounded the earth over it, but you could still see the convexity of it.

The farmhouse was a couple of hundred yards away. They couldn't possibly hear us from that distance, but even so he kept his voice down.

"Stupid," he said again. " 'Twas worse than stupidity that led to the slaughter of the hogs and chickens, but it was stupid all the same. Suppose we drove straight back there? Suppose I'd insisted to Andy that he drive all the way back, because I wanted to inspect the grave site, or have a look at the animals, or for any damn reason at all? He'd have done it, and I'd have seen the carnage, and their great surprise would have been no surprise at all. It's a good sign, that stupidity. If they're stupid in one thing they may well be stupid in another. Give me a hand with these, but take no more than you know you can carry. You don't want to be dropping them, or making any noise with them at all. Better to make two trips."

We made three in all, carrying the stoppered jars and bottles, carrying the can itself, half empty now, carrying the cloth sack of guns and extra ammunition. We stashed everything in the high grass at the edge of the chicken yard. When we were done Mick leaned back against a fence post and caught his breath, then reached for the silver flask in his hip pocket. He took it out and looked at it, then put it back in his pocket unopened.

He brought his head close to mine, spoke in a soft whisper. "As stupid as they are," he said, "they might not have posted a sentry. But we've got to make sure, and I almost hope they have. We can take him out and shorten the odds."

We left our flashlights with the bottles and jars and extra guns. Mick reached into the cloth sack and came out with a suppressor. He made sure it fit his pistol, then took it off and put it in his pocket and the pistol back in his waistband.

We approached the house, picking our feet up and setting them down soundlessly, keeping in the deep shadows, taking a few steps, then waiting and listening, then taking a few steps more. When we drew even with the house I could hear sounds coming through an open window. What I was hearing was a conversation, and one of the speakers had the higher voice of a woman. I thought for an instant that it was Mrs. O'Gara, and then an instant later I realized that it was a television program. They'd taken possession of the farm, they'd killed all the people and animals, they'd set their trap, and now they were watching TV.

Once we were twenty yards or so past the house, I let out a breath and realized I'd been half holding it for a long time, limiting myself to very shallow breaths, as if for fear of disturbing the air. I took a deep breath now. We were past the stretch where they were most likely to hear a stray sound from us, but the task right ahead of us was trickier. We had to look for a sentry without knowing where he'd be posted, or if he was even there at all.

Mick led the way, keeping just to the left of the graveled driveway, and I stayed on the right side, and five yards or so behind. I advanced when he did, stopped when he stopped. It was a long driveway, curving gently to the left as we made our way down it, and following the downward slope of the land itself. It was well shaded, too, by trees and brush, and I had to put my feet down without seeing exactly where I was placing them. My progress was quiet, but not as dead silent as I would have liked it to be.

Ahead of me, Mick stopped dead in his tracks. I wondered why, and then I heard it myself, faint but unmistakable. Dead ahead of us, soft music was playing.

He moved on, cautiously, and I kept apace. The music's volume increased as we got closer to it. Then Mick held up a hand to stop me, and brought a finger to his lips. He reached into his pocket with one hand and drew the gun from his belt with the other, and I could tell he was fitting the suppressor to the weapon.

Then he moved ahead, and deeper into the shadows, and I couldn't see him clearly. I drew the revolver from my shoulder holster and held on to it. I listened carefully and all I heard was the radio, playing a country and western song. It sounded familiar but I couldn't make out the words.

I caught a whiff of something and sniffed the air. It was smoke I smelled, cigarette smoke.

Then I heard what must have been gunshots. I wouldn't have heard them if I hadn't been listening for them, wouldn't have recognized them if I hadn't known what to expect. They were soft popping sounds, the kind you get when you break a bubble from a piece of bubble wrap.

Mick stepped out of the shadows, motioned me forward. I walked without making noise, although we'd gone far enough from the house that they wouldn't be able to hear footsteps. Still, there was no point in making unnecessary noise.

At the side of the drive, a man lay sprawled in a canvas sling chair. He was wearing a Chicago Bulls warm-up jacket and a pair of Levi's, and on his feet he wore black Dr. Martens and white athletic socks. There was a gun in his lap, one of those 9mm's that come with an oversized clip holding ten or a dozen rounds. He'd never get to use them, though, because his days as a gunman were over. He'd been shot twice, once in the center of the chest and once in the middle of the forehead, and if Danny Boy knew the son of a bitch he could put his name on the list.

There was a little portable radio playing on the ground alongside, and next to the radio was a half gallon jug of wine about two-thirds full. There was a cell phone on the ground, also, and a few feet away was the cigarette he'd been smoking. Mick stuck out a foot and stepped on it, hesitated, then stepped on the cell phone, too.

He had Andy's Zippo in his hand, and he spun the wheel and held the flame in front of the man's face. I took a good look and shook my head. He was nobody I'd ever seen before.

"I suppose he could have been one of the muggers," I whispered. "Not Scalzo but the one I never got a good look at. Of course he was wearing soft shoes that night, not Dr. Martens."

"Mayhaps he learned his lesson."

"You taught him a better lesson than I did. Flick the light again, will you? Once in the heart and once in the head, and they're big wounds with hardly any blood from either of them. Whichever shot hit him first, it must have been instantly fatal."

"Jesus," he said, "you needn't investigate the fucking case. We know who killed this one." He closed the lighter, put it away, took the suppressor from the gun, put it in a pocket, then removed the clip from the gun and replaced the two bullets he'd fired. He picked up the casings his gun had ejected, started to pocket them, changed his mind and wiped them on his shirttail, then tossed them on the dead man's lap.

We left him there, the gun and the casings on his lap, the radio playing.

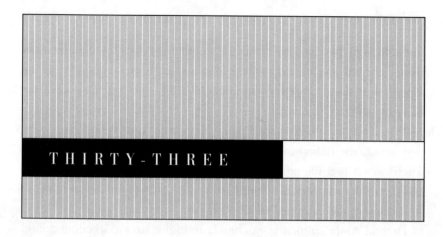

THIRTY-THREE

I STOOD AT the rear of the house. There was a big metal box mounted on it, its door hanging open now. I had a grip on the handle of the main circuit breaker, and I leaned as far as I could to my left, looking around the corner of the house to where Mick was standing. He was wearing his father's apron. I'd tried to talk him out of it, it would make him too visible a target, but he wouldn't hear it. Now his hand moved in signal, and I thrust the handle down and cut off all electrical power to the farmhouse.

The house went instantly dark, of course, and silent. The silence only lasted for a second or two, but Mick was already in motion, lighting the wick of one of his bottles, heaving it, racing a dozen yards to his right to light another wick and hurl another bottle.

Within the house, noise erupted. Men shouted, called to each other, pushed back chairs, bumped into walls and tables in the darkness. I ran back a few yards to where I'd left my stash of jars and bottles, scratched a match, lit the scrap of cloth that served as a wick, and threw it at a ground-floor window. Glass broke and the bottle disappeared inside, and then there was an explosion and I could see flames leaping behind what was left of the window.

There were other explosions in the front of the house. Inside, men were screaming at each other. I lit and tossed my two remaining jars of gasoline, lofting one at a second-floor window, heaving the other at the back door just as someone struggled to open it. It burst on impact and flames blossomed in the doorway.

I got down on the ground. I heard gunfire from the front of the house, and now a shape appeared at a window in the back. I fired at it, and the person I shot at snapped off a couple of rounds in my direction, then drew back from the window.

I got up into a crouch and ran to a position where I could see what was going on in front while still keeping the back door covered. A bullet whined overhead and I hit the dirt, then swung around and returned fire. I didn't hit anything, unless you want to count the house itself.

It was burning briskly now, with flames visible on both floors and at all corners. There was a great explosion, or implosion, as a side window burst on the second floor. A man ran out onto the porch, and I hurried around the side of the house and fired at him. He fired back at me and vaulted over the porch railing and hit the ground running. He was favoring one leg, and I wondered if he and not the dead sentry had been one of the two who'd mugged me. Or had he hurt the leg just now leaping from the porch?

I held the gun in both hands and squeezed the trigger, but the hammer clicked on an empty cartridge. I dropped the gun and yanked Andy's niner from behind my back. He saw me now and fired twice, and one bullet struck me on the right side just below the collarbone. The vest stopped it but the impact knocked me off-balance. I righted myself and aimed and squeezed the trigger, and nothing happened, and I found the safety with my thumb and cleared it and aimed and fired, and he clutched his chest and took a step and fell to the ground. I waited a moment, and when he didn't move I ran up to him and shot him in the head.

I'd left the revolver where it lay. I went back and found it, broke it open, spilled out the empty cartridges and fumbled others from my

jacket pocket. I jammed them into the chambers and snapped the cylinder back in place, and the back door of the house flew open and a
man burst out of the flame-shrouded doorway.

Donnie Scalzo. He had some kind of automatic weapon in his hands
and he triggered off a burst, but he didn't see me and the bullets didn't
come anywhere close. I aimed at him, fired, missed. He let out a yell
and swung the gun around toward me. He fired and missed high, and
I steadied the gun and shot him in the shoulder. He cried out and
turned as if to run back into the house, but the doorway was a sheet of
flame now. He spun around again, one arm hanging, clutching the gun
awkwardly in his left hand now, and I fired and missed, and fired again
and got him in the gut, halfway between the navel and the groin. He
roared and fell and clutched himself, and I remembered how I'd left
him alive the last time. I ran over to him and he looked at me and I
shot him twice and he died.

THERE WAS NO point covering the rear of the house because there was no
way anybody would be coming through the back door. I circled around
to the right and looked around for Mick. The white butcher's apron
made him easy to spot. We were both in front of the burning farmhouse
now, but at opposite ends of it.

Gunfire came from a window, and he fired back at its source. There
was a loud noise that seemed to come from the second floor, a roof beam
giving way, a part of the ceiling falling, something like that. Then there
was a brief silence, and then two men appeared on the porch within
seconds of each other. One burst through the front door while the other
smashed out what remained of the window and stepped nimbly over
the sill.

One was a man I'd never seen before. He had a pompadour like an
old-fashioned country singer and a mustache like a riverboat gambler,
and he held a pistol in each hand and was firing them in turn. I don't
know what he was shooting at and I'm not even sure his eyes were open.
He stood there flat-footed, blasting away with his two guns. I shot at
him and missed, and Mick shot him twice and hit him and he fell back
through the window into the burning house.

The other man was Moon Gafter.

I'd never seen him before, but that didn't keep me from recognizing him. He was tall, at least six-five, with a rawboned frame and that big white moon face. With his long wiry arms and that oversized head he looked like a creature from another planet, or a giant praying mantis.

He looked right at me but I don't think he saw me. He saw Mick, and swung his gun toward the stained white apron. I took aim and got off a shot at him, and the bullet struck him on the left side of the rib cage. He didn't seem to notice it, and I thought he must be wearing a vest himself, but then I saw blood flowing, streaming over his belt and down his trouser leg. But he was still standing, paying no attention to the wound, and he began firing at Mick.

I steadied the gun, aiming for his heart, but when I fired I hit him high on the shoulder. This wound bled, too, but if he felt it he gave no sign. He was shooting at Mick, and now he dashed down the porch steps and ran toward Mick, firing as he ran.

Mick shot back at him and hit him in the chest, and that slowed him down a little, but he kept on coming. I ran toward the two of them and trained the big automatic on Gafter and squeezed off three shots as I ran, and one missed but two struck home, one at the belt line and the other in the small of the back, but they didn't seem to have any effect on him.

Then Mick took a step toward him and fired, and Gafter stopped in his tracks and the gun fell from his fingers. And Mick ran up and stuck the gun in the man's wide open mouth and blew the back of his head off.

"Jesus," he said. "By God, he takes a fucking lot of killing."

I stood there, trying to catch my breath, and there was a burst of gunfire behind me and I threw myself to the ground. I spun around and there stood Dowling himself, the bastard son of Paddy Farrelly, silhouetted against the burning house. He had an automatic rifle like the one Nguyen Tran Bao had used to shoot up Grogan's, and he looked at me, and our eyes locked for an instant just as they had that first night at the bar. Then I fired and missed, and he fired at me just as I threw myself to the ground. That burst was high. Then he overcorrected and the next burst dug up the lawn in front of me.

I looked up. Mick was on his feet facing Dowling, aiming his pistol. He fired twice and missed. Dowling triggered a burst, but it was a short one because the clip was empty. He'd used up too many rounds on pigs and chickens.

I fired at him and missed, and Mick aimed and shot and missed, and Dowling threw his gun aside and vaulted the porch rail and took off, running flat out toward the hogpen and the chicken yard and the orchard beyond.

Mick shot at him and missed, and tried again. There was a click and he threw down the empty gun. Then he was up and moving, running hard, running after Dowling. My revolver was empty. I thought I might have a round or two left in the automatic, but I couldn't get a clear shot. I don't think I could have hit a moving target at that range anyway, but with Mick between me and Dowling I didn't dare try.

I thought Dowling would run away from him. He had twenty-five years on Mick and he must have been fifty pounds lighter, but Mick ran him down and launched himself through the air at the younger man. Then they were both down and I couldn't see what was going on. I saw Mick's arm raised high overhead, and moonlight glinted off something in his hand. The arm descended, and there was a scream, shrill and piercing in the night. Mick's arm rose and fell, and the scream died abruptly. And again the arm rose and fell, rose and fell.

I was on my feet, my breathing ragged, a useless gun in each hand. For a long moment all was still except the sounds of the fire behind me. Then Mick got to his feet. He kicked at something, then walked toward me, pausing long enough to give whatever it was another hearty kick. He kicked it a third time, and of course by now I knew what it was.

It rolled on in front of him like a misshapen soccer ball, and this time when he reached it he bent over and snatched it up, carrying it out in front of him at arm's length. He walked right up to me, gripping Dowling's severed head by the hair. The eyes were wide open.

"Look at the fucker!" he cried. "And isn't he spit and image of his father now, eh? Have ye a leather bag, man? And shall we take young Paddy here round the bars, so all can admire him and stand him a drink?"

I didn't say anything. The only answer came from the house, where a roof beam gave way with a great crack. I turned at the noise and saw the roof sag and sparks erupt outward.

"Ah, Christ!" Mick roared. And he drew his arm back, and, like a basketball player winging one from half court at the buzzer, he hurled the head in a great high arc. It sailed in through a wide-open window and disappeared in the flames.

He stared after it, and then he drew his silver flask from his hip pocket. He uncapped it and tilted his head back and drank until the flask was empty. It was the first drink he'd taken since we found the bodies at Tom Heaney's house.

He screwed the cap back on the empty flask, and for a moment I had the sense that he was going to throw it where he'd thrown Dowling's head. But all he did was put it back in his pocket.

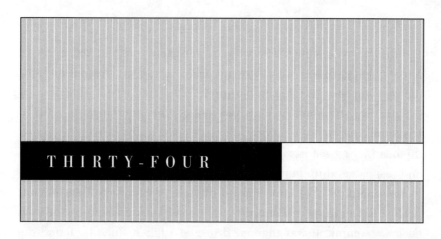

WE THREW OUR guns into the burning house, and the gas can, and the cloth sack of extra guns and bullets. We turned, then, and walked back the way we'd come, up the long drive, past the slaughtered hogs and chickens, past the toolshed, and into the orchard.

"Back through the woods," he said. "It's shorter than taking the road, though slower going. But we wouldn't want to meet anybody now, would we?"

"No."

"Not that there'll be many on the road this late. I doubt the firemen will come at all. The nearest neighbor's half a mile away, and it's good odds no one's even caught sight of the fire yet. By the time anybody gets here 'twill have long since burned to the foundation."

"It was a nice house," I said.

"A sound one. 'Twas built before the Civil War, or at least that's what they told me. The central portion of the house, that is. The porch was a later addition, and the one-story section on the left-hand side."

"I guess that was the best way to get them out. Burning the house."

"I'd say it was," he said, "but if I could have clapped my hands, and if that would have brought them all out in a row, their hands folded in front of them, just waiting to be shot, well, I'd still have had the chore of burning the house down afterward."

"You wanted it to burn."

"I did. I'm only regretful that I didn't hold back a bit of gasoline for the hog house and the hen coop. I'd see them in flames as well if I could. You think it strange of me?"

"I don't know what's strange anymore."

"How could I ever go there again? How could I ever look at the fucking place again? All I'd ever see would be the great corpses of the hogs raked with bullets, and the hens blown apart, and bloody feathers all over everything. And the O'Garas dead as well, and thank God I didn't have to see their bodies. Let the fire have them, eh?" He shook his head. " 'Twas O'Gara's farm, you know. 'Twas his name on the deed. Well, let someone else figure out what to do with it. Let the state sort it out, and take it for back taxes in a couple of years. They can add it on to the adjoining lot, and it can all be state land then. And the hell with it, the hell with all of it."

We'd lost the flashlight from Andy's glove compartment, but he'd kept the better one, the black rubber flash I'd taken from the utility vehicle. He switched it on and lighted the way, and we made our way to the stream and crossed it, but this time we didn't bother finding rocks to step on. We just waded right through it.

He was still wearing his father's apron, and he'd taken the flashlight from one of its pockets. The other pocket was weighed down with his father's old cleaver, evidently sharp enough still for the work he'd put it to.

There was a lot of fresh blood on the apron.

THE CAR WAS where we'd left it, in the clearing across from the little cabin. The 4WD vehicle was still parked in the same spot, too, and Mick watched in amusement as I took a moment to put the flashlight back where I'd found it. We got into the Caprice and the engine turned over as soon as he keyed the ignition.

We rode in silence all the way to the chain with the restricted access sign, which I lowered and replaced as before. As we turned onto the road he said, "There were more of them than we thought."

"Six," I said. "Dowling and Scalzo and Gafter. And the sentry, and that one with the mop of hair like Jerry Lee Lewis. Hard to guess how he fit in with that crowd."

"Hard to say how any of them did."

"And another one. He jumped off the side of the porch, and either he hurt his leg doing it or he was still limping from when I stomped on his foot. I don't know which one it was, him or the sentry, because neither of them looked familiar."

"And you shot him."

"We shot each other," I said. "His bullet glanced off the vest."

"God, did it save you again? You'll be wearing it to bed after all this."

"I'm getting fond of it," I admitted. "You were the perfect target, with that big white apron."

"Less white now."

"I noticed. They couldn't hit you, could they?"

"It wasn't for lack of trying. They were bad shots, the lot of them. Six of the fuckers, though, good shots or not, and we killed them all."

"And got off without a scratch," I said. "Second sight notwithstanding."

"Ah," he said. "I was waiting for you to bring that up."

"I held off as long as I could."

" 'Twas my mother said I had the second sight, and it's not the only thing she was ever wrong about. She never in her life had a decent word for the English, and didn't I tell you how nice they were to me the time I was over there?"

"That's a point."

"I'll give you the straight of it, though. I honestly thought I was going to die."

"I know you did."

"And a damned good thing I was mistaken, with no better priest than yourself to hear my confession. By Jesus, didn't I find a rare lot of bad old things to tell you!"

"You went on for a while."

"I have to say I don't regret it. Oh, there's more than a few of the deeds I regret. A man would have to. But I don't regret telling them all to you."

"I'm glad to hear it."

"And you still stood with me and saw the night through, even after all I said."

"To tell you the truth," I said, "I don't remember very much of what you told me."

"What, were you not paying attention?"

"Close attention. I hung on every word. But they didn't stay with me. They passed through me and I don't know where they went. Wherever such things go, I guess."

"In one ear and out the other."

"Something like that," I agreed. "All I really remember is the first thing you mentioned. About taking out the man's eye and showing it to him."

"Ah," he said. "Well, that would be a difficult one to forget, wouldn't it?"

LATER HE SAID, "I've been thinking of what I might do next."

"I was wondering about that."

"You know, we had a good laugh about the feeling I had."

"The premonition."

He nodded. "It may not have been altogether wrong. There are different ways of dying, and of being reborn. I'm unscratched, but hasn't my whole life gone and died around me? Grogan's in ruins, and the farm in ashes. Kenny and McCartney gone, and Burke and Peter Rooney. And Tom Heaney. And Andy.

"Gone, all of them. And O'Gara and his wife. And the pigs and the chickens, all gone." He smacked the steering wheel. "Gone," he said.

I didn't say anything.

"I was thinking," he said, "that I've no place to go. But it's not true. I have a place to go."

"Where's that?"

"Staten Island."

"The monastery," I said.

"The Thessalonian Brothers. They'll take me in. They do that, you see. You go there and they take you in."

"How long will you stay?"

"As long as they'll have me."

"Do they allow that? Can people stay for a long time?"

"For a lifetime, if you want."

"Oh," I said. "You mean to stay there."

"Isn't that what I said?"

"What'll you do, exactly? Will you become a monk?"

"I don't know that I could do that. I'd be a lay brother, most likely. But 'twill be for them to tell me what I ought to do and when I ought to do it. The first step is to go there, and the second is to get one of them to hear my confession." He smiled. "Now that I've tried it out on you," he said. "Now that I've learned it won't kill me."

"Brother Mick," I said.

AS WE WERE crossing the George Washington Bridge I said, "There's something we're forgetting."

"And what would that be?"

"Well, I'm not sure I should mention this to a future servant of God," I said, "but we've got a dead body in the trunk."

"I've been thinking of it," he said, "ever since we got in the car."

"Well, I haven't. It slipped my mind entirely. What the hell are we going to do with him?"

"It would have been best to leave him on the farm. To bury him there. He'd not have lacked for company. Or even to lay him out there on the lawn with the other dead. He threw in with them, he could lie with them, in the bed he made."

"It's too late for that now."

"Ah, it was too late throughout, for how could we carry him through two or three miles of woods? And I didn't want to leave him where we parked the car, and even if we'd found a shovel and buried him there somebody could have come upon the grave. I'll tell you, the man's as difficult to contend with dead as he was alive."

"We have to do something," I said. "We can't just leave him in the trunk."

"Now I was wondering about that. Isn't it his car? And who has more right to be in its trunk than the man himself?"

"I suppose you've got a point."

"I thought of leaving it on the street," he said, "in his beloved Bronx, with the doors unlocked and the key in the ignition. How long do you think it would take before somebody took it for a ride?"

"Not long."

"And they might keep it for a good long while, especially if we took care to leave it with a full tank of gas. Of course if they had a flat tire, and went looking for the spare . . ."

"God, what a thought."

"Ah, it's a hard old world if you can't laugh, and even if you can. Do you know what I think I'll do? I'll wipe the fucker free of prints, as it's full of mine after all the use I've given it this past week. And then I'll take it over to the piers and run it into the river, with the windows rolled down so it'll sink and stay sunk. Can they get fingerprints off a car hauled out of the water?"

"There was a time when they couldn't," I said, "but they probably can by now. I think they can just about lift them off motes of dust dancing in a beam of light."

"I'll wipe it good," he said, "before I shove it off the edge. Just to be sure."

After a moment I said, "What'll you tell his mother?"

"That he had to go away," he said without hesitation, "on a dangerous mission, and that it might be awhile before she heard from him. That should hold her for the few years she's got left in the world. She has cancer, you know."

"I didn't."

"Poor thing. I'll pray for her, and him too, once they've taught me how."

"Pray for all of us," I said.

I RODE UP in the elevator, used my key in the lock. By the time I had the door open she was standing in front of me, wearing a black robe I'd bought for her. It had white and yellow flowers on it, and tiny butterflies.

"You're all right," she said. "Thank God."

"I'm fine."

"TJ's sleeping on the couch," she said. "I was going to bring dinner over to him but he insisted he could come over for it, and then I wouldn't let him go home. I was afraid, but I don't know who I was afraid for, him or me."

"Either way, you're both all right."

"And you're all right, and thank God. It's over, isn't it?"

"Yes, it's over."

"Thank God. And what about Mick? Is Mick all right?"

"He had a premonition," I said, "and that's a story in itself, but it turns out he's got a touch of astigmatism in his third eye, because he's fine. In fact you could say he's never been better."

"And everybody else?"

I said, "Everybody else? Everybody else is dead."

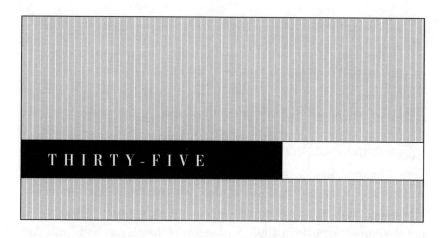

THIRTY-FIVE

"**I**'LL REMIND YOU," Ray Gruliow said, "that Mr. Scudder is here of his own volition, and that he'll answer only those questions I'm willing for him to answer."

"Which means he won't say a goddamn thing," George Wister said.

And that turned out to be pretty close to the truth. There were half a dozen cops in the room, Joe Durkin and George Wister and two guys from Brooklyn Homicide and two others whose function was never explained to me. I didn't much care who they were, because all they could do was sit there while I said essentially nothing.

They had no end of questions, though. They wanted to know what I knew about Chilton Purvis, whom they'd linked to the murder of Jim Faber as a result of information received, which meant that somebody's snitch had indeed come up with the news. They didn't have any evidence to support the snitch's word, however, and so far they hadn't been able to find an eyewitness to the Lucky Panda shooting who would look at Purvis's body and ID him as the shooter.

I couldn't help them out. Anyway, I figured it was their own fault. If they'd coached their witness properly he'd have given them what they wanted.

Maybe one or both of the unidentified men in the room were from the Bronx, because there were questions about Tom Heaney and Mary Eileen Rafferty, which turned out to be the name of Tom's landlady. Tom, I learned, had been shot with bullets from two different guns, and none of the slugs matched any of the bullets retrieved in any of the other homicides in question, although one matched up to a bullet dug out of a corpse in SoHo in 1995. Since most of the players had spent that year in Attica, I figured the gun had some old history attached to it.

All in all, I didn't really give them anything, and I didn't pay close attention, either. I just sat there and watched Ray, and I didn't open my mouth unless he gave me a nod. And he didn't do that very often.

I suppose we were there for about an hour, and then Wister lost it a little and said something nasty, and Ray had been waiting for that. "That's it," he said, getting to his feet. "We're out of here."

"You can't do that," Joe said.

"Oh, really? Just watch us."

"And kiss your license goodbye," Wister said. "I got papers on my desk, formal request for the state to pull your ticket, with all the reasons laid out to make it real easy for them. You walk out of here and I fill out the rest of it and toss it right in the mail."

"And there'll be a hearing," Ray said, "and you'll be subpoenaed, which I know you fellows just love. And by the time the dust settles he'll have his license back, along with a whole lot of newspaper coverage to make him look like a hero."

"He won't look like a hero," Joe said. "He'll look like a fucking criminal is all he'll look like. Which more and more is what he's been looking like anyway."

"That's enough," Ray said.

"No it's not, it's nowhere near enough. Matt, what the hell's the matter with you? You'll lose your license."

I said, "You know something? I don't care if I do."

"Don't say another word," Ray said.

"No," I said, "I'll say this much, and I'm saying it to you as much as to them. They can do what they want, and if the state rescinds my license that's fine. You could fight it, and maybe we'd win, but it's not worth the bother."

"You don't know what you're talking about," Joe said.

"I know I got along fine without a license for over twenty years," I said. "I don't know what the hell made me ever think I needed it. Maybe I make a few more dollars with it than without it, but I always made enough. I never missed a meal, and back when I drank I never lacked the price of the next drink. You want to pull my license? Go right ahead. What the hell do I care?"

We walked out of the station house and down the steps, and when we were out of earshot Ray said, "They'll get your license pulled, and I'll get it back. Not a problem."

"No," I said. "Thanks, but I wasn't just sounding off. I mean what I said. We'll let it go, and the hell with it."

"YOU NEVER NEEDED it in the first place," Elaine assured me. "What, so you can work for a few more lawyers? And they can bill a little higher for your services? The hell with that."

"Exactly my point."

"Besides," she said, "we know the real reason you got the license. You wanted to be respectable. And it's like all those folks on the Yellow Brick Road, baby. You were respectable all along."

"No," I said. "I wasn't, and I'm still not. But the license didn't change anything."

AND THAT WOULD be a good place to leave it, except there's a little more to the story. Like everything else, it's not over till it's over.

That was in September, and in mid-December we got a Christmas card with a return address on Staten Island. It said *Season's Greetings* instead of *Merry Christmas,* no doubt in deference to the Jewish vegetarian he'd once given a ham to, and inside, beneath an unexceptionable printed message, he'd written *God's love to you both* and signed it *Mick.*

Elaine said she was sure he'd sign it Fr. Michael F. Ballou, S. J. I said he was with the Thessalonians, not the Jesuits, and she said goyim is goyim.

Then in late April TJ mentioned that he'd passed Grogan's and had seen a Dumpster at the curb and a construction crew hard at work. I said evidently there'd be a Korean greengrocer in there before long.

And then a week later the phone rang, and Elaine answered it and came to tell me I'd never guess who it was.

"I bet it's Father Mick," I said.

"Ah, Jaysus," she said, "and get along with ye, and haven't the wee folk gifted ye with the second sight your own self?"

"Begorrah," I said.

I picked up the phone and he invited me to come down and see how the work was progressing. "Of course it's impossible to get it so it looks old," he said, "and there are bullet holes they want to cover up, and they ought to be left as they are. There's history to them."

I went over there, and for all of that they seemed to be doing a good job, and getting it more right than not. I said I gathered this meant he was back in business.

"I am," he said.

"You said you'd stay there until they kicked you out."

"Ah. Well, they didn't do that. They'd never do that." He took a drink from his silver flask. "They're lovely men," he said. "The nicest men I've ever met in my life. And they were so good as to let me take my time to realize for myself that I didn't belong there. I half wish I did, but I don't, and they allowed me to see as much."

"And here you are."

"And here I am," he agreed. "And glad to be back, and are you glad to have me?"

"Damn glad," I said, "and so's Elaine. We missed you."

HIS STORY, as I said early on, his story far more than mine. But how could you ever get him to tell it?